Also by **Scott Sigler**

*Infected*

*Contagious*

*Ancestor*

*Nocturnal*


The Galactic Football League series (YA)

*The Rookie*

*The Starter*

*The All-Pro*

*The MVP*


The Galactic Football League novellas (YA)

*The Reporter*

*The Detective*

*The Gangster (coming in 2013)*

*The Rider (coming in 2013)*

*Title Fight*


The Color Series short story collections

*Blood is Red*

*Bones are White*

*Fire is Orange (coming in 2013)*

# THE STARTER

## Galactic Football League: Book Two

**Scott Sigler**

Diversion Books
A Division of Diversion Publishing Corp.
80 Fifth Avenue, Suite 1101
New York, New York 10011
www.DiversionBooks.com

THE STARTER
(The Galactic Football League Series, Book II)

Published in the United States by
Dark Øverlord Paperback,
an imprint of Diversion Books.

For more information, email
info@diversionbooks.com
or media@scottsigler.com

Library of Congress Cataloging-in-Publication Data
Sigler, Scott
    The Starter / Scott Sigler. — 1st ed.
    p. cm.
    1. Science Fiction—Fiction.   2. Sports—Fiction.
Library of Congress Control Number: 2010931183

ISBN: 978-1-938120-10-7

Book design by Donna Mugavero at Sheer Brick Studio
Cover design by Scott E. Pond at Scott Pond Design Studio
Cover art (figure) by Adrian Bogart at Punch Designs

First Diversion Books edition AUGUST 2012

*This book is dedicated to Alan Roark,*
*for showing us that playing hard*
*and leaving it all on the field*
*is the only way to truly live.*

# Acknowledgments

The starting line-up, who make this benchwarmer look All-Pro:

**Adrian "The Bruiser" Bogart**
cover illustration

**A "Future Hall-of-Famer" Kovacs**
partner, talent scout and secret weapon

**Donna "Chalkboard" Mugavero**
interior book design

**Scott "Big Fish" Pond**
cover design

## Special Thanks

Our thanks wouldn't be complete without recognizing the contributions of the rest of Team Dark Øverlord:

**Joe Albietz:** *medical biology expertise*

**Kelly Lutterschmidt:** *copyeditor*

**Arioch Morningstar:** *audio production*

**John Vizcarra:** *continuity coach*

**Carmen Wellman:** *Siglerpedia Czar*

# THE
# STARTER

# BOOK ONE:
# PreSeason, 2683

# 1

# PRESEASON: WEEK ONE

**THEY CAME HOME AT NIGHT.** They came home champions.

Quentin stayed in his room aboard the *Touchback*. He was too nervous about the return trip — wouldn't it be ironic to fight through the war that was his rookie season, win the Tier Two tournament and reach Tier One, then fly back from Earth only to have the team bus crash on the way home? Since he started every intergalactic trip assuming he was going to crash anyway, the concept of such a cruel fate made for a tense flight.

He waited. Waited for the punch-out, for the *Touchback* to slip into normal space.

The ship started to vibrate, shake a little.

*It's fine, it's fine, it's fine, just relax.*

He repeated the familiar mantra in his head, but it didn't help. This was it, he'd die on this stupid ship before he played a single down of Tier One, before he lived his dream.

*It's fine, it's fine, it's fine, just relax.*

He kept his eyes shut. Best not to see it happen. Maybe this time he wouldn't hurl.

*It's fine, it's fine, it's fi—*

The reality wave started cascading over the ship — just because he couldn't *see* it didn't mean he couldn't *feel* it. Quentin's eyes squeezed even tighter, so hard that his upper lip curled. His stomach churned, an oily, queasy feeling that threatened to coax the dinner out of his belly.

The feeling of *splitting*, of *spreading*, of being in several places at once. It pulled at his mind, told the part repeating *"it's fine"* that it was completely full of crap, because any sane sentient knew that things were most certainly *not* fine.

And then it was over.

Quentin Barnes opened just his left eye, just a little, to see if anything was *shimmering*, was *waving*. Everything looked solid. He let his breath out in a long rush, then sprinted for the bathroom as his stomach rebelled.


**QUENTIN HAD JUST FINISHED** brushing his teeth free of the taste of vomit when the computer voice chimed through his room.

[FIRST SHUTTLE PASSENGERS TO THE LANDING BAY]

He spit, then smiled. The first shuttle trip to Ionath City was for key players, for starters who had established themselves as vital parts of the Krakens franchise. That list of players included him.

He walked out of the bathroom and took one last look around. His few belongings were packed into flight crates. Gredok the Splithead, owner of the Krakens, was retrofitting all the players' rooms as part of an overall upgrade to the *Touchback*. Sure, Gredok was a gangster, a thug and a killer, but he took his duties as team owner very seriously — he wanted his players to have facilities that rivaled those of any Tier One team.

Quentin left his room with a strange sense of anticipation. He would spend the next four weeks planet-side. Training, practice, holostudy — all the things needed to prepare for his first Tier One game. The next time he saw this room, it would be for the trip to planet Tower and the season opener against the Isis Ice Storm.

He walked down the corridor, appreciating the orange walls and the black and white carpet more than ever. He loved his team colors. No matter where his football career might take him, he knew he'd have a permanent place in his heart for the orange and the black.

He heard the now-familiar, rapid-fire of pounding footsteps behind him. Quentin automatically put his back against the wall, making room for the sprinting Sklorno.

The Sklorno, it seemed, were *always* sprinting.

A pair of them shot down the corridor. He recognized them — Milford and Denver, two of his fellow rookies from last year. Their big feet hit the carpet hard as they stopped.

"Quentin Barnes Quentin Barnes Quentin Barnes!" Milford said.

"Hey," Quentin said, in a calm voice, lest he excite them further. When Sklorno got excited, Sklorno drooled. Never a fun thing.

Milford and Denver were among the few Krakens taller than Quentin. Denver stood eight feet, ten inches tall, just two inches shorter than Milford. They both wore their Krakens jerseys — Denver was number 81, Milford number 82 — but that was the only clothing that blocked their strange, see-through bodies. Sklorno jersey numbers had to go on the sides, not in front, because their coiled arms stuck out of their chests right where the numbers would ordinarily be placed on a Human jersey.

The jerseys only covered part of their bodies. On the exposed areas, translucent chitin showed the semitransparent muscles flexing beneath and clear blood coursing through them like pumping water, all of it supported by black skeletons. Semi-visible internal organs fluttered here and there.

Nowhere did they have more muscle than in their thick legs that folded backward like those of a grasshopper. Coarse, black fur jutted out of their knee and ankle joints. The legs supported a slender, back-curving body-stalk. On top of that body, the strangest part of a Sklorno — the head.

They each had two raspers, long rolls of skin-covered muscle embedded with thousands of small teeth. Usually the raspers stayed rolled up behind a thick chin plate, but whenever the ladies talked to Quentin, the raspers tended to hang down like a dog with a three-foot-long double tongue. Above the chin plate sat a small crop of coarse black hairs. Out of that hair jutted four eye-stalks. Each stalk moved independently, looking in all directions at once like curious cobras rising up to strike.

"Quentin Barnes QuentinBarnes *QuentinBarnes*!" Denver shouted again. "We are on first shuttle with you!"

Quentin nodded and started to say something, but apparently the conversation was over. The two receivers took off on a dead sprint, headed for the shuttle bay. Quentin followed them, but at a slightly more casual pace.

The shuttle bay's fifty-foot-high domed ceiling held the usual assortment of equipment, machines and stacked metal crates, everything meticulously arranged and organized. Outside of the players' individual rooms, *everything* was meticulous and organized courtesy of Messal the Efficient, the Krakens' team manager.

Quentin looked up, looked to the words that floated in the center of the shallow dome. A sentence made of large, holographic letters ran the length of the bay. The glowing letters never moved, never faded, and they were *never* turned off, even during ship-night. They read: THE IONATH KRAKENS ARE ON A COLLISION COURSE WITH A TIER ONE CHAMPIONSHIP. THE ONLY VARIABLE IS TIME.

The words made Quentin's chest feel all fluttery, stopped his breath short. He'd seen the sign many times during the Tier Two season, but Coach Hokor had changed the words slightly. Before, it had read *The Ionath Krakens are on a collision course with a Tier One berth. The only variable is time.*

Well, they had turned that dreamy prophecy into a hard-won truth. Now Hokor was setting the goal higher, as high as it gets — a Galaxy Bowl championship, a Galactic Football League title. The thought scared Quentin a little, made him wonder if they could live up to such expectations. Scared him ... and also thrilled him.

He wasn't here to chase mediocrity.

He was here to capture glory.

He stared at the sign, then nodded.

Quentin walked toward the shuttle, which was painted in

Krakens orange and trimmed in black and white. A large Krakens logo — the iconic reddish-orange "I" inside a yellow shield, with six white, stylized tentacles spreading off behind it — decorated the side.

Other first-shuttle Krakens filtered into the landing bay. Quentin saw the blue-skinned Don Pine, two-time Galaxy Bowl winner and now Quentin's backup. Denver and Milford, along with Scarborough and Hawick, the starting Sklorno receivers. Mum-O-Killowe, the twelve-foot-long Ki defensive tackle that had gone from rookie to starter in one season, just like Quentin had done at the quarterback position. Aleksander Michnik and Ibrahim Khomeni, the monstrous, knuckle-dragging HeavyG defensive ends, each 525 pounds and nearly seven feet tall. Kill-O-Yowet, the dominant offensive tackle and seeming alpha sentient of the Krakens' seventeen Ki players. Third-string quarterback Yitzhak Goldman, who enjoyed first shuttle privileges because he had been born and raised in Ionath City and, as such, was a local hero. And the big, tattooed, wild-eyed and semi-sane Human middle linebacker, John Tweedy.

Standing next to John was Yassoud Murphy, the Krakens' starting running back by default. *Default* because 'Soud was the only one left on the roster — starter Mitchell "The Machine" Fayed had died, and backup Paul Pierson had lost a leg.

Yassoud and John had become Quentin's closest friends. He worked hard to spend time with everyone on the team, but John and 'Soud were *Human*. Quentin had spent nineteen years of his life being programmed to think that Human was the only race that mattered. Logically, he could separate himself from that propaganda, but emotionally, he still felt more comfortable with his own kind.

"Hey 'Soud, Uncle Johnny," Quentin said.

John turned, his crazy stare-into-nothing changing to a smile. ARE YOU READY FOR SOME FOOTBALL? scrolled across his face. John had a sub-dermal tattoo, thousands of tiny light emitters embedded under his skin. With his cyberlink control, John could dial up any words or phrases he liked. Quentin was getting used to it, but seeing letters dance across John's face was still a bit disturbing.

"Q," John said and held out his fist. Quentin reached out his own for the obligatory fist-bump, then did the same for Yassoud.

"Hey," Quentin said to the running back, "did you *braid* your beard?"

"It's called a Persian, big boy," Yassoud said, then stroked the eight inches of matted, black, curly beard he'd bound together with a thin, orange string. "Orange and black, Q, Ionath-style."

Quentin smiled and nodded appreciatively. Yassoud loved the Krakens just as much as Quentin did.

Most of the first-shuttle team was there, save for Virak the Mean and Choto the Bright, two Quyth Warrior outside linebackers.

"Hey, Uncle Johnny, where are Virak and Choto?"

"Off doing some work for Gredok," John said. "Rumor is they're at Buddha City Station for the heavyweight championship fight."

"No way," Yassoud said. "Oh, yep, I *got* to get on Gredok's good side. Virak and Choto get all the fun."

*Fun.* That wasn't how Quentin saw it. Before he'd arrived last season, Virak and Choto had been football players second, gangland thugs first. Any time they accompanied Gredok, the two were probably involved in something illegal, something that could get them hurt. And if they got hurt, that affected the team. Hopefully nothing would happen. The season was just a few weeks away.

The shuttle's entire side hung open, lowered via a bottom hinge that turned it into a ramp. Head coach Hokor the Hookchest stood at the top of that ramp. It still struck Quentin as strange that Hokor, a Quyth Leader, was technically part of the same species as Virak and Choto. Where Virak was 6-foot-2 and 375 pounds, Hokor was only 3-foot-1, probably 90 pounds if he'd been swimming and his black-striped yellow fur was soaked with water. Leaders and Warriors alike were bipedal, standing on folded legs that had one segment rising up from the hips to a knee, then a foreleg that pointed down, connecting to a long, three-toed foot. Their middle arms had a similar design: upper arm that pointed up and back, then a forearm that pointed down parallel to the upper arm, ending in a thick, three-fingered pincer. Their chests continued up from the middle arms, tapering to a head with a single eye. On either side of and below the eye, a set of pedipalps ended in dexterous, finger-like appendages. The middle hands were for heavy lifting and grunt work, while the pedipalps handled fine skills, like art or computers.

Hokor wore a tiny little orange and black Krakens jacket and a tiny little black baseball hat with a Krakens logo glowing on the bill. He always dressed in team colors.

At the base of the ramp stood three Krakens players, all wearing jerseys that Quentin had never seen before. Krakens home jerseys were black with orange numbers, away jerseys were orange with black numbers — these players wore white. White jerseys with orange numbers and letters trimmed in black. Orange sleeves led to black-trimmed orange flashes running down the flanks.

Where had he seen these before? It hit him — he'd seen those jerseys in the stands, worn by some of the thousands of fans packing Ionath Stadium.

Throwback jerseys.

Paul Pierson wore one of the white jerseys, number 31. Paul refused to wear a realistic prosthetic lower left leg — instead, he wore a chromed post that ended in a metallic foot. The leg had been torn off by Yalla the Biter, a Quyth Warrior linebacker for the Sky Demolition. Since Paul had lost his leg "in combat," as he called it, he wanted the universe to know he'd given his all on the gridiron.

Next to Paul stood the Ki lineman Wen-Eh-Daret, number 66, a right guard who had hurt his back in the Tier Two semi-final game against the Texas Earthlings. The injury had proven more severe than anyone thought, forcing the Ki's retirement. Aka-Na-Tak, the backup, had also been hurt in that semi-final. Aka-Na-Tak was still recovering — he wouldn't see the field until the third week of the season.

Around twelve feet long, the Ki body bent at the middle. Six feet of body stayed parallel to the ground, supported by three pairs of legs. The body bent up at the front. Two pair of arms stuck out near the thick neck and head. The head? That was the stuff of nightmares. A row of five equidistant eyes gave the species three hundred-and-sixty-degree vision. Six leathery lips covered the six black teeth of their hexagonal mouths. Vocal tubes stuck up from the top of the head, making the Ki look a bit like a Human with smooth, short dreadlocks.

Next to Wen-Eh stood the final white-jerseyed player, another Human. Pancho Saulsgiver, number 48. Pancho, the third tight end on the roster behind Yotaro Kobayasho and Rick Warburg, hadn't played much during the Tier Two season. Pancho had been with the Krakens for ten years — an eternity in the brutal world of the GFL.

Ten years.

A missing leg.

A broken back.

And then Quentin understood the reason for the special jerseys.

Hokor spoke in his small but gravelly voice. He was tiny, even downright cute in his little jacket and little hat, but when he spoke, everyone listened.

"Gredok the Splithead cannot be here today," Hokor said. "He has business elsewhere but told me he is proud of all of you." Quentin just hoped that *business* didn't involve Virak and Choto playing the role of gangland muscle.

Coach Hokor continued. "Tomorrow afternoon, Ionath City is throwing us a parade to celebrate our promotion to Tier One. Then we have a week off, then three weeks to prepare for the Isis Ice Storm. Right now it is time to descend to Ionath, a trip that marks the official end of our Tier Two season. As such, we honor the players that are retiring as Krakens."

Hokor's words echoed through the mostly empty shuttle bay then faded out, leaving silence. Quentin didn't know what to say. He imagined his teammates didn't, either.

"These three players wear white," Hokor said. "The white jerseys are the original jerseys the franchise had in the year of its founding, 2662. To wear the white is the highest honor the

Krakens organization can bestow. Pierson, Wen-Eh-Daret and Saulsgiver played hard, they gave everything they had, but all careers must end. Active players, pay your respects to them as you board the shuttle."

Quentin watched the Krakens' starters filter onto the shuttle, each stopping to say something to the three white-jerseyed, soon-to-be-ex-teammates. Quentin watched until he realized he was the only active player standing in the shuttle bay.

He walked up to Pierson. Quentin offered his hand, which the running back shook. Pierson was 29, a decade older than Quentin. Years in the league had aged the man — Pierson looked ready for a rest.

"Sorry you won't be joining us," Quentin said. "Gonna be a hell of a year."

Paul laughed. "I played two seasons in the bigs, with the Dreadnaughts. You think our T2 season was tough? Good luck, brother, I hope you do well."

Pierson's smirk made it clear he thought he would have the last laugh, that *he* had been tough enough to last a decade, but Quentin was not. Pierson radiated disdain and jealousy of Quentin's rising star.

This whole process made Quentin uncomfortable, and he didn't know why. The chrome of Paul's foot reflected the landing bay lights, streaky flashes visible even though Quentin wasn't looking at it.

Wen-Eh-Daret was next. Quentin stood in front of the monstrous creature, unsure of what to say or do. Wen-Eh's black eyespots stared blankly. The pink hexagonal mouth twitched, lip flaps hiding the disturbing triangular teeth. Quentin still didn't understand the Ki all that well — did Wen-Eh want to say something?

The Ki four-armed lineman reached up his two right arms, then smacked them against his tubular chest. If he had been wearing football armor, the movement would have produced a *clack* sound — the Ki equivalent of saying *I will go to war with you.*

The gesture hit Quentin much harder than Paul's condescension. Somewhere during the season, the Ki had accepted Quentin as a fellow warrior. He'd led them into battle, led them to victory. Fighting and winning were all that seemed to matter to the Ki.

Quentin swallowed the lump in his throat, then brought up his right fist and pounded it twice against his chest. That was all that needed to be said.

He finished with Pancho, who stood just outside the shuttle door.

"Quentin, you little rascal, I'm gonna miss you this year."

"You and all the shuckers trying to tackle me," Quentin said, laughing that Pancho had called him *little*. Quentin had two inches and more than a few pounds on the man.

"It was great to be your teammate, Q," Pancho said. "Let me be an old fart and give you some unsolicited advice. Cool?"

Quentin rolled his eyes. "Sure, Pops, go ahead."

"Pro football is a marathon, not a sprint. Just remember that. Paul and I both made it ten years, which is damn near impossible. We were *good* players. You're a *great* one. If *you* last ten years? You'll rewrite every record in the league."

"Just ten? At that point, I'll just be getting warmed up."

Pancho smiled and nodded. "I hope so, Q. Have a great season. Ever been fishing?"

Quentin shook his head.

"If you need a break, just let me know. I'm heading back to Earth, to a little town in a place called Michigan. Anytime you need to get away from it all, you call me."

Where Paul's well-wishing had reeked of bitterness, Pancho's rang with genuine affection. The tight end raised his right fist and banged his chest twice. Quentin did the same, then turned and boarded the shuttle.

All that touchy-feely emotional stuff was fine and good, but those three players just creeped him out. Correction: those three *former* players. All of a sudden, Quentin had to admit he didn't want to be anywhere near them. It was stupid to feel that way, he knew, but those three retired players suddenly seemed almost ... diseased.

Quentin found a Human-sized seat near Hawick, the Sklorno

receiver. He sat and buckled in. She trembled a little, but not as bad as Denver or Milford would have done. Quentin was still trying to deal with the fact that Sklorno now *worshiped* him like some kind of false idol. Hawick was clearly in awe of Quentin, although apparently she wasn't an official member of the "Church of Quentin Barnes," or the *C-o-Q-B* as they called it.

He braced himself as the landing bay catapult tossed the shuttle out into the void. He stared out a view port, taking in the void's star-speckled blackness. The shuttle floated for a few minutes until it cleared the *Touchback*, then the engines kicked in.

The shuttle banked. As it came around, the planet Ionath slid into view. Red, cracked, cratered. From this far up, Ionath was an image of death, of the folly of constant war, of how things were before the Creterakians took over. For all the authoritarian rule of the bats, at least they kept the peace.

A chime sounded. Quentin automatically looked up to holo-icons floating near the roof. Graphics showed an unbuckled seat belt and, next to it, simple pictures of walking Ki, Humans, Quyth and Sklorno. The HeavyG players thought the signs were racist because they showed the rough dimensions of a normal-G Human. Quentin thought that was ridiculous — two arms, two legs, a body and a head were two arms, two legs, a body and a head. You didn't hear the Quyth complaining about their icon, despite the drastic size difference between Leaders, Warriors and Workers.

He unbuckled, then walked to one of the shuttle's larger view ports. Only a few of the Krakens players onboard moved within the cramped space. Some of the vets had seen the orbital approach so many times they were no longer impressed. Michnik and Khomeni were among those, apparently — that, or they were too busy eating the huge sandwiches sitting in their laps. The only movement came from Shizzle, the team's translator and lone Creterakian. Shizzle fluttered to keep his balance on Kill-O-Yowet's shoulder.

Quentin stared out the view port, taking in the ruined planet. He wondered if there might be messages waiting for him when he reached the surface. Maybe his father had seen his game against the Earthlings a week ago. The T2 Tourney didn't get the ratings of Tier One, but it was still broadcast galaxy-wide. Maybe his mother had seen a newscast, seen Quentin's now-adult face and instantly recognized her baby boy.

Maybe. Or maybe he'd never hear from either of them.

A heavy hand hit his shoulder, hit and held. Quentin winced — his shoulder still hurt from the game against the Earthlings a week earlier. The strong hand shook him, the friendly-if-painful grasp of John Tweedy.

"What's *up*, Q? I know you got the tar knocked out of you by those Tex linebackers, but come on, trooper, you should be *happy*. You brought us into Tier One, man. You get a week off! Maybe now you can do something with your money, like get an apartment or something. Hey, maybe you can live near me! We could be shucking *neighbors*, brother!"

When Quentin didn't respond, the words TURN THAT FROWN UPSIDE DOWN scrolled across John's face tattoo.

"Come on, Killer Q," John said. "What's with that mopey sadboy look on your face?"

"It's just ... ah, never mind, I don't wanna talk about it."

"Come *on*, trooper! Uncle Johnny's been in the GFL five years, another three in the lower leagues, all that time trying to get to Tier One. It's been my *dream*, Q! And that dream came true 'cause of you. What's eating ya? Ya need a girl? Wanna go out and paint the town orange?"

"No, that's not ... well, yeah, we *should* go out and hit the town, but that's not what I mean. This Tier One stuff is a big deal, I just wish my parents could see it."

"Why aren't they here? Your dad have attitude? Want me to whip your pop's ass? 'Cause I *will* whip his ass, I assure you."

Quentin laughed. He didn't feel like laughing, but John's always-on intensity could make anything seem funny. "I don't know where they are, John. I don't even know if they're alive. They vanished when I was real little. Happens a lot in the Nation."

Tweedy looked around behind him to the left, then to the right, then to the left again. His eyes lingered on Shizzle, who was farther back in the small shuttle, still perched on Kill-O-Yowet's shoulder.

Tweedy leaned in close to Quentin and spoke in a whisper. "Hey, Q, you told anyone about this?"

Quentin shook his head. "Not really. Warburg knows, some ex-Nationalites in Ionath City, but I guess that's about it. Why?"

Tweedy did the left-right-left look again, the move probably drawing more attention to him than if he'd just talked quietly. "Listen, you might not want to make your situation public, you know? That's the kind of thing Gredok can use against you."

"Why would Gredok use it against me? I'm his quarterback."

John shook his head slowly, as if he couldn't believe he was looking at someone so stupid. The funny thing was that John wasn't the sharpest laser in the kit, but he was so sure of himself and had such conviction that when he thought you were dumb, you actually *felt* a little dumb even if you knew you were right.

"You *challenged* Gredok," John said. "You challenged his authority and won. You know what that means? Don't they have crime bosses on Micovi?"

Quentin thought of Stedmar Osborne and nodded. Stedmar was the owner of the Micovi Raiders, Quentin's Tier Three team back in the Purist Nation. Stedmar was a not a man to be trifled with.

"Yeah," Quentin said. "All teams are owned by gangsters. I know that."

"You *know* that, but you don't *know* it. You get away with stuff because you win games. Gangsters like to win, winning makes money, but the most important thing is respect and control. You challenged Gredok's authority — he's *not* gonna forget that, Killer Q."

Quentin hadn't thought about it that way until this moment. Don Pine had owed millions to Mopuk the Sneaky, a gangster that forced Pine to shave points, even throw games outright. Quentin orchestrated an effort to pay off Don's debt. When Gredok had discovered Pine's betrayal, he wanted to kill the man. Quentin threatened to walk away from the Krakens if Gredok hurt Pine in any way. Quentin had reacted on instinct, done what he had to do for the good of the team, never really connecting the dots that there could be long-term consequences for those actions.

"Anyway," John said, "Gredok's not going to have you whacked. Not yet, at least. But you don't want to give him any more leverage over you, right?"

Quentin nodded. "Then how do I go about finding my parents? We have the season coming up, it's not like I can go out and look for them."

John did the left-right-left look again, then leaned in. I KNOW A GUY scrolled across his forehead in small letters. "Don't you worry about it, Q. Uncle Johnny-Boy The Minister of Awesome will hook you up. You put it out of your head for now."

John turned and walked away, leaving Quentin alone at the view port window.

The shuttle rattled as it entered Ionath's atmosphere. Quentin gripped one of the many hand/tentacle rings lining the shuttle. He looked out at what he now called "home." A Sklorno saturation bombing 124 years earlier had wiped the planet clean of all advanced life. Only bacteria had remained, and not much of that. Ionath had remained lifeless, damn near *sterile*, until the Quyth Concordia colonized it. The Quyth seemed immune to the same radiation that killed every other known sentient in the galaxy. The Quyth were in the midst of a centuries-long process of transforming the planet. Much of Ionath still looked lifeless, lined with massive craters and cracks, but those scars were also blurring under an ever-increasing carpet of orange, red and yellow plants.

The shuttle approached Ionath City. Built in the middle of a ten-mile-wide bomb crater, Ionath City's clear dome glowed like a torch lit up by the lights of thousands of buildings beneath. As the shuttle drew closer to the dome, Quentin stared in amazement as those lights changed. The white, blue, red and yellow glow of a bustling, nighttime cityscape steadily blinked off as a new color steadily blinked on.

That color was *orange*.

The domed metropolis of Ionath City flickered, blinked and, in a span of ten or fifteen seconds, changed into a gleaming black jewel glittering with millions of glowing orange facets.

The orange and the black.

Ionath City welcomed its warriors home.

The pilot dove straight for the huge dome, which obligingly disintegrated a temporary, shuttle-sized hole. The circular roads of Ionath City seemed to guide them in like the concentric rings of a bull's-eye. Straight streets dissected sixteen equivalent sectors, all intersecting at the city center — intersecting at the home of the Krakens.

In Ionath City, all roads led to the football stadium.

The shuttle angled closer. Quentin saw more lights flare up, the sides of buildings coming to life with skyscraper-high motion clips of the orange- and black-clad Krakens players: Scarborough hauling in a pass; Aleksander Michnik sacking a quarterback; Quentin running through the line, a sweat-dripping snarl splayed across his face; Virak the Mean, black and red blood streaking his jersey, pointing out a gap just before the snap of the ball; and then one that made Quentin's soul *hurt* — number 47, Mitchell "The Machine" Fayed, standing over the crumbled, purple-and-white clad form of Yalla the Biter. After Yalla had ripped off Paul Pierson's leg, Fayed had gone headhunting for the linebacker and crushed him in a highlight-reel hit. Quentin blinked back tears for his dead friend. Reaching Tier One had been the Machine's ultimate dream. He'd died just two games shy of seeing that become a reality.

Sixty-foot-tall motion clips of so many players, orange and black giants making the nighttime skyline dance with life. So many Krakens, but the changing images featured one more than all the others combined.

"Zak," Quentin called out. "You seeing this?"

Yitzhak Goldman quickly walked over to stand next to Quentin. The third-string quarterback looked out the window, then took a deep breath that exhaled into a smile saturating every iota of his face.

"Ah, good to be home," Yitzhak said loudly. "Nothing quite like being welcomed home by towering visions of ... well ... of *me.*"

All the players on the shuttle laughed, even the mostly humorless Michnik and Khomeni. Ionath City residents adored Yitzhak, even if most of them didn't really understand he was a third-string quarterback and fairly insignificant to the team's success. That lack of knowledge didn't change the fact that businesses wanted Yitzhak's name associated with their companies, wanted his picture on their products. He was the face of Junkie Gin, the dashboard voice of Hundai Grav-Limos and the chisel-chinned image of Farouk Outdoor's popular anti-rad suits that let the adventurous non-Quyth species explore the vast planet. Compared to the advertising money he earned, Yitzhak's actual salary was probably insignificant.

The shuttle slowed as it approached the roof of the Krakens building and landed feather-light. The side door lowered. Quentin and the others started filing down the ramp, ready for the now-familiar customs check. While the Quyth Concordia was independent of Creterakian control, GFL rules still applied to every team.

Team buses had diplomatic immunity. GFL players could not be searched or detained. This had been implemented to prevent local system police from harassing players based on species bias. For a team to compete, it had to have players from the main races. Immunity allowed teams to move across systems without fear that some of their players would be arrested, possibly even killed. But just because the players themselves couldn't be detained didn't mean the Creterakians would allow team buses be a conduit for weapons or explosives that could be used against the ruling empire. The shuttle had to be searched every time it landed.

Quentin walked out. A red line glowed on the roof. He dutifully took his place on that line, John Tweedy on his right, Scarborough on his left. They all stood, quietly waiting as a white-uniformed, blue-furred Quyth Leader walked up and down the twelve-player line. The Leader's middle arms held something behind his back. Two white-uniformed workers slid a grav-cart into the shuttle.

"I am Kotop the Observer," the Leader said. "I am duly appointed by the Galactic Football League to inspect your shuttle."

Quentin sighed. He knew who Kotop was. Everyone knew who Kotop was because Kotop inspected the shuttle every time it landed. The little Leader insisted on formally identifying himself. Kotop always seemed annoyed that the players were probably using their personal immunity to smuggle in information, drugs or other contraband. The unwritten rule was that whatever a player could carry on his person — as long as it wasn't a weapon — remained totally above the law. Kotop did little to hide his disdain of athletes. He usually had something derisive to say.

"Look at you all," Kotop said. "The conquering heroes return."

Quentin expected Kotop's usual lecture on morals, but this time he sounded different.

John took a step forward and stood with rigid, mock attention. "Mister Kotop Leader *Shamakath* sir! May I ask what is on your mind, Mister Kotop Leader *Shamakath* sir? You seem very ... happy."

"I'm always happy," Kotop said.

The Krakens players laughed.

John stepped back into line.

The two white-uniformed workers pushed their grav-sled out of the shuttle. "No explosives, no weapons," one of them said to Kotop.

"Excellent," Kotop said. "I expected nothing less of such fine representatives of Ionath."

The players looked at each other, confused.

"Kotop, my tip-top," John said. "Aren't you going to tell us we are delinquents that will someday wind up dead or in jail as soon as football is finished with us?"

"Not tonight," Kotop said. He brought his hands out from behind his back. They were holding a little black baseball hat, which he pulled onto his head. The hat showed the Krakens logo on the bill. Across the brim it read: IONATH KRAKENS: 2682 TIER TWO CHAMPIONS.

"Tonight?" Kotop said, "Tonight, I am just a fan, like every being in this city. Congratulations, sentients, and welcome home."

The team laughed and whooped at the unexpected support. They walked across the roof to ride elevators down to their respective quarters, or to cars and taxis. Quentin, however, walked to the roof's far side. He stood there, breathing slowly, staring out at an entire city lit up in orange lights, a city alive with the moving, silent images of his teammates, his friends. Some of the towering buildings showed action clips of Quentin, jersey torn and splattered with blood, fighting for victory against the Sky Demolition, the Whitok Pioneers, the Texas Earthlings.

He looked everywhere, trying to take it all in, trying to capture everything and forever burn it into his brain.

Not that long ago, he'd been an orphan. A low-wage miner, on an unknown colony, in a backwater system.

Now? Now, his image covered towering skyscrapers. Now, he was a *hero*.

He would never, ever, forget this moment.

From *The Ionath City Gazette*

# GFL Schedule Announced, Krakens Face Stiff Competition

*by* TOYAT THE INQUISITIVE

NEW YORK CITY, EARTH, PLANETARY UNION — GFL officials today announced the schedule for the 2683 season. Following their successful season and first-place finish in the T2 Tournament, the Ionath Krakens earned promotion to Tier One.

The GFL has two divisions, the Planet Division and the Solar Division. Ionath was placed in the Planet Division, replacing the relegated Free Birds, who finished the 2682 Tier One season with a record of 1-11.

Each division has eleven teams. The Krakens play each Planet Division team once and also have two cross-divisional games against teams from the Solar Division. Every team gets one bye-week, resulting in a 12-game, 13-week schedule.

*continued on next page*

## 2683 KRAKENS SCHEDULE

| WK | OPPONENT | SYSTEM | 2682 RECORD |
|----|----------|--------|-------------|
| 1 | Isis Ice Storm | Tower Republic | 7-5 |
| 2 | Themala Dreadnaughts | Quyth Concordia | 5-7 |
| 3 | Shorah Warlords (cross-divisional) | Harrah Tribal Accord | 3-9 |
| 4 | To Pirates | Ki Empire | 10-2 |
| 5 | Wabash Wolfpack | Tower Republic | 9-3 |
| **BYE WEEK** | | | |
| 7 | Lu Juggernauts | Ki Empire | 8-4 |
| 8 | Alimum Armada | Sklorno Dynasty | 4-8 |
| 9 | Coranadillana Cloud Killers | Harrah Tribal Accord | 3-9 |
| 10 | Yall Criminals | Sklorno Dynasty | 11-1 |
| 11 | Hittoni Hullwalkers | League of Planets | 6-6 |
| 12 | Jupiter Jacks (cross-divisional) | Planetary Union | 10-2 |
| 13 | Mars Planets | Planetary Union | 4-8 |

*continued from previous page*

## Relegation-bound?

The Krakens' primary objective this season is to win more games than at least one other Planet Division team. The team with the most losses is relegated to Tier Two, to be replaced by one of the teams that reach the championship game of the T2 Tournament.

For reference, keep in mind that the Free Birds won the Tier Two tournament in 2681 to earn promotion, then proceeded to lose eleven games in the 2682 Tier One season and were sent right back down again. In the past ten Tier One campaigns, six of the teams that won promotion were relegated the following season.

## The Magic Number?

The Free Birds were by far the worst team in Tier One. This season, analysts mostly agree that the teams in danger of relegation are the Coranadillana Cloud Killers, the Mars Planets and the Krakens. Ionath likely has to win at least three games to avoid relegation.

## Guaranteed Losses?

Ionath faces almost certain defeat against the Planet Division's dominant franchises, including the Yall Criminals, the To Pirates and the newly renamed Wabash Wolfpack, who went 9-3 last season as the Wabash Wall. As for the Krakens' two cross-divisional games, one is against perennial Solar Division relegation contenders Shorah Warlords. Sadly, the other is against the 2682 GFL Champion Jupiter Jacks.

## Playoff Math

While the odds of the Krakens making the T1 playoffs are just a bit lower than those of every star in the galaxy simultaneously going supernova, reassembling into a bartender and making this writer a Junkie Gin Blaster with a twist of lime, this column wouldn't be complete without providing the actual playoff math. It's simple — the four Planet Division teams with the best record go to the single-elimination Galaxy Bowl tournament. In the case of equal records, the tiebreaker is head-to-head results. In 2682, the four Planet Division playoff qualifiers finished with records of 11-1, 10-2, 9-3, and 8-4. As I mentioned earlier, before the Krakens land eight wins this year, every sentient in the galaxy would die in the burning gases of their suns expanding at nearly the speed of light, leaving this writer to drink his life away as the last living creature (except, of course, for the reassembled bartender). Scientific translation? The Krakens are not going to make the playoffs.

THE CROWD PARTED before the two huge Humans. Quentin and John Tweedy walked down the street, afternoon light playing down through the arcing city dome high overhead. They were trying — and failing — to blend in. They wore nondescript clothes: jeans, sweatshirts with hoods up, sunglasses. Tweedy also wore a strap that circled from his left shoulder to his right hip. It had nine mag-can-sized pouches. Eight carried cans of beer, while one held a pint of Junkie Gin. The strap was the fashion accessory he never seemed to be without, the thing he lovingly called his "beerdoleer."

Other than the beerdoleer, John wore nothing that called attention to his status as a football star. But at 6-foot-6, 310 pounds, there was only one Human on the entire street bigger than he was — and that Human was Quentin. With 380 solid pounds gracing his 7-foot frame, Quentin towered over everyone.

They walked through Ionath City's middle northwest quadrant, the busy nightclub district. It should have come as no surprise that any John Tweedy contact would be in this area, as this area seemed to be the only place he went.

Quentin pointed to one of the towering buildings, where someone was hanging one end of an orange-and-black Krakens banner from a fifteenth-story window, the other end reaching across a narrow gap to a neighboring building.

"They're going all out for this parade," Quentin said. "That why you brought me this way?"

"Sort of," John said. "Our guy's office is on Fifth Ring Road anyway, but I thought you'd like to see the whole city ramping up for the parade."

Quentin nodded. He was happy to see the preparations — banners and flags of orange and black, crowd barriers being put up, general spit and polish on all areas for the parade that would kick off in a few hours. Some fans were already camped out behind the barriers, staking their places for the festivities. If this was how they celebrated promotion into Tier One, Quentin could only imagine what they would do for a Galaxy Bowl victory.

The nightclub district ran along Fifth Ring Road. Fifth Ring was at the mid-point of the dome's convex arc, the inner point where the mostly red, hexagonal buildings started getting smaller, going from the forty-story affairs at the city center to one-story flats at the dome's edge. In the nightclub district, bars and restaurants packed the first two floors of almost every building. Fake exteriors done in hundreds of styles, colorful lights temporarily drowned out by the afternoon sun, holosigns and other decorations calling out to potential patrons. Smooth, red crysteel started at the third floor and rose twenty to thirty stories above.

Fifth Ring looked like the other ring roads: the wide dip of the mag-lev train track in the middle, supporting public transit cars that circled the city. On either side of the track, two lanes of road for cabs, trucks and private cars. Outside lanes always carried clockwise traffic, inside lanes always ran counterclockwise.

Pedestrian traffic tended to match this clockwise/counterclockwise pattern. John and Quentin were on the outside sidewalk, circling north. They walked among a diverse crowd made up mostly of Quyth Workers but also peppered with plenty of Ki, Human and HeavyG sentients. It was only noon and the area was already bustling — by the time the sun went down, the nightclub district would be so packed it could take ten minutes to exit one bar, go down the street a few buildings and enter the next one. Despite the sweatshirt hoods, Quentin saw occasional smiles of recognition. He tried to ignore them and just keep walking.

"It's jumping," Quentin said. "Seems busy for this early in the afternoon."

"Big sports day," John said. "All kinds of stuff going down. Big hover-essedari race out in the wastes, so sentients are packing the bars to watch live coverage. Sklorno soccer championship league tourney is in the final four. That was last night, but it's just broadcasting now. Oh, and in a few hours the Dinolition Derby signal reaches us from the League of Planets. I've got some big bucks on Li'l Pete Poughkeepsie's team."

"Dinolition?"

John stopped in the middle of the sidewalk. "You haven't seen Dinolition?"

Quentin shook his head. "Haven't even heard of it."

**AND YOU BELIEVE IN A HIGHER BEING?** scrolled across John's face. "Oh, man, Q, you're in for a treat. You think things are rough in the GFL? Try being a dwarf in turtle armor riding a seven-ton T-rex into a death match."

"You're kidding, right?"

"Hell, no," John said. "Dead serious. So, yeah, a lot going on makes today a major sporgy.

"Sporgy?"

"An orgy of sports," John said. "Sports orgy. *Sporgy.* And look, man, I want to help you find your parents and all, but I got games to watch so can we just get moving?"

John looked annoyed. He shook his head, then started walking again. Quentin walked with him, not bothering to say that John had been the one to stop in the first place.

"So," Quentin said, "this guy is good?"

"The best. Want a beer?"

Quentin shook his head. He wanted to be totally sober for this. It felt good to finally take a step toward finding his parents. And yet, the fear lingered — what if he found out they were both dead? Then he was alone, no family at all. His teammates, sure, but no real family.

Tweedy drained his beer and tossed the mag-can over his shoulder. It hit a passing Quyth Warrior in the head.

"Hey, Human," the Quyth Warrior said. "You pick that up."

Tweedy stopped, smiled and turned around. Quentin sighed. They were trying to keep a low profile, lest any of Gredok's gang see them, maybe figure out what Quentin was up to.

Quentin turned as well. The offended Quyth Warrior was normal for his species, which was to say he was much smaller than John Tweedy. Quentin had grown so used to being around Virak the Mean, Choto the Bright and his other Quyth Warrior teammates that he'd forgotten how big they were relative to their species, just like he was big for his.

The Warrior wore gray pants that covered his folded-up lower legs. He wore no shirt, exposing his pale orange torso and big lower arms. A few enamels decorated his carapace, but nothing like the full-body art of Virak and Choto. The pedipalp arms on either side of the Warrior's head twitched. Quentin thought he saw a tinge of pink flicker through the Warrior's single, softball-sized eye.

"You talkin' to me?" John said, his smile growing even wider, his face scrolling the bright words FREE TRIPS TO DEATHVILLE, GET YOUR TICKET PUNCHED HERE.

The crowd started to part, giving John, Quentin and the Quyth Warrior plenty of room.

"John," Quentin said. "Now's not the time."

John shrugged. "Not up to me. Up to Mister Happy Public Helper, here." John pointed to the empty mag-can. "What do you say, Mister Happy Public Helper? You want to do something about that trash on the ground?"

The Quyth Warrior looked at John, then at Quentin, then back. The pink color faded, replaced by swirling yellow.

"John Tweedy?" the Warrior said. "Oh, I am a *huge* fan. Can I have your autograph?"

The Warrior reached into one of his pants pockets. Quentin flinched, took a half step back to run, but the Warrior pulled out a messageboard that he offered to John.

John sighed, then took the board and signed it.

"And you," the Warrior said to Quentin. "Are you Barnes? Really?"

Quentin nodded. John passed over the messageboard, which Quentin quietly signed and handed back to the Warrior.

"Oh, thank you! Such an honor! And good luck this season. Go, Krakens!"

The Warrior put the messageboard back in his pocket, picked up the mag-can, then continued down the sidewalk.

"John," Quentin said. "I thought we were supposed to keep a low profile."

"I can't help it if I'm so damn pretty," John said. "It sucks, though — sentients recognize me too fast. Almost impossible to get into a decent brawl these days. I even get recognized when I go to Orbital Station One to see my brother Ju. Now that we're in Tier One, it's going to be even worse."

Quentin thought back to the mines of Micovi, where a similar, minor altercation could quickly escalate into a lethal fight. "John, why would you want to start something like that? What if that Warrior had a weapon?"

"Hard to get a weapon inside the dome, Q. The Quyth aren't big on their citizens and workers getting shot or stabbed every ten minutes. Most conflicts end as a straight-up fight. And when it comes to a straight-up fight? I'm kind of good."

"I noticed," Quentin said, thinking back to the fight at the Bootleg Arms bar. He and several other Krakens had tried to pay off Don Pine's gambling debt to Mopuk the Sneaky. Mopuk, living up to his name, had refused to take the money — a game-tanking GFL quarterback was far more valuable than the millions Don owed. Mopuk's bodyguards tried to attack Quentin, but the bodyguards ran afoul of Virak, Choto, several Ki linemen and John Tweedy. John used his bare hands to kill two Quyth Warrior toughs, one by punching through the single eye to the brain behind, one by snapping its thick neck.

When it came to a brawl, John Tweedy was one bad man.

"I've studied how to fight," Tweedy said. "So many different styles. That's how I spend the off-season, at least when we have an off-season. I even did some pro fighting, did you know that?"

Quentin shook his head. "I had no idea. How did you do?"

"Real good, but you can't succeed in that sport without mods. If I certified as a pro fighter, which you have to do in order to get mods, then no football."

"So why did you choose football?"

"I'm a better football player than a fighter," John said. "I make a load of money in football, but I'd be lucky to earn a living in the Octagon. I can't even beat up my brother, Ju. He had a few pro fights, even sparred again Chiyal North."

"The *Heretic*?" Quentin said. "You're kidding me, right?"

"Nope. Ju is the baddest man I know, and Chiyal whooped him."

"Chiyal is a hero where I come from," Quentin said. "We don't exactly have a lot of intergalactic sports stars coming out of the Purist Nation. Last night's fight ... such a tragedy."

John nodded sadly. "A real shame he died right there in the Octagon against Korak the Cutter, but what a bout! I mean, my man Chiyal used his own *shinbone* to stab Korak. That's why The Heretic is the champ — whatever it takes to win."

"*Was* the champ," Quentin said. "Dead men don't hold titles."

John shrugged. "Korak died first, so Chiyal won the bout. He died the champ. Hey, man, if I had to die to win a Galaxy Bowl? I'd do it in a heartbeat. A championship is immortality, Q. Immortality."

Quentin shook his head and started to argue but stopped when he realized that he felt the same way. Quentin had long ago decided he would do anything needed to win a GFL Tier One title. *Anything.* Was he so different, then, from Chiyal "The Heretic" North, who had died winning the undisputed heavyweight title?

John stopped walking and looked up at a twenty-story red building on his left. "This is it, Q, we're here." He turned to look at Quentin. John stared with wide, crazy eyes. His eyes always looked like that, except for when he was on the football field, when they were wider and crazier, which was bad, or when they crinkled in time with one of his psycho smiles, which was far, far worse.

"Don't you embarrass me in there," John said. "None of your hayseed hick-osity. This is a serious guy I'm introducing you to here. A *serious* guy."

"What makes you think I'll embarrass you?"

John shook his head, the words DUMB SPELLED BACKWARD IS BMUD scrolling across his face. He opened the door and walked in. Quentin followed.

Maybe they were past the edge of the nightclub district because this place looked like some kind of an office building. Quentin looked around, suddenly realized something odd — aside from a couple of nightclubs, he hadn't seen the inside of anything in Ionath City other than the Krakens building.

Outside, all the buildings were varying shades of red. This

lobby? All white. In the middle of the lobby, a Quyth Worker sat behind a circular desk. A couple of scarred Ki wearing green uniforms stood on either side. They looked out of shape, perhaps, but also had that aura of ex-soldiers or former cops. Whatever their past, now they worked office-building security.

John strode to the reception desk like he owned the place. The Ki on either side didn't have to turn their heads to watch him, what with their 360-degree vision and all, but you could tell they were instantly paying close attention to the two massive Humans.

The Quyth Worker behind the desk wasn't like the slovenly ones Quentin often saw in the bars and nightclubs, swilling gin, nearly drinking themselves into a coma. This one was dressed in a tidy green uniform. The Worker reminded Quentin of Messal the Efficient, the Krakens' team manager.

The Worker recognized John, and his one eye flooded with yellow. "Well, Mister Jo —"

John held up a hand, cutting off the worker's sentence. "I'm Mister Smith," John said. "That person you thought you just saw? He was never here."

John pulled the pint of Junkie Gin out of his beerdoleer.

The Worker looked at it greedily, then tapped a couple of buttons that probably turned off cameras somewhere in the lobby.

"Well, Mister … Smith. That is a rather nice gift."

"Look at the label," John said. The Worker did, then started to quiver.

"This … this is actually *signed* by *Yitzhak Goldman*?"

"The man himself," John said. "I'm gonna head up, got some business upstairs. You'll make sure there's no images of us, right?"

The Worker nodded violently, a difficult maneuver considering his relative lack of a neck. "No one will know you and your friend were here."

John rapped his knuckles on the desk twice, then walked around it, heading for the elevators. Quentin followed.

An elevator hissed open, and they got in. John pressed a button for the fifteenth floor.

"John, what was that all about? An autographed bottle of gin?"

"Stuff is like gold," John said. "Really expensive, the Workers are crazy for it. And a signature from Yitzhak? That Worker will do whatever we ask."

"Yeah, but why wouldn't you use my autograph? I'm the starting quarterback."

John pulled a fresh Miller from the beerdoleer and popped the top. The mag-can frosted up instantly. "Get used to it, Q." He drained half the can. "The Quyth are going to root for you like crazy, but no matter what you do, they will always like their own better. Yitzhak is the native son, and that's that."

Quentin still found it odd the Quyth adored a Human that much. Yitzhak wasn't even their species. Zak's family had lived on Ionath going back something like three generations. He'd been born right here under the Ionath City dome. It seemed the Quyth didn't see race — they only saw borders. You didn't have to be a Quyth to be a Concordia citizen; you just had to want to be part of the Concordia. Learn the culture, learn the history, swear allegiance to the Concordia above all others — all others, including your original homeland — and the Quyth would welcome you with open pedipalps.

The elevator stopped. Quentin followed John out. The lobby hadn't looked new, but it had been neat and clean. Everything on this floor seemed damaged. The place smelled musty. The walls had once been smart-paper, but no longer had the ability to flicker images and patterns. Now the material just sagged.

Splatters of dried brown covered one spot.

"John," Quentin said and pointed to the stain. "Is that *blood*?"

John finished his mag-can and tossed it down the hall. "Yeah, probably. A lot of private investigators in this building, some bounty hunters and the like. Everyone needs an office for tax purposes, you know?"

Quentin nodded, although he really had no idea how taxes worked.

John stopped in front of a door marked with a placard that showed one line repeated in fifteen languages. Quentin read the line in English: SUITE 1510 — GONZAGA INVESTIGATIONS.

"Remember," John said. "Don't embarrass me."

He knocked on the door. Quentin heard a buzzing sound, then metallic clicks — which sounded like several big deadbolts sliding back. The door opened, and John walked in. Quentin followed, glancing at the edge of the door as he did. Holes in the thick door were an inch in diameter. The door's frame had matching, recessed circles. When the door was closed and the bars extended, a hover-tank couldn't get through.

The office was a long room with walls and floor made out of irregular, flat, red stones. At the end of the room sat a white desk. Behind the white desk, a man dressed in a business suit made out of some shiny pink material. In front of the desk, two white chairs. Above the two white chairs, something that looked like a stubby-legged horse all done up in a frilly green, blue and yellow material.

Quentin stopped in his tracks. The whole thing made him feel oddly uncomfortable. He pointed to the strange, frilly horse. "John, what is that?"

"That's a piñata," John said.

"What's a piñata?"

"A piñata," the man in pink said, "is *fab*ulous. Uncle Johnny Boy the Awesome, walk your muscles over here and bring that delicious quarterback with you."

Quentin stared at the man. Something ... *off* about him. Something that made Quentin nervous.

John walked to the left-side chair and sat, leaving Quentin standing alone and feeling like an idiot. Quentin walked to the right-side chair and sat, looking up as he did — whatever a piñata was, he was sitting directly under its green, blue and yellow horse ass.

"Quentin Barnes," John said, "meet Frederico Esteban Giuseppe Gonada."

"Gonzaga," the man said. "But that was very close, John."

Tweedy nodded.

"Fabulous to meet you, Mister Barnes. Or should I call you Elder?"

Frederico seemed overly excited about the whole situation.

And the way he'd said *Elder* — all smiles, but the word was laced with hatred.

"Quentin is fine, thanks."

"Well, Quentin, you certainly are a big boy, aren't you?"

"Uh ..." Quentin said. Well, he *was* much bigger than Frederico. Hard to tell while the man was sitting, but Frederico might be six foot even. If so, that made Quentin a full foot taller. Frederico looked athletic but couldn't have been more than two hundred pounds. Next to Quentin, he looked anorexic.

"Soooo," Frederico said, drawing out the word. "Uncle Johnny tells me you're just a lost little lonely heart."

"I'm ... what?"

"You need help finding your parents, your family," Frederico said. "I think you came to the right place. At least your pretty eyes came to the right place."

Quentin stared at the man, then at John. John shrugged.

"Uh, yes," Quentin said. "That's right, I want to find my parents."

"So you can kiss them with that big, pouty mouth of yours?"

Quentin leaned back. Had this guy just called his mouth *pouty*? Why would a guy say that ... unless ...

Quentin grabbed John's arm. "Tweedy, can I have a word with you?"

John nodded. Quentin led him to the back of the office.

"What is this?" Quentin said in a hard whisper. "Why is he talking about my eyes and stuff?"

"He said he thinks they're pretty," John said, matching Quentin's volume. "It's like you don't listen or something."

"Yeah, but ... he's a *guy*. Why would a *guy* think my eyes are pretty?"

Tweedy sighed. "Maybe, backwater, because he thinks guys are prettier than girls."

Quentin stared and blinked, the words hitting home. "You mean he's *gay*? Like ... a homosexual?"

Tweedy dug the heel of his right hand into his right eye. SOME MEN YOU JUST CAN'T REACH scrolled across his forehead.

"Yeah, Q," John said. "Maybe he's gay. Are you going to tell me that after all you've been through with big scary aliens and working in the mines and gangsters and roundbugs, you're afraid of a little gay guy?"

"I'm not *afraid*," Quentin said. "It's just that ... well, you know, it's a ... a ... "

"A what, Q? Is being gay a sin?" DID HIGH ONE MAKE STUPIDITY, OR DID IT EVOLVE ON ITS OWN? scrolled across his face.

Quentin felt his temper rising. "Listen, jerk, don't ridicule my culture, you got that? I was raised to believe certain things."

"*Certain things*. You mean things like all aliens — including your teammates — are actually the spawn of Satan and should be killed on sight?"

"Well, no, that part was ridiculous."

"Why?"

"Because now I know aliens."

"And how many gays do you know?"

Quentin blinked. He looked across the room at Frederico. "Including this guy?"

"Yeah."

"Well ... one."

Tweedy nodded. "Look, man, you asked for help and I delivered. Frederico is the best. You need someone found? You need to sneak into a system? This is the guy. And he's ex-Planetary Union Navy or something. Can fly any ship. If you want to find your parents, hire Frederico — unless you'd rather go to Gredok with your troubles?"

Quentin automatically shook his head. "No way. I'm not giving him any more leverage on me."

"Such wisdom from such a primitive screwhead," John said. "You'd be an idiot not to use Frederico. But then again, Purism produces a butt-load of idiots."

Quentin felt his fingers curl up into fists. "John, I am warning you. You keep insulting my religion, and it's going to go somewhere neither one of us wants it to."

"You don't even *like* your religion."

"I like it enough to defend it."

John rolled his eyes. "Fine. Give Frederico a chance, and I'll lay off. Just talk to him. If you don't think he can cut the gig, we take off, okay?

Quentin looked at Frederico, shiny pink shoes up on the desk, big smile on his face. Frederico saw Quentin looking, put his fingers to his mouth, kissed them, held his hand in front of his face and blew.

"He just blew me a kiss," Quentin said.

"Better than him giving you the finger."

"Yeah, but he just *blew me a kiss.*"

John sighed. "Quentin, aren't you a professional athlete?"

"Yeah."

"He's two hundred pounds, tops. You weigh twice as much as him. Do you think he's got a homo stun gun or something? Maybe a magic spell of gayness that makes you want to dance and sing show tunes?"

"Well ... no."

"Then stop being *you*. You come sit down with me now, or I'm heading to the bar to watch Dinolition. Which is it gonna be?"

Quentin looked up at the ceiling. He knew he was being ridiculous, but it was hard to get past a lifetime of rhetoric. He *had* once thought the Sklorno, the Quyth, and the Ki were Satanic. He'd gotten over that. Maybe he'd get over this as well.

He walked to Frederico's desk and sat in the chair on the right.

John sat in the left-side chair. He pulled a mag-can of Miller from the beerdoleer. "Sorry," he said and reached across the desk to offer Frederico the can.

Frederico took it, popped the top and sipped. He put the can down and stared at Quentin. "So, you're okay with me doing this job?"

Quentin took a deep breath. "Look, I may have reacted, uh, poorly. I, uh, I'm not used to ... to *this*."

Frederico shrugged. "That's fine, you're the client. Pay the bill on time and you can act pretty much any way you like. But please answer my question — are you okay with me being gay? You'll still hire me?"

Quentin nodded. "Yeah, sure. I'll hire you."

"Wow."

"You didn't think I would?"

Frederico shrugged. "You're from the Purist Nation. Everyone from the Purist Nation is a racist homophobic hate-monger."

"Millions of people are from the Purist Nation. Don't judge me as a stereotype. We're not all the same."

"I suppose not," Frederico said. The over-the-top exuberance had left his voice. He didn't sound girly anymore, he sounded like a regular guy. "Now, you know I charge a *lot*, right?"

"Not really spending my money on anything else," Quentin said. "I mean … this is my family, you know?"

Frederico nodded slowly. "I hear you. Well, as long as your money is good, that's what matters to me. I hate you Nationalites, but I'm doing this as a favor for John."

John raised his mag-can in salute and belched.

Frederico laughed and shook his head. "You're one of a kind, Uncle Johnny the Awesome." Frederico waved both hands over his desk. Lines of light flared to life in front of him — a holo-interface. The middle of the desk changed appearance, going from white to clear. Quentin couldn't see from where he was sitting, but there was likely a recessed screen inside the desk. Frederico's fingertips poked at icons made of nothing but light.

"Okay, Quentin," he said. "Tell me what you know."

"Their last name was Barnes."

Frederico entered that. "First names?"

"I don't know."

"What do you mean *you don't know*? They were your parents."

"I was really little," Quentin said. "They were just Mom and Dad to me."

"What happened to them?"

"I don't know. They disappeared when I was two, maybe three. I'm not sure."

"So, probably seventeen years ago? About 2666?"

"Yeah," Quentin said. "How'd you know that?"

Quentin felt an elbow hit his left arm. "'Cause he's *good*," John said. "That's why."

Frederico shook his head and reached under his desk. "I *am* good, John, but this one was easy." Frederico tossed a paper magazine on the desktop. Quentin turned it so he could read the cover — KRAKENS INSIDER: KRAKENS VS. WALLCRAWLERS.

"Game program," Frederico said. "Has your age right in there."

John's eyes widened in stunned admiration. "That's *amazing*. See, Q? I *told* you this guy was good."

Frederico laughed to himself and entered more info. "How about sisters, Quentin? Brothers?"

"Just one brother. They hung him when I was five."

The detective shook his head and made a *tsk-tsk* sound with his mouth. "Right. Let me guess. A really *awful* crime, like ... stealing food?"

"Yeah. How did you know?"

Quentin felt the elbow hit his left arm again. He turned to see John, nodding slightly, eyebrows raised. I TOLD YOU THIS GUY WAS GOOD scrolled across his head.

"You're not my first Nationalite client," Frederico said. "You'd be surprised how unoriginal your story is. They hang people for all kinds of things. They save burning at the stake for heretics, though. Heretics, and what else, Quentin?"

Quentin felt his face flush red.

"Come on," Frederico said. "Who else do they burn at the stake?"

"Homosexuals," Quentin said.

Frederico nodded. "You ever see someone burned at the stake?"

Quentin nodded slowly. He had seen that. Many times.

"So have I," the detective said. He shook his head quickly, like he was chasing away an annoying memory. "Right, and your brother's name?"

"Quincy," Quentin said. "I think. I called him … "

Quentin's voice trailed off.

Frederico stopped entering data and looked at him. "I need all the info I can get, Quentin. A nickname is just as valuable to me as the real thing. What did you call him?"

John sat patiently, also waiting. Quentin knew he wouldn't hear the end of this.

"Fine," Quentin said. "I remember calling him *Kin-Kin*, 'cause I couldn't pronounce Quincy."

Frederico nodded and tapped icons. Quentin tried not to look at Tweedy, but he couldn't help himself. He turned to see John staring at him with a stone-straight face, the words WE'LL FIND KIN-KIN, DIDDUMS scrolling across his forehead.

Quentin sighed and turned his attention back to the detective.

"What else?" Frederico said. "Aunts? Uncles? Who took care of you after High One smote your brother for the horribly sacrilegious crime of murdering bread?"

"I was an orphan," Quentin said. "I was on my own. Should I tell you about the orphanage system?"

"No," Frederico said. "I know quite a lot about that subject, unfortunately. Let's talk money — I charge ten thousand a week, plus expenses. If you don't pay within a day of getting the bill, I drop the case and don't come back no matter what you do. Understand?"

Quentin nodded.

"Good," Frederico said. "Now, listen carefully. Just because I've handled cases like this before doesn't mean I want you to get your hopes up. I'll be honest with you. Odds are that your parents died in a pogrom, that they were incinerated in a mass grave and there was no record keeping of their death. They're just *gone*, and you'll never know different. If they did get out of the Purist Nation, they probably changed their name, abandoned their religion and assumed you were dead. Or more likely, they knew that if they contacted you, an enemy of theirs still in the Nation might find you and kill you to avenge some debt of family honor. The odds of just finding out *what happened* to your parents are about one in a million. The odds of actually finding *them*? Let's just say you can't find a bookie anywhere in the galaxy that would take that bet."

Quentin stared at the pink-suited man for a second, weighing the words carefully before speaking. "So what you're saying is that I'm wasting my money. Wasting ten grand a week, on you. Why should I do that?"

"Ten grand plus expenses," Frederico said. "Don't forget that important little *caveat*. You should hire me because if your parents can be found, I'm the guy to find them. Quietly. I'm assuming you're here because you don't want Gredok the Splithead to know about your family?"

John sat forward quickly, beer sloshing out of his mag-can. "Unbelievable! Is this guy good, or is this guy *good*?"

Quentin smacked Tweedy in the shoulder. "Give it a rest, John. It's obvious that I don't want Gredok to know."

"Yeah," John said. "*Sure*, it's obvious, now that Fred has gone and said it out loud. I didn't see you figuring that one out before."

"I said it on the way here!"

John nodded, eyes wide. "Yeah ... yeah, you're right. It's like Fred knew what we were talking about, like he's *psychic*."

"I *am* psychic," Frederico said. He put his fingers to his temples and stared at John. "Right now, you're thinking ... *this guy is really good*."

John stood up so fast the chair shot out from under him. He pointed a finger at the detective. "You knock that off, Fred, okay? That's just way too freakish. No disrespect to you, man, but I'm—"

"Outta here?" Frederico said.

John dropped his mag-can, took a step back and held up both hands, palms out. "You stop that, Fred, you get—"

"Out of your head?"

John turned and ran out of the office.

Quentin and Frederico watched him go, then faced each other.

"John's great," Frederico said, "but he's a real piece of work."

Quentin nodded. "Tell me about it."

"Look, Quentin, I won't waste your money. I'm extremely talented at everything I do, this included. I'm worth twice as much, so I'm a bargain at this price. And if at any point I figure out I can't help you, I'm done. I won't charge you for work I can't finish. If you come up with something else that might help me — you remember anything — you call me."

Frederico stood and held out his hand. "Now the tough part. Can you shake a fag's hand?"

Quentin felt his face flush red. He was surprised to realize that he didn't even want to touch the man, just like when he'd landed on the *Touchback* and hadn't wanted to touch Don Pine's skin because it was blue. But Quentin had overcome so many preconditioned prejudices there was no point in stopping now.

Quentin stood, towering over Frederico. "Well, you're the first fag I've met, so let's give it a try." He forced himself to meet the man's stare as they shook.

"Know what, Quentin?"

"What?"

"You got really pretty eyes."

Quentin reactively yanked his hand free.

Frederico laughed. "Class is still in session, apparently."

"Yeah, I guess so, and I learned something today."

"Oh? What's that?"

"That *fags* can be total jackasses, just like everybody else."

Frederico laughed louder and applauded. "Now you're getting it. And remember how I said that I excel at everything I do? That includes being an jackass."

Quentin nodded, then walked into the hall to find John Tweedy wearing an empty beerdoleer and standing amidst a pile of three empty mag-cans.

"Q! Are you okay? Did he get inside your head?"

"I'm fine. Just calm down. How about we go get you a beer?"

The big linebacker nodded. "Yeah. Yeah that's a good idea. I'm a little freaked out. That guy is *good*, man."

"We can only hope," Quentin said. "How about the Bootleg Arms?"

John nodded. The two Krakens left the building and headed for the Bootleg Arms, the club owned by Gredok the Splithead.

• • •

## Transcript from the "Galaxy's Greatest Sports Show with Dan, Akbar & Tarat the Smasher"

**DAN:** Hello, fans! I'm Dan Gianni back once again to give you the greatest show in sports. As always, I'm joined by Akbar Smith and Hall-of-Fame linebacker Tarat the Smasher.

**AKBAR:** Thanks, Dan.

**TARAT:** Always happy to be here.

**DAN:** So, guys, we've got a full show today, with just two topics. Why? Because those two topics are so big, so juicy, so tasty, we're going to be inundated with calls.

**AKBAR:** So, I take it we're talking about the Tier Two expansion?

**TARAT:** I'm so excited I could just molt.

**DAN:** Tarat, seriously, please don't. But absolutely, Tier Two expansion! It's so exciting.

**AKBAR:** It's not tradition.

**DAN:** Tradition? What do you mean, *tradition*?

**TARAT:** Tradition means the way things have always been done, Dan.

**DAN:** I know what tradition means, Smasher. What I'm saying is, *what* tradition?

**AKBAR:** There are six Tier Two conferences, Dan. Six, not *eight*.

**DAN:** Well, *now*, there are eight. How can you not be excited about the Whitok Kingdom being brought into the galactic fold with the Whitok Conference? And they're adding a *second* Human conference? It's brilliant.

**AKBAR:** What the hell do you mean, *brilliant*?

**TARAT:** *Brilliant* means that it's inspired, highly intelligent.

**AKBAR:** I know what *brilliant* means, Smasher. I'm saying you can't just go adding leagues like that. And come on, Dan, saying that adding a Whitok Conference is bringing the Kingdom *into the galactic fold*? Isn't that a little much?

**DAN:** Where the heck have you been for the past twenty years, Akbar? This is a major, *major* deal, not just for sports but for politics as well. The Whitok Kingdom isn't controlled by the Creterakians.

This is a major sign that the Kingdom has finally recovered from their losses in the Fourth Galactic War, *and* it marks the first normalization of relations with the Creterakians since the bats ceased hostilities in 2642. Here we are, forty-one standard years later, and Whitok football teams will be part of the GFL. This means the galaxy is finally accepting *peace*, Akbar.

**AKBAR:** Accepting? Tell that to those lunatics from the Zoroastrian Guild. They are crazy with a capital-Z, but I agree with them on one point — being ruled by the bats isn't my definition of *peace*; it's my definition of *subjugation*.

**TARAT:** The Quyth Concordia isn't subjugated. We live free.

**AKBAR:** *The Quyth Concordia lives free! The Quyth Concordia lives free!* Every five minutes with that crap, Smasher. We know, okay? Trust me, we know. And besides, all the Whitok cities are underwater, so tell me how that's going to work for a game played on a field.

**DAN:** Akbar, now, you're just being a pain. What about the Pacifica Dolphins? Their stadium is in the middle of an ocean on Earth. Or how about the Isis Ice Storm? Their stadium is something like a mile underwater. All the GFL requires is a playing field where oxygen-breathing players can operate in standard gravity and standard air pressure.

**TARAT:** The Whitok already have teams playing in the upper tiers, Akbar. Or did you forget about the D'Kow War Dogs?

**AKBAR:** Well, I suppose that's a good point. And I guess going from a six-team T2 Tourney to an eight-team format makes for more drama.

**DAN:** Absolutely. I always thought those first-round bye games were a little confusing. Now it's a straight-up eight-team, single-elimination tournament. The last two teams standing get into Tier One. Makes you wonder if the Chillich Spider-Bears or the Ionath Krakens would have been promoted if they hadn't had first-round byes last week.

**TARAT:** Well, the Spider-Bears would have made it in, they were just fantastic. But the Krakens? Maybe not without that first-round bye.

**DAN:** Speaking of the Ionath Krakens, that brings us to our second topic of discussion — the Tier One teams with the worst records get relegated to Tier Two. Out of the twenty-two Tier One teams that kick off in four weeks, which two are getting sent down at season's end?

**AKBAR:** Wait, you said *speaking of the Krakens*. You're saying the Krakens are going to be relegated?

**DAN:** Oh, come on, there's no question! Quentin Barnes might have been good enough to get Ionath through the T2 Tourney, but the Krak-pack lost their starting running back, Mitchell "The Machine" Fayed. Ionath has no running game, and I don't think their defensive backs can stop *any* Tier One offense.

**TARAT:** I think Quentin Barnes may surprise you, Dan. He's a true warrior in the making.

**DAN:** Warrior? He's from the Purist Nation! No Nationalite quarterback has *ever* led a team to a Tier One championship. *Eh*-ver. He'll be lucky to live long enough to fail and go back to Tier Two. Let's go to the callers. Line two from Citadel in the Tower Republic, go …

**QUENTIN BARNES HAD NEVER SEEN** a real parade before. He certainly hadn't been in one and, *most* certainly, hadn't been a guest of honor.

Back on Micovi, the fundamentalist theocracy frowned on such things. There were processionals, sure — somber marches for the latest martyr, a funeral train for a passed religious leader, that kind of thing. Long lines of people dressed in blue robes, chanting, swaying, self-flagellating, doing everything they could to show their grief and anguish lest a neighbor report them for not feeling *enough* grief and anguish. Not showing enough anguish might lead to an inquiry, probably an arrest and — quite frequently — yet another funeral processional.

There was no shortage of funerals in the Purist Nation.

So, Quentin Barnes had seen lines of people walking down a

street and he'd seen throngs of people lining the sidewalks, but never anything like *this*. So much color. So much noise.

So much ... joy.

Ionath City's rad-free dome was two miles in diameter. A full circle around Fifth Ring Road made for a trip of over three miles. Three *slow* miles. Even with a phalanx of riot-geared Quyth Warrior police dishing out random beat-downs, adoring football fans were still climbing over barriers and running up to the sixteen grav-train cars that traveled down the road's center lev-track.

"This is crazy," Quentin said to Don Pine, who sat on his right. "I've *never* seen anything like this."

Don nodded. He was smiling, waving a cupped hand with a practiced motion. He called it his *princess wave*. "You'll get used to this, Q. At least I hope you do. As many times as I've done this, it's hard to be jaded looking at all these happy faces. Just you wait until you win the big one — this is nothing in comparison."

Quentin found it hard to believe he'd ever think of this teeming mass of sentients as "nothing." The city had placed dividers down the middle of each two-lane road that ran along either side of the lev-track. That let orange- and black-clad fans fill half of the road, and the sidewalk beyond, and the diameter roads that ran deeper into the city. Every window in the red, hexagonal buildings had several heads of various species sticking out of it. Krakens flags flew everywhere, from the small, hand-held kind to giant flags that were probably ten feet high and twenty feet long. Banners, flags, pom-pons, foam fingers, foam pincers, foam tentacles, jackets, hats, jerseys — more orange and black than Quentin had even known existed.

Ionath City's urban dome normally held somewhere around 110,000 residents in claustrophobic closeness. Considering the dome was just about the only place most of the Ionath Krakens players could breathe, that was where they held the parade, and that was where an estimated one *million* additional beings had packed in tight.

Quentin felt an elbow bump on his left arm. He turned to look at Yitzhak, who sat in the seat next to him.

"Q, *smile*, will ya?" Yitzhak said. "Maybe try not to look like an anthropomorphic hayseed?"

"Shuck you, Zak," Quentin said, but he smiled and waved. Hard to think that, just hours earlier, there had been functioning roads, packed sidewalks, grav-cars, taxis, trucks and trains. Now? Nothing but Humans, HeavyG, the three castes of Quyth, some Ki and even a few Sklorno females all wrapped up from head to toe. Sentients lined the barriers, at least a hundred deep.

Quentin didn't know what *anthropomorphic* meant, but he did know the word *hayseed*.

And that wasn't what he was. Not anymore.

"Don't worry about it," Don said. "No one is here to see you, anyway, kid — they're here to see their *hero*."

Yitzhak laughed and stood, holding his T2 Tourney MVP trophy high, waving it at the adoring crowd. Quentin had to smile at the third-string quarterback's exuberance. Zak was soaking up the moment.

The Krakens had earned promotion to T1 with their semi-final win over the Texas Earthlings, while the Chillich Spider-Bears had won their promotion with a semi-final victory over the Citadel Aquanauts. The actual T2 Tourney championship game hadn't mattered. That was why Zak played. Both Quentin and Don Pine had sat out the final championship game, as had most of the starters. The Chillich Spider-Bears had done the same, fielding an entire team of backups. That was just smart football — both teams had already qualified for Tier One, so let the starters rest up for the big time.

So Zak started the championship game, but he didn't care about starters or second string or third string — he'd played his butt off and led the Krakens to a win. The win meant a "championship," and that meant a parade.

Quentin, Don and Yitzhak rode in the front seat of the second train car. Since Ionath City was domed, weather was always controlled and all train cars were open-air.

Public transit train cars had seven rows of species-specific seats that always went in the same order: Quyth Leader and Warrior, then Human, HeavyG, Ki and Sklorno. Human rows had five seats, HeavyG only three to handle the wider bodies. Sklorno rows had those strange, abdomen-supporting seats the ladies required. Ki seats were little more than flat beams that allowed the long creatures to rest their multiple legs. Quyth Workers had their own train cars, as they weren't allowed to use the same facilities as Leaders and Warriors.

The three quarterbacks had a train car all to themselves. City leaders had wanted to stretch the parade out, so each of the sixteen cars in the procession held three to five players or team staff.

The car ahead of Quentin's was the parade's lead car. It held three Quyth Leaders: Coach Hokor the Hookchest, his yellow and black fur puffed up to full thickness; Gredok the Splithead, his glossy black fur as smooth and unruffled as ever; and an orange- and black-furred leader that Don had said was the mayor of Ionath City. The mayor apparently had *white* fur but painted it up in Krakens colors for the big parade.

In the seat behind those leaders rode Choto the Bright and Virak the Mean, who had returned along with Gredok. Quentin couldn't even look at them without feeling a simmering rage. Both of the linebackers had casts on their legs. As tough as the two of them were, apparently there was someone tougher. Quentin thought he'd extricated Virak from goon-duty, but apparently there was more work to be done. The linebacker's primary job was now football, but he was still dangerous enough that Gredok would use him whenever the situation demanded it. For a public event like this, Virak and Choto would stay close to Gredok, their leader, their *shamakath*.

Even Doc, the team's physician, participated in the parade. A Harrah, Doc flew in slow circles around the lead car, his wide, stingray-like wings gracefully pushing him along. Orange and black streamers trailed from his tapered tail.

In the train cars somewhere behind Quentin were all of his teammates: Yassoud, Mum-O-Killowe, Stockbridge, Denver, his fullback Tom Pareless and dozens more — the sentients that had pulled together to put the Krakens in Tier One.

The players of the Ionath Krakens.

*His* players.

His, because now the team was his to lead. Don Pine had said so, passing the torch of leadership in front of High One and everyone else. And all of this screaming, adoring insanity from the fans? Don was right, this was just the beginning. If these sentients thought were happy now, wait until Quentin Barnes rode down these streets, holding the Galaxy Bowl trophy high in the air.

Like they did whenever there was a crowd, his eyes scanned the Human faces, hunting for a familiar one, one he assumed he would remember but could not be sure.

Quentin again felt an elbow hit his left shoulder. Yitzhak leaned in close to Quentin's ear.

"Q, come *on*," Zak said. "This is face-time for you, pay attention to the crowd."

"I am paying attention."

"No, you're staring these sentients down like they're linebackers showing a blitz. This is part of the game, Q. We need to bring your popularity up so we can get you some fat endorsement money."

"I get paid plenty."

Yitzhak threw his head back and laughed. "Yeah, right. Who's your agent?"

"I don't have one."

Yitzhak leaned away, gave Quentin a funny look. "Seriously?" Quentin shrugged. "Gredok bought my existing contract. I don't need an agent."

"Hooooo," Zak said. "Brother, I'll make a few calls. I can help you."

Quentin shook his head. "Thanks, third-string, but I can actually change my own diapers from time to time."

Yitzhak waggled the MVP trophy in front of Quentin's face. "*Third-string?* Hayseed, just run your hands across this bad boy!"

Quentin took the offered trophy. It *was* rather nice. A wooden base with a thin chrome pole that supported a regulation-size football made of faceted crystal. The trophy caught the lights from the sun high above, sparkling with intense, rainbow colors.

"Nice, huh?" Yitzhak said.

Quentin handed it back and nodded. "Yep, I got to admit, that's a sweet piece of hardware."

"Damn right, it is," Zak said. "Now if you don't mind, I'm going to revel in my moment."

Yitzhak raised the trophy high in both hands, smiling and showing off for a crowd that roared in approval.

Quentin sat, his hand waving like an automaton while his eyes went back to searching the crowd.

And then he saw something that held his attention. Off to the right, on the outside of the ring road, a Human wearing a Krakens' jacket. The man visually scanned the parade vehicles much the same way Quentin scanned the crowd. Not looking *at* something, looking *for* something. Something in particular.

Quentin laughed to himself — he *was* looking at the crowd like it was a defense. That Human guy he'd just noticed, for example: the guy's eyes darted around like a linebacker hunting for an open gap, looking for a lineman's pointing foot to give away the direction of the play. And those two big Humans in front of the linebacker-man, they might be defensive linemen …

Quentin stared closer. The two big Humans, they held that same aura of intensity as the first man. And they were right in front of the linebacker-man, one on his left, one on his right.

Positioned in front, just like blockers.

Blockers that were about to clear a hole.

Quentin had spent a decade working in the mines of Micovi, a place where people died almost every day. Sometimes they died from cave-ins. Sometimes from roundbugs. Sometimes from the stonecats that lurked in the bigger crevices, waiting for a miner to stray too far away from the others. But most often, people died because they were killed by other people. Everything from vendettas, to loan sharks making an example, to basic theft gone wrong, or — most often — simple arguments that quickly blossomed into honor fights. To stay alive, you had to learn to read people, read their faces, scan for bad moods, for desperation, for anything that could make one person want to kill another. Sometimes Quentin had to fight. When he did, he made sure everyone understood that to step up to him was to get shredded. Most of the time, however, Quentin avoided fights because he learned to identify dangerous people and stay out of their way. The mines taught him that all the toughness in the galaxy is no armor against a knife in the back.

And the Purist Nation had a lot of knives.

Quentin lived through a decade in the mines, from five years old until he joined the Micovi Raiders football team at fifteen; he stayed alive because he knew how to read people. Read bad people. And that linebacker-looking Human and his two blockers? They looked bad.

"Yitzhak," Quentin said. "Let me hold your trophy for a second."

"No way," Yitzhak said. "Know why? Because you're not the MVP, Q. Sure, you're the franchise and all that, but ol' Yitzhak is the —"

Quentin stood and reached to his left. His eyes stayed on the three Humans, but his backhanded sweep plucked the crystal MVP trophy right out of Yitzhak's clutches.

"Hey," Yitzhak said, a hint of a whine coloring his voice. "Come on, give it back."

Quentin just shook his head. The three Humans pressed toward the barrier, to the line of Quyth Warrior police. Quentin saw that the men would reach the barriers just about the time Gredok's train car passed their position.

A hand on Quentin's right shoulder. "Q, what is it?" Don Pine again, but no humor in his voice this time. Quentin just nodded toward the men.

Don looked, taking it in for a second. "They trouble?"

"Is *who* trouble?" Yitzhak said. "And can I have my trophy back, please?"

The two big Humans leaned forward and threw Quyth Workers out of the way, picking them up and tossing them aside. Orange-and black-clad bodies flew, some shoved away, some pushed down, some diving for cover. The closest cops — one Quyth Warrior, one Ki — turned to address the surging threat. Quentin took it all in, every detail, his brain suddenly as hyper-alert as it sometimes got on the field during games.

The cops did everything right. They brandished shock batons, shouted warnings, moved to the barrier to use it as a partial shield. They did everything right to handle the two *blockers*, but they weren't ready for the third man.

The two big Humans jumped on the barrier and dove at the cops, catching stun batons full in the chest. Both Humans shook from the electrical charge, but their momentum carried them over the barriers and into the cops, pushing the cops back just enough to create a seam. The first Human squeezed through, hurdling the barrier like a running back jumping over a fallen lineman.

Quentin stared, timing the man's run. His left hand held the crystal football, his right the chrome stand connected to the base. A quick bend and the chrome post *snapped* clean.

"You *jerk*!" Yitzhak screamed. "What did you do that for?"

Quentin ignored his teammate. He dropped the wooden base, then held the MVP trophy up to his left ear, just like he'd hold a real football. He timed the man's movements, twisted his shoulders and threw.

*BLINK*

Time slowed to nothing, an almost still-frame rendition of life. He saw that crystal football ripping twenty yards through the air, the tight spiral kicking off a rapid-fire sparkle of rainbow flashes. He saw the crowd, expressions seemingly frozen, some in joy, some in surprise, some in concern.

The rainbow-spinning ball hit the man in the forehead, shattering into a sparkling shower of crystal chunks that — for just a second — looked like an exploding daylight firework.

The man fell to his knees, blood sheeting down his face.

Doc swooped toward the bleeding man, flying fast, orange and black streamers trailing behind in a nearly straight line.

The man's Krakens jacket drifted open. Around his waist, Quentin saw the shiny reflection of plastic wrap and, beneath the wrap, several tubes lined up in neat parallels.

A suicide bomb.

In the train car ahead, Virak the Mean looked right, saw the man, then dove over the train seat in front of him and threw himself on Gredok and Coach Hokor.

Quentin saw Doc reach the man, oblivious to the danger, the Harrah's mouth tentacles reaching for the fresh wound. Doc wanted to help. That was what he did.

Quentin watched the man's weak, numb hands fumbling at his waist, saw dozens of cops rushing in, cops that wouldn't be alive in another few seconds.

*BLINK*

"Down!" Quentin shouted as he reached up and yanked Yitzhak to the floor. He didn't have to worry about Pine because Pine was already diving over the seat back, deeper into the train car.

The world filled with noise and crazy motion. The car normally floated an inch or so above the track. The explosion hit the car like a wrecking ball, knocking it to the left where it cleared the lev-track and crashed into the street. The car's left edge dug into the road's surface, sending up a shower of sparks before it tilted, throwing Quentin, Yitzhak and Pine over the pedestrian barrier and into the packed crowd. Quentin's solid weight crashed into a dense throng of bodies.

He was up and moving almost as soon as he landed. This wasn't the first time he'd been near a suicide bomber. Those guys often attacked in teams. Life on Micovi had taught Quentin many things, but one thing in particular — on a football field, speed *kills*, but when bodies are blowing up around you and you need to get away, speed means *life*.

Quentin ran, his 7-foot-tall, 380-pound athletic body a warning to any sentient stupid enough to get in his way.

**QUENTIN SAT IN A BACK ROOM** of the Blessed Lamb bar, darkness surrounding him except for the low light given off by neon beer signs and the glow of the holojuke. The juke's colored lights played off the steam rising from his plate of habanero falafel biscuits. He hadn't felt hungry, but he'd already eaten one plate and was two biscuits into his second. Comfort food, it seemed, lived up to its name.

He didn't want to be here, here with these people, people that reminded him of the old life. The life back on Micovi. The life of poverty, of constant threat, of subservience. The life of *hatred*.

Yet when the bomb had gone off, he'd ran straight down Radius Eight to Ring Road Four, then circled back clockwise, up Radius One and to this bar, a place full of Purist Nation expatriates. He hadn't even thought about going anywhere else, like to the Bootleg Arms or to the Krakens headquarters at the city center. At first he'd told himself that he'd come here simply because it was close, that it was in the nightclub district. Had he been near the stadium, he surely would have fled to the Krakens headquarters. But he would never know because he *hadn't* run to the stadium — he'd run to the Blessed Lamb. He had run to his people, people who instantly took him in, sheltered him, protected him.

What did it mean that he'd come here first? Was he *really* over his racist upbringing, or was he only deluding himself? When things got dicey, did he just want to run back to what he'd always known?

A man in blue robes quietly walked into the back room. "Your teammates called," he said. "Someone is coming to get you."

Quentin nodded. "Thank you, Father Harry."

Father Harry nodded, then quietly sat down at the table. Father Harry, like most people from the Nation, was no stranger to bombs or bombers. Father Harry came from the same messed-up culture that had made Quentin's childhood a living hell.

"Quentin, are you feeling better?"

Quentin nodded.

"You were both lucky and smart," Father Harry said. "Smart to get out of there, lucky because the reports are starting to come in. Fifteen sentients died in that blast, including eight police officers."

"Was the team doctor killed?"

Father Harry nodded.

Quentin closed his eyes. He hadn't been great friends with Doc, but the Harrah had been the first non-Human to touch Quentin, to talk to him face to face, one on one. Now Doc was gone. Quentin realized that he'd never even learned Doc's real name.

"What about my teammates? Did any players die?"

Father Harry shook his head. "Not that we've heard. A few minor injuries, apparently, but nothing life-threatening."

Quentin nodded. There was nothing wrong with thinking of his friends first, his teammates. He didn't know anyone else in the city. Aside from Doc, the fifteen dead were faceless unknowns. Faceless, except for one thing — they included Krakens fans. They'd come out to celebrate Quentin and his teammates, and now they were gone. Fifteen dead ... and how many wounded?

"I should have stayed," Quentin said. "Stayed, maybe helped people, but I ... I ran."

Father Harry nodded. "I see. Quentin, ask me if I've ever argued with an explosion."

"What?"

"Go ahead, ask me."

Ah. It was *lesson time*, and Quentin was not in the mood for lessons. "Father Harry, I—"

"Humor me, Quentin. Out of respect for your elders."

Quentin sighed. Maybe the people in the Blessed Lamb were racists, but they had always been kind to *him*. They had welcomed him, fed him, and now they had sheltered him. The least he could do was play along with yet another person who wanted to offer him advice.

"Father Harry, have you ever argued with an explosion?"

"No, Quentin, I have not. Ask me why."

"Father, come on, you —"

"Ask me why."

Quentin rubbed his eyes. "Father Harry, *why* haven't you ever argued with an explosion?"

"Because an explosion can't be argued with," Father Harry said. "What a stupid question, I can't believe you asked me that."

Quentin rolled his eyes.

"The last part is a joke," Father Harry said. "One of my favorites, actually. But the first part is no joke. You can't argue with an explosion, Quentin. Just like you can't argue with a bullet or the tip of a knife. Do you know the difference between a hero and a martyr?"

Quentin shook his head.

"A hero is alive," Father Harry said. "A martyr is not. And since you don't seem to follow the teachings of Mason Stewart, you wouldn't even count as a martyr — you'd just be *dead*."

"Now isn't the time for a lecture, Father."

Father Harry smiled apologetically. "No, of course not, and I'm not lecturing you. I'm saying you made the right call. You can't even get a firearm into Ionath City. You can bet whatever explosive the bombers used, the city will have analyzed it and installed specialized detectors for it by the end of the week. The people of Ionath City felt *safe*. They didn't know what real terror was until today. On the other hand, that feeling of terror is something you know all too well. You just keep listening to your instincts, run when you have to, and you'll be fine."

Brother Guido slid into the back room and flipped on the lights. He and his wife, Monica Basset, owned the Blessed Lamb.

"Quentin, your friends are here," Guido said. "Please get them out of my bar. *Now*."

Quentin stood and walked to the front room. Choto the Bright and Virak the Mean were waiting. Even though the two each had a cast on one leg, their aura said that they were not to be messed with. The fifteen or so Human patrons in the bar stared at the two Quyth Warriors, who stared back. The room seemed wired with tension. Quentin wondered at Father Harry's words on how hard it was to get a gun into the city — and wondered if the Purist Nation ex-pats had found a way. If they did have weapons stashed, how long would it take for those weapons to become *un*-stashed?

The Quyth Warriors saw Quentin. They looked simultaneously relieved and annoyed. Quyth Warriors were good at that combined expression. Slightly different hues of red shaded their eyes.

"Quentin," Virak said. "I am glad to see you are unhurt. Gredok wants you back at the stadium immediately."

"Good idea," Quentin said. "Let's go."

He almost pushed his teammates out the door, eager to get them out of the Blessed Lamb. He felt eyes boring into his back as he left. He'd come here for shelter, come to this place where the owners and the patrons deeply loved everyone — as long as *everyone* was from the Purist Nation. He'd come here seeking shelter, and he left with what his Nationalite hosts considered the embodiment of evil. Maybe that was a discussion for another time. As Father Harry had said, you can't argue with an explosion, and Quentin considered an explosion far more reasonable than a religious zealot.

## Transcript of broadcast from Galactic News Network

"Yes, Brad, I'm on the scene at what was a deadly end to a happy day. Ionath City's residents were packed in tight to enjoy a parade celebrating the promotion of their Ionath Krakens from Tier Two up to Tier One. That parade ended in tragedy as a suicide bomber tried to rush the train. It appears that Ionath City Police stopped the bomber, but at a horrible cost. Eight police officers were killed in a blast powerful enough to knock three lev-train cars right off the track and leave a two-foot crater in the concrete. The bomber and his two associates were killed, as were three pedestrians. The full number of injuries remains unknown, Brad, but Ionath City Hospital has been very busy this afternoon."

"Tom, what about the Krakens players?"

"Brad, we don't have conclusive reports yet, but it looks like no players were hurt. The team doctor did die in the blast. The bomb detonated close to the car carrying team owner Gredok the Splithead, a sentient rumored to be involved in organized crime."

"Was Gredok the target, Tom?"

"Brad, it's too early to tell, and we may never know. Krakens quarterback Quentin Barnes was close to the explosion as well. He's from the Purist Nation, a system well known for both bitterness against people abandoning their religion and for terrorist attacks much like the one we had today."

"Tom, if I remember correctly, haven't the Krakens had a Purist Nation player for several seasons?"

"Yes, Brad, tight end Rick Warburg has been on the roster for four seasons. The upcoming Tier One campaign will be his fifth. However, Warburg hasn't had the exposure that Barnes has had. Barnes is shaping up to be a galaxy-wide sports star. It's possible that radical members of the Purist Church were trying to get to Barnes."

"With an explosion like that, Tom, can officials even identify the intended target?"

"No, Brad, they can't. Apparently, all that's left of the bomber is a left shoe and a little green globule. Investigators are typing what flesh remains and running that result through intergalactic criminal and identification databases. What's more important here, Brad, is that city officials are at a loss to explain how explosives were smuggled into the dome. They have identified the chemical components of the explosive. They are confident they will add those chemicals to all entry checkpoints and nano-sweep the city to find any explosives already inside."

"So the danger is over for now?"

"So it would appear, Brad, but the fear is not over. This is the worst terrorist attack to hit the domed area in forty years. Suffice to say, there will be tense times until we know for certain that the three bombers acted alone or until any of their associates still in Ionath City are caught. For GNN, this is Tom Skivvers, signing off."

**NOT THAT LONG AGO,** Virak and Choto would have led Quentin by force, strong pincers gripped on his triceps, perhaps his shoulders. But not anymore. They were his teammates. He was their quarterback. They walked behind him, just a step, the same way they'd walk behind a Quyth Leader.

The front door of the thirty-story Krakens building looked like an army blockade point. High concrete barriers had been erected around the arched front entrance. Beyond them, a dozen police grav-cars and cops on foot — Ki and Quyth Warrior.

Virak and Choto led Quentin right through the police. On the other side of the concrete barrier, Quentin saw more guards, even meaner looking than the police. These guards ran the gamut of races — Quyth Warrior, Human, Ki and HeavyG. There were even a couple of Sklorno wearing their full-body robes so that no area was exposed to the night air.

Beyond the guards, the lobby of the Krakens building.

If you combined a museum and a shrine, you would get something similar to the lobby. High ceilings and black walls created a space that seemed to be vast and endless, like the Void itself. There were even tiny lights positioned high up in the ceiling to represent the constellations and inhabited planets. Glowing team logos marked the nineteen planets that had a Tier One franchise. Most planets had only one T1 team, but Tower, Wilson 6 and Whitok each had two. The sun for Earth's system glowed brighter than all the rest — a tribute to the birthplace of football, even though currently Earth had no Tier One teams. In areas of the ceiling that didn't have GFL planets, animations made of glowing star-dots showed famous Krakens plays and players.

That sprawling, high ceiling arched over twenty-one years of Krakens paraphernalia. Display cases showed jerseys, cracked armor, helmets of five different species, old programs. Many displays held footballs that had one quarter-panel painted white, then lettered with the teams, score and date of famous games or key statistical accomplishments. The back section of the lobby was nothing but red brick — a chunk of wall from City Municipal Field, home of the Krakens from 2662 until it had been torn down in 2673 and replaced with the current Ionath Stadium.

The right side of the lobby showed the Krakens' pride and joy — the golden GFL championship trophy from the 2665 Galaxy Bowl. Slow-motion holos surrounded the trophy, showing key players and plays from that 23-21 win over the Wabash Wall.

Just in front of the Galaxy Bowl trophy sat a small case that contained two things — a single championship ring that would have belonged to Bobby "Orbital Assault" Adrojnik, had he lived long enough wear it, and Bobby's Galaxy Bowl MVP trophy.

Quentin never entered the lobby without passing by the GFL trophy and running his hands over the case containing Bobby's treasures. Quentin would have those things someday, no matter what it took.

Even with Gredok waiting for him, Quentin still angled to the right to pay tribute, to see the physical representation of his life's goals. He didn't dally, merely walked by as he headed for the elevator.

The elevator led them to the top floor of the Krakens building. The place reeked of money, of power; from the smart carpets showing original designs by the hottest artists to sculptures, both static and moving. More guards up here: meticulously dressed, dangerous-looking Humans, Quyth Warriors with exposed torsos that showed countless enamel tats and two HeavyG monsters that were nearly as big as Khomeni and Michnik. Where the heck did one find suits to fit such beasts? The guards recognized Quentin. Some of them even smiled, or gave appreciative nods.

When you're winning, everyone is a fan.

Messal the Efficient appeared out of nowhere, probably sliding out unseen from behind one of the strange sculptures.

"Elder Barnes, welcome," said the perfectly dressed and groomed Quyth Worker. "Gredok is waiting for you. Please follow me."

Quentin did. Gredok apparently kept the entire top floor to himself as his personal quarters. Messal led Quentin through the open area to a heavy door. Inside that door: Gredok's office.

Quentin entered. Sure, Virak and Choto now treated Quentin like a leader, but in the office, that faded away a bit. When Gredok the Splithead was present, there was no question who was in charge, who was the *Alpha*.

The outer room reeked of riches, yet this inner office made it look like a slum. Dim lighting called attention to hanging works of art and sculptures mounted on waist-high pedestals along the room's edge, each lit up by its own spotlight. Quentin didn't know about such things, but they seemed very expensive. Priceless perhaps. Some showed Humans — those works looked as old as old gets. Others showed Sklorno, Ki, Whitok. Some even showed Creterakians: art from the ruling race. The whole thing impressed Quentin, but he would still have traded it all for the football pictures and holoframes in Coach Hokor's office. Great art is in the eye of the beholder, but great football is in the record books.

The art wasn't the only thing on a pedestal. In the room's exact center stood a ten-foot column made of white stone. On top of it, Gredok the Splithead, reclining in a cushy black throne custom-made to his diminutive size. The pedestal and the throne combined to raise Gredok a good thirteen feet in the air. Quentin had to tilt his head back to look into the little Leader's single, softball-sized eye.

"Barnes," Gredok said. "Were you injured in the blast?"

"No."

"No, what?"

Quentin sneered. "No, I am not injured, but gosh, Greedy, thanks for your concern." He knew very well Gredok wanted Quentin to call him *shamakath*, like the rest of the sentients in the syndicate. Well, Quentin wasn't in the syndicate. He was a football player, not a criminal. Quentin would give Gredok the ample respect any GFL franchise owner deserved, but he drew the line at swearing fealty. To anyone.

"Your disrespect troubles me, Barnes," Gredok said. "Sometimes you are so intelligent, and other times — such as the times when you are speaking to someone who could have you killed on a mere whim — you are not."

Quentin shrugged. "The franchise you created kicks major ass, but I'm just not going to grovel at your feet like the rest of those punks in the outer room. I'm your *quarterback*, Gredok, I am not your *property*."

Gredok's immaculate black fur ruffled for the briefest moment, then once again lay perfectly flat. "Now is not the time for that concern. I brought you here to discuss two things."

"My good looks and high bowling score?"

Another ruffle. Quentin realized he was precariously close to pushing it too far, and for no good reason.

"Gredok, I'm sorry," Quentin said. "I'm still a little rattled from the explosion and from Doc dying in the blast. Forgive me."

Gredok's fur settled once again. "I find that choice of words acceptable. Doc's passing is unfortunate, but I already have a replacement for him."

Already? Not even a full day had passed. They still hadn't found all the pieces of Doc's body, and Gredok had a replacement? But that was the nature of business. To Gredok, football was just that — a business.

"Now," the Quyth Leader said, "while I'm sure an athlete of your caliber has a rather impressive bowling score, I do not wish to discuss it at this time. The first thing I brought you here for was to thank you."

Quentin's eyes narrowed in suspicion. "*Thank* me?"

"Your fast reactions may have saved my life."

"Hey, don't flatter yourself, Cuddles. I saw a threat, and I tried to put it down."

"You weren't trying to save me?"

Quentin shrugged. "Naw, just being a good citizen is all. If I'd thrown better, he wouldn't have set off the bomb at all."

"Possibly," Gredok said. "I've seen news coverage of the event. The only fault lies with the design of that trophy — you hit that bomber right in the face from twenty yards away. Had the trophy been solid, not hollow, you would have killed him. The real question, however, is who was the assailant's target?"

Was Gredok for real? That's what gangsters did, killed each other. "What do you mean *who was the target*? It was you, of course."

"You thought I was the target?"

"Obviously."

"So, if you thought I was the target, then you did intentionally save me."

Quentin paused, his brain searching for an answer, finding

nothing for almost three seconds. "Virak and Choto," he said. "I didn't want my starting linebackers to get hurt."

Gredok said nothing. Quentin stared at him, then looked away. His answer had come too late, a feeble attempt to cover up Gredok's accurate observation. Quentin wanted to kick himself.

"Which brings us to the second point," Gredok said. "Who, exactly, was the target?"

The lights dimmed and several holoscreens flared to life, showing replays of the attack. When it happened, it had seemed so obvious the bomber was going for Gredok. But now, with the benefit of multiple angles, Quentin wasn't so sure. The attacker could be rushing toward Gredok's car ... or ... or could be rushing toward *Quentin's* car.

"Many possibilities," Gredok said. "Me, of course, as there are petty individuals who are envious of my business acumen. But also Mayor Kerin the Malleable. Maybe even Coach Hokor."

"Coach Hokor? Who would want to kill a coach?"

"Welcome to Tier One, Quentin. Who would want to kill a coach? Any Tier One team that thinks they might finish last unless the Krakens lose all their games."

"Well, okay, but would someone ... I don't know ... kill for that?"

Gredok's pedipalps twitched side to side. By now, Quentin knew that was a kind of Quyth laughter. Quentin felt his face turn red. He'd asked a stupid question worthy of derision. Bobby Adrojnik had died in a bar fight shortly after winning the Galaxy Bowl. Suspicion had always centered on Gloria Ogawa, the Wabash owner. The next year, without their star quarterback, the Krakens didn't even make the playoffs.

"Tier One is about *money*," Gredok said. "Where there is money, there is a will to kill for that money. Tell me, Barnes, when you worked in the mines of Micovi, where Human life is so cheap, what was the going rate for a petty assassination?"

Why did everyone have to bring up Micovi? "I think you could have someone killed for five hundred credits, if you wanted it done right. If you didn't have that kind of cash, you could hire someone hungry for like fifty."

"Fifty credits to kill a sentient," Gredok said. "And here, there are *billions* at stake. Do you understand?"

Quentin hadn't thought about it in those terms before. He nodded.

"I hope, Barnes, that you can learn these things in time to save me from having to find another quarterback."

Quentin nodded again.

"And if the target could have been Coach Hokor," Gredok said, "then it also could have been ... *you*."

Quentin stared, once again his brain searching for thoughts and finding nothing. Adrojnik had been killed. Adrojnik, the *quarterback*. Gredok was right. Quentin could have been the target. They had no way of knowing.

"We will look into this," Gredok said. "The Ionath Police are good at their jobs, when I allow them to do their jobs, that is, but I won't sit back and wait for them to find the culprit. I will protect my investments. For now, however, I want everyone to stay on the *Touchback* at least until the season opener."

Quentin shrugged. "That's fine with me."

"Really? Some of your teammates whined about not seeing their mates, their offspring. No concerns from you?"

Quentin shook his head.

"Of course not," Gredok said. "Sometimes I forget that your entire life is the game of football. That's one of the things I like about you — you're focused on what matters."

If other Krakens players wasted time with mates and kids, that was their problem. Quentin had nothing to leave behind, but in truth he couldn't wait to get up to the *Touchback* because it meant safety. If someone *was* trying to kill him, he'd rather be in a private spaceship that could punch out than in a city of 110,000 sentients.

"Take this," Gredok said and tossed something into the air. Quentin caught it — a thin, black bracelet. "Put it on."

"If I do, does that mean we're an item? The gossip sites will go crazy."

"You are not funny, Barnes, and I doubt your Human brain could even understand the complexities of Quyth courtship. That bracelet will let my people track you wherever you go in case these mystery attackers send you running again or even kidnap you. I would embed search sounders in your skeleton, but GFL regulations stipulate no mods of any kind. Commissioner Froese is cracking down on such things. Put on the bracelet."

Quentin slid the bracelet over his right hand. It lightly contracted against his wrist. After just a second or two, he couldn't even feel it.

Gredok waved his middle-right arm and snapped his pincer.

"Virak, Choto," he said. "Take Quentin straight to the roof, then shuttle up to the *Touchback*. He is the last of the team to report in. Once you are up, tell Captain Cheevers to take the *Touchback* out of orbit and find a place to hide until I can arrange for military protection. If Gloria Ogawa thinks she can stop me from beating her team, she has another think coming. And Choto?"

"Yes, *Shamakath*?"

"Until further notice, you are to stay by Quentin's side whenever he is off-ship. He goes nowhere without you, understand?"

"Yes, *Shamakath*."

"And Barnes," Gredok said. "Should you give Choto the slip, for whatever reason, it is not you I will punish. I will blame him for failing me. Now go."

Quentin felt big, strong pincers lightly grab each upper arm. He turned, sharing a brief look with each of his teammates. Any delay on his part would make them look bad in front of their *shamakath*. Quentin let them roughly take him out of the office. The second the doors closed on the elevator, they let go and stepped back.

The three teammates headed up to the roof, to the shuttle that would take them off the planet.

**2**

# PRE-SEASON: WEEK TWO

From *The Ionath City Gazette*

## Krakens Players Honored with Post-Season Awards

*By* Toyat the Inquisitive

NEW YORK CITY, EARTH, PLANETARY UNION — GFL officials today announced the post-season awards for the 2682 campaign, a list dominated by the orange and the black.

Ionath wide receiver Hawick was named first-team All-T2 thanks to a breakout season with 47 catches for 829 yards and 9 touchdowns. She averaged 5.2 catches and 91.1 yards per game, and her average of one TD per

game set a new franchise record.

Joining her on the first-team roster is defensive end Aleksander Michnik, who recorded 9 sacks and 56 solo tackles on the season, and Krakens quarterback Quentin Barnes, who was also named the offensive Rookie of the Year.

Second-team all-T2 honors went to offensive left tackle Kill-O-Yowet and linebacker John Tweedy.

Rookie of the Year honors

*continued on next page*

---

*continued from previous page*

for Barnes came as no surprise, at least to this intrepid reporter. Barnes finished with a quarterback rating of 97.2, highest among rookie QBs, while throwing for 11 touchdowns and 1,341 passing yards. He completed 52 percent of his passes, averaging 14 yards per throw. While Barnes had excellent stats for a rookie passer, it was his overall impact on the Krakens franchise that earned him the honor. In the T2 playoff semifinals, Barnes switched from quarterback to running back, where he rushed for 62 yards on 28 carries while catching 4 passes for another 82 yards and a touchdown.

"Barnes was selfless," said Krakens head coach Hokor the Hookchest. "At a critical time against an exceptional defense, he had 144 all-purpose yards and the game-winning score to propel us into Tier One. No question that he deserves Rookie of the Year."

Orbiting Death running back Ju Tweedy was named the T2 Offensive Player of the Year, followed closely by Whitok Pioneers QB Condor Adrienne and Krakens running back Mitchell Fayed (deceased).

Bigg Diggers cornerback Arkham was far and away the winner of Defensive Player of the Year honors, powered by her 11 interceptions.

---

**QUENTIN WALKED DOWN** the *Touchback's* corridor, heading for his quarters. Yitzhak Goldman walked on his left. Pilkie, a Quyth Worker, walked on his right. Pilkie and Yitzhak had been waiting for Quentin in the shuttle bay. Yitzhak said he had something to show Quentin, and Pilkie seemed to be part of the event. The Quyth Worker kept offering to take Quentin's bags every thirty seconds. Quentin didn't need a Worker to carry his bags, he could carry them just fine even though he was so tired he practically stumbled down the corridor.

While he'd somewhat gotten used to the Quyth Warriors and Leaders, the Workers still freaked him out a little. At around four feet tall, they were bigger than Leaders yet significantly smaller than Warriors. Except for the pedipalps, that is — Worker pedipalps were invariably long and knotted with muscle, the result of many years of manual labor. They reminded Quentin of the arms of his coworkers back in the mines of Micovi.

"Crazy times," Yitzhak said. "A bomb, man. Sentients *died*."

"Zak, I'm exhausted," Quentin said. "What is this thing you've got to show me? Let's get it over with so I can go to sleep."

"Quentin, anyone ever tell you you're too intense?"

Quentin shrugged.

"Well, sometimes you are. Try to relax a little. What I want to show you is *in* your quarters. I hope you don't mind, but since you don't have an agent, I had *my* agent put out the word that he was temporarily representing you."

Quentin's eyes narrowed. He'd never even met Yitzhak's agent, didn't even know who the guy was. Or girl. Or *species*, for that matter.

"Representing me ... for *what*?"

"For endorsements," Yitzhak said. "You're about to become a star, Quentin. Companies want to get in on the ground floor."

Quentin hoped the presentation wouldn't take long. He just wanted his bed. His quarters were the same layout as those of the other Human players; a bedroom barely big enough for the bed, a bathroom, a living room with the holotank in the middle. Most of his Human teammates complained about living in such a small space, but not Quentin — he didn't bother to tell them that before he started playing football on Micovi, his entire apartment had been the size of just the small bedroom *and* that he'd shared it with two other miners.

When they reached Quentin's quarters, the door opened automatically and they all walked in. At least, they walked as far as they could. Boxes were everywhere, as were display stands showing all sorts of products. Someone had been in his room, *his room*, messing with his stuff, setting traps for him, trying to take him out.

Quentin stared. He adjusted the strap of his bag. Pilkie moved in fast, reaching out to take it.

"*Leave it*," Quentin said, sharply.

Pilkie flinched as if Quentin was about to hit him.

"Q," Yitzhak said, "relax."

Quentin turned on him. "Don't tell me what to do! And who the hell was in here, huh? You? You plant something in here? *Did you?*"

Quentin's left hand shot out and locked on Yitzhak's right bicep, squeezed hard.

"You gonna make a move, Zak? Well, then, *come on!*"

Yitzhak's eyes widened for a second, but he stayed stock-still. He looked at Quentin's big hand, then back at Quentin.

"Let go," Yitzhak said quietly.

The calmness of Yitzhak's voice contrasted against the rage roiling inside of Quentin, cut through it, made Quentin see the situation for what it was. He was threatening a teammate, using physical force.

Quentin let go.

Yitzhak, still calm as could be, reached up his left hand and massaged his right bicep. "That hurt," he said.

Quentin stepped back. His fatigue won out over his rage, dragging him back down again. "Sorry."

Yitzhak shook his head. "What was that about?"

"Nothing," Quentin said. "I said I was sorry."

"Sorry is not going to cut it, man. You can't act like that around here."

"Act like what?"

"Like you're some petty thug, swinging at everything that makes you mad. What did you think we'd done, anyway?"

Quentin looked away, but Yitzhak persisted.

"Don't clam up on me now," he said. "I'll accept your apology if you tell me what that was all about. You got that mad, why? Because someone touched your stuff?"

"You make it sound like that's not a big deal."

"It's not," Yitzhak said. "It's just a room. I won't accept your apology until you tell me why you did that."

Zak was so calm, so patient. Even after Quentin had all but punched him out, Zak still had that expression of concern on his face. Concern for Quentin.

"Back on Micovi," Quentin said, "your place is kind of ...

sacred. Someone goes in there without your permission, they're trying to steal from you, or ... "

Yitzhak crossed his arms and waited.

Quentin sighed and continued. "Or maybe they're putting a trap in your room, like a hidden roundbug, something to hurt you or kill you. It's a Micovi thing, you wouldn't understand."

"You know what? You're not on Micovi anymore."

Quentin rolled his eyes. "I know that, Zak, I'm not stu—"

"Yeah, you *are* stupid. And you *don't* know it. Not in your heart. Everyone on this damn ship will fall all over themselves to help you, to back you up whenever you need it. So you had to go through some hard times on Micovi? Well, get over it. You can't react with violence all the time."

"Right," Quentin said. "They brought me here *because* I'm violent. I get *paid* to be violent, and I'm just supposed to shut it off?"

Yitzhak nodded. "That's exactly what you're supposed to do. You're in the GFL now. Start acting like a professional athlete and stop acting like some two-bit bully."

Yitzhak was right — that behavior was unacceptable. Quentin felt his face flush red. He knew better. He had to start controlling his reactions.

"Sorry," Quentin said again.

"You've already apologized to me," Yitzhak said. "Maybe you should apologize to Pilkie."

Quentin turned and looked down at the wide-eyed Quyth Worker. Pilkie looked scared, but his eye kept flicking to Quentin's bag. Quentin sighed, slid the bag off his shoulder and held it out.

Pilkie grabbed it and shot off to Quentin's small bedroom. Everything clean would be put away; everything dirty would go into the laundry.

Quentin rolled out his neck and looked around the room. Yitzhak had gone to all this trouble. Since Quentin had made an ass out of himself, the least he could do was check it all out. He casually sorted through piles of stuff, picking up a black baseball bat. He looked at it closely and saw that his face was burned into the wood.

"*Hey*, I didn't give permission for this."

"It's just a mock-up," Yitzhak said. "Companies want you to see what things will look like."

"Yeah, but I play football, not baseball."

"That's the beauty of it, Q — you don't have to *use* the products, you just let them put your name and face on them and collect a paycheck."

Quentin set the bat down and picked up a strange plastic device that dangled with tubes and long, narrow cups. "No idea what this is, but I'm pretty sure I wouldn't use it."

"Probably not," Yitzhak said. "Unless you are a menstruating Sklorno."

Quentin dropped the device like it had suddenly turned into a spider. Pilkie shot out of the bedroom, grabbed the device off the floor and placed it neatly in the pile.

"Quentin, look," Yitzhak said. "I'm not trying to get into your business here, but you are a starting Tier One quarterback. There are only twenty-two starting T1 QBs in the galaxy. You're about to become a *major* star, and people are willing to pay you a *lot* of money just to be associated with you."

"I get that," Quentin said. "I get the whole concept. But all this … " he gestured to the piles of merchandise, "all this *crap* isn't what football is about. And besides, I make plenty of money."

Yitzhak laughed. "That's a good one."

"Why do you keep saying that? I'll make a *million* credits this season. That's a ton of money, Zak. I hate to break it to you, but I'm rich."

Yitzhak laughed again, then the sound faded, the smile slipped from his face. "Quentin, you're serious? You think you're rich?"

Quentin's eyes narrowed. He suddenly wanted to punch Zak in the mouth and wasn't sure why. "Yes, I am rich. Didn't you hear what I said? I don't want to brag or anything, but I make a *million* credits a season. That would make me one of the richest people on Micovi."

"You're not on Micovi anymore. And yeah, a million is a good grab, but you have to understand just how much you can make from endorsements. You could make *ten times* that much, maybe twenty times."

Quentin rolled his eyes. Yitzhak's exaggerations weren't appreciated, even though he knew his teammate was just trying to help.

"Look, Zak, maybe I honestly don't care, okay? My little apartment in the Krakens building is paid for. When I'm not there, I'm here. My food is paid for, clothes, all that stuff. I have a million credits and nothing to spend it on, so why bother?"

"Sure, all that stuff is paid for, as long as you don't get hurt. That's something I've been meaning to talk to you about. Do you mind a little advice?"

Quentin looked to the ceiling and sighed. "Sure, why not?"

"You're a starting Tier One quarterback, which means you're going to get *hit* like a starting Tier One quarterback. Even as good as sports medicine is these days, you are one play away from being finished. There goes your *million credit* salary. What are you going to do then?"

"I won't get hurt."

"I bet that's exactly what Paul Pierson thought."

The name stopped Quentin cold, made the image of a chrome foot flash into his brain. For just a second, Quentin pictured his own leg replaced by such a contraption. He shook his head, forcing the image away — it was ridiculous to think that would happen to him. Still, even if he had a career like Pine or Frank Zimmer, Quentin might be done with football in fifteen years. Yet fifteen years seemed like an eternity ... he'd only been *alive* for nineteen.

Quentin picked up a set of golf clubs.

"Quentin, do you golf?"

"No. Never been. I should pick up the game, though, so I can drive around in a stupid golf cart all the time like Coach does. Are there courses on Ionath?"

"Sure, if you don't mind wearing a rad-suit, there are some of the best courses in the galaxy, right outside the dome. And if your suit fails in any way, it will still hold your biomass together nicely while you melt."

Quentin let the golf bag drop to the floor. "Wow, I can't wait to get out on the links."

Pilkie shot in from nowhere, grabbed the clubs, then vanished. The little guy was crazy fast.

"Zak, maybe we can talk about it later," Quentin said. "I just don't want to deal with this now. I appreciate you trying to help, but I'm going to have Pilkie throw all this garbage out the ... "

Quentin stopped when his eyes fell on a model of a luxury yacht. About a foot long, with sleek lines that screamed *wealth* and *speed*. But it wasn't the model itself that caught his attention, but rather the holocard hovering just above it. He knew that face. Quentin picked up the model.

"*You* like yachts?" Yitzhak said. "I figured you as a pitchman for some swillish, watery beer."

Quentin's head snapped up. "Wait, a *beer* company wants to talk to me?"

Yitzhak nodded. "Yep. Miller Lager. Interested?"

Quentin blinked. Yitzhak was messing with him.

"You're messing with me," Quentin said.

Yitzhak shook his head. "Nope, they were the second company to call."

When Quentin had watched pirated football game coverage back in the Nation, he'd loved those funny beer commercials the former GFL players did. To actually be *in* a commercial like that? Other than a championship ring and the cover image of Galaxy Sports Magazine, that was the biggest level of success a player could imagine.

"Interested?" Yitzhak said. "Not that you have a bad poker face or anything, but it sure looks like you want to know more."

"Yeah, I do. Can your agent set up a meeting with them?"

"No problem. They'll be thrilled to talk to you."

"Miller was the second company to call," Quentin said. "What was the first?"

Yitzhak pointed to the yacht model in Quentin's hands. "You're looking at it. Word is they've been calling everywhere for months, trying to find out who represents you."

Quentin nodded. "Okay. The yacht company and Miller Lager. Please set those meetings up."

"Consider it done. Any others?"

"No. Not interested in the rest. Just Miller and this. I'll have Pilkie get all this out tomorrow, Zak, but if you could take off, I wanna get some sleep."

"Right," Yitzhak said. "I'll get out of your way. Rest up, the free agents arrive tomorrow."

"Free agents?"

"Yep. Free agents tomorrow, rookies the day after. Season begins in three weeks, Q. Gotta load up on new talent."

The helpful third-string quarterback walked out of the room. Quentin sat on his couch — one small cushion was the only uncluttered part of his apartment on which he could sit — and stared at the model of the yacht.

And the face above it, the face that had told him all about the prison ship that had become the *Combine*.

He stared at the face of his countryman, Manny Sayed.


**QUENTIN HURRIED DOWN** the corridor toward the *Touchback's* practice field. He'd slept soundly and awoken to find all the crap cleaned out of his quarters. Pilkie had been a busy boy in the night — quiet, but busy.

The modifications to Quentin's quarters weren't complete. Contractors would be working on the walls during the day while Quentin was out of the rooms.

He'd been called to the practice field to help evaluate the free agent candidates. It excited Quentin to have some control over personnel decisions. He would meet the rookies the next day. They had been selected without his input, mostly because the research on them had been done while Quentin was busy quarterbacking the Krakens in Tier Two. This season, there was nothing he could do about that. After the Tier One campaign finished in thirteen weeks, however, Quentin envisioned himself locked away with Hokor during the off-season, reviewing holo after holo of key free agents and potential rookies from around the galaxy. From here on out, every player decision would have the Quentin Barnes stamp of approval.

He walked down the tunnel, happy to be back in the *Touchback's* familiar surroundings. Despite the parade bombing and the fear it brought, he felt safe up here. Safe and relieved to once again focus on the only thing that really mattered — football. Everything seemed possible. He tasted eternal life in his mouth, felt it on his skin. A logical part of his brain said *this can't last forever*, but his soul knew better. All of his hard work, a lifetime of dealing with a deadly culture, three seasons of putting up with teammates who treated him like a second-class citizen, all of it had led him to *this* church. His church, the Church of Football, a religion he created with his own feet, miracles he made with his own arm.

He exited the tunnel into the *Touchback's* full-size practice field. The nano-grass didn't have a smell, which was a shame — Quentin loved the smell of a gridiron, loved to breathe in the scents of dirt, of plants, of the *essence* of football.

Patches of small, flat, circular, white clipper robots roamed across the green practice field, eating the ever-growing nano-grass and keeping the surface perfectly trimmed. As he walked, the little robots cleared out of his way, then scooted back to their places after he passed.

It was the same ship where he'd spent the last three months, but it felt different. He wasn't the bush-league upstart anymore. He was the *starting quarterback* of a Tier One football team. He *knew* this ship now, knew the eighteen decks that rose up beyond the end zones. Well, no, actually that wasn't true. He knew very little of the ship — pretty much just his quarters, the cafeteria, the Kriegs-Ballok Virtual Practice System and this field. Huh. He'd been so busy doing his job, fighting for this opportunity, that he'd barely explored the ship. Maybe he'd correct that sometime soon. He'd heard rumors that Captain Cheevers was pretty hot. Maybe he'd introduce himself.

At the eighteenth deck, a clear, shallow dome crossed high

above the field. Beyond that dome, black space and twinkling stars. So *many* stars. People said there were something like 400 *billion* in the Milky Way Galaxy alone. Only a fraction had been explored so far, little more than a half billion or something like that. He didn't pay much attention to such things, but he'd heard it would take thousands of years just to see all the stars in this galaxy alone ... just *one* galaxy out of 500 *billion* known galaxies. At best, only a fraction of the Milky Way's stars would be explored during his lifetime.

Quentin jogged to the middle of the field, where Don Pine and four Human players were waiting by a rack of footballs. Hokor, as always, floated about ten feet above the field in his stupid golf cart. Three of the new Humans were dressed in armor and white practice jerseys. One wore street clothes. Don gave Quentin a smile and a wink, the Hall-of-Fame quarterback's way of saying *it's your show, but I'm here if you need me.*

Hokor looked so idiotic in his golf cart. The thing was built for a Quyth Leader's small stature, like a child's toy driven by an angry, one-eyed stuffed animal wearing a Krakens wind-breaker and baseball cap. The visual was a bit comical, but the audio was not — Hokor's cart had powerful speakers, and when he yelled through them, every player winced.

"*Barnes!*" Hokor said. "We picked up a free agent running back to play behind Yassoud, but we need to see if any of these tight ends can replace Saulsgiver."

"Okay, Coach. What do you want me to do?"

Hokor waved to the four new Humans, calling them over. Of the three wearing football gear, only one had a helmet on. The man dressed in street clothes shook Quentin's hand.

"Jay Martinez," he said. "Free agent running back, happy to be here."

The man looked agile, but somewhat small. He wasn't even as big as Yassoud, whom Quentin considered a bit undersized for the position. No one, it seemed, measured up to Mitchell Fayed.

"Jay, I'm Quentin Barnes. Not dressing today?"

Jay tapped his left knee. "Still healing up from an injury I got in the last week of Tier Two. I played for the Damascus Demons in the Union Conference."

Quentin couldn't remember the Demons' record. Damascus was a middle-of-the-pack franchise in the Planetary Union Conference. Martinez didn't seem like a major acquisition. The Krakens had also signed rookie running back Dan Campbell, but with both Fayed and Pierson gone, Yassoud needed at least one more backup.

"Welcome," Quentin said, then turned to the first of three men dressed in gear. His skin was the bright white of a Tower native. Not quite as big as Quentin, but young and solid.

"Pietor Jewell," the man said, shaking Quentin's hand. "I'm still under contract with the Aril Archers in the Ki League, but they'll loan me for the season if you guys want me."

Jewell was a name that Quentin did know. The Archers had entered the T2 Tourney, losing in the first round to the Texas Earthlings. Jewell might not be a super-star, but he was a quality tight end.

"Happy to see what you got," Quentin said. "But, a loan? How does that work?"

Don Pine put a hand on Quentin's shoulder. Don did that whenever the older quarterback wanted to provide a bit of knowledge. Everyone else gave mostly useless advice — Don just shared his experience, then let Quentin figure it out for himself.

"Because Tier Two teams are off when Tier One season is on, and vice versa," Don said, "T2 teams can loan players to T1 teams, for a fee. Helps give the T2 players top-flight experience, which they bring back to their teams."

"And bruises," Pietor said. "We bring those back as well. I got loaned to the Vik Vanguard last year, then went back to the Archers. I've been playing non-stop for three straight seasons; if you guys pick me up, it will be my fourth, then back to the Archers for my fifth."

Quentin nodded, impressed by the man's work ethic but also concerned about that much constant play. Quentin himself had gone from Tier Three straight into a Tier Two season, and now was heading into a Tier One campaign. His body still hurt from the T2 Tourney — he wondered if Jewell's could hold up through another twelve games of elite football.

Pietor stepped back, and the second Human stepped up.

"Claudio Morgaine," the man said. "I was with the Blar Bastion but hoping to catch on with a Tier One team."

The Bastion played in the Sklorno Conference. The franchise had been around for two decades or more and had never made it into the T2 tournament. Quentin couldn't blame Morgaine for wanting to find a way into Tier One.

"Good luck," Quentin said. "We'll see what you've got."

The third Human walked up but didn't offer his hand. Instead, he took off his helmet, and Quentin took in what he assumed to be some kind of practical joke. The man's facial features made him look black or white, maybe even blue, but it was impossible to tell because bright yellow greasepaint covered his skin.

It looked odd, but then again Quentin had touched the slimy raspers of a Sklorno ... a little yellow greasepaint wasn't going to bother him. Maybe the color was a religious statement or something. He offered his hand. "Quentin Barnes."

The man stared at the hand. Quentin let it hang there for an uncomfortable five seconds, then lowered it back to his side. The yellow-faced man stepped back. Quentin leaned in close to Pine.

"Hey," Quentin whispered. "What's the deal with this guy and the makeup?"

Pine shrugged and whispered back. "Heck if I know. His name's Jorje Starcher. Seems kind of familiar to me, but I haven't seen any holos of him yet. He's been with the Moscow Hammers for two seasons."

"Moscow? Never heard of it. That one of those floating cities in the Harrah system?"

"Nope, Earth," Pine said. "It's an NFL franchise, Tier Three."

The NFL. Real bush-league stuff. Better than the PNFL, sure, but not much better.

"Why wouldn't he shake my hand? That annoys me."

Pine put his hand on Quentin's shoulder. "As long as yellow-face can catch, does it matter?"

Quentin thought for a second. "Well, not right now, but maybe down the road, you know? I mean if the guy can play, great, but if he's a jackass, that might be an issue, right?"

Pine smiled. "You are learning *fast*, Q. Yeah, locker room poison is a big problem. But it's too early to tell that right now. How about you put him through the paces, see if he's worth the trouble? If he isn't, no point in considering potential locker room politics. If he is, you evaluate from there. Make sense?"

Quentin nodded. "Yeah, makes perfect sense."

Pine slapped him on the shoulder. "Do your thing, kid."

"Coach!" Quentin called up to Hokor's cart. "What do you want to see first?"

"Ten-yard hooks," Hokor said. "We're going to have to throw short against the Ice Storm, so let's start there."

Quentin walked to the rack of footballs. He grabbed the first one and bent at the knees, a simulation for taking a snap from center. The tight ends lined up eight yards to his left. Pietor bent into a three-point stance: one hand and both feet on the ground, head up, back flat and parallel to the ground.

Quentin took it all in, then looked forward, just as he would for a game-time snap. "Hut-*hut!*"

Pietor shot off the line as Quentin took three steps back and brought the ball up to his ear. Seven yards into Pietor's route, Quentin reared back and threw a laser. Pietor stopped and turned, hands up to catch the timing pass. The ball slid through his palms and hit him in the chest. He winced, then grabbed the ball off the ground and ran back behind Jorje.

Morgaine was next. He leaned into the three-point stance, rocketed out on the "snap." He ran the pattern well enough but just seemed a little slow to Quentin. Maybe the guy would loosen up as they continued the drills.

Quentin bent for the next snap, but Jorje was standing there, hands on hips, just staring at Quentin.

Quentin stood. "Hey, yellow, let's go. You want a shot at this roster slot or not?"

"The universe has decreed that you should throw harder,"

Jorje said. "The cannons of fate cannot change history if the artillery shells of destiny do not finish their parabola of prophecy."

"What?"

"*Starcher!*" Hokor's angry voice boomed from the floating golf cart's speakers. "Starcher, you get in your stance and *run the routes I call!*"

"Destiny," Pine said absently from behind Quentin. "Why does that ring a bell?"

Jorje was still standing tall. "Throw *hard*, young Quentin, lest the doom of millennial atrophy fill our heads with cotton."

"Dude," Quentin said, "are you high?"

"*Starcher!*" Hokor screamed. "Last chance!" Hokor's fur was already fluffed up. Starcher wasn't doing himself any favors by infuriating the galaxy's angriest coach, that was for sure.

Quentin nodded at Starcher. "Okay. You want the heat, you got the heat. Now will you run the damn pattern?"

The big tight end turned and leaned into his three-point stance, weight forward on his toes and on his extended hand.

"Hey," Pine said. "Wait a minute ... I think I know that guy."

"Pine, shut it," Quentin said. This yellow-faced Starcher guy wanted the cannons? Cannons were Quentin's business, and business was good. He'd bounce one off this guy's face and send him home on a stretcher.

"Hut-*hut!*"

Starcher shot off the line. As Quentin brought up the ball and dropped three steps, he instantly saw that not only was Starcher *bigger* than Pietor and Morgaine, he was much *quicker*. Quentin's brain took it all in, cataloging the details for later review. When Starcher passed six yards, Quentin was already in his throwing motion. This guy wanted a strong pass? Quentin would deliver a heater a fraction of a second too soon and see how Starcher liked that kind of destiny.

Quentin threw as hard as he could. The ball shot out, hissing as the white strings and pebbled brown leather split the air. Starcher turned, his hands came up ...

... and the ball slapped into his hands. For just a moment,

Quentin heard a tiny ringing from the air inside the leather ball. The *ping* sound faded quickly but punctuated the sentence that popped instantly and eagerly into Quentin's thoughts: *this guy has world-class hands.*

World-class, and big. The ball practically vanished inside Starcher's mutant-sized hands and his sausage-thick fingers.

They ran drills for another twenty minutes, but all that time only confirmed what Quentin had known from the first pass — that Jorje Starcher was a potential all-star who had somehow slipped through the cracks.

On the final pass, just to be a smart-ass, Quentin threw a ten-yard pass as hard as he possibly could. Jorje — possibly to just be a smart-ass as well — caught it with one hand.

Quentin shook his head and laughed. "Nice job, man."

Starcher smiled, white teeth set in yellow greasepaint skin.

"No," Pine said. "*Not* nice. I know why he's familiar. Jorje Starcher? Are you George Starcher?"

"*Pine!*" Hokor said. "Never mind that."

Don turned to look up at the coach's cart. "Oh, no you don't, Hokor. Don't even try that with me. Are you telling me you brought in George Starcher?"

"Who is George Starcher?" Quentin asked.

"I am," Starcher said. "Polisher of a dirty universe and keeper of the far flame."

"Far flame?" Quentin said. "You *are* high."

"I *knew* it!" Pine said. "Hokor, what the hell are you thinking?"

Quentin looked back and forth between Starcher, Pine and Hokor.

"Come on," Quentin said. "Will someone tell me what's going on?"

"Nothing," Hokor said. "Just run the drills."

Pine's blue face turned a little purple. "*Nothing?* Quentin, you've never *heard* of George Starcher?"

Quentin shook his head.

"Haven't heard of *Schizo Starcher*. No? How about *Crazy George?*"

Actually, Quentin had heard of Crazy George. He looked at the big, yellow-faced Human. Played for the Neptune Scarlet Fliers back in '78, or something? Quentin had never seen him play, but ... yeah ... now he remembered. He'd read an illegal, pirated feature written by Yolanda Davenport. She'd covered George's philosophy blog or something, made him the subject of one of those *colorful personalities of football* pieces. Quentin remembered not because of Starcher, but because the story showed a picture of the young, blue-skinned reporter. Oh, how that picture had wracked a fourteen-year-old Quentin with such guilt — she was the most beautiful woman he had ever seen, but it was sinful to be attracted to someone with blue skin.

"Crazy George Starcher," Pine said. "He's been kicked off more teams than I've played on."

"But he played for Neptune," Quentin said. "That means he's got Tier One experience."

"That's right," Starcher said. "I have decorated the highest halls of legend."

"Sure," Pine said. "And he was *kicked off* the Fliers for being bug-nuts crazy. Then a season with the Titan Triangles in T2, who *cut* him, and another T2 season with the Lipton Engineers, who *also* cut him. Then, it seems, Mister Painty Face changed his name and fell all the way to the NFL."

Quentin heard what Pine was saying. He respected Pine's opinion above all others, but the fact remained that Starcher had Tier One experience ... and those *hands*.

Starcher raised his right hand and looked up dramatically, maybe to the dome, maybe to some star above. Quentin looked up but didn't see anything.

"Donald Pine speaks the truth," Starcher said, every word dripping with the drama of a preacher. "I changed my name because the name was offensive to the hidden Old Ones of the firmament, and one *does not* want to offend the hidden Old Ones of the firmament."

"C'mon, Don," Quentin said. "Maybe the guy straightened out his life or something."

Don looked stunned at the question. "Look at his *face*,

Quentin! Does that look like the face of a man who has straightened out his life?"

"Didn't you just tell me to see if he can catch the ball? Well, he can."

"That's why so many teams have given him a chance," Pine said. "Don't you want to find out why those same teams let him go? I'm going to take a wild stab in the dark here, Quentin — they let him go because he's rat-shucking *crazy*."

Maybe Pine was right. But Starcher had the speed, size, moves and hands of an All-Pro. Just the one pass told Quentin that Starcher was better than Yotaro Kobayasho, the Krakens starting tight end, and *way* better than that racist Rick Warburg. Who knew how good Starcher would be after a few weeks of practice, after learning the Krakens offensive system?

"*Pine!*" Hokor shouted. "This is not your decision! It is mine."

Pine glared at Hokor then looked at Quentin. "Q, it's your show now. If you tell Coach *no way*, he won't sign Starcher. There's a reason this guy was in Tier Three. Don't sign him."

Hokor stayed silent, watching. So did Starcher, and so did Pine. They were all waiting for Quentin's words. Maybe it actually was Quentin's decision after all.

Starcher spoke first. "I am ... I have thoughts," he said. "Visions, if you will. But I ... " His voice trailed off. It seemed very difficult for him to say what he needed to say. The dramatic tone dropped away, and Quentin heard the words of a desperate man. "I don't always think like maybe you think, but I know that I can still *play*. I can. I will work hard. I just want one more chance."

Quentin stared into the man's eyes. There was crazy in there — and after nineteen years on a colony ruled by religious fundamentalists, Quentin Barnes *knew* crazy — but there was also pain. The pain of having the ability and the desire, but no outlet for it. Quentin knew that pain firsthand.

To give George Starcher that chance, all Quentin had to do was look past the odd behavior and the yellow greasepaint. Quentin had learned to look past a lot of things in the months since he'd left Micovi.

"Screw it," Quentin said. "Starcher, you'll have to prove it in the locker room and in practice before you get a chance to prove it on the field. You have to do what Coach tells you to do, but first you have to make *me* happy before you ever see a down of playing time. This is my show. You want in? You do it my way. That work for you?"

Crazy George Starcher smiled and spread his arms. "Destiny delights us with opportunity only seldom. I would be a fool to turn her away, and I—"

"Starcher," Quentin interrupted. "Put a sock in the crazy-talk. My way or the highway. I want a simple *yes* or a simple *no.*"

Starcher put his hands at his sides, clearly trying to control his emotions. "Yes," he said.

Quentin felt Don's hand on his shoulder.

"Quentin, don't," Pine said. "You'll regret this."

Quentin knew Pine had the experience, the wisdom, but Quentin wanted the kind of dominant tight end that Starcher could clearly be, that Quentin *needed* him to be. The road to a Tier One GFL championship would be a bumpy one.

"Coach," Quentin said. "Sign this guy."

Pine kicked over the rack of footballs, then strode toward the tunnel.

### From "Species Biology & Football"
#### *written by Cho-Ah-Huity*
### Sklorno Twins: A Rare Form of Double Trouble

Sklorno egg clusters produce broods of eight, ten or twelve children. It is always an even number because eggs sprout from both sides of the mid-line reproductive channel. That means if there are ten broodlings, there are five sets of identical twins. So why don't we see an endless parade of Sklorno twin sisters dominating professional football?

Because as a species, the Sklorno are rather hungry.

The egg cluster develops inside the mother's body. By the end of her four-month term, she will double or triple in weight. Her tail will grow to five or six times its original length and mass. As the egg cluster develops, the mother's body undergoes physical changes that will allow for the depositing of the egg cluster. The mother's body widens at the hips, greatly reducing the Sklorno's speed. Hence, motherhood is an automatic end to any GFL career.

Each pair of eggs within the cluster can be male or female. Male eggs hatch while the cluster is still inside the mother, so males benefit from a "live" birth. What is that benefit, you ask? The benefit is that as soon as they are born, they can move away from any sisters that remaining in the cluster. If the males do not move away — far away, I might add — they are not going to live long.

Three to five days after the mother passes the egg cluster, Sklorno female infants burst free. Within hours of hatching, they have full coordination and differ from adults in little more than size. While the hatchlings already possess well-developed physical capability, mental maturity doesn't arrive for three to four weeks. In short, the infant Sklorno females are small killing machines with no sentience whatsoever. They attack any moving thing that is their size or smaller, and, if they succeed in killing it, they eat it.

This immediate kill-or-be-killed environment has put heavy evolutionary pressure on speed. The faster the Sklorno female, the more likely that she will find slower, weaker prey and the more likely that she will avoid larger pursuers. Only the females that avoid being eaten live to see sentience.

This sounds like a brutal, primitive system. The casual observer might logically assume that the now highly advanced Sklorno separate the hatchlings. That casual observer would be wrong. As a species, the Sklorno are already dealing with enormous overpopulation pressures. Protecting each hatchling is not high on the list of priorities. Almost every Sklorno adult killed and ate three, four or more of her brood-mates before sentience manifested. To the Sklorno, this process is considered an ancient rite of passage, a fact of life as basic and necessary as reproduction itself.

Because twins are identical, they have the same size and speed. They can't escape each other, driving them to an almost immediate confrontation. A *lethal* confrontation. This is why you see very few adult twins in Sklorno culture.

The one exception to this rule is that of conjoined twins, which occur about once in every 100,000 births. Normally, these twins are conjoined in a way that slows them down and makes them easy prey for their brood-mates. Occasionally, however, the twin sisters are joined by a tentacle, an eye stalk or some other way that doesn't interfere with running. When this happens, it is a powerful combination indeed. Now instead of two individuals fighting for survival, the conjoined twin sisters act as a single organism — bigger and stronger than all of their brood mates.

Once sentience occurs, the conjoined sisters always opt for separation surgery. They remain emotionally close, however, and usually stay together as they go through life.

Several sets of twin Sklorno succeeded in the GFL, including Adleburgh and Bamburgh, receivers for the Yall Criminals and the Hall-of-Fame cornerbacks known as "Sisters of the Holy Shutdown" who anchored the secondary for the Hittoni Hullwalkers during their championship seasons of 2671 to 2673.

**THE TOUCHBACK REMAINED** in orbit around Ionath, isolated and safe from attack thanks to a generous no-approach cushion provided by flights of Quyth military fighter-craft. Gredok, it seemed, had called in some markers to make sure no one came after his players.

Quentin stood in the waiting area just outside the *Touchback's* landing bay, marveling at how so much could change in such a short time. Through a view port, he watched the orange and black shuttle sliding out of the void and through the bay's big airlock doors. It had returned from the former prison station now known as the *Combine*, rookies in tow.

Had it really only been thirteen weeks since *he* had arrived as a rookie? Walking out of the shuttle and into his new home, his new life? Until then, he'd never seen anything but Purist Nation space. Never seen an actual alien other than the bats, let alone played football with them.

John Tweedy walked up and stood next to Quentin. Tweedy was bouncing from foot to foot, rolling out his neck and flexing his muscles. He looked a lot like he did every time the defense took the field. I EAT ROOKIES AND CRAP CORNFLAKES scrolled across his face tattoo.

"Pretty wild, eh, Q? I mean, the rookie stink is barely off of you, and here you are, welcoming in a new crop."

"Bite me, Tweedy. That stink is yours. Where I come from, we wash with soap and water."

"Where you come from, Country, running water is probably called a *miracle*," John said. "Just wait until your people discover that wild new invention, *eee-lec-tris-it-eee*. Then the real fun will begin."

"You're hysterical."

"I know," John said.

"And why do you call me *Country*?"

"It's a figure of speech, Your Hickness. Hey, they done with your room upgrades yet?"

"They're finishing now. I get to program everything tonight."

"Did they put in one of those primitive water showers you're always whining about?"

Quentin shook his head. Since leaving the Purist Nation, he'd had to suffer through the "civilized" version of personal hygiene in the form of nannite showers — little swarms of microscopic robots that scoured your skin free of dirt and oil.

"They wouldn't put in a water shower," Quentin said. "Gredok wouldn't spring for it when the nannite showers work fine for everyone else. I got him to put a weight bench in, though."

"You had a weight bench put in your room? Why not use the weight room in the gym?"

Quentin shrugged. "I'll use that as well. I want the bench in my room so I can work out first thing in the morning."

John stared at him. "I know you already work out at lunch.

And after practice. You work out in the morning, too?"

Quentin nodded. "Morning lifting, then passing routes in the VR room, then running, then team and position meetings, then lunch, then practice, then I run again after practice, then holo-review in my room for two hours, then I lift again, shower and go to bed."

John shook his head. "Boy, you're not well."

"You got that right. I got a disease, and a championship is the only cure."

John rolled his eyes. "Oh, man, that's corny. You practice that one?"

Quentin laughed. "Actually, yeah. Working on corny phrases and some pregame chants to get everyone pumped up. Want to hear them?"

"Not now," John said. "Leave me be for a while to think about how you out-work me and everyone else who has ever played the game."

Quentin watched the shuttle settle onto the landing bay deck, watched the bay doors slide shut.

[PRESSURE EQUALIZED] a computer voice called out moments later. [LANDING BAY NOW SAFE TO ENTER]

The waiting area doors hissed open. Quentin, John and most of the team filtered into the landing bay.

"The rookies are almost all offensive players," John said. "We get just one DB this time. Hey, I wonder if we got another quarterback? We could use a real quarterback, not the backwater pansy we got now."

"John, you bore me," Quentin said.

Yassoud walked up to join them. He'd replaced his orange beard string with a gold one that gleamed under the landing bay's lights.

"Boys," Yassoud said, "I hear we got a running back in that shuttle somewhere."

John smiled. "Probably our new starter. You'll be lucky if we even keep you around for punt returns."

"Shuck you, Tweedy," Yassoud said.

The shuttle's side door lowered.

Hokor and Gredok were the first to exit. Shizzle flew out and flapped around the landing bay, but he wasn't the only flier. A Harrah eased out in that species' half-flying, half-floating style. He wore an orange and black backpack that looked just like the one Doc had worn on the sidelines. This Harrah was bigger, though, and his skin looked ... tauter, almost artificial.

"Must be the new doc," John said.

"Looks ... weird," Quentin said. "Something wrong with him?"

"Him or her," John said. "I can never tell the difference with the flappies. Looks like *it* has had a ton of cosmetic surgery and not very good surgery at that."

Gredok stood and stared at the gathered team, who quickly fell silent and waited.

"My growing network of scouts discovered these highly talented players," he said. "Make these rookies feel like a part of our little family. And this," Gredok gestured up to the floating Harrah, "is Doc Patah. He is our new team physician. I'm sure that all of you will be getting one-on-one time with him soon enough."

With that, Gredok walked through the much larger football players that parted to let him by. Doc Patah flew along behind him. Watching the Harrah, Quentin felt a stab of sadness at the death of the Krakens former physician. Quentin hadn't even known the Harrah's real name, just called him *Doc* like everyone else on the team. That wasn't right. The team doctor was a lifeline to victory, keeping players healthy, patching them up so they could continue to produce. Quentin made a mental note that he would get to know this Doc Patah, treat him like the invaluable part of the team that he was.

The first rookies out were two long-limbed Sklorno wearing orange Krakens jerseys, numbers 31 and 13. Again, Quentin thought about how much had changed in his life. Three months weeks ago at the *Combine*, he'd met Denver and Milford — the first Sklorno he'd ever seen in person. Their translucent, flexible chitin skin and fluttering muscles had been so disturbing up-close. Now? Nothing he hadn't seen a thousand times. Well, that wasn't quite true — he'd seen Sklorno a thousand times, sure, but never any as *big* as these two.

Wahiawa and Halawa. He already had their stats memorized. Both stood nine feet, six inches tall. Both weighed 325 pounds. Because of their size and speed, they had been placed in developmental football leagues at just eighteen months old. When they were full grown at six years of age, they joined the Chachanna Football Collective, one of the Sklorno Dynasty's Tier Three leagues. After two years there, the eight-year-old Awa sisters were now Krakens.

"Man," Yassoud said. "They look like clones."

"Twins," Quentin said.

"I thought Sklorno babies ate each other?"

"Most of the time, they do. These two shared an eye stalk at one point, so they were like the same sentient or something."

"Wimps," John said. "It's much cooler when they eat each other. I wish I'd eaten my brother when we were kids." I HATE JU scrolled across his face.

Quentin laughed to himself as he recalled John's brother, the All-Tier-2 running back for the Orbiting Death. The Krakens had fought a pitched battle against the Death just a few weeks earlier. "The Mad Ju," as the press called him, had put three Krakens linebackers out of the game, *including* John.

"Hey," Yassoud said. "They each only have three eyestalks instead of four. You see that?"

Quentin nodded. "Yeah, they had to cut that eyestalk off to separate them, so they each only have three."

He just hoped three eyestalks would let Halawa see his passes because he was excited to have such a big receiving target. Nine-foot-six. Taller than any veteran Krakens receiver. Even her legs looked larger than others of her species: giant, folded leaping machines. He'd be able to throw the ball up high to her in the corner of the end zone. She'd jump on those big legs, reach up with the two long tentacles that stuck out of her chest. Very few defensive backs — if any — could go high enough to stop her from coming down with the ball.

Tweedy started laughing. "Oh, no, man, you *have* to be kidding me. *That* is Mitchell Fayed's replacement?"

The mention of the dead running back drew Quentin's attention. Coming down the shuttle ramp he saw what had to be a mistake. As big as the Awa sisters were for Sklorno, this guy was little for a Human. He wore a jersey with the number 21.

"Wow," Quentin said. "He's small"

"Damn near a midget," Tweedy said. "Oh man, we are *sooooo* desperate."

"A midget?" Quentin said. "What is that?"

Yassoud and Tweedy looked at him.

"What?" Quentin said. "What are you looking at?"

John shook his head and rolled his eyes. "Never mind, Q. I forget that the Purist Nation isn't big on people with congenital defects."

"We don't have any congenital defects in the Purist Nation."

John and Yassoud both started laughing. Quentin didn't get the joke. Quentin sighed and looked over the new rookie running back. Number 21, Dan Campbell. At 6-foot-2, 230 pounds, he wasn't small by normal Human standards, but in this landing bay, the only Human smaller than him was Arioch Morningstar, the Krakens kicker.

"Hey, 'Soud," John said. "You might as well hang up the cleats right now, chief."

Yassoud shook his head. "I've got ten grand says the midget doesn't make it out of training camp."

"I'll take that bet," Quentin said. He'd memorized Campbell's stats as well. A *Combine* 40-yard dash of 3.6 seconds, fairly fast for a Human, but nothing really special. Campbell's acceleration and agility numbers, however, were nearly off the charts. Maybe he wasn't the fastest guy in the league, but when he got the ball, he would hit his top speed almost instantly.

"You're on," Yassoud said. He and Quentin shook hands, and the bet was official.

Next out of the shuttle came a Ki, bigger than most of his kind, but nothing out of the ordinary for an offensive lineman.

"Shun-On-Won," Quentin said. "Played Tier Three in the KRAFL." Quentin pronounced the word *kra-full*, an acronym for the Ki Rebel Alliance Football League.

John crossed his arms over his chest. "Sure doesn't look like much."

And according to Shun-On's scores at the *Combine*, the Ki rookie *wasn't* much. He charted firmly in the middle in every category — nothing that bad, nothing that great.

"That's the best we could do?" Yassoud said. "If this Shun-On-Won doesn't work out, then I don't have a right guard to block for me. I don't think Aka-Na-Tak is going to make it."

"He'll be back," Quentin said. "Aka-Na will be back."

If only Quentin felt as confident as he sounded. Aka-Na-Tak still hadn't recovered from injuries sustained in the game against the Texas Earthlings. The lineman was out another two to three weeks.

"This is crap," Yassoud said. "How am I going to run the ball with no line?"

And then number 38, the final rookie, walked down the ramp.

Quentin looked at her, already feeling animosity. But that was silly — she was here for a reason and that reason didn't conflict with Quentin's goals. Rebecca Montagne, also known as *Becca the Wrecka*. Six-foot-six, three hundred and thirty pounds of muscle. She wore her long, black hair tied back in a tight ponytail. Big, solid, athletic and yet still clearly feminine — a strange combination.

"Awwww, *yeah*," John said. "'Bout time we got some *ladies* in here that don't spend all their time worshiping Quentin and drooling all over the place."

"Ew," Yassoud said. "Tweedy, you serious? That chick is a HeavyG girl. Her butt is bigger than yours."

"Exactly," Tweedy said. "Uncle Johnny likes 'em healthy. Quentin, what's her name?"

"Rebecca Montagne. Fullback. Played Tier Three in the NFL on Earth, for the Green Bay Packers."

"Wait a minute," Yassoud said. "Rebecca … why do I know

that name? I know, she's got a cool nickname ... what is it? Oh, it's on the tip of my tongue."

"Becca the Wrecka," Quentin said.

Yassoud snapped his fingers and smiled. "That's it!"

"Wrecka?" John said, his eyes even more alive at the possibility that this HeavyG woman was somehow known for violence. "Why do they call her that, Q?"

"Because of the way she hits when she runs the ball."

John looked to the ceiling, raised his hands as if in prayer. "Quentin, you've got to thank your High One for delivering an angel like this to me. She hurts people while running the ball? That is all kinds of mean, I like it. The Packers run the fullback a lot?"

Quentin shrugged, but Yassoud snapped his fingers again. "Wait, now I remember why I heard of her," Yassoud said. "The Packers were trying some bush-league stuff in the NFL, running the option offense. Where the quarterback carries the ball."

John looked from Quentin to Yassoud, then back to Quentin again. A smile crept across his face. Quentin saw the smile, felt his own face getting hotter, redder. There was no reason for him to get this angry. Becca was there to play fullback, to block for Yassoud or whoever played running back. Worse, John Tweedy always knew when Quentin was upset and never missed a chance to exploit it.

"Oh, man," John said. "Quentin, was Becca the Wrecka a *quarterback*?"

Quentin gritted his teeth and nodded.

Tweedy stared blankly at Quentin for a few seconds, then threw his head back and laughed. YOU'RE KILLING ME, WHITEY flashed across his face.

Quentin nodded angrily. "She's here to be a *full*back, John, so just keep on laughing."

John did, even harder. His hands dropped to his knees, as if he could barely stand. "Hooo," he said, trying to suck in a breath, "you better hope that she ... that she knows her role and doesn't come after your spot."

"She's a *fullback*, John. Tom Pareless is retiring after this season, and we needed a fullback to replace him. You take the best athlete available for the position, and Hokor thinks she can start next year as our *full*back."

Quentin knew that, Hokor knew that, and Rebecca Montagne had better know that. Whatever position she wound up playing, if she played at all, Quentin would *make sure* she didn't entertain any ideas of playing quarterback.

That was his position, and if Don Pine couldn't take it from him, then no one else should even try.

**JUST AS HE'D PROGRAMMED** the night before, the lights in his small bedroom flicked on at 5:30 in the morning. Quentin Barnes sat up. He'd already been awake for ten minutes, maybe fifteen, but he'd forced himself to stay in bed. Soon his body would adapt to the new schedule. It was time to make *everything* obey his will … his body, his drive, his team, even time itself.

Everything would align.

He would make it so.

Because he had a championship to win.

The smart-paper walls of his apartment were white when he awoke. As he walked out of the bedroom to the living room, every wall faded into a sequence of still pictures that slowly painted a chronological history of the game. Quentin bent, stretching his hamstrings, his calves, his groin, feeling delicious pain in his muscle fibers as black-and-white, two-dimensional images showed faces like Tittle, Unitas, Baugh, Layne, Thorpe, Pollard, Nagurski. He stretched his arms as the two-dimensional images changed to full-color, with faces like Campbell, Butkus, Landry, Brown, Staubach, Bradshaw, Rice, Tatum, Montana, Lewis. The images then changed to three-dimensional holograms, faces like Adrojnik, Cuh-En-Shaka, Jacksonville, Tarat the Smasher, Smith, Pikor the Unquestioned, Zimmer, Pine.

All of them, the faces of champions.

Quentin finished his stretching routine, then started it all over again, forcing himself to go farther each time, to feel *more* pain, to hear everything his body had to say. You *listened* to pain, but you didn't *obey* it. Pain was a servant, a reminder that you were one of the few sentients lucky enough to be alive at *this* moment, at *this* time in history.

The holotank flicked on at 6:00 a.m., exactly when he finished his second round of stretching. Before moving on to his next task, he waited just long enough to see what game the computer randomly selected.

Super Bowl LXXIX, the Grand Rapids Lions versus the Mexico City Conquistadors back in the ancient times when there was the NFL and nothing else, when there was only one planet playing football, centuries before the Lions moved to Thomas 3. He'd never watched this game. The recorded crowd filled his room with a roar as he moved to the weight bench.

The rig consisted of a padded bench and a horizontal bar above it. The bar was steel, with soft, black handles on either end. Right at the middle of that bar, another bar connected, making a "T," the T-post leading into a vertical slot in the wall. The wall had other attachments sticking out of it, individual handles that could be pulled or pushed, giving Quentin any number of weightlifting options. He would use all of the attachments for a full-body workout. His favorite — by far — was the tried and true bench-press.

He lay back on the bench, then reached up to grab the padded handles, his hands shoulder-width apart. In the space between his hands, the bar showed a readout in red letters: *400 lbs*. He looked up at the ceiling, where the smart paper showed the silver and blue Lions rushing out of the tunnel, preparing for the biggest game of their lives. Every player he saw up there was long-since dead, the game having taken place more than six centuries earlier. *Dead*, but not *forgotten* — every player was forever notched in the glory of history, every player was eternal.

"Give me music," Quentin said. The room computer faded out the game noise. The first song on his playlist faded in. His favorite band, Trench Warfare, the long, melodic guitar intro to their hit *Combat Bats*. He would watch the game and listen to the music.

He couldn't work out and watch Trench Warfare — the band's lead singer, Somalia Midori, was far too distracting for that.

Quentin lowered the bar to his chest, then pressed. The four hundred pounds went up smooth and easy. He lowered the bar and repeated, watching the ceiling as the players took to the field. He hit ten reps before his muscles started to burn.

Another half hour of weights, then it was time to hit the virtual practice field for twenty minutes before the 7:00 a.m. position meeting.

**QUENTIN'S PRACTICE CLEATS** pressed into the corridor's carpet. He approached the Kriegs-Ballok VR practice room and through the door saw Hawick — his top receiver — streaking across a sapphire-blue surface marked with blazing white yard lines. Sapphire blue and white: the home field colors of the Isis Ice Storm.

She was running an inside-slant route, one that would take her at a shallow angle from near the sidelines to the middle of the field. Running with her was Stockbridge, the Krakens left cornerback.

The wide door framed the scene — Quentin saw a ball rip through the air. His eyes had only a fraction of a second to comprehend that the ball looked a little *too* real to be a holographic projection, then Stockbridge stepped in front of Hawick and caught it.

An interception.

Quentin stepped through the door and looked left, in the direction of the pass, expecting to see Don Pine or possibly Yitzhak.

But he saw neither.

Instead, he saw Rebecca Montagne. She froze as if she'd been caught doing something wrong.

"Rookie," Quentin said, "what do you think you're doing?"

She stared at him with wide eyes. "Uh ... I'm, just, you know, uh ... throwing the ball."

"Montagne, you are a *fullback*. Fullbacks do not throw the ball."

Her shocked stare vanished as her eyes narrowed. Quentin saw aggression there, attitude.

"I'm a *quarterback*," she said. "I'm playing fullback because the offer was on the table and I wanted to get into Tier One."

"And you are in Tier One *as a fullback*. If you were a Tier One *quarterback*, someone would have picked you up for that. But they didn't. So stop wasting my receivers' time."

Hawick and Stockbridge walked up, their walk faster than most Humans' *run*.

"But Quentin Barnes," Hawick said. "Rebecca Montagne was not wasting our time, she was here early so we —"

"Shut *up*," Quentin said. Hawick and Stockbridge visibly winced, as if he'd raised a whip to beat them down, a whip they'd felt land hundreds of times before.

"Hey," Rebecca said. "Be mad at me if you want, but you don't have to be a jerk to them."

Quentin turned on her. "What was that, *rookie*? Are you telling me what to do?"

Her eyes grew wide again. Quentin was a good six inches taller. He towered over her.

"Well, *rookie*? Are you? Are you telling me what to do?"

She shook her head. That brief bit of attitude seemed long gone.

"Good," Quentin said. "This room is reserved for *quarterbacks* in the morning, you got that? You want to use it, come late at night, although I bet you'll have your hands full just learning to block like you're supposed to. Now get out of here."

Rebecca looked to the ground, then ran out of the practice room. Quentin watched her go, making sure she didn't stick around. The *audacity* of that rookie. Taking snaps? *Throwing?*

"Quentin Barnes," Hawick said, her meek voice barely audible over the holographic crowd's steady drone. "We stand miserable in our shame for disappointing one as godlike as you. Would you like us to kill ourselves to atone?"

Quentin sighed and stared at the ceiling. Hawick wasn't kidding. It was hard being looked at as a religious figure — you had to be careful about what you said to your *subjects*.

"Room, off," Quentin said. The sapphire blue field and the

crowd vanished. With them went the sound. Quentin turned to face Hawick and Stockbridge, who were shaking violently in fear.

"Hawick, I'm sorry I yelled. You did nothing wrong, you have nothing to be ashamed of. Please, tell me what's on your mind."

The Sklorno's shaking vanished, as instantly as if they'd never been afraid in the first place. Sklorno switched emotional gears at the drop of a hat.

"Rebecca Montagne meant no harm," Hawick said. "She was helping us to catch glorious passes to further your glory. She was here before you, so we thought we would practice."

Quentin gritted his teeth. "Room, on. Hawick, line up, let's work out-routes to the sidelines. Bump-and-run coverage."

Hawick scrambled to the line of scrimmage, while Stockbridge practically fell over herself moving into close-cover, defensive back position. Quentin couldn't be angry with them for working with Montagne. Just as he did, the Sklorno lived for football. In their minds, any missed chance to play was a chance that would never come again, a chance that was lost forever to the sands of time.

"Hut-*hut!*" He dropped back five steps and planted, throwing the ball even before Hawick cut to the outside. Her big feet dragged inbounds as she extended her tentacle arms. She caught the ball firmly just before those feet scraped onto the white sideline. Perfect throw, perfect catch, but it didn't chase away the words that rang in the back of Quentin's head.

She was here before you.

**QUENTIN THREW THE OUT PATTERN** for the thirtieth time in a row, again hitting Hawick's outstretched tentacles. If she could get off the line without being stuffed by a defensive back, and he delivered on-target, the throw could not be stopped. This season, he planned on using more short, controlled passes. Tier Two defensive backs had caused him no end of trouble — and now he was in Tier One, where they would be even better, where they would be some of the greatest to ever play the game. He couldn't go head-hunting against talent like that, couldn't constantly be throwing the deep ball unless he softened up the secondary by throwing multiple short passes underneath, drawing the defenders in close. When that happened, when they came up to stop the short pass, that would give him the opportunity to throw long. Hawick and Scarborough were as good as any Tier One receiver — if they could get a step on the defense, Quentin could hit them for six every time.

"*Barnes!*"

Quentin smiled when he heard the high-pitched, gravelly voice. He turned to face Coach Hokor. Not so long ago, hearing Hokor's piercing shout would have made Quentin wince, made him dread the inevitable laps of punishment. But those days were gone for good.

"Hey, Coach," Quentin said. "Ready for the position meeting?"

"Of course," Hokor said. "I respect the fact that you are working out early — again — but we have receiver practice in fifteen minutes. Why are you running my receivers to exhaustion?"

Quentin turned and looked at Hawick. Her raspers dangled all the way to the floor, drool running off in rivulets to pool at her feet. Beneath her clear chitin skin, he saw her heart fluttering madly, her three lungs expanding and shrinking, expanding and shrinking.

He turned back to face Hokor and shrugged. "She better get used to it, Coach. The whole team better get used to it. Some things we can't control, but one thing we can *always* control is how hard we work. *No one* will work harder than the Krakens."

Hokor's pedipalps twitched up and down a little. The Quentin of thirteen weeks ago might have mistaken that for laughter, but he was getting to know Quyth Leaders — his coach, in particular. That kind of twitch meant Hokor was trying to hide excitement. Trying, and failing. Gredok the Splithead could disguise emotions at will, but Hokor? Despite the little coach's gruff exterior, Quentin was rapidly reaching the point where he could read Hokor like a messageboard.

"Hawick, Stockbridge," Hokor said. "Go to the practice field and sit down until we start drills."

Hawick shivered, the motion making little bits of spittle fly off her tongue. "Yes, Coach Hokor the Hookchest! Yesyesyes!"

She sprinted out of the virtual practice room at top speed, completely missing the fact that Hokor wanted her to rest. Stockbridge ran as well, only a step behind the faster receiver.

As they ran out of the VR practice room, Donald Pine and Yitzhak Goldman walked in. Both were dressed for the day's practice — full football armor and red *do not touch* jerseys.

"Let's begin the quarterback meeting," Hokor said. "First of all, we have Media Day coming up next week. That will cost us a half-day of practice, so we need to make this week count."

"A half-day?" Quentin said. "Can't we just do some holophone interviews or something?"

"It is mandatory," Hokor said. "A league requirement. And as the starting quarterback, you *will* do it, Barnes."

"Why would they want to talk to me? I haven't even won a Tier One game yet."

Don laughed. "Win or lose, there's still news coverage. You're the starting quarterback, that makes you a media darling whether you like it or not. If you want, I'll walk you through the process, tell you what to expect."

That made Quentin instantly feel better. Don's experience as the best player in football, his confidence, his calmness, all of these things helped Quentin get a perspective on his new duties as team leader.

"Yeah," Quentin said. "That would be great."

Don nodded once, then looked at Hokor, letting the coach continue.

"The Ice Storm finished with seven wins last year," Hokor said. "Their five losses were all close games. They were just a few tipped passes away from *nine* wins and a trip to the Tier One playoffs."

Quentin nodded. Since the schedule had been released, he had studied the Ice Storm in depth. Hokor was right — Isis *was* a playoff-caliber team.

"Offensively, we have a primary problem," Hokor said. "Isis puts significant pressure on the opposing quarterback. Their linebackers are among the best in the league at pass coverage and at blitzing. We will not have a strong running game this week."

"This *week?*" Pine said. "How about this *season.*"

"Back off, Don," Quentin said. "Murphy will come through."

Pine shook his head. "He's not the solution."

"If he's not, then who is? Campbell? Martinez?"

"Maybe," Don said. "Maybe we land someone else. For this week, however, I'm guessing the solution is the fleet feet of our starting quarterback."

Hokor grunted in agreement. "Today we will be working short patterns to keep the pressure off of you, Barnes, and rolling you out of the pocket to give you more time to throw. With Aka-Na-Tak out, I don't think our replacement right guards can protect you for drop-back passing. Combine that with our weak running game, and play-action won't buy you time, either. If we roll you out to the sides, your speed will give you time to throw and keep you from getting killed in the pocket. So let's get out there and practice those patterns with the receivers."

Quentin nodded and started to run off the practice field, but Hokor stopped him.

"Barnes, this is just the first game of a long season. Our game plan revolves around you not taking big hits, so you don't get damaged. But that *also* means that you have to work on *sliding.* No head-to-head collisions with defensive players. I don't want you taking the kind of punishment you took against the Earthlings."

Quentin laughed and shook his head. "Hell, Coach, you can count on that. I don't feel like getting beat up like that again. And besides, you know you don't have to tell me something more than once."

Yitzhak snorted. He was trying to choke back laughter. Pine looked away, his lip quivering.

"What?" Quentin said, annoyed at once again not being part of the in-crowd. "What is so damn funny?"

"You ... " Pine said, then he bent over at the waist, shaking his head and trying to hold it in. Yitzhak couldn't stop his snorts anymore and laughed as he ran for the practice field door.

Pine stood, pursed his lips, shook his head, blinked away tears, then walked off the field.

"Coach," Quentin said. "What are those guys laughing about?"

Hokor said nothing. Quentin looked down at his coach, whose pedipalps quivered. And this time? They quivered side to side, they quivered with *laughter*.

"I really don't know what they find so funny," Hokor said. "But, as you say," — the pedipalps quivered faster — "you don't have to be told twice. Now get your butt on the field. It's time for practice."

Quentin snarled and jogged off the field. He hated not getting the joke.

**QUENTIN PULLED ON HIS HELMET** as he jogged to the 50-yard line of the *Touchback's* practice field. Pine and Yitzhak were already there, waiting by a rack of footballs. Beyond them, the Sklorno receivers: veterans Hawick, Scarborough, Mezquitic and Richfield; last year's rookies Denver and Milford; and this year's rookie Halawa.

Damn, but Halawa was a *big* girl.

Hokor was once again in his little cart, floating fifteen feet above the field. Quentin looked at him, wondering how the diminutive coach had gotten to the field before him.

"*Barnes!*" Hokor called over the cart's speakers. "Line them up. Out patterns, right then left."

Quentin nodded and clapped his hands together three times, so hard it stung the skin of his palms. "You heard the coach! Ten-yard outs. Right side first. Let's go, ladies, we have a lot of work to do to get ready for the Ice Storm. All snaps on a two-count, all on two."

The Sklorno quivered with unbridled excitement. Hawick lined up first. Last year she had been the Krakens' number-two receiver, but after her season, it went without saying that she had become the Krakens' main threat. In line behind her was Scarborough, who had been the Krakens' top receiver for the past three seasons. At twenty-five years old, she was the most senior Sklorno on the team. She had lost a step or two but could still fly down the field like a space fighter, still jump high and still scrap and claw for every ball thrown her way.

Quentin bent in a mock-snap position. He looked over at Hawick and winked.

Hawick saw his wink, then shook so much he thought she might spontaneously combust. Drool flew everywhere around her.

"Hut-*hut!*"

Quentin pushed away from the line, looking to his left, taking three powerful steps back before planting with his back foot and turning to the right. His shoulders snapped around and the ball rocketed out of his hand in a flat parallel with the ground. The ball magically reached Hawick just as she turned, tentacles outstretched, already reaching for the ball that she knew would be there.

Feet dragging inbounds, she caught the ball cleanly before she slid out.

*Yeah. Perfect. Just like this season is going to be ... perfect.*

Quentin grabbed the next ball from the rack and bent as Scarborough lined up. Scarborough shook even harder than Hawick. The Krakens' oldest receiver, it seemed, was an early member of the Church of Quentin Barnes.

"Hut-*hut!*"

Scarborough ran the route just a hair slower than Hawick. Hawick had become the team's leading receiver, true, but everyone knew the real reason for her breakout success was that opposing defenses had put their top cornerback on Scarborough. Now Hawick would draw the top defender, which meant Scarborough would usually play against a lower-caliber, number-two defensive back. That would create good match-ups for the Krakens and might give Scarborough one last, great season.

After this season, however, there was little doubt that Milford would take over as the number-two receiver. She and Denver had been rookies alongside Quentin. Both of the second-year receivers could flat-out fly, but their cuts weren't yet quite as crisp as Scarborough's and Hawick's, their acceleration not quite as marked. Denver was faster, had more long-term potential, but needed another season or two to become all she could be. Milford, however, was ready right now. With a few more games under her belt, she would become a major threat. When Quentin looked at the Krakens receiver slots one through four, he felt strongly that he had one of the best lineups in all of Tier One.

After Milford came Mezquitic, the former number-three receiver. She was thirteen years old, a fifth-year player, and should have been coming into her prime. She wasn't as fast as Denver and Milford, however, and her vertical leap had gone down a half-inch over the past two seasons. Sklorno vertical leaps usually went up about a quarter inch a season for the first five or six seasons, plateaued for the next three or four, then finally started dropping off around year ten. If, that was, the receiver lived that long. Sklorno had the highest death rate of any species in the GFL. Mezquitic was slowing down, and no one knew why. She'd probably taken too many hits. The repetitive trauma had begun to take its toll.

After Mezquitic came Richfield, the final receiver. Her primary role on the team was as a kick returner, bringing back punts and kickoffs. She was slimmer than her Sklorno teammates, standing at 8-foot-5 but weighing only 273 pounds. Richfield simply didn't have what it took to be an every-play receiver, but she did have a crazy knack for finding holes on those kick returns. That ability let her pick up five to ten extra yards on every return, yards that were critical for field position. Every now and then she would hit a hole clean and take it to the house.

Richfield ran her out-route slower than the others had, but still disciplined and efficient. She returned the ball to the rack, then got back in line. Quentin's eyes drifted to the front of the line, to the last receiver on the roster.

Halawa.

He *still* couldn't get used to her size. Scarborough was 8-foot-6, 295 pounds. Halawa was a full *twelve inches* taller and weighed a solid 320 pounds. Her body wasn't as thick as Scarborough's. In fact, Halawa was a touch skinny for that height, but the rookie receiver was only eight years old. She would grow, probably adding ten to fifteen pounds in the next two seasons alone.

"*Barnes!*"

Hokor's speaker-powered scream brought him back. He'd drifted away, hadn't realized he'd been just staring at Halawa.

"Barnes, do you mind?"

Quentin gave Hokor a quick wave. "Sorry, Coach. Halawa, on two, on two. Huuuut … *hut!*"

Quentin dropped back as Halawa shot off the line. He looked left at first, as he'd done on all the passes, then at three steps stopped, turned right and threw.

High One, she was *fast*.

Way faster than Scarborough, than Hawick, than even Denver. Her speed caught him off guard and he hurried his throw. The split-second the ball left his hand, he was mentally kicking himself — he'd thrown it too far out of bounds.

And then Halawa *stretched*. Her big feet scraped against the nano-turf field, kicking up small sprays of green dust as her elegant body extended horizontally and her long, muscular tentacles reached out. Her body was parallel to the ground, just a few inches above it, and her toes only a half-inch inbounds when her tentacle tips snagged the ball out of the air.

Had it been a game, that would have been a complete pass. A complete pass that would have been *impossible* to defend. Big. Fast. Athletic. A natural receiver.

Quentin felt his pulse racing, combining the visuals of Halawa with the size and hands of Crazy George Starcher. He'd had a good receiver corps even before they had arrived. Now? It had the potential to be the best in the league.

"*Baaaarnes!*"

Quentin shook his head clear. Wow, he had to stop drifting away like that.

"Sorry, Coach! Okay, ladies, five more each on this pattern, then switch to the left. On two, on two … ready … hut-*hut!*"

# 3

# PRESEASON: WEEK THREE

From **"Species Biology & Football"**
*written by Cho-Ah-Huity*
**Quyth Warriors & Football: A Star-Studded Caste**

The Quyth have one of the galaxy's most unusual life cycles. Along with the Leekee, the Quyth are the only known sequential hermaphrodites to achieve sentience (although the Leekee reproductive cycle involves multiple species and is far more complex). All Quyth are born male. At a certain age and under the right conditions, Quyth Leaders change their sex and become female, capable of producing egg sacs.

It is those egg sacs that give the Quyth their unique caste system. The egg sac is a soft, spherical membrane usually about 23 to 25 centimeters in diameter. That is about the same size as a regulation basketball or soccer ball. A sac usually contains anywhere from four to eight small eggs. Every egg contains a Quyth Leader larvae — it is only after hatching that the caste system manifests.

Larvae hatch from eggs, then remain in the sac for about four weeks. In an interesting bout of parallel evolution with Humans,

Quyth have a pair of testes. The first larva to eat its way out of its egg is blind, yet is capable of swimming within the sac fluid and navigating via a sense of smell. As his brothers come out of their eggs, this first-born instinctively establishes his dominance. He does this in two ways, first with a physical attack, and then with chemical warfare.

For the physical attack, the first-born cuts off the testes of half of his sac-mates. These castrated Quyth grow to become the Warrior caste. Quyth Warriors are much larger than Leaders. On average, Warriors are over twice as tall and weigh six times as much. This large growth rate is actually a form of gigantism that is naturally controlled by a regulatory hormone produced in the Quyth's testes.

The first-born allows half of his brothers to keep their testes but bombards them with a hormone that permanently alters their brain structure, making them docile. The Quyth affected by this hormone become the Workers. Fascinatingly, the docility hormone only becomes active when it mixes with the growth-control hormone, which is prevalent in Workers because they still have their testes. Hence, the hormone has no effect on the castrated Warriors.

Quyth larvae stay in the sac for two to four months after hatching from their eggs. About a day or two before the brood exits the sac, the single Leader finishes the job and castrates the Workers. As the brood enters the world for the first time, there is only one individual capable of eventually breeding.

Hormonal control continues through childhood, into adolescence and then adulthood. Warriors naturally imprint on their Leader brother but can switch allegiance to another Leader. Sometimes this is a conscious decision, but often it is due to circumstances of proximity, overcrowding or mandatory military service.

Warriors naturally desire to follow a Leader. Evolutionarily speaking, the reason is simple — the Warrior cannot reproduce, so if his genetic line is to survive, he must ensure that his Leader brother breeds. Modern Quyth civilization has hijacked this instinct. That same imprinting tendency results in Warriors following military officers, employers, criminals, community organizers and, yes, sports coaches and team owners.

While Workers become docile followers, Warriors retain high levels of natural aggression. Contact sports — both lethal and nonlethal — provide a critical outlet for those urges. When you combine a Warrior's size, strength, speed and natural aggression with the innate desire to *follow*, it is no surprise that Warriors make excellent soldiers and athletes.


**MESSAL THE EFFICIENT LED QUENTIN** and Don Pine down the *Touchback's* corridors toward the practice field. Media Day had arrived.

"So," Don said, "not to treat you like you're an idiot or anything, Q, but how about you go over my rules?"

Quentin sighed. Sometimes, Don walked a fine line between being a source of invaluable wisdom and an annoying nag.

"Think before I talk," Quentin said. "Don't rush my answers. A pause actually makes me look smarter, more introspective."

"Uh-huh," Don said. "And when you do answer, what do you *not* say?"

"Anything bad about my teammates or the franchise. And nothing that could be locker room fodder for our opposition."

"Good," Don said. "And what *can* we say about the opposition?"

"That we are excited to play them," Quentin said. "Whatever team the reporters are asking about, I say that the team is a quality organization that has a lot of threats. Ionath will practice and prepare, then play as hard as we can on the field."

Don's wide smile showed white teeth that blazed from between his blue lips. "Nice, Q. Nice. Just remember the *think before you talk* part, you're not so good at that."

"Thanks."

Don shrugged. "This isn't the time for me to beat around the bush. If you get flustered, just take a breath. It's a bit of a zoo out there."

"Whatever," Quentin said. "How bad can it be? They're just reporters."

They turned a corner into the tunnel that led to the practice field.

"It can get bad," Don said. "Just trust me on that. And if it gets too bad, Messal will step in and bail you out. Right, Messal?"

"Abso*lute*ly, Mister Pine. You couldn't be more correct. I will stay near Elder Barnes every moment and offer assistance if needed, although I'm confident Elder Barnes will exceed everyone's expectations."

"Thanks," Quentin said, and then the three of them walked onto the practice field where Quentin saw something he'd never seen before — sentients other than his teammates or coaches out on the turf. Dozens of them, maybe hundreds. Many were from the species that made up the GFL: Humans with their skin-tones of tan-pink, brown, black, bleach-white, blue; HeavyG with their shades of light brown and tan-pink; Sklorno females covered head to toe in robes of more shades and colors than Quentin could count; multi-legged Ki dressed in the fine clothes so common to that culture's noncombatants; Quyth Leaders, their fur a myriad collection of shades and striped patterns; floating Harrah that ranged from the utterly smooth skin of young adults to the bony, scaled skin of the elders.

And there were also Creterakian civilians dressed in their crazy, harlequin-esque suits of every horrible color-clashing pattern you could imagine. The civvy bats circled around the heads of the Krakens players. Quentin shuddered. He reminded himself to move slowly, to be respectful — even though these were civilians, where there were bats there were entropic rifles.

And a new creature. Leekee, the amphibious sentients that made up a big part of the Tower Republic's population. Quentin had seen them swimming in the aquatic centers of Ionath City, and in his one visit to Hudson Bay Station, but never out of the water. Hunched-over bipeds built low to the ground, the small Leekee had long, vertically flat tails. The line of that tail continued onto their back as a ridge-line of small spikes ending at their pointy head. The Leekee all had bright-blue skin marked with wide, black stripes. The stripes were thick at the spiky back ridge, tapering to points on the sentients' smooth sides. Leekee bodies looked streamlined and muscular. A small, yellow eye dotted either side of the pointy head.

A hand on his shoulder.

"Kid," Don said. "You all right?"

Quentin looked at Don's blue face, then back to the circus out on the practice field. "I don't know, man. This has nothing to do with football. I think I'll skip it."

"Can't," Don said. "League requirement. Trust me, you don't want to get on the wrong side of Commissioner Froese. And this has *everything* to do with football. The media covers what we do in the GFL. That coverage is for the *fans*. Fans watch the broadcasts, and that brings in advertising revenue. Fans buy jerseys, memorabilia, team clothes — just about any kind of crap you can imagine as long as it has a team logo. Fans buy *tickets* and pack the stadiums every Sunday. Know what you and I do for a living if not for those fans?"

Quentin shook his head.

"Well, I don't know, either," Don said, "but it sure wouldn't be football, and I'm sure I wouldn't like it. Without fans — and therefore, without the media — we would be universe-class athletes playing on some stone-filled field, practicing with a club team after we get out of work. What jobs have you had before football?"

"I worked in the mines," Quentin said. "Only job I ever had."

"Oh, right. Well, without fans, you're *still* working in the mines, Q. This is Media Day. In Tier Two, every football fan on Ionath wanted to know more about you. Now you're in Tier One, and every football fan in the *galaxy* wants to know more. Media scrutiny is part of the job you fought for, my friend."

Quentin looked out at the collection of reporters circling around his orange-and-black-clad teammates. It looked like a feeding frenzy, like giffler fish ripping apart brimler-ants that fell into the steep-walled quarry lakes back on Micovi. *Hundreds* of reporters, so many body shapes, colors, floating holocameras.

"Maybe you can do it with me?" Quentin said. "You know, just for the first time out there? Just kind of ... stay close."

Don leaned back and sucked in air through clenched teeth. "Yeah, I don't know if that's a good idea. If you and I are standing together, every question is going to be about who will start, whether I've still *got it*, stuff like that. The focus should be on you, not on a quarterback controversy. Messal will be with you, though."

Don was right. At some point there would be a quarterback controversy. When the Krakens lost, fans would be screaming for Don Pine to replace Quentin Barnes. It was just the way of things. Quentin didn't need to fuel that fire ahead of time.

"All right," Quentin said. "Any final advice?"

"Yes. *Don't* be yourself."

"Huh?"

"Quentin, anyone ever tell you you're too intense?"

Quentin nodded.

"That's someone's nice way of saying you're an overbearing jerk," Don said. "Just relax, answer the media's stupid questions. Don't say things like you think we'll win eight games and go to the playoffs."

"But we will win eight games," Quentin said. "We will go to the playoffs."

Don sighed and looked to the sky. He took a breath, then looked at Quentin again. "Kid, remember all those times I gave you advice and you ignored it?"

Quentin looked down. He *had* done that, too many times, and every time Don turned out to be right. If Don thought Quentin was an overbearing jerk, then maybe Quentin was an overbearing jerk. "Am I really that bad?"

"In the locker room or the practice field? No. You are exactly what you need to be. Outside of those places? You're a mouth machine that needs a new muffler."

Quentin laughed. Don Pine had such a way of putting people at ease.

"This is part of our life, Quentin. Just get out there and be nice."

Don patted Quentin on the shoulder twice, a manly *go get 'em* pat, then jogged out onto the field. Quentin watched him go, watched the reporters recognize him and flock to him.

Quentin waited another couple of minutes, then walked onto the field himself, Messal the Efficient just a step behind.

**AS A KID, QUENTIN HAD WATCHED** Church holos about Earth history. Most of those movies were about the persecution of the chosen people. Some of them even went back to medieval times. Holos like that were filled with heroic tales of those in service to High One. They were also full of swords, knives, spears: all kinds of pointy things designed to poke holes in bodies. As Quentin looked out at three dozen microphones jabbing toward his face, that was all he could think of. Too many sentients yelling at him all at once, all asking stupid questions.

"Quentin!" a bleach-white Human reporter from Tower shouted. "Quentin, Harold Moloronik from Grinkas NewsNet. Do you think the Krakens will be relegated this year?"

"Uh … " Quentin said, then paused, trying to channel his inner Donald Pine. *Think before I speak.* Quentin took a slow breath, then gave his answer. "Our goal is to win every game. If we play hard, things will take care of themselves."

"Quentin!" A Creterakian civilian dressed in a fuchsia suit, perched on the shoulder of a smallish, fat Ki. "I speak for Ron-Do-Hall, Ki Empire Sports Fest. Rumor is that Yassoud Murphy isn't cutting it as your starting running back. Is that why the Krakens brought in Jay Martinez and Dan Campbell?"

Quentin started to talk, then stopped. Think first. He'd been about to say that Yassoud needed to step it up in practice. 'Soud's performance thus far did not speak well for the season. But Don had told Quentin not to say anything bad about his teammates.

"Yassoud is our starting running back," Quentin said. "Martinez and Campbell practice hard. I know they will contribute to the team."

"Quentin!" shouted a voice from below, a Leekee who had

slithered his way between the legs of the other reporters. "Kelp Bringer from the Leekee Galaxy Times."

"Kelp Bringer?" Quentin said. "That your real name?"

"Rough translation. Why? You want to hear the real pronunciation?"

The Quyth Leader reporters took off running, while the Human and HeavyG reporters immediately started shaking their heads, but Quentin only noticed that after he'd already nodded. The streamlined, four-foot-long, black-striped blue sentient let out a five-second string of piercing noises that ranged from ear-splitting high notes down to lows that Quentin felt vibrate through his stomach and privates. It was an assault of sound. He winced and covered his ears, as did all the other Humans and HeavyGs.

"Okay, *okay*," Quentin said. "I think *Kelp Bringer* works just fine. It's like my favorite name of all time."

The collection of reporters laughed. Quentin smiled. He'd made a joke, and they had laughed. Maybe this wouldn't be so bad after all.

Quentin took an automatic step back — he saw something moving on Kelp Bringer's back ... *several* somethings, *spindly* somethings.

"Uh ... Kelp Bringer, you got ... something on your back there."

Kelp Bringer twisted his pointy head to look. The spindly things were right in front of his yellow eyes. "What?" he said. "I don't see anything."

Quentin pointed. "Right *there*, those buggy things crawling on you."

There was a pause, then a single laugh. Kelp Bringer's stripes changed from black to an iridescent yellow, a color that just looked angry. Another Human giggled, and then all the reporters started laughing.

But this time it wasn't because he'd said something funny. Quentin felt embarrassed — he didn't know what he'd said, but he knew it had been something stupid. Again.

"Those *buggy things*?" Kelp Bringer said. "What are you, some kind of racist?"

Quentin felt his face flush red just as fast as the Leekee's stripes had turned yellow. "What? *Racist?* But I ... and you ... no, uh ... sorry?"

"These *buggy things* are my symbiotes."

"What is a symbiote?"

The clutch of reporters laughed even harder.

Kelp Bringer's stripes changed from yellow to a neon orange. "Are you mocking me, Human?"

Quentin shook his head, hard. "No, I ... look, I have no idea what's going on here. You're the first Leekee I've seen in person."

The laughter faded instantly.

Kelp Bringer's orange stripes shifted back to yellow, then to mostly-black. "You're serious?" he said. "You've never met my kind before?"

"Sorry, no," Quentin said. "No offense or whatever, but ... ah ... where I come from, there are only Humans."

Quentin noticed that all the reporters were suddenly keying that information into palm-ups and messageboards.

"Ah," Kelp Bringer said. "Yes, you're from the Purist Nation. Fine, I will accept your apology, but only if you answer my question."

Quentin nodded, grateful to put the embarrassing moment behind him.

"So my question is, how does it feel to start the season with a certain loss against the Isis Ice Storm?"

*Think before you speak.* "We are excited to play the Ice Storm. They are a quality organization. We'll practice and prepare, and play as hard as we can."

"So you're predicting a win?" Kelp Bringer said. "You are going on record saying the Krakens will win big against the Ice Storm? Maybe three or four touchdowns, you think?"

Quentin hadn't said anything of the sort. What was this weird-looking sentient talking about? "No, I didn't say that. That's not ... I'm not predicting anything."

"Quentin!" A Quyth Leader shouted. Apparently the Leaders had returned to the mix just as quickly as they'd left. "Pikor the

Assuming, UBS Sports. How do you feel about the assassination attempt on your life?"

"Assassination ... well, we don't know the guy was coming after me."

"Assuming he was," Pikor said, "how does it feel to know eight police officers died to protect you?"

Quentin hadn't thought about it that way before. "I ... uh ..."

Microphones moved in closer, a phalanx of stabbing black points.

"Quentin!" a reporter shouted, her voice drowning out the other dozen sentients screaming exactly the same name. "Sara Mabuza, Earth News Syndicate. Since someone *is* out to kill you, wouldn't it make more sense to start Don Pine, so there's no team setback if the assassins strike again?"

The reporters switched from dead police to a quarterback controversy without missing a beat? What the hell was wrong with these sentients?

"Look, guys," Quentin said. "I'm the starting QB, okay? And I don't feel comfortable marginalizing the loss of those police officers by discussing it here, on Media Day for a football team. Doesn't anyone have questions about the Krakens?"

"I do."

Quentin looked left, toward the source of the voice. When he saw her, everything else instantly faded away. Purple skin, much deeper and richer than the blue skin of Don Pine. Glossy, black eyelashes framed bright blue eyes, blue that *popped* thanks to artfully applied white eye shadow. A *perfect* mouth, shaped so thick and full that he immediately wondered what it would feel like to kiss it. Hair the color of snow, worn short but meticulously styled. She couldn't possibly be more beautiful.

"Yolanda Davenport," she said. "Galaxy Sports Magazine."

Quentin nodded, still unable to look away from her eyes. "You ... you had a question about the Krakens?"

"Sure do. I want to know how Ionath's starting quarterback would feel if he saw himself on the cover of Galaxy Sports?"

Quentin just blinked. He felt stupefied by her looks, and yet she was dragging his brain from one promised land to another — the hallowed ground of the ultimate recognition of athletics, the cover of Galaxy Sports Magazine.

"Uh … " Quentin said. "He'd feel … amazing, I guess."

She smiled. He'd been wrong, she *could* be more beautiful. Her thick, dark lips framed white teeth that blazed brighter than the yard lines.

"You *guess*? Well, that's not a very definitive answer. If the Krakens stay in Tier One next year, we might just have to find out."

"Quentin!" another reporter screamed, so loud his head reactively snapped around to look. This one, a bat, fluttering in place, dressed in a lime-green bodysuit with blue paisley trim. "Kinizzle, Creterakian Information Service. Now that you've played a year in the GFL, would you say you've stopped being a racist? Or is that still active?"

"What?"

"Regarding your hateful nature," Kinizzle said, "which of your teammates would you most like to kill?"

They were baiting him, and he'd had just about enough. "You listen to me, you little piece of—"

"And Elder Barnes' time is up!" Quentin looked down to see Messal the Efficient, who now stood between Quentin and the reporters, who had to tilt their microphones up and back to avoid poking them into Messal's one big eye. "Thank you all for coming out, but Elder Barnes has several private interviews scheduled. Thank you!"

Quentin felt Messal pulling at his left hand, leading him back to the tunnel. Quentin entertained one final, brief thought of ripping off the bat's wings and drop-kicking him through the goal post, then let Messal lead him off the field. Reporters kept screaming his name, screaming asinine questions, but he ignored them.

Was this what it would be like from now on? No. He had not yet played a single down of Tier One ball. Once the season began and the Krakens faced off against some of the best teams in the history of the sport, he knew things would get even worse.

• • •

**QUENTIN WALKED UP TO THE LINE,** looking from left to right, taking it all in. His offense, dressed in practice whites, facing off against the Krakens' defense, dressed in practice blacks. The *Touchback* remained locked in orbit above Ionath City, making ship time roughly match city time. Noonday sun poured through the practice field dome, which Captain Cheevers had shaded slightly to block the worst of the light and heat.

Quentin's short passing game was looking strong, but his deep-throw timing just wasn't connecting. The Krakens defensive line kept generating too much pressure.

The left side of the Krakens' offensive line was doing fine. Kill-O-Yowet didn't have much trouble with the pass rush of right defensive end Aleksandar Michnik. Kill-O was in his ninth year as a pro and was the kind of dominant left tackle that every quarterback dreamed of. He was also the alpha male among the hierarchical Ki. Kill-O kept the rest of his kind playing hard.

Just inside of Kill-O was Sho-Do-Thikit, the Krakens' left offensive guard. Sho-Do was a fantastic football player but was having some trouble stopping Mai-An-Ihkole, the Krakens' right defensive tackle. On each snap, the two linemen tore into each other with a frenzy that sent black blood flying. In his twelfth year, Mai-An was finally coming into his own. If he could battle Sho-Do to a standstill, push him back, even get pressure on Quentin every fourth or fifth play, it boded well for Mai-An's season.

Bud-O-Shwek, Quentin's center, seemed flawless at both run- and pass-blocking. Quentin had no worries that Bud-O would protect him at all times.

On the far right side of the line, offensive tackle Vu-Ko-Will did battle with left defensive end Ibrahim Khomeni. Ibrahim seemed to have lost a step or two, or maybe he didn't play that hard in practice. At any rate, he only occasionally got past Vu-Ko to lightly touch Quentin's red *do-not-hit* jersey.

Between Bud-O and Vu-Ko, however, lay the real problem — rookie right guard Shun-On-Won. Shun-On couldn't stop defensive tackle Mum-O-Killowe, who seemed to be in Quentin's face before Quentin could even complete a five-step drop and look downfield for a pass.

While the violent and ill-tempered Mum-O was a star in the making, he shouldn't have been in Quentin's grille on *every damn passing play*. Shun-On-Won couldn't block for crap. He looked a mess — helmet visor cracked, jersey torn, black blood dribbling down from his upper right forearm, all results of a constant beating at the hands of Mum-O-Killowe. And this was just *practice*. What would happen in a real game?

Quentin bent behind center. "Green-ten, hammer route!" he shouted down the left side of the line. At the sound of *green*, heads turned his way. That word meant an audible, Quentin changing the play at the line of scrimmage. Calls of other colors, like *blue* or *red*, meant nothing. He called out a color every play to maintain consistency, so the defense wouldn't know when he switched a play.

"Green-ten, hammer route!" Quentin shouted down the right side of the line. His offensive players heard the call, then stared straight ahead once again, ready to run the play.

His call of *hammer route* had changed the play from a deep drop-back to a quick pass. Instead of streaks and post-patterns that might go twenty yards deep and take several seconds to run, all receivers switched to predetermined shorter routes: five-yard hook patterns, inside slants toward the center of the field or the well-practiced out patterns that took the receivers to the sidelines. No receiver would run a pattern deeper than five or six yards. He could call an audible like this if he saw the defense was running a linebacker blitz, so he could get the pass off before he was sacked. Or, he could call it because his offensive line couldn't block the defensive tackles.

The audible also changed the assignment of rookie running back Dan Campbell, who was lined up in a single-back set behind him. Instead of going out on a pass route, Dan would fake a handoff and help Shun-On-Won block Mum-O.

"Hut ... hut-*hut!*"

The offensive and defensive lines smashed together, Ki and HeavyG bodies squeezing out grunts of rage and effort and pain.

Quentin stepped back and to the right, stretching the ball out toward Campbell. Campbell raised his left elbow high, left hand on his sternum, right hand at his belt, pinkie touching his stomach, thumb pointed out. Quentin stabbed the ball at Dan's belly, then pulled it back at the last second as Dan's arms snapped shut, faking the handoff.

Quentin ran one more step away from the line, then planted and turned. He instantly had to jump right to avoid Campbell, who was flying backward thanks to a hit from the onrushing Mum-O-Killowe.

Last season, the sight of the four-armed, twelve-foot-long monster might have made Quentin pause, but such things had now become commonplace. He reacted on pure instinct, shuffling another step right even as Mum-O's long body compressed and *gathered*, the thing a Ki would do right before launching for a tackle. In that split-second pause, Quentin saw tight end George Starcher hook up at five yards, just past the end of the line. Starcher instantly saw that Mum-O was blocking Quentin's line of sight, so the big tight end shuffled to his left to make a clear passing lane. Quentin saw this, processed it in less time than it takes to blink and flipped a hard pass at Starcher.

The ball had no sooner left Quentin's hands than Mum-O-Killowe's body violently expanded like a striking snake — an angry, 580-pound snake. He smashed into Quentin, drove him backward into the nano-turf. It was a hard hit, but Mum-O hadn't followed, hadn't let his weight land on top of Quentin. Quentin would feel that hit through the next day, for sure, yet from Mum-O, it was just a love-tap.

Quentin rolled to his feet, seeing that Starcher had caught the pass and carried it another five yards before John Tweedy brought him down. Had this been a real game, Starcher's automatic adjustment would have turned a blown block and a sure sack into a first down. Rick Warburg or Yotaro Kobayasho, as good as they were, wouldn't have reacted as fast. Whatever Crazy George Starcher had in his head, it was worth the trouble.

"*Mum-O-Killowe!*" Hokor's speakers blared. "*Did you just hit my quarterback?*"

The Ki lineman growled something low and nasty.

"I'm fine, Coach," Quentin called up to Hokor's cart. "Just a little tickle, that's all."

Mum-O growled something else, then scuttled back to the defensive side of the line. Quentin's offense ran back to the huddle. Shun-On, the rookie right tackle, was the last to arrive, limping along on sore, tired legs, leaving a thin trail of black blood in his wake.

Quentin shook his head. Just over two weeks away from the first game of the season against the Isis Ice Storm. Unless Shun-On-Won started playing better, or unless Coach put someone else in the lineup, the first three games were going to be very, *very* rough.

**QUENTIN STEPPED OFF THE ELEVATOR** onto Deck Eighteen, the *Touchback's* top deck. He'd been up here only once before, during his first tour of the ship after arriving as a rookie. That time, he'd been seeing the sights. This time, he'd been summoned.

Summoned by his coach and the team owner to discuss a personnel decision. Quentin had run down to the Ki locker room to take a bath and scrub up proper, with hot water and soap. He knew the nannite showers in his quarters *technically* got him cleaner, but when he bathed in water he just felt better, more ready for the world. Hokor and Gredok would never know the difference, but it just felt more ... respectful ... to clean up the best he could.

Gredok was a criminal and a killer, but he was also the team owner. He spent the money needed to find players like Starcher and the Awa twins. Keeping Gredok happy — happy and *spending* — was as much a part of the game as overcoming racism or eating with the team. In any context that involved pure *football*, Quentin would go out of his way to show Gredok proper respect.

Maybe showing that respect could go a long way toward patching things up with the black-furred Quyth Leader.

Quentin had even dressed in his best clothes. Or tried to, only to realize he didn't even have a suit. A quick call to Messal the Efficient resulted in Pilkie showing up at Quentin's quarters, a sport coat in hand. It fit okay but was tight in the shoulders and back. Another call and Messal said he would acquire a new wardrobe. For now, however, Quentin had to make due with the ill-fitting sport coat.

He had fixed his hair, he'd shaved, and his body felt relaxed from the Ki pool's near-scalding water. Oh, that reminded him ... he had yet to sit down for a meal with the Ki. The Ki, who ate their food *alive*. One thing at a time. Maybe making nice with Gredok first, then eating live animals.

Quentin walked into the administration area. Orange walls complemented the white-and-black carpet. Once again he took in the furnishings that catered to every species, two each for Human, Quyth Leader, Sklorno, HeavyG and Ki. He admired the holoframes showing twenty-one years of Krakens greats, all moving in an endless repeat of some glorious play.

He walked past the holoframe of the greatest Kraken of all. No matter where you went in the *Touchback*, the stadium, the Krakens building, you were never far from a reminder of Bobby Adrojnik. The holoframe showed the baby-faced quarterback being held aloft by two Ki linemen. He held the GFL championship trophy high, pumping it up and down so it caught the field lights, his moment of achievement captured forever in computer memory. The image reminded Quentin of Bobby's short career, which in turn reminded Quentin of the bombing at the victory parade. Was someone out there *really* trying to kill him? He put the thought out of his mind. For now, up here on the *Touchback*, he was safe.

Quentin left the holoframe behind and walked past doors and desks. Some of the desks had staff: Quyth Leaders, Workers, a few Humans. There were even a couple of Sklorno males, the tiny, furry "bedbugs" that went insane during the football games when their females soared high to fight for passes twenty-five feet in the air. Had all of these sentients been here the first time Quentin had visited Deck Eighteen? And why hadn't he seen any of them during his months on the ship?

He suddenly realized why, and it embarrassed him. The *Touchback* was a big ship, but not *that* big. The reason he hadn't seen these staffers was because they weren't allowed to circulate on the player decks.

As he passed the staffers, everyone smiled at him or gave their species equivalent of a smile. They were clearly excited to see him up here. The fact that they weren't allowed on the field, on the player decks, it reminded Quentin of the places on Micovi he hadn't been allowed to go because he was an orphan, because he wasn't part of an upstanding church family. Restaurants, clubs, some shops, the decent grocery stores — he hadn't been allowed to set foot in those places. Not until he became a football star, anyway.

Quentin tried to nod at the stares and smiles. He realized they were looking at him the way he had once looked at the rich Churchies back on Micovi, the people who enjoyed privilege, prestige, who ate the finest foods while poor children were hung for stealing bread. Well, shuck this — these sentients worked for the same team that he did. He would take it up with Gredok, but later in the season. One thing at a time.

He reached Hokor's control room and pushed the buzzer next to the door. The door opened and Quentin walked in. Part of his brain took in this room he'd never seen before. The entire back window looked out onto the practice field eighteen decks below. A dozen holotanks lined the window. Only two were on. One tank showed highlights of a big HeavyG offensive lineman dressed in a silver, gold and copper uniform. The other showed a Sklorno in practice whites. Halawa, Quentin realized.

A small part of his brain took this in, but the majority of his thoughts centered on the control room's occupants. Coach Hokor, Gredok the Splithead ... and Donald Pine. Hokor sat behind a black desk, Gredok sat in a chair off to the side, and Pine was in one of two chairs in front of the desk.

Quentin felt a rush of jealousy and annoyance at seeing his blue-skinned teammate, who wore an immaculate suit perfectly tailored to his athletic frame. Quentin felt instantly silly and inadequate in his poorly fitting, borrowed sport coat. Quentin had been called in to talk personnel with the top two people in the Krakens organization, and yet Pine was already there, giving his opinion before Quentin could. Was Pine making a play for the starting job?

No. No, Pine was a mentor, a friend. Quentin had to stop reacting to things with anger. If Pine was here, there was a reason, and that reason was probably to *help* Quentin.

"Barnes," Gredok said. "Have a seat. Nice coat."

Quentin felt his face turn red.

"I just talked to Messal," Gredok said. "I appreciate that you are improving your image, it reflects well on the organization. I told him to send your measurements to my tailor. He's the best, you know. I'll pay for it all."

"Thank you, Gredok, but I'll pay for it."

Gredok stared but said nothing. Quentin couldn't make out the owner's mood. Hopefully he hadn't offended Gredok by turning down the hospitality. Quentin was young, sure, but he'd been around organized crime his whole life — you did not want to be indebted to a sentient like Gredok the Splithead. Not for clothes, not for a flippin' bowl of soup, not for anything.

Coach Hokor's upper left pedipalp gestured to the open chair next to Don. Quentin sat.

"Barnes," Hokor said, "we have an opportunity. The regular season starts in just over a week, and we have shortcomings. We have a chance to improve those shortcomings, but we wanted to talk to you about it first."

Quentin looked around the room, quickly taking in each face. The first face was the clear, one-eyed, cold stare of Gredok. Nothing to read there, but Quentin knew that Gredok was reading him. Quentin took a quick, deep breath and forced himself to be calm. If Gredok wasn't going to show emotion, Quentin wouldn't either.

Coach Hokor's eye swirled with a touch of green — the color

of stress, sometimes anxiety. His fur seemed a bit more fluffed than usual.

Finally, Quentin looked at Pine. Pine looked ... sad? Corners of his mouth turned down, just a bit, eyes soft.

Quentin looked back to Hokor. "Okay, Coach. What's this opportunity?"

"We have a major issue at right guard," Hokor said. "Would you agree?"

Were they going to buy a free-agent right guard? Maybe an All-Pro? Quentin fought to keep himself calm. A high-level right guard would solidify the offensive line, give him time to throw.

"Yes, Coach. I would agree."

"Put yourself in my position," Hokor said. "If you were me, what would you do about Shun-On-Won?"

Quentin thought for a moment. Two weeks into practice, and Shun-On hadn't shown significant improvement. He just wasn't good enough. There was no way around it. Sad for the rookie, but that's the way it was. Still, Quentin was the team leader, and if someone had to make a tough decision that benefited the franchise, he would be the one to do it.

"Shun-On is a liability," Quentin said. "But we have Aka-Na-Tak coming back in Week Four."

"Week *Four*," Gredok said quietly. "We could be oh-and-three by then. Winless. In last place."

Quentin shook his head. "Not gonna happen, Gredok. We'll win at least one, maybe two."

Quentin automatically looked at Pine for confirmation. Don just raised his eyebrows, then dropped them back down again. An unreadable reaction.

"Barnes," Hokor said, "we have a trade offer for Michael Kimberlin, right guard from the Jupiter Jacks."

Michael Kimberlin? Quentin's eyes flashed to the holotank showing the player dressed in silver, gold and copper. Kimberlin. An All-Pro, a veteran and one of the few non-Ki offensive linemen in the GFL. While the HeavyG was probably in the final few years of his career, there was no question that Kimberlin could instantly solve the Krakens' offensive line problem. Probably solve it permanently — when Aka-Na-Tak came back from injury, he wouldn't have a starting job waiting for him.

This should have been good news, exciting news, but Quentin sensed a coldness in the room. Nothing from Gredok, of course, but Hokor seemed bothered, and Quentin picked up even more of that sadness from Pine.

"Kimberlin," Quentin said, knowing he had to ask the next question, knowing he would hate the answer. "Who do the Jacks want for him?"

"They need receivers," Hokor said. "Scarborough and Denver."

Quentin just stared. That was a ridiculous offer. "Scarborough is my top receiver. And Denver, she's … she's our future."

Quentin almost bit his tongue after he'd spoken her name. He had been about to say *she's my friend*. That was his first thought. An alien, one of the Satanic races … his *friend*.

"It's a good offer," Hokor said. "Both teams prosper. The Jacks have a second-year right guard. They think he's going to give them ten seasons. That means they can afford to deal Kimberlin."

"But we can't afford to deal Scarborough," Quentin said. "Like I said, she's my top receiver."

"Was," Gredok said. "Hawick is our top receiver now."

Quentin felt his anger welling up. He fought to control it.

"Gredok, you know Hawick had that year because of double-coverage on Scarborough. Okay, sure, *now* Hawick is our number one, but we can't win without Scarborough."

Don leaned forward. "You sure about that, Q?"

"Yes, I'm sure."

"What about next year?" Hokor said. "Scarborough is getting old. This could be her final season of high production. Do we want to pass up a player like Kimberlin, who will give us three, maybe even four, seasons to hold onto a receiver whose best years have passed her by?"

"Then what about Denver?" Quentin said. "She's in her *second* year. She's the fastest receiver we've got. She's only going to get better in seasons to come."

"Seasons to come," Gredok said. "Such an interesting phrase. Tell me, Barnes, how much benefit is that to the franchise if those *seasons to come* are back in Tier Two?"

Quentin shook his head. "We're *not* going back. No way. I won't let it happen."

Don reached out his hand as if he was going to touch Quentin's shoulder, but he stopped himself and put the hand back on his knee.

"It *can* happen, Q," Don said. "It can, and if our offensive line can't protect you, it *will*."

Quentin felt his face getting hotter, redder. Were these jerks serious? Denver had played her heart out. The team adored her. Quentin had to control his anger, talk reason here.

"So we trade our number two and our number four receivers," he said. "And we get a right guard that will only last a few years?"

"Long enough to find a better one," Gredok said. "I am developing the best scouting agency in the galaxy. All we need to do is stay in Tier One for this season and I can give you a team of all-star talent."

Quentin stood before he even knew he was doing it. "We *have* a team with all-star talent. We are *not* going down to Tier Two! I object to this trade."

Coach Hokor's black-striped yellow fur fluffed out, then settled back down. "That's why we called you here, Barnes. Normally, we'd pull the trigger on a trade of this caliber, but these are two of your top receivers. The decision is yours."

The words stunned him. "It's ... *my* decision?"

Don nodded. "I told them they needed your take, Q. You're the guy who has to deal with a weak offensive line. It's great to throw to Denver and Scarborough if you have time to throw, which you won't, at least not until Aka-Na-Tak comes off injured reserve."

"But he comes back in Week Four."

"Quentin, *think*," Don said slowly. "This is Tier One. This is the promised land of football. Every ... game ... *matters*. A season is only twelve games. Lose the first three, and it could already be too late. And you're forgetting something else here."

"Yeah? Am I, *Pine?* What am I *forgetting?*"

Don leaned back. Now he was the one trying to control his patience. "Aka-Na-Tak is a second-string player to begin with. How good do you think he is? When he comes back, is he good enough to protect you?"

Quentin stared at Don, stared and blinked. Quentin hadn't thought of that. Aka-Na-Tak *was* a second-stringer. He was better than Shun-On-Won, sure, but how *much* better?

As usual, Don Pine, the veteran, the two-time Tier One Champion, the former league MVP, was thinking several moves ahead.

Quentin sat back down and let out a slow breath. "Okay, Don. I'm listening. You tell me — if it was you, what would your call be?"

That sad look on Don's face again. "It sucks, but I'd make the trade. You can't win if you spend half the game looking for your teeth."

The office fell silent. They were waiting for him to decide. The future of two receivers hung on his decision. No, the future of two receivers, an All-Pro lineman and an entire *franchise*. His other teammates. All those people in the administrative offices.

But most importantly, the future of Denver. She'd been on that landing deck with Quentin back on the *Combine*. They'd been rookies together, fighting to take the Krakens into Tier One. She worshiped Quentin — literally, *worshiped* him. If they made the trade, if *he* made the trade, what would that do to her?

"No," Quentin said finally. "Scarborough is too valuable. And Denver has just too much up-side. We can't make this trade."

Coach Hokor leaned forward, yellow-furred pedipalp hands pressed against the black desktop. "Are you *sure*, Barnes? When you are lying on your back after your fifth or sixth sack of each game, will you be *sure* then?"

Quentin nodded. He'd taken beatings before. He'd just have to keep taking them for a little while. He could win with the offensive line he had. He knew he could.

"I'm sure," Quentin said. "I promise you, we will not go oh-and-three."

"We'd better not," Gredok said. "All I can say is that if we leave this decision up to you, and we go winless for the first three games, then the result is on *you*, Barnes. Not on Hokor, on *you*."

There was no way around it. His coach, his mentor, his owner, they all wanted to make this trade. If passing on it was the wrong call, they might never again trust him to make the smart decision.

But smart or not, he knew he'd made the *right* decision.

Quentin stood. "Is there anything else, Coach?"

"No," Hokor said. "You may go."

Quentin left the control room and headed for his quarters. He'd made the right decision, sure, but if they didn't win, did the right decision even matter?


**TWO DAYS AFTER** the stressful trade discussion, Quentin, Yitzhak Goldman, Virak the Mean and Choto the Bright walked down the corridor toward the *Touchback's* landing bay. Manny Sayed had flown in to discuss Quentin's endorsement for Manny's luxury yacht company. Gredok wouldn't let Krakens players return planet-side, not with the season so close and potential bombers possibly lurking in Ionath City.

Yitzhak came along to counsel Quentin, while Virak and Choto were there for security. As far as Gredok was concerned, everyone was a threat — including a fat, old, one-legged, Purist Nation businessman. The two Quyth Warriors walked in front, each wearing a gun strapped on his right side just below the head. It was interesting to see how fast Virak's and Choto's demeanor changed, from on-field bad-ass football player to intimidating, cold-eyed, gangland enforcer. They had much more experience as the latter, and it showed.

"Q," Yitzhak said. "You limping?"

Quentin shook his head and tried to walk straighter, but his leg hurt like crazy. When he didn't focus on each step, he did limp. In practice earlier that day, Quentin had felt pressure and scrambled for yards instead of taking a sack. He'd dodged Aleksander Michnik's huge HeavyG arms, only to be leveled by Mum-O-

Killowe. Coach Hokor was furious with both Quentin, for not sliding, and Mum-O, for hitting a starting quarterback. Quentin had thought his days of running laps as punishment ended when he became the starting QB — he'd been wrong.

"You've got to stop insulting Mum-O-Killowe," Yitzhak said. "I don't get that. Why are you making him so mad? He's going to kill you on the practice field."

"We have to figure out what's up at right guard," Quentin said. "If I make Mum-O mad, then he comes at me as hard as he can, just like he would in a game. We need to know if Shun-On can really block for me. If he can't, we're going to have to try someone else at right guard. Maybe Cay-Oh-Kiware can step up."

Yitzhak shrugged. "If he can make the switch from left guard to right guard, sure. We should try that Zer-Eh-Detak kid. I know he's only eighteen, but that's the biggest damn sentient I've ever seen. Regardless, Quentin, your little science experiment won't matter if you miss the first game because you're digesting inside Mum-O's belly. And it's not just our right guard you have to worry about — Vu-Ko-Will has to block Ryan Nossek. Kind of sucks to be you, Q."

Quentin had been thinking a lot about Nossek, the Isis Ice Storm's All-Pro defensive end. Vu-Ko, the Krakens' right tackle, would have to defend against that gigantic HeavyG. Nossek had led Tier One in sacks last season. He'd also killed four sentients in his career. Many considered him the best defensive end in football. Quentin would square off against him in just eight more days.

"Just promise me something," Yitzhak said. "*Please* tell me that when we play the Ice Storm, you're going to *slide* and stop taking head-on hits if you scramble?"

"If I don't have blocking, I have to run. I can't slide every play, Zak. I have to make things happen out there."

Virak the Mean stopped and turned. "The Quyth have a saying, Quentin."

"Which is?"

"It's hard to make things happen when you don't have a head."

"That's not really a Quyth saying, is it?"

"Close enough," Virak said, then he continued down the corridor.

Quentin followed and said nothing. He knew Yitzhak, Hokor and even Virak were right. He had to start treating his body like a precious resource. But every slide felt like an admission of weakness. He'd never slid in the PNFL. Of course, back then he'd been bigger than almost everyone else on the field. He wasn't in the PNFL anymore.

They reached the landing bay and boarded the orange-and-black shuttle. They waited for the airlock to cycle, then the catapult hurled the shuttle out. It would be a short trip — Manny's luxury yacht was also in orbit, only a click away.

As the shuttle approached, Quentin took in the yacht's long, flowing, curved lines. It possessed a sleekness that the *Touchback* did not. The Krakens' team ship was an old military vessel, built for efficiency, for combat. The yacht, which was maybe a tenth the length of the *Touchback*, was built for comfort, built for looks. It seemed more a work of art than a functioning vessel. The yacht's glossy, orange hull reflected the stars and the approaching shuttle's running lights. Long, swooping black lines trimmed with white ran the length of the yacht's hull.

"She's a beauty," Yitzhak said. "Wow, that is really a top-of-the-line craft."

"Yeah?" Quentin said. "I've never been on a yacht, just seen them in holos."

Yitzhak nodded. He, at least, was getting used to the fact that Quentin knew little of the finer things in life. Zak didn't judge, didn't poke fun. Most of the time, anyway.

The shuttle carefully slid into the yacht's tiny landing bay. While the *Touchback's* landing bay could hold several large craft, the yacht's had barely enough room to lower the shuttle doors. Virak and Choto walked down the ramp first, pedipalp hands on their guns. Beyond them, Quentin saw Manny Sayed standing there, clearly surprised to see two gangland toughs ready to throw lead at the first sign of trouble.

"Oh, my," Manny said. "Please, dear sentients, there is no cause for alarm. My crew and I will cooperate in any way possible."

"That is good," Virak said. "We are very much on edge after the terrorist attempt during our victory parade."

Manny sighed and looked up to the low ceiling. "Yes, of course, I should have thought of that. Let me announce to my crew that they must cooperate and stay calm. Acceptable?"

"Yes," Virak and Choto said together.

Manny raised a jeweled hand to his mouth and spoke. Quentin heard Manny's words echo through the landing bay. The same words were probably echoing through the entire ship.

He'd met Manny Sayed on the trip from Micovi to the *Combine*. The overweight man wore flowing, blue robes that signified a confirmed member of the Purist Nation church. Manny also bore the church's primary sign of identification: an infinity symbol tattooed on the forehead. He had the robes and the symbol, true, but he also wore garish, expensive jewelry. Such a display would be frowned upon in Purist Nation space. Outside the system, no one seemed to care. He had also cut his robes shorter than normal, exposing his bare lower right leg and its jeweled sandal. He'd lost his left leg in the Creterakian takeover. A jewel-studded platinum prosthetic stood in its place.

Manny smiled at his guests. "I have informed our crew to stay out of our way. Now, Quentin, if your associates are satisfied, may we begin the tour and talk about your possible endorsement of Sayed Luxury Craft?"

Virak and Choto stepped apart, allowing Quentin and Yitzhak room to walk forward.

Manny extended his hand. "Praise High One for blessing your journey."

Quentin shook the offered hand. "Praise to the High One for bringing us together. It's good to see you again, Elder Sayed."

The traditional Purist greeting. Scripted words, but it surprised Quentin to find that he *meant* them, that it felt good just to say them. Manny was another reminder of home. A home that Quentin hated with all his soul, but still, it was *home*.

Manny turned and gestured that Quentin should walk side by side with him. Manny's jewelry *clinked* with every movement, his prosthetic foot *clonked* with each step.

"This vessel is the Marquis model," Manny said as they walked. "It has its own shuttle, suitable for four beings. We sent the shuttle out to make room for the *Touchback's* shuttle, which is quite a bit larger. The Marquis model also has one lifeboat, suitable for five sentients, or maybe three of your size.

As they walked, Quentin took it all in. The ship looked brand new. There weren't even any scuffs on the landing bay's metal deck.

In the corridor, everything looked extremely expensive, from the dark wood of the walls to the polished metal trim and moldings. Smart carpets, framed artwork, everything clean and new and sparkling. He'd only seen one place that so reeked of money and power — Gredok's quarters in the Krakens building.

Quentin barely noticed that Virak and Choto followed along. As big as the Warriors were, they seemed well practiced at fading into the background.

The corridor led into a large salon. Thick couches and chairs made of some kind of cured animal skin, tables and chairs of a rich, exotic wood and walls made of smart material. Classy sculptures sat in each corner. Holoframes dotted the walls, showing slowly shifting images of the galaxy's great artworks.

"This is the standard display," Manny said, gesturing to the smartwalls and holoframes. "But, just for you, we programmed a special configuration."

He snapped his fingers. The images and holos shifted to a football theme. Quentin was a little embarrassed to see himself in all of the images. Like the buildings of Ionath City, the walls around came alive with many versions of Quentin Barnes in action.

Manny continued the tour. The yacht had the main salon, a spacious bar (which John Tweedy would just love, Quentin knew), a beautiful kitchen, a dining room that would seat fifteen sentients, a bridge and five staterooms each bigger than the last. The master stateroom alone was larger than Quentin's entire quarters on the *Touchback*.

"This is really cool," Quentin said. He felt a little strange being in such a place, like he didn't deserve to be surrounded by such grandeur. Finery like this belonged to the upper classes, not to a dirty orphan from Micovi.

"I have one more thing that might interest you," Manny said. He led them to the back of the master stateroom, to the bathroom. With a sweeping gesture, he showed a large shower — metal-tile floors and walls, six shower heads that would spray from all angles.

Quentin smiled. "Manny, only a Nationalite would have thought of that."

"I figured that you would like it."

Yitzhak leaned in and squinted his eyes. "Hey, that's not a nannite shower. Does that thing shoot *water*?"

"Don't worry about it," Quentin said as they left the stateroom. "It's a Purist Nation thing, you wouldn't understand."

Manny led them back to the stateroom. "This ship is called the *Hypatia*. But, if you choose to endorse my modest little company, you can name her whatever you like."

Quentin laughed. "What, is that part of the advertising or something? I can say 'I like these boats so much, I named one?' How is that going to sell your ships?"

"It's up to you," Manny said. "You'll own her, after all."

Quentin looked around as if he hadn't really seen the ship at all when he'd first walked through. "Yeah, I don't know. How much does it cost?"

"The Marquis is our top-of-the-line model. With punch drives, you can go anywhere in the galaxy, even use the primary shipping lanes just like a transport. The *Hypatia*, as she sits right now, would go for fifteen million credits."

Quentin let out a long whistle. He made just over one million a season. He felt almost relieved that such an ostentatious display of wealth was outside his means. Despite his newfound fortune, there was always a reminder of wealth's ever-increasing levels.

"I can't afford that," he said. "But it's very classy, Elder Sayed. If it would help your business, I'd be happy to endorse your ships. What would I get paid for that?"

"Uh, Q?" Yitzhak said. "I don't think you understand. What Manny is saying is that if you endorse his company, you get the *Hypatia*. She's yours."

Quentin playfully pushed Yitzhak away. "Yeah, right. Come on, Zak, I wasn't born yesterday."

"Mister Goldman is right," Manny said. "We can't have you endorsing our ships without knowing what it's like to own one, Quentin. The *Hypatia* is the fee for your endorsement. Sign with me, and she's yours."

Quentin stared at Manny, then looked around the salon. Everything in the room spoke of prestige, of *position*. "This *can't* be for me."

Yitzhak laughed. "Q, they painted it orange and black and put in a water shower. Who else would it be for?"

"But all this?" Quentin said. "Mine? I'm just ... " he started to say *an orphan*, but caught himself. "I'm just a second-year quarterback. I haven't won anything."

"You will," Manny said. "Quentin, I believe you are about to become one of the best-known names in the galaxy. I am willing to gamble on that with this big investment."

"But I can't fly," Quentin said. "Could I even afford the crew you have up here?"

"They're mostly for show," Manny said. "You could learn with just two weeks of training. Sail the galaxy solo. Now, if you sign to endorse my company, you will represent us for the next five years. We get two full commercial shoots per off-season, one per regular season. We have the right to use your face, name, image and likeness in any ad we choose."

"Oh, no," Yitzhak said, his tone suddenly shifting from happy and amazed to serious, even borderline angry. "Quentin gets final approval on all ads."

Manny nodded. "Acceptable."

"And no regular- *or* post-season shoots," Yitzhak said. "Forget it, Manny. You can't expect a starting quarterback to take time away from the season or the playoffs."

Manny looked to the ceiling as he thought, then spoke.

"Acceptable. But I will require a commercial shoot one week after the close of the season. That should allow enough time for any bruises and breaks to heal. I need that photogenic face to be *very* photogenic. Until then, I will use GFL-licensed still shots and news footage to make one commercial. Acceptable?"

Yitzhak looked at Quentin. "That sounds fair, Q. Do you agree?"

Quentin nodded, not really understanding what was happening. He felt that both men were negotiating in good faith, and he trusted Yitzhak. Did this mean his backup quarterback was also his agent?

"Fine," Manny said. "Quentin, we have a deal?"

Quentin chewed at his lower lip. "Look, Elder Sayed, I just don't see why people are going to buy yachts because I have one. I want to make sure that … you know … you get a fair deal."

Manny's smile widened. He patted Quentin on the shoulder the way an uncle would do to a beloved nephew.

"Quentin, my boy, that's for me to worry about. If there's one thing Manny knows in this universe, it's what rich men will do with their money to feel young again. I appreciate your concern, but I know exactly what I'm getting into."

Quentin looked at Yitzhak, who simply nodded.

Such a beautiful ship. More than a ship, a *home*. And all his? He'd never even dreamed of such a thing.

"Okay," Quentin said. "Manny Sayed, you have a deal."

Manny suddenly started clapping, the *clink* of jewelry loud in the salon. "Excellent! I'll make the adjustments to the contract right now, then we can sign. Mister Goldman, will you review the changes?"

Yitzhak nodded, then wandered around the salon. He ran his fingers over the wooden trim, over sculptures, along the crysteel walls.

"This ship is really something, Q," he said. "What are you going to call her?"

"It already has a name."

Yitzhak shrugged. "*She* has a name. You own her, you can call her whatever you like."

Quentin thought a name might pop into his head, but none did. "I don't know, Zak. The *Hypatia* sounds kind of ... classy." It did sound classy. Sounded like something a rich man would own.

Manny waddled over to Yitzhak and handed him the contract box. Yitzhak concentrated, reviewing the details. Quentin looked out a view port at the *Touchback*, a kilometer away. *That* was his favorite ship. The *Hypatia* was beautiful, to be sure, but for all her gloss and polish, she did *not* have a built-in football field.

Manny brought the box over and offered it to Quentin. Quentin slid his index finger inside. Manny did the same. The machine quickly recorded their genetic makeup, linked up to the Intergalactic Business Database, verified their identities, then gave a low beep to indicate the transaction had been recorded.

"Congratulations," Manny said. "You, my young friend, have one of the best ships in the galaxy. I know many a high-ranking Elder that will be very jealous."

Quentin nodded, but those words bothered him. He knew what it was like to feel jealousy over the possessions of others ... he'd never thought he could make someone feel the same. He didn't *want* to make someone feel the same. Still, the deal was done, and if Manny was happy and successful, then that was the most important part.

Yitzhak ran his hand over the polished metal trim one more time. He put his hands at his sides, stared at the surface a little longer, then turned and nodded at Manny.

"I'll take one."

Quentin laughed at the joke, but Manny clearly didn't get it.

"Excellent," Manny said, his fat face breaking into a wide smile. "You see, Quentin? Five minutes in, and your endorsement has already brought me a sale. Mister Goldman, I'll have my customization team contact you, and we'll start building models and material sample decks for your review."

Quentin smiled sheepishly, a little embarrassed for his new sponsor. "Manny, relax. Zak is messing with you."

"No, I'm not," Yitzhak said. "Seriously, Manny. This is beautiful work. I want one for myself."

Quentin's smile faded. "Zak, what are you doing? You can't buy one of these."

"Why not?"

"Because he just said they are like fifteen *million* credits. And not to be a jerk or anything, but I'm the one endorsing Manny, okay? So it wouldn't be cool if you tried to cut in on that."

"I don't need an endorsement, Quentin," Yitzhak said. "And I know how much they cost. Trust me, big fella, I can afford it."

Quentin looked from Yitzhak to Manny, assuming there still was some kind of a joke, but that now he was the target. Manny had his right hand up, palm flat, a projected holo-interface floating in the air above his skin. His left pointer finger tapped at floating icons, moving information around. Quentin saw Yitzhak's face in the icons, realized that Manny was creating a customer profile.

There was no joke. Yitzhak was buying a shucking *yacht*.

Manny looked up from his hand. "This just for in-system cruising, or you want the punch drives?"

"Punch drives," Yitzhak said. "Gotta have the punch drives."

"But ... how?" Quentin said. "I mean, it would take me ten seasons to buy one. More, even. Pine couldn't buy one."

"Pine *wasted* his money," Yitzhak said. His tone made Quentin wonder how much Yitzhak knew, if he knew that Pine had gambled away his fortune, if he knew that Pine had thrown games to pay back part of that debt.

"Okay," Quentin said, "I see your point with Pine. But, I mean ... *I'm* the starting quarterback, and I couldn't afford this."

Yitzhak shrugged. "I tried to tell you, Q. You really don't make that much."

Manny looked up again. "Will you want a courtesan suite?"

"I'm married," Yitzhak said.

"So that's a yes?"

Yitzhak laughed. "*Happily* married, Mister Sayed. So, *no* on the courtesan suite."

"Married?" Quentin said. "You mean, like a wife?"

"And two kids," Yitzhak said. He held out his hand and tapped his wrist, calling up a palm-holo. A smiling brunette with her arms around two little boys, both dressed in miniature Krakens uniforms. Their numbers, of course, were both 14 — Yitzhak's number.

Yitzhak was smiling, seemed to be waiting for something. People with kids expected some kind of comment.

"Uh, cute," Quentin said. "Couple of little future quarterbacks."

Yitzhak smiled wider and nodded, then tapped away the palm-up. "That they are. Next to marrying Ahava, little Shem and Kaleb are the best things I've ever done."

Quentin held back a snort. Yitzhak had the accomplishment of being a professional quarterback in the GFL, and getting married and having kids were the *best things he'd ever done*? With perspective like that, no wonder he was third string.

"You should meet them," Yitzhak said. "Shem wants one of your jerseys, which is a little annoying for Daddy. I haven't seen them since Gredok sequestered us on the *Touchback*. Once he lets us go back to Ionath, we'd love to have you over for dinner."

Right, dinner with some old couple and a pair of brats? Quentin could think of far more fun things to do.

"Sure," he said. "We'll see if we can set that up."

Yitzhak laughed and shook his head. "Yeah, right. You just keep going out with your bachelor buddies Tweedy and Yassoud. I remember those days, Q. It's cool. But if you ever want a home-cooked meal, you let me know."

Manny finished his data entry. "Mister Goldman, we will be in touch. Quentin, we will leave the crew on board for security purposes for the rest of the season, no charge. She'll just stay in orbit around Ionath until then, but you can take her at any time. The crew can go with you, or call for a shuttle down to the surface, whatever you prefer. We'll be in touch about that first commercial. Acceptable?"

Quentin looked to Yitzhak, who nodded.

"Acceptable," Quentin said to Manny. "I guess I'll see you then."

They shook hands with the man, Manny's jewelry ringing in time. Virak and Choto led Quentin and Yitzhak back to the shuttle.

Quentin used the ride back to concentrate, to focus. All

these thoughts of yachts, of business, of Manny and of the Purist Nation were interesting, but they wouldn't win football games. The time for such things was over. Preseason preparation was almost complete.

In the next few hours, the *Touchback* would begin the flight to the planet Tower. A six-day trip, punching from one shipping-lane point to the next.

And on the seventh day, he would play his first game in Tier One.

# 4

# PRE-SEASON: WEEK FOUR

From **"Species Biology & Football"**
*written by Cho-Ah-Huity*
**HeavyG: Built for War (& Football)**

Contrary to popular opinion, the HeavyG are not just "really big Humans." *Homo sapiens* are the ancestral species, true, but the HeavyG's genetic makeup has changed so much that they are classified as a completely separate sentient race — *Homo pondus*.

While HeavyG and Humans *can* mate, and often do, only one half of one percent of those couples can produce a pregnant female. Of those pregnancies, only one one-hundredth of a percent produce a living child. This means that offspring are produced only once for roughly every two million matings, a level of reproductive isolation clearly indicating speciation between *Homo sapiens* and *Homo pondus*.

First and foremost in this speciation is the difference in size between the races. The average Human male stands five feet, eleven inches tall and weighs one hundred seventy-five pounds. The average HeavyG male, on the other hand, stands six feet, three inches tall and weighs three hundred forty-eight pounds. This is a massive difference in height-to-weight ratio. HeavyG are not only taller, but are far denser than Humans.

The HeavyG were created on Vosor 3. The high-gravity planet had a wealth of mineral resources, but "normal" Humans could only work there for short periods of time. An extensive genetic engineering project by the League of Planets set out to create a Human variant that could live an entire lifetime on Vosor 3.

To achieve this, the HeavyG race has thicker, denser bones. They also have higher levels of muscle density. These are just two of the morphological differences that make breeding between the species nearly impossible, and they are only the beginning.

It is this structural variation that led to the HeavyG species' role in football: one of strength, balance and high speed over short distances. Those attributes are what make the HeavyG the ideal defensive end.

Despite being taller and having shorter legs than their Human counterparts, HeavyG players have a lower center of gravity,

Defensive ends (marked "DE") want to attack from the outside in, forcing all play back inside where their teammates can help. The DE attacks blockers with his inside shoulder, trying to keep his outside shoulder and arm free. Keeping any ball carrier inside of him is called "keeping contain." A DE must work to keep blockers off his outside shoulder, lest he get "hooked" and lose contain.

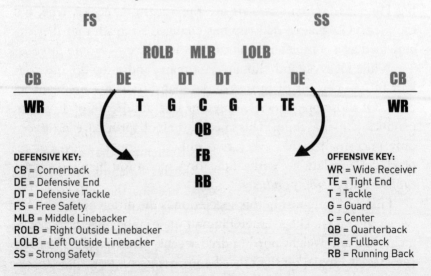

DEFENSIVE KEY:
CB = Cornerback
DE = Defensive End
DT = Defensive Tackle
FS = Free Safety
MLB = Middle Linebacker
ROLB = Right Outside Linebacker
LOLB = Left Outside Linebacker
SS = Strong Safety

OFFENSIVE KEY:
WR = Wide Receiver
TE = Tight End
T = Tackle
G = Guard
C = Center
QB = Quarterback
FB = Fullback
RB = Running Back

thanks to heavier hips. The HeavyG also have relatively longer arms — with their arms at their sides and their palms pressed flat against the outside of their legs, the tip of the index finger on most HeavyG males will touch the ground. Long arms, short legs and a heavily muscled upper body is what led Human reporters to dub HeavyG players the "Gorillas of the Gridiron." A "gorilla" is an extinct Human-like animal from Earth's history. This association is compounded by the fact that most HeavyG sprint as a quadruped, using their hands as well as their feet just as gorillas once did.

A defensive end has to perform three main functions. To show you these functions, we'll use Ionath Krakens standout defensive end Aleksander Michnik, number 91, as our example.

**1: Force the play back inside.** Remember that the defensive end (often listed as "DE," pronounced "dee-ee") is usually the widest defensive player on the line of scrimmage. If a running back or quarterback approaches Michnik, it is his job as a DE to attack from the *outside-in* and force the ball carrier back inside toward the other defensive players, such as defensive guards, nose tackles and linebackers. If the ball carrier runs *outside* the defensive end, there is often no one to stop that ball carrier for many yards. Running backs and quarterbacks will try to get outside the defensive end, then turn up the sidelines for long gains. Even if a DE is rushing the quarterback, he does not want to let that quarterback scramble and escape outside.

**2: Stop the run.** A defensive end like Michnik tends to line up in a three-point stance and attack forward upon the snap of the ball but attack forward while *under control*. This means he moderates forward momentum so he can quickly stop, go left or right, or even back up if necessary. Remember that an offensive lineman is constantly pushing and hitting Michnik, so Michnik must be able to press forward while keeping that offensive lineman at arm's length. If it is a run play, Michnik can separate from the blocker and either make the tackle or turn the ball carrier back inside. Michnik has to make sure the offensive lineman or other blocker doesn't "hook" him. A hook happens when the blocker gets on Michnik's outside shoulder and turns him back inside, allowing the ball carrier an unimpeded path to the outside.

**3: Rush the passer.** If Michnik determines it is a pass play, his job is almost always to *get to the quarterback*, either to make the quarterback hurry a throw or to sack him outright. To reach the quarterback, Michnik has to go around or through the offensive lineman. To go *through* requires brute strength. To go around requires strength as well as the agility needed to make moves like the *spin*, the *swim* or, what Michnik is famous for, the *rip*. Quarterbacks throw the ball about three seconds after the snap. Therefore, the DE must have a combination of strength, balance *and* short-distance speed. On long-yardage situations, like a third-and-seventeen, for example, there is a high degree of probability that the offense will throw. In these situations, Michnik can rush forward in an all-out attack because he isn't worried about stopping a running play. This single-minded effort to get to the quarterback is colloquially called *pinning your ears back*, in reference to the behavior of a small, warm-blooded Earth animal known as a "dog" that is used as a Human pet or used to attack foot-soldiers and criminals.

Because Michnik is so adept at running on all fours, he is faster and more agile than the Ki offensive linemen that usually block him. This agility often allows Michnik to overcome a Ki's superior strength. Long reach and low center of gravity help a HeavyG hold offensive linemen at arms' length — this allows Michnik to stand his ground against blocks, giving him time to identify the run or the pass and react accordingly.

For pass rushing, Michnik's mass and huge upper body allow him to take the punishment dished out by offensive linemen. A HeavyG player's natural tendency to sprint forward on all-fours makes their center of gravity almost as low as that of the Ki. Michnik's short, thick legs keep driving him forward even as his massive arms and mallet-like fists come up to slap or punch at the backpedaling offensive lineman.

So why don't coaches use the HeavyG size and speed in offensive positions, like receiver and running back? First, the average HeavyG player is significantly slower than the average Human player. More significantly, to run at top speed, a HeavyG has to run on all-fours, which makes it impossible to carry the ball. With ball in hand, a HeavyG can only run on two legs and one arm, slowing him considerably. Finally, the HeavyG player's big hands and slower reaction time make it hard to *catch* the football. Ionath Krakens head coach Hokor the Hookchest is famous for saying that HeavyG players can't "grab their own butts with both hands." It is somewhat unclear what this euphemism means.

HeavyG dominate the defensive end category, but a few of the larger members of the species succeed in defensive interior positions and even on the offensive line. Five percent of defensive tackles are HeavyG, while seven percent of starting offensive linemen come from the species.

A few female HeavyG have also found success in the GFL. Females have relatively shorter arms and longer legs than the males. Physically, HeavyG women appear more similar to Humans and gravitate toward the same positions occupied by Humans. HeavyG women play at fullback, tight end, quarterback and — in the rare example of Jan "The Destroyer" Dennison — at linebacker.


**QUENTIN WALKED TO THE LINE**, pausing before he bent behind center. He cupped both hands to his facemask.

"Hey, Mum-O! You call that last tickle a *hit?*"

The Ki adolescent rose up so he could see over the massive Zer-Eh-Detak, who was lined up as the offensive right guard.

"*Barnes!*" Hokor shouted from his golf cart. "Stop antagonizing Mum-O-Killowe! I'm out of players to put at right guard!"

Quentin ignored the coach. That was easy. Ignoring the pain in his right ribs and his left thigh? Not so easy. Baiting Mum-O into playing all-out carried a powerful price.

"Mum-O, you are a weak warrior. My gramma back on Micovi used to hit harder than you do, and she only had one arm. If you're not going to play hard, go home — you are an embarrassment to the franchise."

Mum-O reared up on his back two legs, waving his other four legs and his four arms while roaring at the top of his lungs. Terrifying. Quentin would have been scared, but he already hurt so bad it couldn't get any worse — so what was there to be afraid of?

Mum-O dropped into his eight-point stance, rear legs madly kicking at the nano-grass. In front of Mum-O, Zer-Eh-Detak prepared to block. The backup right tackle was twelve feet, eight inches long and 680 pounds, easily the biggest sentient Quentin had ever seen. Zer-Eh was almost a foot longer and a hundred pounds heavier than Vu-Ko-Will, the starting right tackle, but Zer-Eh was also only eighteen years old — could he handle Mum-O's psychotic assault?

This had to work. It *had* to. An enraged Mum-O had blown past Shun-On-Won so many times that Hokor had given up, tried playing Cay-Oh-Kiware at right guard instead. Mum-O had ripped past Cay-Oh six times in ten plays, so Hokor had tried backup left tackle Shut-O-Dital. Mum-O knocked Shut-O out of commission in three plays, sending the inexperienced lineman to visit Doc Patah in the training room.

So, if Zer-Eh didn't step up, the Krakens were out of options. They'd go back to Shun-On-Won, and Quentin would spend the coming Sunday getting the tar knocked out of him.

"Blue, sixteen!"

*Come on, Zer-Eh, step up.*

"Blue, sixteeeeen!"

*We need you to be the man, Zer-Eh, if you can block him, you win a starting spot.*

"Hut-hut!"

Quentin turned to the right and handed off to Dan Campbell. The rookie running back dashed forward as Mum-O immediately drove in, pushing the bigger Zer-Eh around like a child. Mum-O separated from the block, gathered and *shot* forward.

Campbell ducked the tackle so fast, it was like he'd known it was coming. He ran along the line, looking for a hole, but Virak the Mean dragged him down.

"Huddle up!" Quentin called out. As his players ran back to

the huddle, he glanced at the sidelines. There was Yassoud Murphy, arms crossed, just glaring. 'Soud hadn't been running the ball hard enough for Hokor's liking, so now the coach was giving Campbell first-string reps. Campbell *was* running hard. The rookie showed phenomenal reaction time and head-snapping moves. He wasn't big or fast, but Dan reacted to holes almost instantly and drove his body into them at top speed. If Yassoud didn't improve his game in a hurry, Campbell was going to take over as the starting running back.

"All right, all right," Quentin said to the huddle. "Campbell, nice run."

The baby-faced runner grinned back, his mouth an open smile as he sucked in air.

"It *would* have been a nice run," Quentin said, "if we had blocked for him. Zer-Eh, this is your chance to take the starting position. You up for it?"

Zer-Eh let out a long, deep bark.

"Then let's pass the ball," Quentin said. "Eagle-set, forty-two red wing on two, on two, ready? *Break!*"

Quentin walked to the line as his blockers settled into position. He knelt behind Bud-O-Shwek, the center. To Bud-O's left, the offensive guard Sho-Do-Thikit. To Bud-O's right, the mountain of pebble-skinned flesh that was Zer-Eh. Quentin scanned the defense. Mum-O-Killowe again lined up right in front of Zer-Eh. Straight ahead, John Tweedy waited in his middle linebacker position. Virak the Mean stood on John's left, Choto the Bright stood on John's right.

Under John's helmet, Quentin could see the man's facial tattoo. HERE COMES THE JUDGE, it said.

*Great, they're blitzing. Just great.*

Quentin started to audible, then stopped. If Zer-Eh couldn't pick up a blitz in practice, the Ki wasn't going to pick one up in the game. They had to see how he fared. Groaning to himself, Quentin continued with the play.

"Blue, twenty-two! Blue, twenty-two! Hut ... *hut!*"

Quentin took the snap and backpedaled. He saw Mum-O

drive to the inside, toward center. Zer-Eh should have stayed in his position, let Bud-O, the center, pick up Mum-O's angling attack. Instead, Zer-Eh went with Mum-O, reacting instead of sticking to the blocking scheme — and that opened a hole for the blitzing John Tweedy.

Quentin realized a second too late that he was still watching Zer-Eh's struggle against Mum-O-Killowe, and in that second John Tweedy closed. Quentin's head rocked back. He felt himself go airborne, carried by a pair of huge arms. His back hit the ground as 310 pounds of linebacker drove into his chest.

From somewhere, Quentin heard a sympathetic *ohhhh* — one of his teammates reacting to John's hit.

Quentin opened his eyes to see John's crazy face far too close, separated only by the space of two facemasks.

"Uncle Johnny, I have a red jersey on, remember?"

"What, you let Mum-O tee off on you, but I can't have any fun?"

"Truth be told? I'm really not having any fun at all."

DIDDUMS HURT HIS WIDDLE CHESTERS-WESTERS? scrolled across John's face.

"Hey, Q? I suspect Zer-Eh isn't going to work out at right guard."

"Wow, you think? Now get off me, John, before people start to talk."

John got to his feet, then reached out a hand and helped Quentin to his. Quentin limped back to the huddle, his head hurting, his chest throbbing. Zer-Eh was only two plays into his trial, but Quentin's instincts said he just wasn't ready. The Krakens' starting offensive line averaged 46 years of age — Zer-Eh was only 18. He was a project, drafted for his massive size, but it would probably be another three or even four seasons before he had the coordination necessary to react to attacking defensive tackles and linebackers.

Quentin had to face a harsh fact: backup players were backup players for a reason. There was only so much money to go around, only so much room on the roster to pay for expensive second-stringers. Ki were usually resilient, and teams could often count on a consistent offensive line for five seasons or more before any change was required. Bud-O-Shwek, the center, was sixty-three years old and had twenty-three professional football seasons under his belt, all without missing a single snap. Ki didn't injure easily, but the problem was that when they *did* get hurt, it was usually quite severe.

Quentin looked up to Hokor's floating golf cart, then shook his head.

"Zer-Eh-Daret!" Hokor screamed through the speakers. "Get out of there. Shun-On-Won, back in at right guard. Run the same play, and can *somebody please block?*"

Quentin watched the huge Zer-Eh scuttle off the field and Shun-On scuttle back on. Hokor had tried everything possible, every option at their disposal. Unless Gredok landed a free agent right guard, Quentin would have to go to war with the army he had.

A free agent ... or ... a *trade*.

Quentin reached the huddle and looked over his teammates, eyes lingering on Scarborough, on Denver, on their bodies quivering with excitement, eyes shining with deep reverence.

No. No trade. Shun-On would get better, *had* to get better, and that's all there was to it.

Time was up. The *Touchback* was already en route to Tower, three punches into an eight-punch, six-day flight.

Just *four days* away from their first game against the Isis Ice Storm and the start of the regular season.

**CAPTAIN KATE CHEEVERS LIKED SUNLIGHT.** No matter where the *Touchback* went, she always angled the ship so that the clear dome faced the closest star. The practice field had a full complement of lights, but she only lit them up when the ship was on a planet's dark side or during punch-space flights when there were no stars to see.

The *Touchback* had reached Grasslop, the sixth stop of the trip to Tower. The distance from the fifth punch — the planet To in the Ki Empire — to Grasslop was the longest of the eight-punch trip, requiring a full day for the engines to recharge.

A long trip was no excuse not to practice. That's what the *Touchback's* built-in field was for. Captain Cheevers had put the *Touchback's* belly toward the planet, dome facing out, so the strange yellow-green light of Grasslop's star illuminated the field.

That was how everyone knew something major was about to happen, when something blocked out the light of the sun.

Everyone looked up at the source of this strange eclipse. Through the practice field's dome, they could only see a portion of a ship, clearly larger than the *Touchback* by a factor of five or more. Gun turrets bristled from a clean, white hull. Quentin could see the corner of a red, white and blue image — the GFL logo.

John Tweedy walked up to stand next to Quentin.

"John, what the *shuck* is that?"

"GFL war cruiser," John said.

"The GFL has a war cruiser?"

"Yep," John said.

"How about that?" Quentin said.

"Yep," John said.

"And *why* does the GFL need a war cruiser?"

"Because when Commissioner Froese makes a visit, he doesn't mess around. And because it's got a punch drive. Which means he got the *Touchback's* travel itinerary so he could catch up to us here."

"Is that bad?"

HE DIDN'T COME HERE FOR SCOTCH AND COOKIES scrolled across John's head.

"Yeah," John said. "I'm guessing it's bad."

[ALL PLAYERS REPORT TO THE LANDING BAY] the computer called out. [ATTENDANCE IS MANDATORY, REPORT IMMEDIATELY]

"Huh," John said.

Quentin sighed. "Well, I guess practice is over."

"Yep," John said.

Quentin and John started walking to the end-zone tunnel. His Human, HeavyG, Sklorno, Quyth Warrior and Ki teammates did the same.

"Uncle Johnny, what do you think this is all about?"

"Mods," John said. "Someone is about to get busted."

• • •

**AN ENTIRE PROFESSIONAL FOOTBALL TEAM** — in white and black practice jerseys and full armor — packed into the *Touchback's* landing bay. The ship's orange-and-black shuttle sat unused, over-shadowed by the larger, white-painted visiting craft. White, with a big GFL logo on the side, the small words "official diplomatic vehicle" painted underneath.

In truth, Quentin thought of it as a *shuttle* only because he didn't know the proper word for something that looked like a fly-ing tank, complete with front-mounted guns, a cannon-turret up top and a smaller turret-gun underneath.

He nudged John, then nodded toward the craft. "What is that thing?"

"M-58T combat tank," John said. "Combo gunship and troop transport. The Commissioner never leaves home without it."

"A *tank?* That big warship outside? What's he need all this for?"

John's face wrinkled. He sighed. BMUD SPELLED BACKWARD IS QUENTIN scrolled across his face. "Well, hayseed, the Com-missioner's job is to tell owners what to do and punish them if they are caught breaking GFL regulations. Maybe you didn't notice, but owners don't like being told what to do."

"So they … they would try to kill the Commissioner?"

"Maybe. Gangsters like Gredok want their own people in control. The Commissioner has the backing of the Creterakian Empire, so owners can't control him. Commissioner Froese calls the shots. Whatever he says goes."

The tank's side door lowered. Quentin took a step back when he saw what came out — two Sklorno dressed in white combat ar-mor, each carrying a large energy rifle in her tentacles. Small GFL logos decorated their armored midriffs, just below their tentacle arms. Big, armored feet made metallic *clacks* as they stepped out onto the landing bay's deck.

"Just be cool, Q," John said. "Be cool, don't panic."

"Why would I panic?" Quentin hissed. "I'm not a little kid, John, I—"

Quentin froze, motionless, as perhaps a dozen Creterakians swarmed out of the tank. They flew as a flock, spreading out, then snapping back together as they circled the landing bay. Each wore a white bodysuit with a little GFL logo across the small chest, and each carried an entropic rifle.

Terror stabbed through Quentin, rooting him to the spot. "That is why I told you not to panic," John said. "I know you aren't that fond of our tiny flying overlords."

Most of the Krakens groaned in annoyance or made their species-equivalent sound. No one liked being rousted by the bats. Quentin's teammates seemed to be treating this like some minor traffic stop. He, however, had seen too many people die from those entropic rifles. The sight of a bat wasn't *like* life and death, it *was* life and death.

"Here comes the man," John said, his voice full of excitement, maybe even reverence.

"The Commissioner?"

"No, he comes after," John said. "This here would be the greatest linebacker to ever not play the game. Leiba the Gorgeous."

Out of the tank walked something Quentin had seen only in history holos — a Quyth Warrior in power armor. The white armor covered polished metal coils and joints beneath. When Leiba moved, the armor *buzzed*, like a stop-start version of an insect swarm. The heavy, white helmet provided only a black, horizontal slit to see through. Holstered sidearms hung in armored cases from each hip. Leiba held a long shock-prod in both of his armor-covered middle arms.

Quyth Warriors were impressive creatures to start with, GFL-sized ones even more so, but with the power armor, Leiba was pushing eight feet in height. He looked like a walking wrecking machine. Leiba turned his head slowly from side to side, taking in everything, taking his time.

Quentin whispered to John. "You said he was the greatest to ever not play the game? What's that mean?"

"Oh, he played," John said. "Two seasons with the Vik Vanguard. Led the league in tackles both years. No one could stop him."

"He get hurt?"

John shook his head. "He quit. Wanted to get into league administration, of all things. Became the Commissioner's bodyguard so he could learn the ropes. If Leiba had kept playing, he would have probably been the best linebacker of all time. Oh, shush it, here comes the Commish."

After the parade of white-clad lethality, what walked out next made Quentin squint to make sure he was seeing it right.

"It's ... John, what is that? A robot toy or something?"

John squeezed his eyes shut and pinched the bridge of his nose. "Backwater," he said, "remember when the rookies arrived, and Yassoud and I told you about midgets?"

Quentin nodded.

"Well, *that* is a midget. Only don't call the Commish that, or he'll string you up."

"So what do I call him?"

"You call him *sir*."

Coach Hokor walked across the landing bay to face Commissioner Froese. They were the same height, exactly, and could look at each other eye to eyes.

"Commissioner," Hokor said, loud enough for the team to hear. "To what do we owe this honor?"

"We need to speak to one of your players," Froese said. Quentin would have expected a tiny voice, but the Commissioner's words boomed through the landing bay.

Froese turned to face the gathered team. "Dan Campbell, please step forward."

There was a pause, a murmur. Krakens players looked around. Then, a scuffling sound. Quentin saw a smaller body at the back of the pack, pushing through the team.

"There he is!" Froese screamed. "Seize him!"

It was Campbell, running for the landing bay door. The Creterakian flock swarmed down, flying in front of him and flapping their leathery wings as they leveled their entropic rifles. Dan paused, then took a step forward and stopped, as if he was thinking of taking his chances. Another pause, then he lowered his head and rushed them.

Quentin winced as he waited for a dozen entropic rifles to turn Dan Campbell into a puddle of rancid goo and a cloud of stinky smoke, but the shots never rang out. The two armored Sklorno hit Campbell from behind. Dan's forehead bounced off the deck, instantly split and bleeding.

Quentin heard the stop-start buzzing of an insect swarm.

John grabbed his arm and yanked him to the side just before Leiba the Gorgeous stomped past.

Campbell pushed away the Sklorno tentacles, came to his knees and threw an elbow at a midriff. The sound of bony elbow hitting armor echoed through the landing bay, followed by Dan's sound of surprised pain.

Leiba closed the distance and shoved his shock-stick into Dan's stomach. The rookie running back twitched, his face screwed into a tight-eyed mask of pain, then he fell into a fetal position.

Leiba reached down and grabbed Dan's ankle. The power-armored Quyth Warrior dragged Dan across the deck to the white-painted tank.

"Commissioner!" Hokor said. "Tell your goon to unhand my running back!"

"Your running back has mods," Froese said. "We have a statement from the doctor that installed them. Synthetic nerve augmentation, new technology that slipped past our detectors at the *Combine*."

Hokor's one big eye tracked a twitching, prone Dan Campbell's slide across the floor, leaving a trail of blood in his wake. Leiba effortlessly tossed Dan into the tank's dark interior. The Quyth Warrior turned to face the landing bay, his head once again scanning from side to side.

Hokor turned back to Commissioner Froese. "If it's new tech, how did you find out?"

"We have other means of collecting information," Froese said. "Campbell's doctor ... *talked*. That's all you need to know, Hokor."

"If you're wrong, we want Campbell back."

"We're not wrong. We have every reason to believe the Krakens franchise did not know about this violation. There will be no fine."

The Sklorno guards walked past Leiba and into the tank, followed by the flying, white-suited Creterakians. Froese walked up the ramp, his little feet padding on the metal surface.

"Hey," Quentin said. "Wait a minute."

Froese stopped and turned. Quentin felt a hand grab his elbow.

"Q," John hissed. "What are you *doing?*"

Quentin shook his arm free. "Where are you taking Dan?"

Froese paused a moment, staring until the wait felt uncomfortable.

"Barnes," Froese said. "That is none of your business."

Quentin instinctively looked into the tank, fighting back his fear at the Creterakians inside. Someone had to speak for Dan. "That's my teammate and I want to know where you're taking him."

Froese put his little hands together and cracked his little knuckles. "Creterakian law stipulates that Campbell's mods must be removed. We're taking him to the hospital onboard the *Regulator*."

"The *Regulator?*"

Froese inclined his tiny head to the landing bay doors. "My ship. The *Regulator*."

"I want to know Dan will be safe," Quentin said. "I want your guarantee."

"*Barnes!*" Hokor shouted. "This is not the place for you—"

Without looking away from Quentin, Froese raised a hand, cutting the coach off in mid-sentence. Froese kept staring, again waiting until the whole landing bay felt full of awkward air.

"Barnes, you don't get to ask me for a guarantee of anything. You are an employee of the Galactic Football League, a rather privileged position. As for your teammate — excuse me, your *former* teammate — he broke not only GFL regulations but also Creterakian law. He has mods. Those mods have to be removed."

"These synthetic nerve things ... can you take them out safely?"

Froese shrugged. "There's always a first time for that. I didn't put the mods in him, Barnes. He made his choice. He knew what would happen if he was caught. Well, he got caught."

"Okay, sure, but—"

"Enough," Froese said. "I have a schedule to keep. But don't worry, Barnes, I've been reading up on your history. I've had sentients keeping an eye on you. I think that soon, you and I are going to have a nice face-to-face chat."

The Commissioner smiled for the first time. He had red teeth. Quentin didn't know what to make of that, not one bit. The small man turned and walked into the white tank. Leiba gave the room one more scan, then walked inside. The door lifted and closed shut with a hiss and a clank.

"Q," John said. "What was he talking about? Have you done anything that puts you at risk? Do you have mods?"

"No," Quentin said. "You know better than that."

"Then what was he talking about?"

Quentin shrugged, but he wondered the same thing. Quentin was as clean as clean gets. Unless ... could Froese know about what Quentin had done to clear Don Pine's gambling debts? Or even worse, did Froese know the To Pirates had tried to get Quentin to throw games? Maybe Quentin needed to come clean on that. But he *hadn't* thrown games. He hadn't done anything wrong. Reporting that now would create suspicion where there was nothing to be suspicious about. The team didn't need distractions like that, not now.

[PLEASE CLEAR THE LANDING BAY IMMEDIATELY. PLEASE CLEAR THE LANDING BAY IMMEDIATELY]

Quentin felt a tap on his shoulder. He turned to face a smiling Yassoud Murphy.

"I believe that we had a bet about Campbell making it out of training camp?"

"What? Are you kidding me? Dan Campbell is probably going to *die*, and you want *money?*"

Yassoud held his hand out, palm up. "A bet is a bet, hayseed. The idiot got mods, that's his problem. No wonder he was so agile."

Quentin filed out of the landing bay with the rest of the team. "Fine," he said. "I'll pay you tonight."

"Good deal. Because if you wait until tomorrow, I'll have to start charging you interest."

Yassoud seemed far too happy with the situation, but Quentin couldn't really blame him — his top rival for the starting running back position was out of the picture. That, *and* he'd won a bet. For Yassoud, that was about as good as it got.

As for Dan Campbell, his GFL career was over, and he'd soon undergo forced surgery that might prove fatal.

The Krakens faced off against the Ice Storm in just two days. There wasn't enough time to find a free-agent replacement for Campbell, and any free agents left unsigned most likely weren't even at Yassoud's level. If Yassoud didn't deliver as the starting running back, the Krakens were in even more trouble than before.

# BOOK TWO:
# REGULAR SEASON, 2683

# 5

# WEEK ONE:
# IONATH KRAKENS at
# ISIS ICE STORM

**Transcript from the "Galaxy's Greatest Sports Show
with Dan, Akbar & Tarat the Smasher"**

**DAN:** Welcome back from the commercial break, and remember
to patronize our sponsor, Kolok the Daring's Spindly Spider
Snacks, with that deep-fried taste of tarantula. Now in nacho
flavor. Tarat, what do you think of those nacho-flavored tarantula treats?

**TARAT:** I have to say that I don't like many things the Earth has
produced — no offense, Akbar.

**AKBAR:** None taken.

**TARAT:** But these big spider treats you breed there? I can't get enough
of Daring's Spindly Spider Snacks. I'm having one right now.

**AKBAR:** Oh, God, I can't even look at that. Tarat, don't bite it in
the middle! Spider juice is getting all over the counter! It makes
me want to vomit.

**DAN:** Akbar, *come on*, that's our sponsor! Try one.

**AKBAR:** I'll quit the show before that happens. Can we get to the
news?

**DAN:** We've been waiting, and waiting, and waiting, and *finally*, kickoff is here. Akbar, Smasher, in just a few hours the Tier One season begins as the Coranadillana Cloud Killers, pride of the Harrah Tribal Accord, play host to last year's Galaxy Bowl runner-up, the To Pirates.

**AKBAR:** Oh, Coranadillana is going to get *destroyed*.

**TARAT:** That outcome is highly probable, Akbar, but it is not a for-gone conclusion. Last season the Cloud Killers lost four games by three points or less, which is why they signed kicker Shi-Ki-Kill away from the Orbiting Death in Tier Two.

**DAN:** A bitter pill for the Death to swallow, Tarat, considering the Cloud Killers and the Death have such an intense rivalry.

**TARAT:** They haven't been able to play each other in the past few seasons, with the Cloud Killers in Tier One and the Orbiting Death in Tier Two, but you are correct, Dan. Those two plan-ets are just a single, short punch away from each other and share a great deal of commerce. One of the truly great rivalries of the GFL.

**AKBAR:** Well, unless the Orbiting Death earn promotion this season —

**DAN:** Which they will.

**TARAT:** I also think so.

**AKBAR:** — then that rivalry doesn't really matter. What does mat-ter is that all twenty-two Tier One teams are playing this week, no bye-weeks until Week Three.

**DAN:** You got that right, Akbar. This week and next, all twenty-two teams have to step up and battle.

**AKBAR:** Including our two newly promoted teams, the Ionath Krakens and the Chillich Spider-Bears.

**DAN:** It's going to be a hard season for both squads. Really, it's too bad they don't play each other, at least one of them would get a win this season.

**TARAT:** Dan, I think those teams will each win at least one game.

**DAN:** I'm kidding, Smasher. But seriously, it's silly they don't play, the two planets are only a single punch apart. Practically neighbors.

**TARAT:** I have often thought the Quyth Concordia should annex Chillich, which is practically in our sovereign space.

**DAN:** Smasher, hey now, we don't need to start talking about a new war between the Concordia and the Sklorno Dynasty, do we?

**TARAT:** It would be more like a minor skirmish that we would win.

**AKBAR:** Smasher, ever the pacifist.

**DAN:** At any rate, Chillich is in the Solar Division, the Krakens are in the Planet Division, and the two teams don't play each other this year. The Spider-Bears open with a road game at the Bord Brigands, while the Krakens travel to the Tower Republic to face the Isis Ice Storm.

**TARAT:** I feel bad for the Krakens. Not only did their rookie running back Dan Campbell get busted for mods, but now Ionath has to play its first Tier One game at the *Fishtank*. That is an extremely difficult place to play.

**DAN:** It is, Smasher, and the Ice Storm has something to prove this year. They just missed the playoffs last season, they've got some new talent, and they are talking big smack about making a run for the title.

**AKBAR:** Hey, as long as they have Ryan Nossek rushing the quarterback, the Ice Storm is in every game.

**TARAT:** Nossek is the best defensive end in the game. I think Quentin Barnes is in for a long afternoon.

**DAN:** More likely Don Pine is in for a long afternoon.

**AKBAR:** What do you mean *Don Pine*?

**TARAT:** He means that he thinks Don Pine will start instead of Quentin Barnes.

**AKBAR:** *I know* that's what he means, Tarat! I'm saying it's a ridiculous statement. Dan, you're not going to start a quarterback controversy before the season even begins, are you?

**DAN:** What? Me? Who? Start something? Where am I? What am I doing here?

**TARAT:** Dan, Quentin Barnes has officially been named the starting quarterback.

**AKBAR:** Oh, don't encourage him.

**DAN:** For *now*, Barnes is the starting quarterback, but with two-time league MVP Don Pine on the bench, how much rope does Barnes get before he hangs himself?

**AKBAR:** Couldn't you at least wait until the first snap to say the Krakens need to pull Barnes?

**DAN:** No! I *never* wait, and that's why we have the galaxy's top-rated show. We get the story before the story even happens! In fact, I want to hear what the peons out there think about this brewing quarterback controversy.

**TARAT:** But I'm confused. There isn't a controversy.

**AKBAR:** Too late, Smasher.

**DAN:** Line three from Chachanna, you're on the space, go.

**CALLER:** Quentin Barnes is a god!

**DAN:** A Sklorno fan of Barnes, who'd have thunk it?

**AKBAR:** This is always so uncomfortable ...

**CALLER:** Do not blaspheme Quentin Barnes, or he will cause the suns to supernova and destroy you all!

**TARAT:** I don't think he can do that.

**DAN:** Caller, tell me more about this Cult of Barnes because I know our non-Sklorno fans just love to laugh about ... I mean ... love to *hear* about it. Continue!


## From "Tower Republic: Birth of a Nation"
### by Shellfish-Related Gatherer

Like so many nations in the history of all races, the birth of the Tower Republic came from a combination of war and isolation.

In 2469, a League of Planets expeditionary flotilla, sweeping near the galactic core, discovered a G-class star. As was the custom in those times, each star surveyed was named for an expedition crew member. Because this expedition had already surveyed and cataloged over five hundred systems, stars had been named after all of the command crew, the surface explorers, the engineers and even the maintenance crew. So it was that this particular G-class star was named after Earnest Tower — the flagship's third-shift short-order cook.

The Tower System, as it is now known, proved to have one habitable planet. Originally called "Tower 1," as it was the first planet in the system, the world is now known simply as "Tower."

The surface of Tower is ninety-five-percent liquid. While all the surface liquid is covered by ice, the planet's internal geothermal temperature creates a thick temperate zone that flourishes with life. The planet's oceans and the ground beneath them are home to ample natural resources.

Like many frontier planets, Tower quickly became a haven for free-minded Humans seeking a new start. Tower exported animal protein, clothing and mineral wealth. The population grew steadily via immigration, reaching five million beings by the time it became a voting member of the League of Planets in 2527.

The year 2527 fell in an era known as The Age of Colonization, when almost every government in the galaxy had embarked on a major campaign of discovery and acquisition. As the most far-flung planet in the League, Tower became the home of the Sixth Expeditionary Fleet. The League planned on using the Sixth Fleet to explore that sector of the galaxy, but its very first mission proved to be both historic and disastrous.

In 2531, the Sixth Fleet set out on a peaceful mission to contact the Portath, a sentient race that lived inside a dense nebula. While no one had made contact with the Portath, it was known that they had discovered audio broadcast technology and achieved FTL capability. To date, no video signals have ever been received from the race. The Sixth Fleet sailed into the nebula now known as the Portath Cloud and was never heard from again.

A search and rescue attempt was in the planning stages when the galaxy heard the first direct message from the Portath. Transmitted in passable English, the message simply said, "To enter the cloud is to die."

The League of Planets reacted immediately, secretly sending a task force of seventeen warships to Tower. League officials weren't going into the Portath Cloud until they knew more, but they also weren't about to leave their newest planet undefended.

The year 2538 saw the beginnings of Tower's independence. It was then that the expansion-minded Purist Nation launched an offensive on the far-flung planet. The League of Planets immediately declared war, unwittingly falling for the political trap the Purists had set.

To close the First Galactic War, the Purist Nation had signed a peace treaty with the Planetary Union. That treaty clearly stated the Union would not allow forces hostile to the Purist Nation to pass through Union space. Since the primary shipping lanes between Tower and the League of Planets went through Union space, the Union government found itself in a very uncomfortable position. Because the League had declared war, the Union — by the dictates of their treaty — could not allow League ships to pass through Union space.

The Purist Nation had planned for this. They knew they could get the majority of their forces to Tower before the League could send their navy around the broad swath that is Union territory.

In effect, this political strategy completely isolated the young planet Tower from any help. A fleet of over one hundred Purist Nation ships closed in and demanded the complete surrender of Tower. Purist forces, however, did not know about the seventeen League warships that had been sent to protect against potential aggression from the Portath Cloud seven years before.

This fleet of seventeen ships, led by Captain Aurelius Markos, launched what is perhaps the biggest gamble in the history of galactic warfare. Instead of staying back at Tower and defending the planet against overwhelming enemy numbers, Markos bypassed the Purist Nation fleet and launched a surprise attack against Stewart, the Nation's home planet.

The armada sent to conquer Tower was forced to turn around and defend Stewart. The technically superior League warships inflicted heavy damage, recording a seven-to-one kill ratio, but the Purist navy's numbers were too much to overcome. Now with only fourteen ships, most of those damaged, Markos fled Stewart.

Eighty Purist Nation ships pursued Markos, hoping to crush his small fleet and then move on to an undefended Tower. To avoid that outcome, Markos again initiated a surprise strategy. With the entire Purist flotilla in pursuit, he took his forces straight into the Portath Cloud.

Markos kept a tight formation, intentionally slowing his ships to allow Purist Nation forces to close in. Once the Purist ships followed him deep into the Cloud, Markos scattered his fleet and ordered every ship to fend for herself. That is the last known communication from this hero of the Tower Republic. Seven Tower ships escaped the Cloud. Seven, including Markos' vessel, were never heard from again. All eighty ships of the Purist Nation flotilla vanished with all hands aboard. They sent no messages. If they ejected contact buoys, those buoys were never found. It is assumed they were destroyed.

The Purist Nation admiralty could not contact their ships. They did receive one key communiqué, however — a direct message from the mysterious government of the Portath Cloud: "Attack again, and we will destroy you."

Details of what happened from this point forward are sketchy at best. A persistent rumor is that several Purist Nation spies were discovered on Tower and that Tower's intelligence agency successfully sent false information that the planet had achieved a secret alliance with the Portath.

It is important to note that the church leaders of the Purist Nation could not say for certain what had happened to their flotilla. They knew that eighty ships had entered the Portath Cloud but did not know if those ships had been lost to Markos, to the unknown Portath, or to a cosmic accident. What they did know is that they had instantly lost thirty percent of their overall naval strength. Considering Tower's possible alliance with the Portath, and considering that League forces were closing in to reinforce Tower, Purist Nation leaders sued for peace.

Tower had fought its first war and won. Their government, the League of Planets, had done little to assist. By the time those League reinforcements reached Tower, they were greeted not by a League planet, but by the new, independent government of the Tower Republic.

Tower's birth as a nation had long-reaching political ramifications. League officials blamed the secession of Tower on the

Planetary Union's blockade. The Union blamed the Purist Nation for unmitigated aggression and manipulation and quietly abandoned the Treaty of 2535. Both of these developments would directly contribute to the Third Galactic War.

**THE REALITY WAVE TICKLED** Quentin's soul as the *Touchback* slipped out of punch space. He inhaled sharply and deeply, the natural reaction to holding one's breath for too long. It took two more deep breaths before he could open his eyes.

He didn't throw up. He breathed slowly, wondering if he was finally getting used to space travel. Maybe soon he could actually sit in the viewing lounge with his teammates and share the experience of seeing a new world with them. One could only hope.

With the punch-out over, he ran out of his quarters and headed for the *Touchback's* viewing lounge. Two dozen Krakens were already there, staring out the large windows. Quentin didn't even break stride as he entered, running to an open space at the window. He slid to a stop, hands locking on the rail that ran along the clear crysteel.

"Easy, kid," Don Pine said. "A big boy like you could go right through this window."

Don was on Quentin's right. Quentin smiled at him, gave him a nod. "I'll be careful, Gramps."

"Not enough speed," said a metallic voice on his left. Quentin turned and found himself facing Doc Patah.

"He wouldn't go through the window, Don, because he's *slow*," Doc Patah said, his voice coming from the speakerfilm mounted on his backpack. "Why is he slow? Because he's limping."

"I'm not limping."

"Q, don't bother," Pine said. "Doc Patah has been talking about you for the last fifteen minutes."

"Talking about me?" Quentin said, feeling a little self-conscious. "Why, what about me?"

"That your limp means something is wrong with your leg," Doc Patah said.

"I'm not limping."

"Limping," Don said. "Limp-a-loo-laa."

Quentin felt his face flush red. He thought he'd been hiding the limp, but obviously not. "Well, whatever. Everyone plays with pain, right, Don?"

Don nodded. "Sure, *after* they get things checked out with the doc."

"Yes, *after*," Doc Patah said. "I will expect you in the Tower Stadium training room after we land."

This was not how Quentin envisioned starting things off with the new doctor. "Well, if you knew I was limping, why didn't you come see me?"

Doc Patah spun in place, an effortless move for a floating creature. His sensory pits were only a couple of feet from Quentin's face.

"I do not come to see you," he said. "I am a *doctor*, the finest surgeon you are ever likely to meet. You are a professional athlete. If you choose to be *tough* and not protect the team's investment in you, that is your concern. Gredok hired me to be your doctor, not your babysitter. I am not some star-struck Human girl that will chase you all over the galaxy."

Babysitter? What did that mean? "But, okay, Doc, but I —"

"One hour after we land," Doc Patah said, then flapped his wide wings and shot through the viewing lounge. He left the room with barely a hiss of air, leaving Quentin to stare after him.

"What a jerk," Quentin said, turning back to lean on the handrail and look out the window. "Don't you think so, Don? Isn't he a jerk?"

Don shrugged. "Too early to tell."

"Well, what's he so mad about?"

"I don't think he's happy to be here," Don said. "He is, after all, one of the *finest surgeons you're ever likely to meet.*"

"He is?"

Don leaned away from the rail and pointed down the windows to Virak the Mean. "Back on Ionath, did you notice Virak had a cast?"

Quentin nodded.

"Well," Don said, "apparently one of Gredok's little off-field activities resulted in Virak getting into a fight, blowing out his leg. It should have put him out for four, maybe five, weeks. Doc Patah operated on him, and boom — we have Virak back for preseason. Yeah, I do think Doc Patah is the best."

"How did Gredok hire him, then?" Quentin said. "I mean, if Patah doesn't want to be here, and he's so special and all, why be here?"

Don laughed, shook his head and again leaned on the handrail. "Kid, you are a piece of work. Patah is here because Gredok wanted him. What Gredok wants, Gredok gets. How about we just enjoy the view, okay?"

Quentin nodded, remembering why he'd come to the viewing lounge in the first place. As he looked out the window, that fluttery sensation blossomed in his chest, his stomach, even his toes. Thoughts of Doc Patah and Gredok vanished because he was looking out at Tower, at *a whole other planet*. Even the rich kids back on Micovi, would *they* ever get to see this planet? Winning on the football field was the biggest reward for his hard work, his dedication, but the perk of seeing the galaxy ran a close second.

Tower seemed to glow slightly from the inside, a scratched, yellow-glass globe hung against the backdrop of dead black space. It was a small planet, probably two-thirds the size of Ionath and farther away from its star. Quentin knew that the smooth, yellowish surface was mostly ice, lined with cracks that were hundreds or thousands of miles long. A crescent of shadow marked Tower's night-time side. In that darkness gleamed a spot of concentrated lights. A mountain city rising up out of the ice and sparkling like a multi-faceted jewel. But it didn't look very big. Barely looked larger than Ionath City.

"Don? Is that Isis?"

"Yup, home of the Ice Storm."

"I thought Isis had like a hundred million residents."

"You're only seeing a part of the city," Don said. "Just the tip of the iceberg, so to speak. The city follows the mountain slope right down through the ice and into the water. Most of Isis is submerged."

"I hate going under water. It's dangerous."

"Q, you are in *space* right now."

"Well, I hate that, too."

Don laughed. "Yeah, I've noticed. Don't worry about it, I've played here a dozen times. Tower loves its football, Q. You're going to have a good time."

Tower football had come on strong in the past decade. The Republic's Tier Two conference was very competitive and had produced three T1 teams: the Bartel Water Bugs, the Isis Ice Storm and the Wabash Wolfpack. The League of Planets, Planetary Union, Quyth Concordia, Ki Empire and Sklorno Dynasty each had three teams in the bigs. That three-team credibility spoke volumes about the quality of Republic football when you considered it had only about three billion citizens — the wealthy Ki Empire had five times that, the League and Union had ten times as many citizens, while the Quyth and Sklorno had more than *fifty* times as many citizens.

The Tower Republic wasn't just a modern-day competitor at football's highest levels, it was also deeply rooted in the sport's history. The Tower Terrans and Wabash Wall had been among the twelve teams that founded the GFL. The Republic could boast of three GFL titles: the Wabash Wall in '69, the Terrans in '70 and the Bartel Water Bugs in '80.

Don turned away from the window and leaned his right elbow on the handrail. The reflected light from Isis came through the window, giving half of his blue face an oddly greenish tinge.

"Think you're ready, kid? Ready for the bright lights of Tier One?"

Quentin stared out the window, stared at a planet he would have never seen were it not for football. More sentients would see him play on Sunday than lived on his entire home colony. No matter what the season would bring, it would all begin here.

"I'm ready," he said quietly. "High One help me, Don, but I'm here to *win*. I'll die before I waste the chance that I've got."

"Let's hope it doesn't come to that. You die, I go back into the lineup, and I have no desire to ever meet Ryan Nossek again anywhere but at a dinner table with a pair of steaks separating us. Don't put an old man into the meat grinder, Q. Show some of that *mercy* your people claim to have all the time."

Don was making a joke, trying to lighten the mood with a sarcastic dig on the Purist Nation. Quentin heard the joke, maybe even appreciated the humor, but the message didn't make it from his brain to his lips. There was no smile. He stared out the window, trying to soak up every iota of this moment. The time for jokes and laughter was over.

The time for war was here.

**HIS LEG FELT BETTER ALREADY.** No more limping. Fifteen minutes with Doc Patah, and the pain was gone. Quentin walked into the Human locker room and began his pregame ritual.

*BARNES, #10*, it read above the locker. The little electronic numbers and letters changed every week, changed for the players visiting Isis stadium. This week, though, they were *his* name, *his* number.

He opened the locker and stared at the contents. His Krakens away jersey waited for him, a black number 10 trimmed with white, set against the team's trademark blazing orange. Quentin reached in and took it out, fingers feeling the rough Kevlar fabric.

Human teammates circulated around him: Don Pine, Yitzhak Goldman, John Tweedy, Rick Warburg, Arioch Morningstar, Tom Pareless, Rebecca Montagne and more. A part of his brain knew they were there. A small part. Most of his brain, however, focused on his uniform, focused on the *ritual* — the placing of the pieces, imagining himself in them, on the field, leading the team, proudly carrying the burden of responsibility, accountability.

He set his jersey flat on the floor, smoothed out the fabric around the numbers, made sure that the small letters above the numbers — letters that spelled out KRAKENS — were clean, readable. He imagined himself in that jersey, throwing, running and, yes, even *sliding*.

Quentin stood, careful not to tread on the jersey. He pulled his Koolsuit from the locker. He stepped into the legs of the rubbery material, pulled it up around his hips, slid his arms through the sleeves, then pressed the self-sealing chest flaps together. The suit fit perfectly, covering every part of his body save for his hands, neck and head. The microtubule material circulated coolant, helping to regulate his skin temperature throughout the game.

Shoulder armor came next. Quentin held the rig in his hands, fingers brushing over the layers of thick, black, curved plates. Padding beneath the plates rested against his Koolsuit-covered body, while the plates themselves helped protect him against the insane amounts of force generated by Ki defensive linemen, HeavyG defensive ends, blitzing Sklorno safeties and Human or Quyth Warrior linebackers. The plates absorbed that force, dissipating it instead of transmitting it to the wearer. Some of it, anyway — when the big sentients hit you as hard as they could, it hurt.

He slid his arms through the shoulder-armor sleeves, the black plates clattering slightly with each movement. The armor was thicker on his right arm and shoulder, thinner on the left shoulder and left arm ... his throwing arm. Micro-sensors automatically adjusted the armor's fifty-six adjustable spacers, giving him a perfect form fit in just seconds. Quentin rotated his arms, mimicked a throwing motion, a hand-off, a straight-arm. Everything felt right, everything felt perfect.

He pulled the lower-torso armor from the locker, wrapped the rig around his lower back and locked it home at his stomach. Micro-sensors adjusted the fit and linked into the shoulder armor, giving him flexible protection from the top of his pelvis up to his neck.

Next came hip and leg armor. Orange-enameled alloy protected his hips, thighs, knees and lower legs. Finally came his armored shoes, Nike All-Space Enforcers. He stepped into the shoes, which automatically locked into and bonded with the leg armor.

Quentin lifted his orange jersey like a holy relic, staring at it for a long moment. He pulled it on over his armor. He reached into his locker for his helmet. Even more than the jersey, the helmet was iconic of the Krakens, of the *team*. Ionath helmets were a deep, glossy black with orange facemasks. The helmet's front-center, above the facemask, showed an orange design trimmed in red piping — six orange-fading-to-white points stretching up, across and down the helmet's sides. Many people mistook the six-armed design for flames, like someone would paint on a tricked-out hovercar. Actually, it represented the six-tentacled Quyth sea creature for which the team was named.

Quentin pulled the helmet on, knowing he would turn and walk to the meeting room where he'd see fifty-two other black helmets. Those helmets had many shapes, from Ki to HeavyG to Sklorno to Quyth Warrior, but the black was always the same, the six-armed orange pattern was *always* the same.

The *same*, because even though they were different species, come kickoff they were all of the same tribe.

They were all *Krakens*.

A rage slowly built inside of him. A coldness, a feeling of pent-up damage to be dealt, an overpowering sense that there were those dumb enough, *arrogant* enough, to try and take what was his.

Season opener.

His moment had come.

Quentin stood and walked out of the Human locker room and into the central, communal area.

"It's time," he said. Calm, but loud enough to be heard. The various races filtered out of their respective locker rooms. The team gathered around him — five species merging into a single soul-crushing species that wore the orange and the black. The players formed a tight circle, leaving him just enough space to turn and take a step, maybe two, before he turned again, looking each teammate in the eye or the eyes.

"We need to take care of the ball," Quentin said. "We need to play smart."

"Hell, yeah!" John Tweedy said. "Yeah! Kill 'em!"

Some of the Krakens looked intense and angry, or even totally psychopathic like John. Most, however, wore only a thin veneer of confidence. Just a handful of players possessed Tier One experience. Quentin didn't have any. He'd played a single season of Tier Two, but that didn't change anything — football was football.

"They think we're weak," Quentin said. "They think you all are a bunch of *Tier Two* players."

The looks around him grew more intense, angrier.

"Football is football," Quentin said. "They're a little faster than what we faced last year, a little bigger, but we're ready for them. Let's go out there and let them know who we are. Who are we?"

"Krakens!" the team shouted as one.

"*Who are we?*"

"*Krakens!*"

"All right, let's go play some football!"

The tight circle of players parted for him. He walked out of the locker room and into the tunnel leading to the field. His team followed close behind. The soundproofing in the locker room must have been top-grade because as soon as they stepped into the tunnel, he heard the crowd's low, rumbling roar. John Tweedy, the defensive captain, walked on his right. Kill-O-Yowet, his huge Ki left tackle, scuttled along on his left.

They stopped at the mouth of the tunnel, staring out at a capacity crowd of 150,000 blue- and white-clad sentients. Quentin looked around the strange stadium that the locals called the Fishtank. When he'd seen the field hours ago, during a short walk-through practice, the place had been almost empty. The stadium's clear dome showed a seemingly endless ocean, lights from surrounding buildings playing off of floating particulate and plankton to create a slightly glowing, translucent cloud. Now, just minutes before kickoff, he couldn't see the surrounding buildings anymore. He couldn't see them because *thousands* of Leekee swarmed across the other side of the dome. *Ten* thousand, maybe more, hard to make out at this distance, but even from here, he could see that they all looked like Kelp Bringer — bright blue bodies with black stripes. The species that had looked a bit misshapen and awkward during Media Day on the *Touchback* moved with a lightning-fast, fluid grace when in the water.

Air-breathing sentients packed the stands, a solid wall of blue-and white-garbed Ice Storm fans. Three decks. Between each deck, a fifteen-foot-high ring of thick glass. Behind that glass, more liquid, more Leekee — their equivalent of VIP seating, probably. Liquid luxury boxes. Only one section in the north corner showed a concentration of orange and black, a combination of local supporters and Krakens super fans who had made the long trip from Ionath.

All enclosed stadiums were loud, but the Fishtank was on a whole different level. He could feel the sound rocketing back and forth, up and down, a kinetic force that would only get worse as the game wore on.

*"Sentients of all races,"* called the announcer, her voice booming off the roof and echoing throughout the underwater stadium. *"Please welcome our visiting team, the Ionath ... KRAK-ennnnnns!"*

Right on cue, Quentin stormed onto the sapphire blue field, his orange- and black-clad teammates at his back. Most of the 150,000 football fans in attendance screamed for his blood. Quentin reached the visitors' sidelines, and his teammates packed in around him, jumping up and down as one multi-legged creature, pushing and pulling, awash in the pregame ritual of war chants and adrenaline. He saw John Tweedy screaming things that John Tweedy thought were sentences but were really just unintelligible syllables of rage. Crazy George Starcher, face painted red this time. Rebecca Montagne, looking more than a little shell-shocked. Michnik and Khomeni, just standing there, bobbing their upper bodies in time instead of jumping, knuckles touching the ground each time they dipped. Scarborough, Denver and the other Sklorno receivers, leaping far too high and squealing with glee. Mum-O-Killowe, Kill-O-Yowet and the other Ki players, clumped mostly together, eyes hidden by their wrap-around helmet visors.

And then, the announcer called out the home team.

*"Residents of Isis, citizens of the Tower Republic, members of the Tri-Alliance and visitors from across the reaches of known space. You are all now part of ... the Fishtank! Please welcome*

*the defenders of the Republic's honor, your ... Isis ... IIIIIIIICE ...
STORRRRRRRRRRRRRM!"*

They raced out of the tunnel, a sentient tornado of blue and
white. Snow-white helmets decorated only on the left side with the
Ice Storm logo: six metal-blue swords in a snowflake formation,
gleaming with chrome highlights that matched chrome facemasks.

Their jerseys were white on top, fading to a light blue in the
middle that blended into leg armor — light blue at the waist blend-
ing to navy blue at the shins and shoes, ending with shoes of blue
so dark they looked damn near black. Chrome numbers with dark
blue trim decorated shoulder pads, chest and back. Even their belts
and shoe clips were chrome.

Aside from the uniforms — which Quentin thought were just
about as cool as cool could get — what he noticed was the *size* of
the players. The Krakens had big players, but the Ice Storm squad
just seemed a bit larger across the board. In particular Quentin
had trouble looking away from number 76.

Number 76 ... Ryan Nossek, All-Pro defensive end, HeavyG
and big as a tank. The sack leader of Tier One.

A quarterback killer.

In Nossek's six-year career with the Ice Storm, he had four
confirmed kills: one Sklorno receiver, a Human tight end and two
quarterbacks. He'd also ended the careers of two additional quarterbacks. One, a backup for the Sala Intrigue, now had a successful bedding company. You could see his commercials in just about
every GFL broadcast. The other, a former starter for the Shorah
Warlords, hadn't made one coherent sentence in the three years
since Nossek blindsided him.

Nossek was a killer, true, but all the hits had been clean. He
was widely respected in both the media and among GFL players. None of that mattered now — Nossek was the enemy, and
Quentin was going to put him down.

Nossek stopped walking and looked across the empty playing
field. He seemed to be searching for something, seemed to find it
when he locked eyes with Quentin. The gigantic HeavyG slowly
raised one massive hand and pointed at Quentin.

Mind games? This joker wanted to play *mind games*?

Quentin extended both hands at shoulder height, palms up, then flipped his fingers repeatedly, making them touch the heels of his hands. The gesture said *come get some*.

Nossek smiled and nodded.

The crowd roared so loudly neither team could hear the whistles of the flying Harrah refs waiting at the center of the field. Quentin saw the refs beckoning captains from both teams to come out for the coin toss.

He felt a rush in his chest as he jogged out, John Tweedy on his left, Hawick on his right. Quentin was the offensive captain, John the defensive captain. Hawick was this week's honorary captain, a reward for her fantastic Tier Two season. Such prestige made her shake uncontrollably, of course, but she'd earned the right.

The three Krakens reached the 50-yard line and stood at the edge of an Ice Storm logo painted onto the field. A Harrah ref floated seven feet above the logo. The ref, or "zebe," as Don Pine called them, wore a black-and-white striped jersey with a matching black-and-white striped speaker backpack. Two yellow penalty flags dangled, just waiting to be tossed. Just a few feet on the other side of the ref, the Ice Storm captains: Nossek, linebacker Chaka the Brutal and quarterback Paul Infante.

The players nodded at each other. Quentin waited for one of the Ice Storm captains to say something, to talk trash, but they did not.

"Players," the zebe said, his mechanized voice echoing across the packed stadium's sound system, fighting for dominance over the still-shouting crowd. "Because this game is played in Creterakian-controlled space, we will use a Creterakian coin for the toss."

The Harrah held out a tentacle, which was thick and flat like a squashed snake. The tip of the tentacle showed a round coin with the image of a planet — Creterak. "This is tails," it said, then flipped the coin once. The other side showed the six-eyed head of a bat. "This is heads. Krakens, you are the visiting team, who will call it?"

"I will," Quentin said. He'd share the wealth later in the season; use the coin toss as a bonus, a reward for people playing particularly well. For this game, however, his *first* game in Tier One, the honor was his.

"Call it in the air," the zebe said, then tossed the coin high in a rapidly spinning arc.

"Heads," Quentin said.

The coin spun as it fell, hitting the white and chrome Ice Storm logo, bouncing once, then falling flat. Seven sets of eyes leaned in to see.

"Heads," the zebe said. "Krakens, do you wish to kick off, receive or defer?"

"We want the ball," Quentin said.

"You sure?" Nossek said. The big HeavyG smiled, his demon-deep voice dripping with amusement. Seven-foot-three, easily five hundred pounds, long arms leading to massive fists that hung just an inch from the ground. "*Sure* you want the ball, young'un? You might want to enjoy the day a little first."

Tweedy took a step forward. "You want some?" THE BIGGER THEY ARE THE MORE I GET TO EAT flashed across his face.

Nossek sneered. Quentin realized that Nossek was just trying to affect someone's game by getting into their head. Apparently that worked on the high-strung John Tweedy, who started to take another step forward but stopped when Quentin's hand snapped up, palm on John's chest.

"Easy," Quentin said. "Let's play smart."

Nossek smiled and nodded at Quentin. The giant seemed as polite and professional as could be. He was going to try and kill you, but if he *didn't* kill you, he'd happily help you up and pat you on the back.

"Ice Storm," the Harrah referee said. "Which end zone do you wish to defend?"

Paul Infante, the quarterback, answered. "That one," he said, pointing to a south end zone painted in blazing white with metallic letters that spelled out ICE STORM. Past the end zone, a waving sea of blue-, white- and chrome-clad Isis fans ready to blast Quentin and his teammates with deafening noise.

The Harrah ref spun in the air, long tail pointing toward that end zone. "The Ice Storm will defend the south end zone. Sentients, prepare to play ball."

The crowd's roar hammered at Quentin. He turned and ran off the field, Tweedy and Hawick only a step behind him. His orange-clad teammates waited for him on the sideline. Krakens players packed in around him. So much mass, so much strength, so much energy and anger, pressing in on him from all sides.

When Quentin spoke, his words came out as a scream: guttural, short and clipped, his head bouncing forward with each syllable.

"Let's set this season off right. We get the ball, we show them the Krakens are for real. *Destroy* on three. One … two … three!"

"*DESTROY! DESTROY! DESTROY!*"

The kickoff return team ran onto the field, just as the Ice Storm's kickoff unit did the same. Richfield waited to receive the ball. The kickoff and kickoff return teams were mostly comprised of backup players, second stringers who contributed by playing on various special teams. Second-stringers were a bit more expendable — because both teams accelerated to reach top speed before smashing into each other, more players died on kickoffs than on any other play.

Suddenly, the arena air filled with spinning images of Ice Storm sword-flakes, holograms sparkling in chrome and white and deep blue. The sound system played a roaring wind that screamed in time with the spinning images. Quentin had never seen anything like it. This was the first Tier One game he'd ever seen in person. It was more than just a game; it was a show — a pageant. Even in his season of Tier Two he'd seen nothing like this. He could only guess at the expense of such a stadium-wide holographic system. The Ice Storm had been in Tier One for twenty-four seasons and, as a result, apparently had money to burn.

The crowd ate up the light show, screaming in time with the ebb and flow of the projected wind. Over 150,000 sentients playing along and enjoying every moment. Maybe the Leekee watching from up above were screaming as well, or making whatever noise aquatic creatures made.

The sound and swirling sword-storm vanished, allowing full vision of the white-lined, sapphire-blue field and the two teams preparing for action. Quentin focused on the ball sitting on a tee at the 35-yard line.

That same ball would be in his hands in only minutes.

The Ice Storm kicker raised his hand. The zebe blew his whistle, signifying the game was officially under way. The Human kicker ducked his head for a moment, then ran at the ball. His teammates ran with him, a wall of white and chrome and blue. The kicker nailed the ball, which sailed deep into air thick with the screams of Ice Storm fans.

Richfield waited as the ball descended. Perth, Kobayasho, Kopor the Climber and Rebecca Montagne formed up in front of her. When the ball landed in Richfield's tentacles, her four blockers were already going full speed forward, trying to punch a seam in the onrushing tide of blue and white. The Ice Storm's "wall breakers" shot in, a pair of Sklorno speedsters that crashed into the wave of orange and black. Quentin caught a brief image of Rebecca launching herself, smashing into one of the white- and blue-clad wall breakers, a combined impact that had to be around forty miles an hour. Both players dropped to the ground, the irresistible force hitting the irresistible force.

Richfield shot into the coalescing pile of bodies. Quentin hoped to see her pop out the other side en route to a long return, but the pile collapsed and the zebes blew their whistles.

Quentin felt the butterflies roiling in his chest and stomach. The kick return team ran off as the offense ran on. Rebecca was slow to get up. The Sklorno she'd hit didn't move at all. Whistles kept blowing long after the play was dead. White-backpacked Ice Storm docs flew from the Isis sideline rushing to the fallen player.

Quentin heard the hum of a med-sled flying onto the field, then the echoing voice of the field announcer.

*"Player down on the field, number twenty-three, North Branch."*

Starting off a game with an injury was bad luck. Quentin didn't want his team to dwell on it, so he gathered his huddle.

"All right, all right," he said. "Focus on me, on me. Here we go, Krakens. First and ten, Richfield got us to the thirty-three, so we have good field position."

He knew what was happening somewhere behind him — the med-sled was hovering over the fallen player, lowering thousands of nano-fiber wires that would engulf her, allow her to be lifted without changing her position or moving her in a way that could further aggravate her injuries. Quentin saw some of his teammates' eyes straying over his shoulder.

"Hey!" Quentin said. "Focus on me, got it?" The eyes snapped back to him. "This is a simple game. We run the ball, we catch the ball, and I throw the ball. We block, we execute, just like in practice."

The med-sled hummed again. Quentin didn't turn to look — the Sklorno player was being taken to the tunnel, to the stadium's emergency hospital somewhere underneath the stands. All stadiums had hospitals. Rarely did a game go by where at least one player didn't need immediate, life-saving surgery.

Surgery that didn't always work.

But such was the GFL, the life-and-death game that he and the rest of these sentients had chosen. Death was always just one snap away. If you thought about that too much, you would play with hesitation and be ineffective. To succeed in the game of football, one needed to play with reckless abandon.

"Here we go," Quentin said. "Just like we practiced, three plays in a row, no huddle. I-set dive left, then I-set *counter* left, followed by quarterback boot right. That's two runs right behind Kill-O-Yowet, then a boot where Shun-On-Won and I make Nossek look silly. Ain't that right, Shun-On?"

The rookie Ki lineman barked out a string of unintelligible vowels. Quentin didn't have to understand the words to feel the hate they contained — Shun-On-Won couldn't wait to take on the Ice Storm's All-Pro defensive end. This was the rookie's chance to prove himself as a player, as a warrior.

"First play on three," Quentin said. "Second two plays, we go on first sound. Ready? *Break!*"

The Krakens sprinted to the line. Quentin walked up slowly, taking it all in. The Ice Storm ran a 4-3 defense: four defensive linemen up front, three linebackers playing three or four yards behind them. That left four defensive backs — two cornerbacks near the sidelines, safety and strong safety four or five yards behind the linebackers. HeavyG defensive ends, Ki defensive tackles. The Ice Storm linebackers were all Quyth Warriors, and they were all excellent. The Storm's only weak spot? The cornerbacks. If Quentin could stay in the pocket long enough to let Hawick, Scarborough and Denver get deep, he knew he could notch some big plays. The key word being *if.* So much now depended on Shun-On-Won's ability — could the rookie handle the pressure?

Quentin took his spot behind Bud-O-Shwek. He knelt and slipped his hands under the Ki's posterior. Bud-O's pebbly skin felt cold and hard, a familiar, welcome feeling that foreshadowed the snap.

"Blue, forty-seven!" Quentin shouted. "Blue, forty-*seveennnn.*"

The defense shifted, flexed. Hands and tentacles clutched at nothing, mouths twitched, eyes widened. This was it ... game time.

"Hut-*hut!*" Quentin screamed, pausing only a second to see if his hard count drew the defense off-sides. It did not.

"Hut!"

The roar of the crowd was nothing compared to the clash of bodies at the line of scrimmage. The Krakens' offensive line shot forward, met instantly and forcefully by the Ice Storm defenders. Quentin turned to his left, pushing away from the line. Tom Pareless, the fullback, ran by, driving toward the line. Once he passed, Quentin extended the ball. Yassoud lifted his right elbow high, right hand against his chest, left hand palm up, left pinkie against his belly. Quentin placed the ball on Yassoud's stomach. Yassoud's arms clamped down, both hands wrapping over the football's pointy ends.

The hole seemed to open up as Kill-O-Yowet's huge bulk drove forward, pushing back the opposing defensive tackle. Pareless slammed into the tiny hole, blocking the Quyth Warrior linebacker, who tried to fill the gap. Yassoud ran in, helmet and shoulder pads leaning far forward. The hole was there, then gone — a multi-jointed Ki arm reached out and hooked around Yassoud's waist, slowing him just enough for the middle linebacker to close and land a solid hit. Armor clacked and rattled, Yassoud hit the ground after a three-yard gain.

Whistles blew. Quentin stepped forward. The Krakens jumped up, rushing back to the line as the zebe placed the ball.

"No huddle!" several defensive players called out. "No huddle!"

Going without a huddle kept the defenders from swapping out players, in hopes of catching them in a formation that didn't properly match up with the offensive set.

Quentin waited only long enough for his line to settle into their stances.

"*Hut!*"

Bud-O-Shwek snapped on first sound, slapping the ball hard into Quentin's hands. Quentin turned to the right this time, seemingly showing a mirror image of the last play. This play, however, was a *counter* — start out right to hopefully draw the defense in that direction, then after the handoff, the running back cut left. Pareless again ran past, again Quentin reached out with the ball, and again Yassoud took it. The second-year runner immediately cut to the left, following Pareless through the hole to the left of the center. The Ice Storm linebackers weren't fooled by the misdirection; they came up and filled the gap almost instantly, stopping Yassoud for just a two-yard gain. Armor cracked, players grunted, and bodies crashed to the ground.

Third down and five.

The Krakens hopped up, again scrambling back to the line of scrimmage, all except for Yassoud, who got up slowly.

"Come on, Murphy!" Quentin shouted. "Move, move!"

Yassoud stood and jogged to his tailback position. His slow pace gave the Ice Storm time to swap out players. A defensive lineman ran off and a defensive back ran on, giving Isis five defensive backs for the third-down passing situation.

Quentin bent behind Bud-O-Shwek, surveying the defense. The defenders weren't set, maybe he could still catch them on their heels.

"*Hut!*"

The ball smacked into his hands on first sound and the line erupted. Quentin pushed back to his left, watching Pareless rush by, then extended the ball with his right hand, offering it to the oncoming Yassoud for what looked like the third running play in a row. At the last second, Quentin pulled the ball back, planted his right foot and pushed off, turning his body all the way around until he was running right, parallel to the line of scrimmage.

In front of him, the entire offensive line had driven to the left upon the snap of the ball, taking the defense with them either by force or because the defenders wanted to follow the play. Quentin sprinted to his right when most of the defenders were still moving in the other direction, now fighting not only blockers, but their own momentum to chase after the quarterback.

Shun-On-Won had pushed to the left like his line mates. After a one-second delay, however, he had planted his six feet and stopped, suddenly driving to his right. Shun-On scuttled parallel to the line of scrimmage as a lead blocker for Quentin. A boot play like this could catch undisciplined defenses sleeping, let an athletic quarterback roll out toward the sidelines, give him time to throw or room to run.

Ryan Nossek was not undisciplined.

The HeavyG defensive end had "stayed home," meaning he hadn't over-pursued down the line. His job was to make sure plays didn't go outside of him, where running backs and quarterbacks could turn up the sidelines and rack up big gains. When Nossek saw the boot play, he came in on all fours. He ran upfield but also to his left, staying outside of Quentin. This angle would stop Quentin from getting to the right sidelines, force him to either stand and throw or tuck the ball and run back inside where Nossek's pursuing teammates could help.

Quentin should have done just that, cut back inside, but he kept running to the sidelines, trying to look downfield to see if Starcher was open. Shun-On scuttled toward the oncoming Nossek, then gathered his tubular body, compressing it like an accordion. Shun-On expanded, blasting forward like a long-tailed orange and black comet. Nossek bent and dipped his right shoulder, then ripped his thick right forearm up just as Shun-On reached him. The forearm hit just under Shun-On's chest, lifting the Ki lineman enough so that he sailed over Nossek's ducked head.

Quentin had only a split second to think *wow, that was really shucking amazing*, and then Nossek stepped forward and reached. Quentin tried to plant and turn away, but the defensive end had speed that belied his 550 pounds. Arms as big as Quentin's waist reached out, hands the size of autocannon rounds grabbed, lifted and slammed the quarterback into the sapphire-blue turf.

Quentin blanked out, but only for a fraction of a second. The crowd's concussive roar brought him out of it. He opened his eyes to see a smiling Ryan Nossek staring down at him.

"Come on now, young'un. It doesn't hurt *that* bad. First one is just a love tap. Here on out, I'm bringing everything I got. You should think about heading to the sidelines so I can say hello to my old friend Don Pine."

The giant stood and reached down, grabbing Quentin's hand and pulling him to his feet.

Quentin slapped the bigger man on the side of his helmet, a friendly-yet-patronizing gesture that said *nice hit*. "Next time? Big man, there won't *be* a next time."

Nossek smiled, turned and ran to his sideline, leaving Quentin to do the same. Quentin jogged to the bench. His first drive in Tier One? Three and out, a sack, a ringing in his head and possibly the lamest comeback of all time.

Not a strong start.

**THE ICE STORM RETURNED** Arioch Morningstar's punt to their 42-yard line, giving them prime field position. They took only four plays to advance forty yards before Paul Infante hit wide receiver Angoon in the end zone on a high cross. Quentin had to admire Infante's accuracy, nailing Angoon at the apex of a 20-foot leap, slicing the ball between Perth and Berea, the Krakens' free safety and cornerback, respectively.

Extra point good: Ice Storm 7, Krakens 0.

"*Barnes!* Get over here!" Hokor's voice coming from the speakers in Quentin's helmet. Quentin ran down the sidelines to the 50-yard line, where Hokor waited. The fuzzy yellow-and-black Quyth Leader wore a little orange Krakens jacket and a VR headset on top of his tiny ballcap. Quentin knelt. Hokor put a pedipalp on Quentin's shoulder pad.

"Barnes, don't let that last drive worry you."

"Do I look worried?"

"No. Keep running the ball and see what Yassoud's got. This season is a marathon, not a sprint, and I need to know what my running back is capable of long term. I also need to make sure Nossek doesn't kill my starting quarterback, so we're going conservative."

Quentin wanted to say *screw that, let's throw that sucker.* But he kept quiet.

The kickoff went out of the end zone, giving the Krakens the ball on the 20-yard line. Quentin ran onto the field as a little holographic Hokor face popped up in his helmet visor.

"X-set, off-tackle right," Hokor said. "And Barnes, *do not audible*. Just run the plays that I call."

"Don't I always, Coach?"

Hokor said something that might have been a Quyth-language curse, then the holo blinked out.

Quentin called the play, Yassoud ran the ball, and the offense went nowhere. Aside from one run that gave Yassoud a fifteen-yard gain, he couldn't hit the holes cleanly, couldn't break tackles and couldn't get more than two or three yards a play. Quentin threw only seven times, completing three, getting hit twice and finding out that when he'd told Nossek there wouldn't be a next time? Yeah, he'd been wrong about that. When the Krakens ran into the tunnel at the half, the Ice Storm was up 24-0. Quentin's head hurt almost too bad to tell Messal he needed another helmet to replace the first one, which had been cracked in two.

• • •

**THE KRAKENS GATHERED** in the communal locker room, already looking beaten and bedraggled. Blood dripped. The sound of armor welders and unrolling tape provided an audio backdrop as Hokor walked up to the holoboard.

"We have to make adjustments," Hokor said. "We're not giving Yassoud enough of a hole, so we will adjust to the Storm's defensive scheme. We gave up twenty-four points, but I'm not that worried about the defense. If we can *run the damn ball* and pick up some *first downs*, well, then the defense won't be out there every damn minute! But first, we did get some bad news. North Branch, the wall-breaker who went down on the opening kickoff, she's dead. When you shake appendages after the game, make sure you give your condolences."

"*Dead?*" A female voice. Rebecca Montagne. "But … how?"

John Tweedy stood up and pumped his fist. "Because you blasted her, man! How about that, Krakens? First play of her first game, and Becca the Wrecka *got a kill.*"

There were murmurs of approval from the Humans, deep grunts and clacking of chest armor from the Ki linemen. The Sklorno squealed and jumped up and down, their armored eyestalks coming only inches from the fifteen-foot ceiling. The Krakens players weren't celebrating the death of another player, necessarily, but their job was to hit as hard as they could — if another player died from one of your hits, you deserved respect. Quentin said nothing. It was sad that North Branch had died, but it was a violent game and bad things happened to good players.

Rebecca shook her head. "But I didn't *mean* to. I just … I just hit her. I'm *supposed* to hit her!"

"Montagne!" Hokor said. "Sit down, we have halftime adjustments to make."

"But Coach, I didn't mean to kill anyone, I—"

"*Montagne!* Sit down and *shut up!*"

She looked stunned, as if it was news to her that the galaxy's most violent team sport might result in death.

Quentin quietly walked over to her as Hokor outlined blocking schemes for the second half.

"Becca," Quentin said in a whisper. "You okay?"

She looked at him with haunted eyes. Clearly, she was not okay.

"Relax," Quentin said. "It's okay. This is upper tier football. These things just happen."

"*Just happen?* That sentient is dead, Quentin."

"Yeah, and she won't be the last this season, not by a long shot. You need to focus on halftime adjustments. We can talk about it after the game. Right now, you put it out of your mind, understand?"

She looked away, the expression on her face showing she thought Quentin either a simpleton or a heartless ghoul. Well, he was neither. He was the quarterback, and his team was getting whipped.

Quentin walked away from her and focused on the holoboard. A 24-point deficit was damn near impossible to overcome unless they could get some offense together. They had to make adjustments, then go out and kick some ass.


**THE KRAKENS DID NOT** "kick some ass." Ice Storm did, and plenty of it. Isis added three more touchdowns and two field goals in the second half. The Krakens' offense sputtered, save for one of the few plays in which Quentin had time to throw, and he hit Hawick for a 78-yard touchdown pass. Most of the pass plays, however, he'd barely had time to complete his drop-back and look downfield before someone was in his face. He'd been hurried seven times, knocked down another eleven and suffered five sacks (three by Nossek, two by the Storm's left tackle, the player Shun-On-Won was supposed to block). Basically, Quentin got the crap kicked out of him for sixty minutes.

End result: Ice Storm 51, Krakens 7.

In the Human locker room, Quentin slowly peeled off his armor. He tossed the plates, wraps, armor and shoulder pads on top of the blue-stained orange jersey already sitting in a heap on the floor.

Man, did his head hurt. Beat-up players surrounded him. They all felt humiliated by the lopsided loss, yet an odd sense of optimism remained. The Ice Storm was a damn good team building on last season's success. Isis had several years of Tier One experience, *and* they were fully rested from the long off-season. The Krakens, on the other hand, had finished a brutal Tier Two campaign only four weeks earlier. Nobody wanted to lose 51-7, but at the same time no one had assumed the Krakens could go undefeated. Quentin and his teammates now had their first taste of Tier One blood.

"Nice game, kid."

Quentin turned to see Don Pine, already fully dressed in a flashy black suit and matching hat.

"Sure," Quentin said. "If you can call losing by six touch-downs *nice*."

Don shook his head and spoke in a quiet, subtle tone of voice. "Let it go. The instant a game ends, it's gone. You need to move on and start thinking of next week. Forget it. And let the team *see* you're forgetting it. They look to you now, remember that."

Quentin considered the words and nodded. Don was right. Everyone watched Quentin, unconsciously monitoring his moods, if not outright following his lead. At times, he'd have to put on a happy face.

Quentin turned to see Messal the Efficient standing only a foot away. Those little Workers sure moved quietly.

"Elder Barnes, it is time for the post-game press conference."

"No thanks, Messal," Quentin said. "I'll pass."

Hints of green washed across Messal's single eye. "Elder Barnes, I apologize for my lack of clarity. Clearly I am to blame for any confusion. What I meant to say was, we must go to the press conference now. You are scheduled."

"I heard what you said. You heard what I said. *I'll pass*."

Now green *flooded* Messal's big eye. He turned and looked up at Pine.

"Q," Pine said, "you're the starting quarterback. Post-game press conference is mandatory."

"Whatever. We got whipped by forty four points. Nobody wants to hear the losers talk."

Don laughed. "Kid, are you serious?"

Quentin stared at him, then nodded.

"Elder Barnes," Messal said, his words coming faster and with more urgency, "if we don't get to the media room right now, we will be *behind schedule*."

"Shuck off, Messal, and I mean that in the nicest possible way."

"Quentin," Don said. "Seriously, these are *mandatory*. Win or lose, you have to go and answer stupid questions from people who don't know anything about football."

"That doesn't even make any sense."

Messal started hopping lightly from foot to foot. The motion made him resemble a Human child that had to pee.

Don shrugged. "No, I guess it doesn't make any sense, but you gotta do it."

"Why?"

"Because. It's *mandatory*."

Quentin waved a hand in annoyance. "Rules are for pansies. You used to be the biggest star in the GFL. What happened when you skipped a press conference?"

"I never skipped one," Don said. "Do you need some help with the cliché answers or something?"

"Elder Barnes, *please!* We are now *late!*"

Quentin reached out and grabbed Messal's left pedipalp.

"Messal, I like you, but if you don't get out of my face right now, I will start getting angry. Human eyes don't turn black when we get angry, but I assure you, you will have no question about my state of mind. You get me?"

Messal blinked twice, pranced side to side once more, then nodded. Quentin let go of the pedipalp. Messal scurried away.

Quentin looked at Pine again, who had a smirk on his face.

"What?" Quentin said. "Is it time for someone to correct Quentin's behavior again?"

Pine chuckled soundlessly, his shoulders bouncing a little as he looked to the ceiling. "Quentin," he said, "you are endlessly entertaining, you know that?"

Quentin hated to be laughed at, but sometimes he just had to roll with it. Don didn't mean any harm. Quentin had learned that the hard way last season. Time to change the subject.

"You got dressed fast," Quentin said. "John and I are grabbing some dinner later, seeing downtown Isis. He's got a submarine lined up or something. You want to join us?"

"No thanks. I'm heading out with Ryan Nossek and some of the Ice Storm guys."

"*Nossek?* The guy who knocked the living crap out of me out there?"

Don nodded.

"But ... he's from the *other team*."

"Sentients are sentients, kid. Just because they play for another team doesn't make them poison. And I'm dressed fast because that's what happens when you don't play. While I'd rather be playing, I have to say leaving the locker room with no bruises, breaks or concussions is kind of a welcome experience."

Quentin didn't know if Don was being serious or facetious. Just because Quentin would do anything, to anyone, to take every snap of every game, he still felt odd doing it while a legend like Pine rode the bench.

Don's eyes narrowed. "Kid, you're not feeling sorry for me, are you?"

Quentin looked away, his face turning red.

"Well, knock that crap off. You earned your starting job. You want to feel sorry for me? Do it when you've got *three* Galaxy Bowl rings, and you can make fun of me for only having *two*."

Quentin's eyes shot to Don's right hand, where the sparkling rubies set in a pair of big, gold rings sparkled in the locker room lights. Don smiled a friendly smile, but the message was clear — Quentin had a long way to go before he was on Don's level. All careers end. Not all end with as much glory as that of Donald Pine.

"Besides," Don said, "there was no reason to take you out. You were throwing well."

"I only had one touchdown."

"You were fifteen of twenty-eight for a hundred eighty-two yards. Not All-Star numbers, but considering your offensive line let you get roughed up all day, I'd call it a solid job. Most importantly, know what you didn't have?"

Quentin smiled. "No interceptions."

"Bingo. Know how many picks I gave up in my first Tier One game?"

"Four," Quentin said quickly.

Don smiled. "You been studying up on the old man?"

Quentin shrugged, trying to play it off. The truth was he had been studying Don Pine's career: every game, every snap, every off-field transgression.

Quentin wrapped a towel around his waist and stood, trying to roll his back out to loosen the knots and shake off the deep pain radiating from the spot where Nossek's helmet had hit him in the kidney. "I gotta hit the showers."

"You mean with *water?* Swimming with the *salamanders* again?"

*Salamanders* was a racist term for the Ki, and the way Don said it meant he was mocking Quentin for his racist beliefs. *Former* racist beliefs, that was, but like any other sensitive subject under the sun, it was open for locker-room ridicule and mockery.

"Up yours, blue-boy."

Don laughed. "Seriously, though, you're going to *bathe?* In *water?* You're civilized now, Q, use the nannite shower."

"Bathing *is* civilized."

"Dude, you know the dirt and sweat that comes off your body? Where do you think it goes? It goes *into the water.* The water you're bathing in. Taking a water-bath is like soaking in your own filth. It's disgusting."

Quentin shrugged. "Then I guess I'm disgusting."

"You can take the boy out of the mines ... but listen, Q, mind if I give you some pointers about talking to the Ki?"

Quentin fought down a burst of annoyance. People just loved to give him advice. But Don was far more experienced in football and in life — and the old guy was usually right.

"Sure," Quentin said.

"Your offensive line did a crap job for you today. If you go hang out with them, talk to them, it's like you're saying *hey, it's no big deal.*"

"So what then? The silent treatment?"

Don nodded. "For some of them. Kill-O-Yowet played his salamander ass off for you. He's also the Ki alpha male on the team, so you have to give him the respect he deserves. And by talking to him, you're showing the Ki *race* respect, even if you don't respect the other individuals."

"That sounds complicated."

"Every race has its own set of ingrained politics. Learn what those politics are, or get used to losing. The Ki culture has all kinds of warrior code crap — hierarchies, unwritten rules, unspoken traditions."

Quentin rolled his eyes. Why couldn't everyone just play football? "Unwritten? Unspoken? How in the void am I supposed to learn all of that?"

"By watching and learning. And by listening to me. Do you want to win a championship?"

Quentin felt the rush in his chest. Any thought, any mention of a title, galvanized him. He nodded.

Don spread his blue hands, palms up, as if to say *well there you go.*

"Okay," Quentin said. "I can talk to Kill-O. Anyone else?"

"Sho-Do and Bud-O did okay, but they have to do better. You can *look* at them, just don't *talk* to them. Vu-Ko-Will had a bad game, but that's to be expected when you're up against Nossek. Vu-Ko is also the oldest player on the team and number two in the alpha hierarchy, so you have to acknowledge his presence. Once you've done that, just pretend he's not there. Trust me, he'll be so ashamed of his performance he won't want to engage you anyway."

"Got it," Quentin said. "And Shun-On-Won? The rookie?"

Don shook his head. "You don't even *look* at him. Act like he doesn't even exist. He's responsible for three of the sacks. That's not going to change unless he ups his game. It's a warrior culture, Q — where they come from isn't as nicey-nicey as the GFL."

"A Sklorno *died* today," Quentin said. "The GFL doesn't sound nicey-nicey to me."

"Compared to where the Ki come from? One death is like a day in the park with the wife and kids. For them, this game is combat. In combat, failure usually means corpses. Shun-On failed, so you act like he's dead to you."

"Sounds harsh," Quentin said. "I mean, he's a rookie. This was his first game."

Don spread his hands again. "All I can tell you is what I know. But it's your team, Q, you do things your way."

Quentin thought for a second, then nodded. "Okay, I'll find Shizzle and go in."

"Shizzle? What do you need that little Creterakian for?"

"To translate," Quentin said. "I don't speak Ki."

"Yes, but they understand *you* just fine. Besides, you can tell what they mean by the tone of their grunts. You're the one who needs to do the talking. You don't need a translator."

"Well ... Shizzle will also, you know, tell me who's who."

Don's eyes narrowed. "Quentin, you've come so far. Are you going to tell me you think all Ki look alike?"

"It's not *racist!* They *do* all look alike. If they don't have jerseys on, you can't tell them apart."

"I can," Don said, then turned and walked off. Quentin stared after him for a second, feeling both angry and embarrassed. He wasn't responsible for evolutionary shucking biology. They *did* all look alike.

Quentin left the Human locker room and went looking for Shizzle.

**STILL DRESSED IN ONLY A TOWEL,** but now with Shizzle perched on his shoulder, Quentin entered the Ki locker room. It was empty, filled only with discarded jerseys, armor and dirty joint braces streaked with black blood. Quentin and Shizzle walked through the littered floor, heading for the Ki baths.

Shizzle was known for his garish outfits, but this one really took the cake. The material was pink, maybe, but it was hard to tell when tiny lights made waves of green, blue and yellow cascade over his football-shaped body. The material ran down his flat, two-foot-long tail and even covered his membranous wings. He had a rig on his head that seemed to be the Creterakian version of sunglasses: pink frames holding black lenses over all three pairs of eyes. Two eyes looked straight forward, two looked straight down, and one sat on either side of the head, looking left and right.

"I do wish you'd find another interpreter for this," Shizzle said.

"We don't have another interpreter."

"Then take a language course. I'll never understand your species' shortcoming in learning the tongues of other cultures. I speak over three hundred languages."

Quentin stopped at the door to the baths. "Don't give me that, Shizzle. This is what your race *does*. You guys can learn a language in a week. We're not wired that way."

"Then your physiology is flawed."

Quentin did not need this, not now. Interpreting for the team was Shizzle's job. The little bat was starting to make Quentin mad.

"Tell you what," Quentin said. "How about we make a deal — if I take a language class, then you come out and suit up for a practice. We'll see how well *your* physiology works on a football field."

Shizzle stayed quiet for a second. "Point taken," he said.

"And why don't you want to go in there with me? What are you, racist?"

It shocked Quentin how liberating it felt to say those words, instead of having those words said to him.

"It's not *racism*," Shizzle said, "it's *terror*. When the Ki are in areas with the other races, I'm fine, but their baths? Where it's dark, and no one is around? I feel like I'm going to wind up on their dinner table."

"So you eat with them, how bad can it be?"

"Not *at* their dinner table, backwater, *on* it. I'm about the right size for a Ki feast. In fact, I think I'll opt out. You don't need me for this."

"Shizzle, you are going in there with me."

"No, backwater, I am n—"

Quentin's hands shot up and grabbed the football-shaped body. Bat-like wings flapped in panic. Six-eyed sunglasses clattered to the floor.

"Stop!" Shizzle screamed. "Stop it! Stop it!"

Quentin shook him to quiet him down. "You *shut up*. I'm trying to unify a team, and you will help me. Do you understand?"

"Yes! I'll go in! Please don't *hurt* me!"

Quentin looked at the disgusting creature, the race he'd hated his whole life, the race that had subjugated his people. He looked, and saw ... fear. Shizzle feared for his life.

Quentin let go. The Creterakian flapped away, started flying a circle around the ceiling, trying to stay out of Quentin's reach. Another stressful moment, and Quentin had again reacted with violence. He put his hands over his face, felt that sensation of self-hatred well up in his throat. Yitzhak's words echoed in his thoughts: *you're not on Micovi anymore.*

"Shizzle, I'm sorry."

"I will go in with you!" Shizzle kept circling around the ceiling. "Just don't hurt me!"

Quentin looked up, watched Shizzle flying. The Creterakian weighed all of ten, maybe twelve, pounds. Quentin's left foot probably weighed more. "Honest, I'm *really* sorry. I shouldn't have done that."

Shizzle stopped flying, clung to a ceiling fixture. "Whatever you say, Quentin. Can we go in now? I will do my job, just don't shake me again."

Quentin wanted to find a hole, crawl in and not come out for a decade. But despite his horrible behavior, he didn't have time for that. He had a job to do, a job that was in the Ki baths. He could try and make it up to Shizzle some other time.

Quentin opened the door. Thick steam billowed out, catching the glow of purple lights from inside. He walked in, wrinkling his nose against the stench of mildew and post-game Ki stench, something that made him think of dead fish mixed in with rotting chicken entrails. The sound of hissing water jets and low-range Ki growls played off the black tile walls.

His eyes adjusted to the low lights, revealing a scene most Humans would consider a nightmare. A large pool of black water filled with a wriggling, entwined pile of long, tubular bodies. Wet, orangish skin gleamed, as did the reddish-brown spots of enamel that dotted it. Add in staring black eyes, muscular multi-jointed arms, pinkish hexagonal mouths lined with black teeth, and you had a squirming, multi-headed ball of pure terror.

Quentin tossed his towel, shook Shizzle off his shoulder, then dove into the water. Near-scalding temperatures scraped at his skin, initially shocking, then soothing, relaxing. He arched his back and rose. His head popped out of the surface only a few feet from the massive ball of entwined Ki.

It was no small feat to hide his instinctive fear, his natural revulsion. He controlled it for two reasons. First, these were his teammates, and he would not disrespect them by acting like some backwater racist brat. Second, this activity, coming into their private area and showing no fear, helped them bond to him — and to win a championship, you needed an offensive line that would follow you to hell and back.

As the glowing Shizzle flew laps around the small pool, Quentin stared into a dozen sets of eyes, wondering if he'd recognize something specific, something familiar. All the Ki looked pretty much the same — he normally used jersey numbers to tell them apart.

And then, shockingly, he realized one of the Ki's eyes were a little more round than the others. It's mouth, not perfectly hexagonal, but skewed a little. He saw those things and knew, without a doubt, that this one was Kill-O-Yowet. And there, the small, pink scar above the left-center eye, that was Aka-Na-Tak, the injured starting left guard. And *that* head, half-buried in the tangle, he saw an eyelid that was a little more droopy than the others — Shun-

On-Won, the rookie he now recognized despite only knowing him for four weeks.

"Shizzle," Quentin said. "You can go."

The garishly dressed bat didn't need to be told twice. He looked like a blur of foggy light as he shot away from the pool and back to the communal dressing room.

Quentin looked into the eyes of the Krakens' alpha Ki.

"Kill-O-Yowet. Thank you for protecting me today."

The Ki grunted a reply. Quentin didn't understand the words, might *never* understand the vocally complex Ki language, but Don was right about one thing — you didn't need to fully understand words once you got used to their tone. Kill-O's grunt was the Ki equivalent of self-deprecating modesty. Had a Human expressed an identical sentiment, he might have said something like: "yeah, I *protected* you so well you were sacked five times." Still, while football was a team game, an individual always knew when he or she had played well. Those five sacks? Not one had come from a sentient that Kill-O had been assigned to block.

The packed ball of Ki slithered and writhed a little. Some heads slid in, some slid out. Water rippled across the pool, splashed against the sides. Quentin stared into many, many eyes ... then recognized Sho-Do-Thikit, the left guard, and Bud-O-Shwek, his center. He nodded at each of these players in turn.

Other black eyes stared at him. They seemed to be waiting ... almost *hoping*. How about that? The big, bad Ki had accepted him as a war leader, and as such, they wanted his approval. Or, at least, his acknowledgment.

Well, they weren't going to get it. If they wanted recognition, they would have to earn it.

Quentin swam to the edge of the pool, right under a stream of hot water that arced down from a spout high up on the black tile wall. The water splashed on his head. He shut his eyes tight against the heat. He sank down to his chin, soaking in — as Don had said — not only his "filth" but the "filth" of his salamandery teammates.

Aside from the sound of small waves and splashing fountains, there was no noise.

Except for ... crying?

Quentin opened his eyes. Yes, it was crying. A woman's crying, from the other side of the gigantic pile of tangled Ki. He swam around the pile. On the other side, he saw a thick Human head, fountain water splashing off of long, black hair.

No, not a Human head, thicker, blockier ... a HeavyG head.

Rebecca Montagne.

Quentin felt his face flush red. He was *naked* in front of a woman? Sinful! Apparently, it didn't bother him to be naked in front of members of another species, but having a woman in here made him instantly self-conscious. He calmed himself — his body was underwater, water that looked black. She couldn't see anything of his, nor could he see anything of hers.

"Becca? You okay?"

She looked at him briefly, a disembodied, black-haired head floating on a black, liquid surface. Her eyes looked very dark under the dim purple lights. Dark, and a bit ... exotic. Then she shook her head.

"No," she said. "I'm not okay."

He swam closer, careful to keep a couple of yards between her and his nakedness. "Hey, didn't anyone tell you there's no crying in football?"

He meant it as a joke, but she closed her eyes and started crying harder. "I didn't ... *mean* it," she said, choking out the words. "I didn't mean to hurt her."

Quentin nodded. He couldn't leave; he had to talk his teammate through this. She was the same age he was, maybe even a little older. Don Pine would know exactly what to say, but Don Pine wasn't here.

"Becca, this is football. Beings are going to get hurt. Beings are going to *die*. It's just the way it is."

"I *know* that," she said between sobs. "I've been playing since I was twelve. I've hurt beings before, ended careers, I've seen beings die. I just ... "

Her voice trailed off. Quentin finished the sentence for her. "You just never killed one yourself."

She nodded. The mist and the splashing fountain water hid her tears. Quentin wondered what the ball of slithering Ki were thinking of this, of watching a teammate crying over the death of an opponent.

"Look, Montagne, you're going to have to deal with this. You can't let this affect your play."

"Affect my play? A sentient *died* today, Quentin. Died because I killed her."

"Because you did your job. Because you executed your position."

"My position?" Rebecca shook her head, again staring at Quentin like he was some kind of ghoul. "North Branch is *dead*, and you're talking about executing a position? Is that *all* you think about? Football?"

Quentin blinked a few times, then gave her the honest answer. "Yes. That's pretty much it."

She said nothing, just cast her gaze back to the black water's surface.

"Montagne, you're in Tier One now. If football isn't all you think about, then *make* it all you think about. We don't have room on the roster for someone who doesn't."

Her eyes snapped up again, glaring at him like he'd said something completely unbelievable. She turned, put her hands on the tile sides of the pool and pulled herself out of the water.

Quentin's eyes went wide as he saw a glimpse of her naked behind before he quickly turned away. He heard her feet slapping against the wet tile surface, then the hiss of the door as she left the pool room.

He wondered if he had ever felt as embarrassed as he did at that moment.

QUENTIN, JOHN TWEEDY AND YASSOUD MURPHY walked out of the locker room and into Isis Stadium's private landing bay. It was much larger than the *Touchback's* landing bay and needed to be — there were fifteen shuttles just from broadcast companies alone, all lined up neatly along the bay's edge. Shuttles and stream-lined personal cars moved across the wide space, stopping on top of yellow-lined platforms mounted flush in the black grate deck. Every twenty seconds or so, one of the platforms would lower, dropping those cars into the shadow below, or rise up, delivering a new car dripping with water.

Yassoud was still limping. The normally outgoing, loud run-ning back seemed uncharacteristically subdued. Quentin wasn't surprised. Yassoud had carried the ball twenty-three times for a whopping forty-seven yards, an average of two yards per carry.

John seemed despondent that his life-of-the-party drinking buddy was not being the life of the party. "Lighten up, 'Soud," John said. "It's a long season, we'll do better next week against the Dreadnaughts."

"Whatever," Yassoud said. "If I don't get some blocking, it won't matter who we're playing."

John and Quentin said nothing. Better blocking would help, certainly, but Yassoud was no Mitchell Fayed. Sometimes a run-ning back had to go beyond just hitting the hole, had to make things happen on his own. Quentin knew that Yassoud would improve. What did they expect out of him in his first Tier One outing? A game or two of poor production was almost to be expected.

"So, John," Quentin said. "Where are we going?"

"*Out*," John said. "I've only been on Isis once, and I can de-scribe it in two words — awwwwwwwwwe-some. Ionath City has the one big dome, right? Well, Isis is so big they couldn't fit it all under one dome, so there are *hundreds* of domes with businesses and residences inside. And there's *thousands* of buildings that are self-contained, outside of the domes. They even have some bars that are right down on the ocean bed, man! And there's a *crap*load of party-subs that float around the city. If you don't know their current coordinates, you can't find them, let alone get in."

Quentin saw that look in John's wild eyes, that look that said the man would be out all night and wouldn't go home without at least one bar fight.

"What about curfew?" Quentin said. "We have to be back on the *Touchback* for the trip back to Ionath."

It had taken five and a half days to reach Tower and would take the same to get back for next week's home opener against the Themala Dreadnaughts. Hokor wanted a full practice at Ionath Stadium before the game, which meant the Krakens departed that night.

"Don't worry about it," John said. "I promised Coach I'd have you back by midnight Isis time. Trust me, I will *not* let you miss the bus."

"Why?"

John grimaced. "Coach mentioned something about castration. I'm not sure of the details, but suffice to say I don't really want to find out if he's joking or serious. I hired us a private sub, Q. Trust me, I'll have you back in time."

Despite the lopsided loss and throbbing head, Quentin could barely contain his excitement. Another foreign planet, another exotic city. Isis was rumored to be among the most beautiful places in the galaxy. John led them out onto the busy landing bay. He seemed to be counting off the yellow numbers next to each platform. When he found the one he wanted, they waited.

They weren't waiting long before the platform lowered, creating a rectangular opening thick with shadow. Moments later, a streamlined, deep-blue ship rose up out of the opening, lifted by the elevator platform below it. Water dripped off the vehicle, which was about the size of a large grav-car.

The driver's side door rose up on a hinge. A fat, bearded Human stepped out. He nodded at John. "Are you Mister Tweedy?"

"That I am, governor! Call me Uncle Johnny. This is our ride, boys, let's hit the town."

The fat man walked around, opened a rear door for them and they climbed in. Quentin marveled at the spacious interior — it reminded him of Stedmar Osborne's limo, the vehicle that had taken him to Micovi's lone spaceport. The vehicle windows looked out onto the bay's other ships and empty stalls. The vehicle's roof was also clear, showing the bay's high ceiling.

The driver closed the door. As soon as he did, music filled the vehicle. Quentin instantly recognized the song: *Combat Bats* by Trench Warfare.

"Nice! That's my favorite band."

John and Yassoud laughed.

"Wow," John said. "What a coincidence."

Quentin looked at them for a second, then looked away. There was always a joke he didn't get.

He felt the vehicle lower. The windows went dark as the elevator platform dropped the ship into the hole. Quentin heard various machinery humming, the clank of metal-on-metal, the hiss of air, then the burbling of water.

Acceleration pushed him back into his seat. Instantly, the windows filled with light, filled with a view that took his breath away. The underwater city of Isis sprawled out before him. Buildings and domes littered the ocean floor as far as he could see, clear and bright when near, hazy and darker in the distance. The water looked slightly murky. There were also floating spheres covered in lights both steady and flashing. Billboard signs glowed brightly, advertising Human products as well as products that must have been of use only to Leekee. Most of the latter seemed to be things catering to the health of their spindly symbiotes. And it wasn't just the buildings and floating spheres — a hundred feet or so above the tallest buildings, Quentin saw the hulking shapes of massive, streamlined submarines, some as large as the *Touchback*, some even bigger.

The limo banked. Quentin saw the spectacular design that was the Fishtank, home of the Isis Ice Storm. The beautiful stadium reminded him of ancient football temples back on Earth: a white cylinder rising up out of the ocean floor, capped by a clear dome. He could see through the dome to the empty stands and the sapphire-blue field below. Above the stadium, an enormous, shimmering, slowly spinning hologram of the Ice Storm's sword-snowflake logo.

The limo banked again, revealing the sprawling grandeur of Isis. Lights and shapes as far as the eye could see, personal ships whizzing through the water at all depths, each leaving a stream of thin bubbles that slowly floated toward the unseen surface. The ships seemed to follow a traffic pattern, but they were packed in so tightly and moving in the same directions that they looked like schools of strange fish.

"Wow," Quentin said. "This is madness."

"Nope," John said. "This is Isis. Enjoy the ride, Q."

"Oh, I am. Where are we going?"

"Never mind where we're going and eat your broccoli," John said.

The ship shot toward a thick stream of traffic, banked at the last second, then melded into the school. Quentin felt his hands squeezing the seat — some of the ships were only inches from his window. Particulates shot past the window, blurring things even more, making the buildings and domes outside waver, shimmer. Quentin sat unmoving, mesmerized by this city of water until the vessel suddenly broke free from the school and banked to the right, diving toward a canyon between tall buildings.

Down near the ocean floor, Quentin saw hundreds of streamlined bodies swimming in all directions — Leekee, he realized, the Isis equivalent of pedestrians. He saw groups of Dolphins, smooth skin modified with bright colors and designer patterns. Harrah, too, as at home in the water as they were in the air.

"I don't see any Whitokians," Quentin said. "They're underwater types, aren't they?"

"Not here, they aren't," John said. "There's a lot of hatred between the Leekee and Whitokians, left over from the Third Galactic War."

"Wasn't that like a century ago?"

John shrugged. "Something like that. History ain't my thing."

Quentin saw another odd sight — *Humans*. A few wore breathing masks, but most swam along with the Leekee, Dolphins and Harrah. They wore various kinds of clothing, some skin-tight, some loose and rippling with motion, but no masks.

As the ship drew closer to the pedestrian traffic, Quentin pointed down to one of the Humans. "John, how come they don't drown?"

"They're Amphibs," John said. "Genetic mods, breathe as easy in Tower's oceans as they do on its surface. And check out their feet."

Quentin looked closer, realizing that none of the maskless Humans wore shoes. They had longer feet and longer toes with skin running between the digits.

"Fish-people?"

"Amphibs," Yassoud said. "*Fish-people* is offensive. Oh, and don't call them *frogs*, either. Or *phibbies*."

"I can call them *Amphibs*, but they are offended by *phibbies*? That doesn't even make any sense."

Yassoud shrugged. "Hard to keep track of the sheer number of things that offend sentients these days, but that's their preference."

The ship evened out, once again traveling with other small passenger vehicles, only now the school wasn't as tightly packed. Quentin realized there was a level below that the cars didn't travel because all the pedestrian swimmers were beneath that level.

The ship evened out, once again traveling with other small passenger vehicles. A few minutes later, it banked left out of the traffic and into a building's opening. Darkness covered the windows. Quentin waited, barely able to contain his excitement. Burbling, hissing, clanking, light blaring in from above. He was in a loading bay again.

"Where are we?"

"Never mind where we are," John said.

"And eat your broccoli," Yassoud said.

"What is this *broccoli* that you guys keep talking about? Is that food?"

Before they answered, the fat driver opened the door. Quentin stepped out, his feet landing on the elevator platform grate. Water beaded down the limo's smooth, blue hull to drip onto the grate, then drain through it.

"Mister Barnes," the driver said. "Do ya mind if I have yer autograph?" He held out a messageboard, which Quentin took.

"Sure thing, man." He signed it and handed it back. "There you go."

"Thanks. Tough game against the Ice Storm, but I thought ya played great."

Quentin nodded acknowledgment, then looked around. Another landing bay, but full of larger, longer ships that had to be the underwater equivalent of cargo haulers and buses. It looked very industrial, like the part of a business that customers usually don't see.

"Q," John said. "Come on, this way."

Quentin followed John and Yassoud, then realized that the driver was walking along as well.

"Hey, John? Why is the driver coming with us?"

"He's more than a driver. If anyone messes with you, you let the driver handle it, right?"

Quentin flashed a glance over his shoulder. The guy couldn't be more than six feet tall. Fat. Out of shape.

"Seriously, Uncle Johnny? *That* dude?"

"He's not what he appears to be, Q. Don't worry about it, probably won't come into play."

They walked into a dark hallway. Quentin heard the growing roar of a crowd. Not the mass of a hundred-thousand-plus at a GFL game, but it was still a lot of voices packed tightly together. The sound echoed through the halls.

Quentin felt a poke in his chest. It was John's hand, pushing a lanyard with a plastic badge-chip. Quentin took it. His own holo-face smiled up from the badge, right under the words BACKSTAGE PASS, ALL ACCESS.

"John, what is this?"

They reached the end of the hall just as the crowd roared loudly enough to shake the walls. Quentin found himself in some kind of luxury box, like the ones that Stedmar sat in for the Raiders games back on Micovi. The box's entire far wall was clear, showing a view of a packed audience and a stage. On that stage, a band.

The first notes of a melodic guitar intro roared to the crowd. The crowd roared back. Quentin recognized those notes — the long, melodic guitar intro of *Combat Bats*.

"No ... way."

"Oh, yep," Yassoud said, or rather, shouted, just so he could be heard over the screaming throng of fans packed into the theater below. "A little present for you, Q, from John and me."

Quentin's heart hammered. His chest felt all cold and tingly. A blue-skinned woman wearing nearly nothing strode into the center of the stage, her hands raised as if in victory. Confidence and absolute control radiated from her like a miniature sun.

"High One," Quentin said. "That's Somalia Midori."

"It is," Yassoud said.

"This is Trench Warfare," Quentin said. "I'm at a Trench Warfare concert."

Quentin felt John's hand pushing into his chest again. He looked down, quickly, to see a mag-can of Miller Lager. Quentin grabbed it, his eyes snapping back to the stage, his hands opening the can as if on autopilot.

"Your favorite band," John said. "You look like a kid that just got a hover-bike for Giving Day, Q. How many concerts have you been to?"

Somalia was pointing one hand at the crowd, holding the other to her ear. The crowd's roar cranked up to an insane level.

"I've never been to one before," Quentin said. "Concerts are illegal in the Nation. How did you guys pull this off?"

"We called the theater," John said. "We told them you were a fan of the band, and next thing you know, we've got box seats and backstage passes."

"Because *I'm* a fan? Why did we get all that? The band doesn't know me."

John drained his Miller and pulled another. "Quentin, I know you haven't figured this out yet, but you're a Tier One quarterback. You are a *star*, my friend. You'll find people want to do all kinds of things for you."

Quentin wasn't about to complain, but what John said was hard to believe considering that the Krakens had lost the game.

The drummer unleashed a booming roll that shook the theater.

Somalia held the mic a half-inch from her face, cupping it in both hands. She screamed out her primitive *four three two one!* and the band ripped into the first verse.

Quentin felt an elbow hit his shoulder.

"Q," John said, "I think you're missing something."

"Which is?"

"You have a backstage pass. After the show, guess who you get to meet?"

The words seemed to knock all other thoughts out of his brain. "I get to meet ... *her?*"

John laughed, but Quentin could barely hear it as the band hit the first chorus and the crowd went wild. Trench Warfare ran around the stage, attacking their song with the intensity of a blitzing linebacker. Quentin tried to look at all the band members, take it all in, but in truth it was almost impossible to take his eyes off of Somalia Midori.

**QUENTIN HAD A SET** of very familiar, very comfortable emotions. Among them were cold-calculating anger, all-out rage and wide-eyed wonder. One emotion he wasn't used to, however, was feeling *nervous.*

He and John and Yassoud waited in a room filled with beat-up furniture and semi-functional holotanks. Graffiti covered the walls. The place smelled of stale beer. Around twenty sentients were in the room, all wearing backstage passes hanging from lanyards. Two of the sentients had big feet and long toes. Quentin also noticed that their skin looked *thick* and that they had five parallel slits on either side of their necks. He tried not to stare.

The room doors opened. Trench Warfare's five members rolled in, sweaty and exhausted but full of satisfied joy. They looked like Quentin felt after winning an important game.

In the middle of them, *her.* Somalia Midori. She locked eyes with him and strode over. What little clothing she wore clung wetly to her sweat-shined blue skin. The purple mohawk was also heavy with moisture, yet still looked thick and inviting. It hung down the left side of her face, cascading over her shoulder. The shaven right side of her head gleamed under the room's lights.

She stopped only a few inches away, their chests almost touching.

*Tall*, Quentin thought, realizing that Somalia had to be six and a half feet tall. Just six inches shorter than he was.

"I hear you're my biggest fan," she said. "That true?"

"Uh ... well, I don't know."

"He's a *huge* fan," John said. He stood at Quentin's right shoulder, all smiles and wild-eyed giddiness.

"I don't know," Somalia said, not taking her eyes off of Quentin's. "I got infinites of crazy-massive fans, we clear? What's so special about Mister Tall Quarterback here?"

Quentin shook his head as if he were apologizing, and he didn't know why. "Oh, nothing, nothing special. I ... I've just been listening for awhile."

John leaned in, looking from Somalia to Quentin and back again. "Quentin here is from the Purist Nation," John said. "Ask him what would have happened if he'd been caught with your music."

Quentin's sensation of embarrassment deepened. He didn't know why, but he hadn't wanted this woman to know where he was from.

John's statement didn't seem to bother her. Instead, it made a small smile creep across her perfect, blue lips. She still hadn't broken eye contact with Quentin, not even for a second.

"So?" she said. "What would have happened?"

"Oh, it's no big deal, I—"

She put her hand on his chest. "No, seriously. Enough with the shy and all. What would have happened?"

Quentin glared at John, who simply shrugged. THE TRUTH WILL SET YOU FREE scrolled across his face tat.

Quentin turned back to face Somalia. "Depends on how many songs. Up to five gets you a public whipping. Five to ten, a whipping and a month in jail. More then ten banned songs is considered an act of sacrilege."

Her smile faded. "Sacrilege? What happens then?"

"Depends on the judge."

"And if the judge is grumpy?"

"Public hanging," Quentin said. "Rare, but it does happen."

"Seriously?"

He nodded.

She stared at him, disbelieving. "We have seventy-two recorded songs. How many of those did you have?"

"Seventy-two. Plus all the live recordings I could find, so ... probably a hundred."

She blinked rapidly, and her mouth opened a little. "You're telling me that if you'd been caught with our music, you could have been *executed* for it?"

Quentin nodded.

An appreciative grin slowly broke across her face. She extended her hand. "I guess you are a crazy-massive supernova fan, then. I'm Somalia."

Quentin shook her hand, feeling the wetness of her sweat, the warmth of her skin, the strength of her fingers. This was a real handshake, not the polite grasp of a socialite.

"I'm Quentin," he said. "Quentin Barnes."

"You're cute," she said. "I think you and I should get a drink."

Quentin's breath froze in his throat. Was Somalia Midori asking *him* out for a drink?

"I ... uh ... I'd love t—"

"He'd *love* to, but he can't," John said. "Our ship leaves tonight. In fact, we have to get going right now or we're in trouble."

Somalia frowned at John. "Well, aren't you just a good boy obeying the boss. Come on, what's the worst they can do to you?"

John's smile faded. "You really don't want to know. Q? Say your good-byes."

"John, no way! We can't leave now, you—"

"Promised I would have you back in time, that's what I did," he said. "My neck is on the line if we don't leave now. Are you going to make me have to face Hokor's wrath?"

Quentin looked at John, then at Somalia.

She had such a sexy smile. Her deep-blue eyes blazed with confidence and mischief. "Do you really have to go?" she said. "Just one drink?"

Quentin wanted to say yes, but John was right. If they didn't make curfew, they'd make the entire team wait.

"Sorry," Quentin said. "Maybe … maybe some other time?"

Her smiled widened. More of a sneer, really, a sneer that made his insides melt.

"I hope so," Somalia said. "Super-star fan of fans, here's to our paths crossing again."

John and Yassoud pulled Quentin away. He stumbled, still looking back at Somalia, who watched his every move with the eager intensity of a cat watching a wounded mouse.

They reached the hall and moved quickly toward the landing bay.

Yassoud slapped Quentin on the back. "Have fun?"

"High One, yes," Quentin said. "Thanks, guys, that was amazing."

"Don't mention it," John said. "The girls always dig the quarterbacks. Ain't that right, 'Soud?"

Yassoud nodded. "The ladies love the long ball."

"*Lady?*" John said as they entered the docking bay. "I'm not sure I'd call Somalia Midori a *lady*. What do you think, Quentin, you ever meet a *lady* like her?"

Quentin shook his head, thinking of Somalia's confidence, her aura of aggression. "We don't have women like that back in the Nation."

The fat driver held the door for them. Minutes later, they were once again soaring through the waters of Isis, headed for the shuttle that would take them up to the *Touchback*.

The night had been simply unbelievable, but rocking out was just a temporary escape. The Krakens were 0-and-1. So were the Themala Dreadnaughts. One week from now, one team would still be winless.

Quentin would make sure that team was *not* the Ionath Krakens.

## GFL WEEK ONE ROUNDUP
(Courtesy of Galaxy Sports Network)

| | | | |
|---|---|---|---|
| Armada | 13 | **Wolfpack** | 28 |
| **Brigands** | 42 | Spider-Bears | 21 |
| Cloud Killers | 15 | **Pirates** | 24 |
| **War Dogs** | 24 | Criminals | 13 |
| **Ice Storm** | 51 | Krakens | 7 |
| Jacks | 20 | **Planets** | 21 |
| **Astronauts** | 56 | Atom Smashers | 3 |
| **Intrigue** | 21 | Water Bugs | 14 |
| **Warlords** | 37 | Scarlet Fliers | 20 |
| Dreadnaughts | 10 | **Hullwalkers** | 35 |
| Vanguard | 0 | **Juggernauts** | 21 |

The GFL's 25th Anniversary season is under way, and surprises abounded in Week One.

The Mars Planets registered a shocker, traveling to Jupiter and delivering a 21-20 upset against the defending champion Jacks. The New Rodina Astronauts made a loud announcement of their intentions this season with a 56-3 blowout win over the Jang Atom Smashers.

Both of the newly promoted teams dropped their Tier One debuts. The Ionath Krakens were manhandled by the Isis Ice Storm, 51-7, while the Chillich Spider-Bears suffered a 42-21 loss at the hands of the Bord Brigands.

### Deaths

**North Branch,** special teams player for the Isis Ice Storm, died on a clean hit from Ionath Krakens rookie Rebecca Montagne.

## Offensive Player of the Week

New Rodina quarterback **Rick Renaud**, who threw five touchdowns in a 25-for-32, 293-yard performance.

## Defensive Player of the Week

Mars cornerback **Matsumoto**, who registered two picks on Jacks QB Shriaz Zia. Matsumoto returned the second pick 62 yards for the winning touchdown.

**6**

# WEEK TWO:
# THEMALA DREADNOUGHTS at
# IONATH KRAKENS

## PLANET DIVISION

1-0  Hittoni Hullwalkers
1-0  Isis Ice Storm
1-0  Lu Juggernauts
1-0  Mars Planets
1-0  To Pirates
1-0  Wabash Wolfpack
0-1  Alimum Armada
0-1  Coranadillana Cloud Killers
0-1  Yall Criminals
0-1  Themala Dreadnaughts
0-1  Ionath Krakens

## SOLAR DIVISION

1-0  New Rodina Astronauts
1-0  Bord Brigands
1-0  D'Kow War Dogs
1-0  Sala Intrigue
1-0  Shorah Warlords
0-1  Jang Atom Smashers
0-1  Neptune Scarlet Fliers
0-1  Jupiter Jacks
0-1  Chillich Spider-Bears
0-1  Vik Vanguard
0-1  Bartel Water Bugs

## From "The GFL for Dummies"
### by Robert Otto
## English Language & Imperial Measurement System

Much debate has been made regarding the use of the Human-oriented language "English" as the official language of the GFL. Even more debate has focused on the use of an archaic, arbitrary, Earth measurement system known as "Imperial." To understand the reasons for these rules, one must look at two factors: the origin of football and the Creterakian Empire's needs.

### The Name of the Game

The term "football" applies to several Earth-invented sports. The first game to use that name is now commonly known as "soccer." Soccer is played with a round, inflated ball. In this game, ten of the eleven players on each side are not allowed to use their hands. The primary controlling appendage is the foot, hence the original name *foot*-ball. This game's origins are unclear but date back some two millennia to possibly as early as 400 B.C. on the Earth historical timeline (ErT).

Over the centuries, many variations of the game arose, all of which allowed the use of the hands. These sports included Gaelic Football, Australian Rules Football, Rugby League, Rugby Union and American Football, or Gridiron. The term "football" persists for many of these variants, although the Creterakian Empire Bureau of Species Interaction (EBSI) has dictated that these sports be officially referred to as the following:

**Soccer/Football:** *Football*
**Gaelic Football:** *Gaelic*
**Australian Rules Football:** *Footy*
**Rugby League:** *Leagueball*
**Rugby Union:** *Unionball*
**American Football:** *Gridiron*

The adoption of these names has been spotty, at best. The fact that the primary Gridiron league is known as the Galactic *Football* League is no small source of confusion.

### History of Gridiron

Gridiron, also known as "American football," is an off-shoot of the game rugby. Variations of Gridiron were active in the late 1800s ErT, but the current version is primarily attributed to Walter Camp, known as the "Father of American Football." Among the changes Camp initiated were the forward pass (where players are allowed to throw the ball downfield to a teammate), the line of scrimmage, the addition of a helmet and other protective equipment, the concepts of "down" and "distance" and changing the players from fifteen to a side to eleven. While both forms of rugby involve mostly nonstop action, Gridiron comes to a complete stop after every play. Teams stop, plan their next play, line up and run the play. This constant stopping is one of the main things that differentiate Gridiron from the other football variants.

Camp began these rules changes in 1878. Therefore, League of Planets historians have officially declared 1878 as the first year of modern Gridiron. At the time, the game was played with the Imperial Measurement System unit known as a "yard." As Earth cultures progressed and most governments switched to the metric system, practitioners of Gridiron steadfastly refused to change from "yards" to "meters."

The Creterakians finished their conquest of the galaxy in 2642. At that time, Gridiron had been played for over 750 years with "yards" being the official unit of measurement.

When League of Planets social scientist Demarkus Johnson created his plan for the Galactic Football League in 2658, he recommended the game be used with existing rules. Hence, "yard" continues to be accepted as the primary unit of Gridiron measurement.

### English-Only

Johnson also suggested creating a new language for football, with unique terms for all aspects of the game using sounds that could be pronounced by all races. Creterakian officials refused this suggestion, however. The ability to quickly master any vocal language is innate for Creterakians, and as such, they have difficulty comprehending that other species can't do the same.

The Empire implemented the GFL to facilitate inter-species cooperation and understanding. They wanted a single language for the game but did not want to spend time creating a *new* language. The Creterakians understood and spoke English, the game of American Football used English, and that was that. Because the Empire and the EBSI control the GFL, all official communication related to the game or its coverage is done in English. Language-specific coverage is allowed on a system-by-system basis, but the prevalence of English-language usage by players, coaches, owners and GFL officials means that the vast majority of media personnel must also speak English. This emphasis, combined with the galaxy's ravenous appetite for all things GFL, means that English is the fastest-growing language in the known universe. Sklorno Prima, of course, is the galaxy's most common tongue, but that will soon change — it is estimated that ninety percent of Sklorno are learning English so that they can better understand the game of Gridiron.

**QUENTIN REARED BACK** a big foot and kicked his locker, denting the metal-grate frame. "Fined? I've been *fined*?"

Messal the Efficient trembled. His eye flooded an opaque, neon pink.

"For *what*? Who fined me?"

"Commissioner Froese," Messal said. "He fined you for missing the post-game press conference after the Isis Ice Storm game."

"He can fine me for *that*?"

"Yes, Elder Barnes. You were fined thirty thousand credits, Creterakian."

Creterakian. What was the exchange rate for that in Quyth money? "Uh, is thirty thousand a lot?"

"*A lot* is a relative term, Elder Barnes."

"Is it a lot for *me*?"

Messal trembled. He clearly didn't want to answer the question.

"Come on," Quentin said. "Out with it."

"This year, you make one point two million credits, Creterakian, this year," Messal said. "After Creterakian income taxes, Quyth Concordia income taxes, Ionath City income taxes and GFL union dues, you make 720,000 credits."

"But ... but that's not fair," Quentin said. "The taxes are like forty percent!"

Messal nodded.

"So, I work my ass off, and the government takes *forty percent* of what I make?"

Messal nodded again. His cornea glowed a solid pink. Quentin knew he was terrifying the poor Quyth Worker, but he couldn't stop. Messal, unfortunately, was the only available target for Quentin's temper.

"So let me get this straight," Quentin said. "If I go by the Earth calendar year, I work from January to *June* before I make a penny for myself? Five months of working to give the money to other people?"

"It could be worse," Messal said. "You could own a home and pay property taxes. Mister Tweedy pays over half his income in taxes."

"Remind me to never own a home," Quentin said. "So ... I still don't get it. How much do I *actually* make *per game*?"

"There are twelve games in the season, Elder Barnes. You earn sixty thousand credits per game, after taxes."

Quentin stared at the much smaller Quyth Worker, trying hard to remember that Messal hadn't made the fine, trying to remember that ripping Messal's pedipalp arms off of his skull would neither solve anything nor punish the guilty parties.

"And I was fined *thirty thousand*," Quentin said. "So I just basically got fined for an entire *half* of a football game, a half where my life is at risk on every snap?"

"Yes, Elder Barnes."

"For not going to a press conference?"

"Yes, Elder Barnes."

"Well, you can tell them I'm not going to pay the fine."

Messal's trembling grew so bad the Worker dropped down to all fours, his middle arms keeping him stable. Quentin sighed. Messal was just the messenger.

"Messal, this isn't your fault. You tried to get me to go, so just tell them I won't pay and that's that."

"The money is already docked from your account," Messal said. "Your GFL contract stipulates that the league has a direct connection to your finances in order to receive payment for fines."

They already had his money. Quentin wondered what other things were in his contract that he didn't know about. He made a mental note that he should actually *read it* sometime soon.

He'd lost his pay for half of a game. He'd never really given his salary much thought, but that was changing. At one point, just getting paid to play football seemed like the greatest blessing ever. Now? Now he realized that sentients who barely set foot on the field, sentients who were never in danger, made more than he did. At least two governments and a league that took itself *way* too seriously were helping themselves to his money. And if he suffered major collision? It wouldn't be the league or the governments getting carted off the field on a med-sled, it wouldn't be the league or the governments with a prosthetic leg, and it wouldn't be the league or the governments lying in a casket being lowered into the ground.

Quentin had chosen a career where each minute of work might be his last. When he thought of it that way, he knew he'd been wrong — money *did* matter.

Just one more thing to worry about. He'd deal with it later. Money mattered, but *not* if the Krakens kept losing.

Quentin picked up his helmet and walked out of the locker room.

**QUENTIN'S CLEATS CLACKED** against the concrete floor of Ionath Stadium's tunnel. Clacked and *echoed*. There would be no echo here on Sunday, not with 185,000 sentients packed into the stands.

Aside from the echoing clack, all he heard was the distant sound of his team out on the field, warming up for practice.

He walked out of the tunnel, blinking against the blazing sunlight that poured through the city dome. That sunlight lit up a hundred and eighty thousand empty seats, seats that reached up on all sides, surrounding the field. Usually the stadium was completely empty for practice, but now he saw a few sentients moving in the stands. Maybe twenty, spaced throughout the massive temple dedicated to the glory of football. He held a hand to his forehead, shielding his eyes against the sun. Squinting, he could just make out a Ki halfway up the first deck. A cop. A cop with a gun.

The *Touchback* had come back to Ionath City at night. Atmospheric fighters had escorted the shuttle down to the roof of the Krakens building. Kotop the Observer had inspected the shuttle, as usual, but this time accompanying him had been a squad of Quyth Warriors dressed in full military armor. The city, the national government, Gredok the Splithead — perhaps all three — weren't taking any chances that terrorists would take another shot at the newly promoted Tier One franchise.

The team was already gathered at the 50-yard line, right on top of the six-armed Krakens logo painted onto the field. Quentin slowed, then stopped at the twenty-five. He did another slow 360, drinking in the view. If you didn't stop and look with your *eyes* once in a while — not with a brain that already stored hundreds of memories of this place — you could lose sight of the fact that Ionath City Stadium was simply amazing. Stands reached up and out, stretching toward the horizon hidden somewhere beyond. Seats made for all the races, all seats blazing orange except for those in black that spelled out a hundred-yard-long IONATH on the home side and a hundred-yard-long KRAKENS on the visitors side.

Two decks sandwiched an oblong ring of clear crysteel, windows that led into hundreds of luxury boxes. Twenty-two giant pillars rose up from the top decks, done in a style that Quentin had been told was called "Roman." The pillars were made from some kind of marble, apparently imported all the way from Earth. Each pillar rose up forty feet, and each supported a colorful, vertical banner hanging down its length. Last season, those pillars had held the banners of other teams in the Quyth Irradiated Conference. There were only ten teams in the Irradiated. The other twelve columns had stood blank. Quentin had never given the blank columns a second thought. Now, however, each gleaming pillar held a colorful banner — one for each of the twenty-two Tier One teams. This stadium had been *built* with the expectation that the Krakens would be a permanent part of the galactic football elite.

Quentin was here, here at *this* moment, because he was leading this franchise in its first Tier One appearance in six years. He knelt and rubbed his hands over the field's blue surface, let his fingertips drag through the soft coolness of the Iomatt plants. He plucked a few of the circular leaves. Each circle was smaller than his pinkie nail, a slightly translucent blue. He held one up to the sky, used it to block out the sun. Light streamed through the thin plant, silhouetting its tiny veins like dark blue tentacles. Quentin held the plant to his nose, breathed deep — it smelled like cinnamon.

It also smelled like home.

He brushed his fingertips together, letting the leaves fall back to the surface. He stood, put on his helmet and jogged to the center of the field to join his teammates for their final practice before their first home game of the season.

**THE GRAV-CAB STOPPED** in front of an apartment building at Sixth Ring and Second Radius. Choto the Bright got out first, looked up and down the street, then waved Quentin out.

"It looks safe," Choto said. He dressed as he normally did, bulky gray pants, no shirt, always preferring to show off his scars, chitin welds, enamels and engravings. "You should be fine here. John is smart enough to live in a place with security."

A Ki guard stood on either side of the big double doors that led inside. The Ki wore neat blue uniforms with matching blue helmets that hid their eyes and protected their heads. They both stood stone-still, a clear deterrent to anyone who might plan bad things. Things like attacking the members of the Ionath Krakens who lived inside the building.

"Thanks, Choto," Quentin said.

"I'll just stay in the lobby and read." Choto reached into a side pocket of his pants and pulled out a small rectangular object. Quentin leaned down a bit to see the gold lettering embossed into the green leather cover. The title said HOT MIDNIGHT.

"What is that? Is that an actual *book*? Like made with dead plants?"

"Yes, it is," Choto said. "I have been trying to learn more about Human culture, so I am reading the texts of the ancients. The only way to properly read them is as the ancients did, on dead plants. Have you ever heard of this author, Gunther Jones?"

Quentin shook his head.

"Very influential," Choto said. "Extremely misunderstood for his time. Kind of like William Shakespeare."

"Who?"

"Never mind," Choto said. "You go on inside, I'll be in the lobby. And Quentin, *please* don't think of leaving without me. If I lose you, Gredok will have my shell."

"I won't," Quentin said, marveling at how Gredok had controlled the situation. Quentin might risk Gredok's anger, but if his teammate Choto would suffer the consequences? Then no matter how much it bothered Quentin to have a keeper, he wasn't going to slip away. Gredok knew that.

Quentin walked to the doors, then hesitated. Did he need to show his identification or something? As if answering his thoughts, the double doors opened and a Quyth Worker scurried out.

"Elder Barnes?"

Why did every damn Worker insist on calling him *Elder*? "Call me Quentin, please."

"Of course, Elder Quentin," the Worker said. "Please, come inside. I am Pizat the Servitous."

"Servitous? Really? Is that even a word?"

"If you say it is, it is," Pizat said. "If you say it is not, it is not. Please, come inside."

Quentin did. As he passed through the doors, he saw they were made of two-inch-thick crysteel. That kind of armor might be found on a space fighter.

The lobby's opulence stopped Quentin in his tracks. Everything looked like it belonged on a movie set, or in some documentary about how the rich and famous lived. Tall plants arced gracefully, statues exuded class, and diamond trim lined the wooden wall panels. A step up from his small apartment in the Krakens building, that was for sure.

"This is some place," Quentin said. "How long has John lived here?"

"Mister Tweedy has lived here for five years," Pizat said. "We had the privilege of selling him his suite shortly after he signed with the Krakens. Obviously, our building caters to Humans. Several Krakens players live here, including Don Pine."

Pine lived here? Quentin realized that Pine had never invited him into his home, as John had done. Was there a reason for that? Maybe Pine didn't want to be caught slumming with a hayseed hick like Quentin. No, that wasn't fair — Don had to have a reason for not showing hospitality. Didn't he?

"Here is the elevator, Elder Quentin Barnes," Pizat said. "Mister Tweedy is on the fifteenth floor, suite 15-B. If you need anything else, don't hesitate to hit any comm button and simply ask. The building staff will be happy to assist you."

Quentin took the elevator up to the fifteenth floor. He didn't have to look for suite 15-B because wild-eyed John Tweedy was waiting for him outside the elevator.

"Q! Come on in, brother. I just have to finish this call. Come with me."

He followed John down the short hall and through the door to suite 15-B. Inside, football memorabilia seemed to cover every wall and rest on every flat surface, from the entry way into the living room. Pictures and holoframes of John in various uniforms from his career, mostly with the Krakens, but also others: a team with bright blue jerseys and silver helmets decorated with a blue lion on the side; a team with black jerseys and yellow numbers, black helmets with a single yellow stripe down the middle; and a team with green and gold uniforms. John looked oldest in the Krakens pictures and progressively younger through the others.

John picked up a remote control and hit a button. The room's central holotank flared to life, showing a tiny Human woman wearing a jersey that was half Krakens orange with black numbers and half black with metalflake-red numbers — the jersey of the Orbiting Death. The woman's shoulders were practically in her ears. She looked somewhat hunched over, making her even smaller than she already was. A big smile broke across her face.

"Well!" she said. "Jonathan, is this your little friend Quentin?"

"That's him, Ma," John said. "Quentin, say hello to Ma Tweedy."

Families. Quentin never felt comfortable around families. "Hello, Missus Tweedy."

"Call me Ma," she said. "I've been watching you this season, Quentin. You're not playing too bad, but you gotta start sliding."

John leaned and whispered in Quentin's ear: "Ma knows a *lot* about football."

"Jonathan! No whispering!"

"Sorry, Ma."

"So," Ma Tweedy continued, "Quentin, you gonna start sliding? I mean, if you like getting hit in the mouth, I can send some of my friends from the shipyard to smack you in the face with lead pipes, if you're into that kind of thing."

John leaned in again. "Ma does admin at a shipyard on Orbital Station One."

"*Jonathan!* Whispering!"

"Sorry, Ma."

"So, Quentin," she said. "How about it? You going to start taking care of yourself and stop taking hits?"

"Uh ... yes."

"Yes, what?"

"Uh ... yes, ma'am?"

"Such a polite boy," she said. "And ... Jonathan, did you take your brother off of hold?"

"Oh, sorry," John said. "I forgot."

"Don't lie to your mother, Son. Put him on.'

John hit another button on the remote. Ma Tweedy's image narrowed and slid to the side as a second image appeared. Quentin instantly recognized the big face — John's brother, Ju.

"Dillhole," Ju said. "Did you leave me on hold?"

"*You're* the dillhole," John said.

"Julius! Jonathan! *Language*."

"Sorry, Ma," the two men said in unison.

"Ma," Ju said. "Don't go using my full name in front of other people, okay?"

"Shut it," Ma Tweedy said. "You and your fancy nicknames. It says Julius on your birth certificate and that's what I'll call you. Quentin, John tells me you have a fancy new yacht?"

"Yes ,ma'am."

"And you have the Wolfpack in Week Five?"

"Yes, ma'am, we're gonna win that."

"There's a difference between dreams and delusions, Quentin. You ain't beating them unless you get some pass blocking. But that doesn't matter — you have three days off in your bye-week after you play the Wolfpack?"

"Uh ... yes, ma'am."

"Good," she said. "John tells me you got no family in Ionath City, so you put my son in your fancy yacht and you come visit me at Orbital Station One. Don't bother saying no because I'm already planning to make my tuna noodle casserole."

"*Sweet*," John and Ju said in unison.

"Uh, Missus Tweedy I—"

"Can't wait to see you in person," she said. "Any friend of Jonathan's is welcome in my home any time."

"Ma," John said. "I gotta get going. I love you!"

"Love you too, Son. I'll let you boys go now, I know you have all kinds of fancy things to do while your mother sits here alone in her apartment. But I don't mind. And Julius! You stop seeing that no-good gangster girl! You're going to get yourself shot and break your poor mother's heart!"

"Ma!" Ju said. "Do you mind not airing the family laundry in front of strangers?"

"Quentin *is* family. Julius, you just keep it in your pants lest someone cut it off. Good-bye, boys! Remember that Mommy loves you!"

Her face blinked out. Ju's face expanded to fill up the holotank.

"Ha-ha," John said. "You got yelled at."

"You're an idiot," Ju said. "Quentin, I guess I'll be seeing you after Week Five."

"Okay," Quentin said, not having any idea of what else he could say.

"Screw you, John," Ju said, then the holotank blinked out.

John started laughing.

"You jerk," Quentin said. "You timed that call, didn't you?"

WHO, ME? scrolled across John's face. "Hey, you're the one with the sweet ride. OS1 is just a short punch away, not even half a day. Once you've had my mom's tuna noodle casserole, you'll thank me."

"John, I'm not going."

"Gotta go," John said. "Ma said you're going, so you're going. Don't argue with Ma, Quentin. Besides, if I don't get you out of here, you'll spend your three days off studying, right? So you're coming with."

Quentin closed his eyes and sighed. "Okay, fine. I'll take you."

"*Sweet!*" John said.

Quentin walked to a frame on the wall that held a blue jersey with silver numbers. "Thomas 3 Lions? You played for them?"

Tweedy pounded his chest three times. "Glory be to Thomas 3!"

"Right," Quentin said, now remembering that John hailed from Thomas 3 and was exceedingly proud of his home planet. "I don't recognize the other teams."

"The green and gold is from Fionas University, Tier Four."

"University? You took classes in college?"

"Wouldn't exactly say I took classes," John said. "But I did play for the team. Two years, then I got drafted by the black and yellow team, the Pittsburgh Steelers."

"No *way*," Quentin said. "The Steelers? They've been around, like, for centuries."

"Over seven hundred years," John said. "Old NFL team, like the Lions were, but the Steelers stayed on Earth when most of the other NFL teams moved to new planets."

"Cool," Quentin said, impressed that his friend John was so steeped in tradition. "Hey, what is a steeler, anyway?"

"It's people who steal stuff."

"Really? I don't think it's spelled the same."

John crossed his arms and gave Quentin that head-shaking, *you're not that bright* look.

"Well, Quentin, maybe if they're dumb enough to steal, they're dumb enough to not spell so right."

Quentin just nodded, making a mental note to ask his room computer about the name later that night. "Is Pittsburgh a cool city?"

John laughed. "There isn't a cool city left on Earth, Quentin. Everything is just so ... so *old*. Run-down. The Steelers were Tier Three, but it was still really fun to get paid to play football. We won a Super Bowl before I got picked up by the Lions and moved into Tier Two, right on my home planet."

"That must have been cool."

John nodded and smiled. BIG MAN ON CAMPUS = JOHN TWEEDY played across his forehead. "It was awesome. I went from a small town to Fionas U, then the Steelers, and then I came home as a T2 player for the biggest team on Thomas 3."

Quentin wondered what it might be like to go back and play for the Purist Nation's only upper-tier team, the Buddha City Elite of the Planetary Union Conference in Tier 2. Would he be welcomed as a hero or as a traitor to the religion? Well, hopefully, he'd never have to find out. The only way he was going back to the Purist Nation was if the Elite made it into Tier One and the Krakens had an away game against them.

"Come on," John said. "Let me show you around the place." The apartment wasn't some sprawling mansion, but in the landlocked circle of Ionath City, the amount of space John did have had to carry a high price tag. Everything in the three-bedroom place looked new. New and expensive.

In one room, John had an old-fashioned workout equipment. Racks of circular, black, metal plates, different sizes marking different weights. Quentin hadn't seen weights like that since he'd left Micovi. He saw a bench press with a gleaming, chromed bar, a squat rack, a curl bench and other workout machines.

"Nice," he said. "The real thing, huh?"

John nodded. "One of the first things I bought with football money. Antique set, something like four hundred years old. With all the biometric workout machines we get from Hokor, you really can't find stuff like this anymore."

"You can where I come from," Quentin said. "Back home, sets like you've got here *are* state of the art."

"You guys *have* discovered fire, right?"

Quentin rolled his eyes and looked around the room. Only then did he realize that the walls, ceiling and even the floor were action shots of John's brother, Ju, dressed in the black uniform of the Orbiting Death.

"Hey, John? Miss your brother much?"

"Whatever," John said. "It's motivation, so if we play each other again, I can beat his ass."

Quentin said nothing, remembering how "The Mad Ju" had ripped the Krakens for 179 yards and four touchdowns. The Krakens had won 35-31, but any ass-kicking by the Tweedy family had come from Ju.

"Why don't you guys get along?"

"Because Ju's a selfish idiot. He only thinks about himself, doesn't think about what his actions do to others. You know the Orbiting Death owner?"

"Um ... Sikka the Death, right?"

"Yeah, a *nasty* gangster, man. Real nasty. He and Ju are good buddies. Wanna know how dumb Ju is?"

Quentin nodded.

"One of Sikka's lieutenants is Anna Villani. Her girlfriend is Grace McDermot. Ju is seeing Grace on the side."

"Seeing? You mean, like *dating?*"

"I wouldn't exactly call it *dating*," John said. "Ju thinks no one knows that, and even if they did, nobody will touch him because he's buddy-buddy with Sikka the Death and because he's the biggest star on Orbital Station One."

"So, your brother is seeing the girlfriend of a powerful gangster in the organization that owns his team?"

John nodded. "Yep."

"Sounds stupid."

"*Beyond* stupid," John said. "You play with fire, you're going to get the horns, Quentin. Remember I said that."

"How could I forget?"

John stared at one of Ju's pictures. In the picture, Ju had his big head and wide shoulders lowered, blue eyes peeking out from just under the flat-black helmet. It was an excellent shot, capturing what it must feel like to be a defensive back stepping up to tackle a walking tank like Ju.

"Someday," John said, "my little brother is going to get in trouble he can't get out of, and you know what? His big brother John won't be coming to bail him out this time."

"This time?" Quentin said. "There have been times before?"

"Ju and trouble go together like peas in a glove. But that doesn't matter. He's on his own. Let's get out of here, I can't even stand his stupid face."

John finished the tour in the entertainment room, where a large holotank showed the hovering logo of a video game: MADDEN 2684.

"John, no *way!* The new version of Madden? That doesn't come out for another *week*, how did you get it?"

"Because people love Uncle Johnny. And guess who they have as quarterback for the Ionath Krakens?"

"No ... *way.*" Quentin sat in one of the room's two big recliners. He slipped on the fingertip controllers that were sitting on the armrest. John did the same in the other chair. Within seconds, both players selected teams. Quentin chose the Ionath Krakens, of course — and so did John.

"Krakens versus Krakens?" Quentin said. "You don't want another team?"

"If they have you as the quarterback, who do you think they have as the inside linebacker?"

Quentin smiled and nodded. "Ah, I see, and in the video game, there's—"

"No red jersey," John said, finishing Quentin's sentence. "Prepare to be knocked into the Stone Age, backwater."

"Bring it, Uncle Johnny." Moments later, Quentin stared into the holotank at something he'd never dared believe he might actually see — a lifelike representation of himself. He'd played the various versions of Madden more times than he remembered, played as all the great quarterbacks — Zimmer, Adrojnik, even Don Pine, although he'd never tell Pine that. And now he was playing *himself*. It was a surreal experience.

Quentin selected a play and watched his team line up. So realistic, just like watching a game on the holo. His offense wore orange visitor jerseys. John's defense wore the home black. Quentin saw the video-game version of John Tweedy creep up behind the noseguard, just a little. Quentin's fingers tapped open air, calling up an audible. He twitched his left thumb, snapping the ball. Sure enough, John's holo-linebacker roared through the line on a blitz. Quentin's holo-quarterback calmly threw to the holo-tightend — in this case, Rick Warburg — who caught the ball right where John's holo-linebacker would have been.

"Jerk," John said. "You see everything. I should know better than to blitz against you."

"Yeah, you should. John, I have to say, your apartment is awesome."

"Thanks."

"What's a place like this go for, if I can ask?"

"Sure," John said. "Cost me seven million."

Quentin paused the game. "*Seven* million? How can you afford that?"

"That's a season's pay," John said. "Not that weird."

"You make *seven million* in one season?"

"Yeah," John said. "Why, how much you making?"

"One-point-two," Quentin said quietly. "I thought it was a lot."

"Q, one-point-two million is league minimum."

"League … minimum? You mean, like as in … *minimum*?"

John nodded. "Yeah, brother, sorry to be the one to tell you. What does your agent say?"

"I don't have one."

"Hoooo," John said. "Well, that explains a lot."

"Minimum. Is that what Yitzhak makes?"

"Oh, no way," John said. "Yitzhak makes more than that for sure. Becca the Wrecka probably makes league minimum, though."

"She makes what I make," Quentin said absently.

"Should I ask her out?"

"What?"

"Like on a date," John said. "Is that weird? To date someone on your own team?"

"Yeah," Quentin said quickly. "It's weird, don't do it." Quentin sat back in the chair again. Becca made as much as he did? A backup fullback? And why did he care if John dated her? What business was that of his? And league *minimum*? One-point-two million had seemed like a fortune, and it *was* a fortune, but if other people were making so much more …

It was all too much, too overwhelming. He didn't want to think about anything but football. "Let's just play the game, Uncle Johnny. I'm done talking for a little while."

John shrugged, then unpaused the game. They continued with the Krakens versus the Krakens until the game finished (Quentin won 28-10), then Quentin let Choto take him home. The entire way there, he thought about a conversation he needed to have with Gredok the Splithead.

A conversation about money.

It would wait until season's end, but it *would* happen.

**QUENTIN WALKED DOWN THE TUNNEL** toward Ionath Stadium's field. In Earth Standard Time, the system that everyone used to track all things football-related, it was Saturday. Today they'd have a walk-through practice — get a decent workout, but not push too hard, and no hitting. Tomorrow the Themala Dreadnaughts would come calling. The Krakens had to be rested and ready.

He walked past a Human cop, one of the dozens guarding Ionath Stadium.

"Hey, Mister Barnes," the guard said. "Hey, do you mind signing this for me?"

The guy looked left and right, then held out a messageboard. It seemed a little suspicious, but then again, if the guy had already got past Gredok's guards and wanted Quentin dead, Quentin would be dead. Quentin took the messageboard, signed it, and handed it back.

"There you go."

"Thanks, Mister Barnes!"

Quentin nodded at him, then started to walk out of the tunnel.

"Hold it, Quentin. I've got some questions for you."

Quentin stopped. Same guy, but his voice sounded different ... familiar. Quentin turned and peered at the smaller man's face. The eyebrows were different, and he had a mustache, but the shape of that face ...

"*Frederico?*"

"Frederico Esteban Giuseppe Gonzaga," he said. "And you actually figured out it was me? You should be a punch-drive scientist, you know that?"

"Why did you have me sign that messageboard?"

"Just messing with you," he said. "And testing my disguise skills."

The words *disguise* and *messageboard* clicked together in Quentin's thoughts, sparking a memory.

"You were our driver on Isis."

"Wow, can't put one past you," Frederico said. "Oh, wait, I guess I did."

"What were you doing there?"

"Sometimes John hires me to be his bodyguard."

"*John Tweedy* hires *you* to be his *bodyguard?*"

"Don't look so shocked, Quentin. There's more to conflict situations than being big and fast. I can fly just about any ship known to man, and some that aren't. Considering that you seem to be a magnet for trouble, you might keep my skills in mind."

John was the most dangerous sentient Quentin had met. If he hired Frederico as a bodyguard, what did that say about Frederico's abilities?

"How do you know how to fly ships?"

"I used to be a navigator in the navy."

"Which navy?"

"None of your business," Frederico said. "Look, I need to talk to you."

"So why didn't you schedule it? Messal would have set it up, you don't need this silly disguise."

"Oh, but I do," Frederico said. "Let's just say that Gredok is not my biggest fan."

"Look, Fred, I have to get out there for practice."

"Not until you tell me about your involvement with the Zoroastrian Guild."

"The who?"

"You heard me."

Quentin shrugged. "I don't know what you're talking about."

"You're lying," Frederico said. "A splinter cell was behind the parade bombing."

"A cell of what?"

"What are you, deaf? The Zoroastrian Guild."

Quentin felt his temper rising. He'd have to watch his control — if he lost it and hit a normal size man like Frederico, a single punch could do major damage.

"Look," Quentin said. "I don't know anything about this Zoro Guild, and ... hey, wait a minute, don't *you* work for *me?*"

"Not if you're involved with the ZG," he said. "I'm not working for anyone associated with those psychos."

"Well, since I am *not* involved with them, then I guess you're still working for me. So how about you treat your client with a little re*spect.*"

The last syllable came out harsh and clipped. Quentin realized he was leaning forward a little and that his eyes had narrowed into a scowl. He stood straight again, breathed deeply through his nose and forced himself to relax.

Frederico seemed to consider Quentin's words for a few seconds. "I have to know," he said. "I needed to see your face for this, know if you're telling the truth. I am not someone you want to cross, Quentin. Trust me on that."

"I have no idea who these Zoro dudes are."

"Are you telling me you have never even *heard* of the Zoroastrian Guild?"

"No, I never ... " Quentin's voice trailed off as a memory popped into his thoughts. A memory of being restrained on an X-rack, a room full of Creterakians asking him rapid-fire questions.

"The *Combine*," Quentin said. "The bats asked me about it when they were giving me the shock treatment."

"And that's it?" Frederico said. "That's the *only time* you heard of them?"

Quentin nodded.

"You don't watch the news much, do you?"

"Sure, I do," Quentin said. "ESPN and Galactic Sports Net, I watch them all the time."

Frederico stared at Quentin for a long time. He stared hard. Quentin fought an urge to look away. Quentin had refused to back down from far bigger sentients, far *meaner*, but there was something in Frederico's eyes that seemed ... merciless. Frederico's stare was akin to only one other sentient that Quentin knew: Gredok the Splithead.

"Okay," Frederico said. "I believe you."

"Damn right you do." Quentin had meant the words to be tough, but for some strange reason, this much smaller Human bothered him. Threw him off his game. Maybe even ... *intimidated* him? Just a little?

No, that couldn't be it. It was because Frederico was gay. Had to be. Quentin was trying hard to adjust to his new environment,

but the fact remained that he'd spent nineteen years being indoc-
trinated in hate. It had to be the gay thing because no way could
he be intimidated by a man that was a foot shorter and weighed
half as much. No way.

"So, Fred, now that you're finished calling me a liar, who …
wait a minute, you *are* finished calling me a liar, aren't you?"

Frederico nodded.

"Fine," Quentin said. "Now that you're done with that, who
are these Zoroastrian guys?"

"For lack of a better word, they are the resistance."

"Resistant to what?"

"To Creterakian rule," Frederico said. "The ZG is committed
to overthrowing the Creterakian Empire and returning self-rule
back to the controlled governments."

"Which ones?"

"*All* of them. That's one of the spooky things about this outfit.
It's got members from the Union, the League, the Ki Empire *and* the
Ki Rebel Establishment, the Sklorno Dynasty, Tower Republic, et
cetera. All these sentients work together against a common enemy."

"What about the Purist Nation?"

Frederico laughed a humorless laugh. "Where do you think
the Guild got started? It's committed to hate and murder, just like
your religion."

"Purism is *not* my religion."

"What? You don't worship your ridiculous imaginary friend
anymore?"

Quentin took a step closer and pointed a finger at Frederico's
face. "I don't care who you are, Frederico. You don't bad-mouth
High One in front of me. High One is not Purism, and Purism is
not High One. I worship in my own way."

"Get that finger out of my face."

"Oh, yeah? And what if I don't? What are you goi—"

Frederico moved faster than Quentin could have imagined,
definitely faster than Quentin could react. One moment the finger was inches from Frederico's nose, the next, it was buried in
Frederico's fist — buried and bent backward.

Quentin sucked in a breath at the pain. He dared not move. The pointer finger on his throwing hand, and Frederico could break it with just another ounce of pressure.

"I told you not to point at me," he said.

"Uh … " Quentin said.

"I told you, Quentin, I am not a sentient you want to cross. Understand?"

Quentin nodded.

Frederico let go of the finger. Quentin flexed his hand and made a fist over and over, working out the pain.

"Back on the subject," Frederico said. "When I found out the bombers were Zoroastrians, I made the most obvious connection."

"Which was?"

"That you were with the Guild. You decided that you liked football more than you liked overthrowing our tiny, winged over-lords, so you turned your back on the Guild. No one turns their back on the Guild. They tried to off you. But if what you say is true, that you don't know them, then I *don't* know what's going on."

"Could the Guild have been targeting Gredok? Or the mayor, or something?"

"Doubtful," Frederico said. "The Guild doesn't care about some crime boss or a low-level politician from a free system. Those Humans that did the bombing? They knew it was a one-way trip. For that, you need conviction."

"Or you need to be ordered by someone with conviction."

Frederico nodded. "All right. I believe you weren't involved. I'll take care of it."

"You going to call the police?"

"No, I'm going to give the remaining cell members' names and locations to Gredok."

Quentin stared at the man's cold eyes. One could only imagine what Gredok would do to the terrorists.

"I thought you and Gredok didn't get along."

"We don't," Frederico said. "But this? He'll appreciate this. It will be one less favor I owe him."

"How many favors do you owe him?"

"None of your business."

Quentin sighed. "Okay, fine. Gredok still doesn't know you're working for me?"

Frederico shook his head. "No, and if he finds out, there will be problems for me. Hence the disguise."

"At least it's better than that ridiculous pink suit."

"Whatever," Frederico said. "Once Gredok has his boys take care of the ZG cell, you'll be safe."

"Not that I don't appreciate this, but you better not bill me. I didn't pay you to protect me."

"No, but John did."

"John hired you to protect me? Why did John think I needed a bodyguard?"

"Quentin, I know you're technically smarter than John, but sometimes you should just keep that pretty mouth shut so I don't question that assertion."

"What's that supposed to mean?"

"It means you're an idiot," Frederico said. "John thought you needed a bodyguard because *someone blew up a bomb and killed sixteen sentients*. Are you a moron?"

The way Frederico said it, well, yeah, Quentin did feel kind of moronic. John had tried to protect Quentin? Quentin felt a rushing sensation in his chest, the sense of *family*.

"So what now?" Quentin said. "How do you *protect* me now?"

"I really don't know how to pursue the case. It's difficult for the Zoroastrians to get a foothold in Quyth space. Because the Concordia is free, there aren't many sentients here willing to sacrifice themselves to blow up Creterakians. So, I think you're safe for now. At least in Ionath City, you're safe."

"What about the other cities? What do I do about the road games?"

"Hope for the best, I suppose. Gredok's security forces are no joke. And the home teams will protect you because there are huge fines from the league if visiting players are hurt or killed."

The clack of cleats from farther up the tunnel ended the conversation. Frederico smiled, then walked deeper into the tunnel. He passed Don Pine, who was walking out.

"Hey, Q," Don said, "were you talking to that guard?"

"Not really," Quentin said. "He just wanted an autograph."

Don nodded. "Oh, cool, but keep that quiet. If Gredok finds out the guy could lose his job."

"Noted."

"You ready for practice? Tomorrow is your first home game as a starter, my friend. It will be glorious."

"I'm ready."

"Great, let's head out there before Hokor blows a gasket because you're thirty seconds late."

Quentin and Don walked out of the tunnel to join their teammates at the 50-yard line.

### Live feed from UBS GameDay holocast coverage

"Hello, football fans, and welcome once again to Sunday Football on UBS. This is Masara the Observant, here with Chick McGee, our very colorful color commentator."

"Thanks, Masara. We know it's not Sunday for most of you fans, or even if you even know what a *Sunday* is, but welcome all the same. We're here at Ionath Stadium, the Big Eye, for the Krakens home opener against the Themala Dreadnaughts."

"Chick, both teams have one loss and no wins. How important is this game for them?"

"Well, Masara, how important is it for you to remember to take your incontinence medicine in the morning?"

"Chick! That's not—"

"Sorry, Masara, sorry, folks at home, but this game is even *more* important than avoiding an inadvertent public pooping. A win puts one team back in the playoff hunt, and leaves the other at the bottom of the Planet Division, sitting right on the relegation bubble. And wait, what's that? Yes, the Dreadnaughts are coming onto the field! Soon the Krakens will rip out of that tunnel, and this place will go insane."

**QUENTIN STOOD IN THE TUNNEL** of Ionath Stadium, waiting for the announcer to call his team onto the field. His hands ran up and down his jersey, left hand tracing the "0", right hand tracing the "1," fingertips feeling the Kevlar texture. Black jerseys this time … *home* jerseys. Out there, just past the mouth of the tunnel, Ionath Stadium awaited. *The Big Eye.* His house. In the stands sat 185,000 Krakens faithful, waiting, clapping and chanting.

*"Let's go KRAK-ens!"* clap, clap, clap-clap-clap. *"Let's go KRAK-ens!"* clap, clap, clap-clap-clap.

The Themala Dreadnaughts had already taken the field, escorted by a powerful chorus of boos. The Dreads had ended last year in seventh place with a record of 5-and-7. They were a strong Tier One franchise, but they weren't the Isis Ice Storm. The Krakens could win this game, *had* to win this game.

Quentin felt his insides twist and turn as the powerful sound system carried the announcer's words throughout the stadium.

*"Beings of all races, let's hear it for, your, Ionath, KRAAAAAA-KENNNNNNNS!"*

He sprinted out of the tunnel, his teammates at his back and sides. The roar of the home crowd seemed to make the air boil and bubble, every atom filled with excitement and rage and the primitive desire to *destroy the enemy*.

With thousands of adoring fans screaming in support, the Krakens gathered at the sidelines and began their pregame ritual. Quentin led that ritual, led it with passion and intensity, but a part of his brain couldn't shake free a pair of thoughts …

… would his offensive line protect him, give him time to throw?

… and would Yassoud finally step up?

Quentin would find out soon enough.

• • •

**THE DREADNAUGHTS WON** the toss and took the ball. They wore deep-yellow leg armor free of any stripes or decorations. The numbers on their white jerseys were crimson with yellow trim. Their crimson helmets had a simple decoration: stylized, crimson "TD" letters trimmed in yellow and black.

Themala had a good running game led by fleet-footed tailback Donald Dennis. Their passing game, however, suffered the same problem as that of the Krakens — a lack of blocking. Dreadnaughts quarterback Gavin Warren could deliver the ball if he had time to set up and throw. With the outside pressure of Michnik and Khomeni, the Krakens' defensive ends, and inside pressure from Mum-O-Killowe, Quentin didn't think Warren would have much time at all.

The Dreadnaughts managed a first-down run on their opening play but were off the field five plays after the kickoff. After a short punt return, Quentin led his offense onto the field for a first-and-ten at their own 38-yard line.

Just like the game against the Ice Storm, his first three plays were already scripted — two runs and a pass.

"Okay, boys and girls," Quentin said, "let's do it just like we practiced. Sweep left, on *two*, then we go no-huddle. Next play is off-tackle left on two. I'll go with a hard-count, try to draw them off-sides. Let's open up that hole for Yassoud. Third play, wing-set right, roll-out pass, we go on my *first sound*, you got that? My first sound.

"Ready? *Break!*"

The Krakens ran to the line of scrimmage. Quentin walked up, feeling the atmosphere of electricity that permeated the Big Eye. He surveyed the defense, the stats and tendencies of each player ripping through his thoughts. The Dreadnaughts were good, damn good, one of the top twenty teams in the galaxy, but they were not as good as the Isis Ice Storm.

He could move the ball on these guys.

The Dreadnaughts lined up in their base defensive formation, a three-four. A HeavyG nose guard and two Ki defensive tackles would comprise most of the pass rush. Then came four linebackers, two inside LBs that lined up behind the defensive line and two outside LBs that lined up on the ends. The outside LBs could play down in a three-point stance, like defensive ends, or a few yards off the ball, like traditional linebackers. The formation took advantage of the Dreadnaughts' defensive speed but didn't provide the same overpowering outside pass rush Quentin had faced against the Ice Storm. As long as he could keep an eye on those linebackers, guess where they were going to go and watch to confirm those guesses, his foot speed would keep him out of trouble and give him time to throw.

Quentin slid his hands underneath Bud-O-Shwek, feeling the coolness of Bud-O's enamel-pebbled skin.

"Red, twenty-nine! Red, twenty-nine! Hut ... *hut!*"

The lines collided. Quentin pivoted on his left foot, sweeping his right foot around as he turned his back to the line. Tom Pareless ran left, parallel to the line of scrimmage, eyes up and looking for a block. Yassoud was a few steps behind Tom, his eyes looking back to Quentin, waiting for the pitch. Quentin finished his turn, tossing the ball out ahead of Yassoud, leading him. The ball hit Yassoud in full stride. The running back hauled it in and kept running to his left, looking for room to run. Pareless turned upfield, moving with the black-jerseyed lead blockers, and Yassoud followed. Tom lowered his head and leveled a white-jerseyed Quyth Warrior linebacker, opening up a huge hole. Yassoud shot into that hole, then cut outside — he picked up fifteen yards before the Dreadnaughts' safety brought him down.

Quentin ran to the line, waving the rest of the team up with him. Yassoud's strong run filled Quentin with hope, hope that his friend could put in a big game and build some confidence. The Krakens scrambled into position. The Dreadnaughts did the same, their linebackers getting into place before anyone else. They had prepared for the Krakens' no-huddle offense.

Quentin let his players settle in, then called the snap-count.

"Blue, sixteen! Blue, sixteeeen! *Hut!*"

He waited a fraction of a second to see if the Dreadnaughts jumped off-sides, but they did not. His team would go on the next sound.

"*Hut!*"

Quentin turned to his left. Pareless shot by. Quentin extended the ball for Yassoud, who practically tore Quentin's arm off taking it. Yassoud drove into a hole created by Pareless and Kill-O-Yowet. Quentin watched, everything moving in that strange, slow-motion sensation he experienced on the field. He saw a white-jerseyed linebacker slip through a block, filling the hole. Quentin waited for Yassoud to cut back inside to the seam that was just forming there, the seam that would have given Yassoud at least a 5-yard gain, but 'Soud didn't cut back. Instead, he lowered his shoulder and went head to head with the linebacker.

Yassoud lost that battle. The Quyth Warrior linebacker knocked Yassoud backward, putting the Human flat on his ass.

Second and ten on the Dreadnaughts 47.

"Move, move!" Quentin called, waving his team to the line of scrimmage for the third precalled play. Yassoud was slow to rise.

"Murphy!" Quentin screamed. "Get up, let's go!"

Yassoud rose, but not fast enough. Once again, the defense had time to swap personnel, defeating the purpose of the no-huddle offense. Yassoud stumbled to his position at tailback. Quentin felt anger and annoyance swirling in his chest, but he forced it away to concentrate on the next play.

He surveyed the defense. They had pulled one defensive back and brought in a defensive tackle, effectively switching from a three-four to a pass-rushing four-four. Yassoud stayed behind Quentin as a single back, but Tom Pareless lined up as a right wing, just behind and outside of tight end George Starcher (who had painted his face with red stripes this week). Hawick was lined up wide right, almost to the sidelines. A cornerback covered her, and Quentin could see the safety cheating that way to provide help. That meant one of the four linebackers would probably be in single coverage on Starcher: Quentin had the defense right where he wanted them.

"*Hut!*"

The lines collided as he pushed off of his left foot, going back and also to the right. He sprinted right, the rush of pure speed

coursing through his veins. Tom ran right as Quentin's lead blocker, waiting to stop the first defensive player that came in. Hawick
drove off the line, shooting straight downfield on a streak pattern.
The Themala cornerback had no choice but to turn and run with
her, clearing out the shallow right side of the field. George Starcher
blocked down, hitting the defensive end, then bounced off and ran
to his right; a shallow, 5-yard pattern. The Quyth Warrior linebacker had him covered.

Quentin took two steps toward the line of scrimmage, like
he was going to tuck the ball and run. The linebacker covering
Starcher came up immediately, but Quentin then shot to the right,
still parallel to and behind the line of scrimmage. The Quyth
Warrior linebacker tucked and rolled to the side, just a few yards
behind Quentin and closing fast.

Quentin waved his right hand, urging Starcher to deepen the
route, but Starcher was already doing just that, automatically
moving to the open space. The linebacker closed. Quentin threw
a bullet before the linebacker sprang out of his roll and brought
Quentin down. The ball hissed out, a throw hard enough to kill,
but Starcher's huge hands grabbed it as if it were a floating child's
balloon. The big tight end turned upfield.

Watching Starcher run was like watching a sprinting tree, big
legs punishing the ground with each step. The three defensive
backs converged on him. He threw a forearm at the closing cornerback, crushing her to the ground, then shook off the strong safety
and made it another twenty yards before the free safety drove him
out of bounds.

Quentin's first pass of the day, and it picked up 38 yards. First-
and-ten on the Themala 9.

Starcher had just *known* where to go, instinctively, or almost
like he'd read Quentin's mind. And Quentin knew full well that
Starcher would do that all day.

Hokor's fuzzy yellow face popped up in Quentin's helmet VR.
"*Barnes!* Good job on that play. Run the same thing. Warburg is
coming on to spell Starcher after that big run. The linebacker will
follow Warburg out on the pattern, you turn it upfield."

"No, Coach, leave Starcher out here, I need him for that play." Warburg started running onto the field. Quentin held up a hand, palm-out, signaling Warburg to stop. At the same time, Quentin tried to wave Starcher back onto the field.

"*Barnes!* Just run the plays that I call!"

"I will, Coach, but send George back on here or I'm not running anything."

Warburg hesitated, then started again toward the huddle. Quentin held his hand up again, far more emphatically this time. Rick Warburg stopped again, a man isolated by confusion in front of 180,000 sentients.

"*Barnes!* We're going to get a delay of game penalty!"

"Then you better send George out here, right now."

A second later, Quentin saw George Starcher's big body lumbering onto the field. Warburg looked at Quentin. Even from a distance of some twenty yards, Quentin could see Warburg's expression of hate. Hate could wait, a touchdown could not. Quentin called the play as soon as Starcher reached the huddle, then followed his team to the line. The crowd screamed for blood. Past an end zone painted in the blazing Krakens orange, beyond the goal posts, Quentin saw the sea of fans dressed in orange, black and white. No one wearing crimson and yellow here.

He forced his attention back to the game, saw that the Dreadnaughts were again in a three-four. That gave them more speed. Would the play still work?

It would work. He smiled, his hands tapping out a quick *ba-da-bap* on Bud-O-Shwek's rear. Quentin settled in under center.

"Blue, twenty-two," he called. "*Bluuuue*, twenty-two … hut-hut!"

The lines clashed. Quentin pushed to his right. Everything seemed to slow to a crawl.

*BLINK*

Quentin's brain soaked up every last detail as he ran right. The defense seemed to be moving in slow motion. The left inside linebacker blitzed forward, but Tom Pareless threw a waist-high block that sent both Pareless and the linebacker to the turf. Quentin watched Starcher block down, then spin with a ballerina's grace and run toward the sidelines, just like the last play. Quentin tucked the ball and started to cut upfield, to run for the touchdown, when he saw that Starcher had a step, just a *step* on the Quyth Warrior linebacker covering him. Still running forward, Quentin raised the ball and fired it as hard as he could.

The linebacker reached out a pedipalp to knock the ball away. The stadium was too loud to hear the *snap*, but Quentin saw it, saw the pedipalp hand bend back the wrong way. The ball kept going, deflected downward by the impact. Quentin watched, amazed, as George Starcher reacted instantly, diving down, big hands strangling the ball just before it hit the ground. George landed on his back in the orange end zone ... touchdown.

*BLINK*

Everything snapped back to normal speed, the crowd's roar deafening this close to the end zone. What a catch! George started to get up, but Quentin ran at him and tackled him out of pure joy. Hawick jumped on the pile and squealed, as did Scarborough and a few other teammates, hundreds of pounds of sentients weighing down on Quentin.

"Nice catch!" he screamed into George's face. "That was really something!"

"I told you to throw *hard*," George said. "The fates that be let not the straight arrows of fortune go awry."

"Starcher, I don't know what the hell you're talking about most of the time, but you make catches like that and you can keep on babbling whatever you like!"

Hands and tentacles pulled Quentin to his feet. He knelt and reached down to the turf. He picked up a few torn, orange-painted circular leaves. Some of the paint had flaked off due to cleats or crashing bodies, revealing the translucent-blue plant material beneath. Quentin held the ripped leaves to his nose and inhaled deeply.

The smell always reminded him of cinnamon.

He ran to the sidelines as the field goal team came on. Arioch Morningstar kicked in the extra point, and the Krakens led 7-0.

• • •

**"MY FATHER-MOTHER, CHICK,** did you *see* that throw?"

"Barnes was on a full-out sprint to the right, Masara, and he fired that ball in at terminal velocity. There wasn't a passing window, so Barnes *made* one by brute force alone."

"I'm *stunned*, Chick! I think Barnes threw the ball so hard he broke the pedipalp-hand of Tibi the Unkempt."

"Masara, I haven't seen anything hurled with that kind of velocity since I drank those two bottles of Junkie Gin after an all-you-can-eat Quyth barbecue. I was projectile-spewing legs and thoraxes all over the place."

"Chick! That's not something we—"

"Sorry, Masara, sorry, folks at home. Let's get back to the action on the field."

**THE TWO TEAMS BATTLED** for the rest of the half. Quentin hit Starcher three more times, as well as completing passes to Denver, Hawick, Scarborough, Milford and even one to Rebecca Montagne when she came in to spell Tom Pareless. Despite all the completions, he couldn't get the Krakens into the end zone again. Arioch Morningstar hit two field goals, and the defense gave up a long run. At the end of the half, it was Ionath 13, Themala 7.

**FIVE MINUTES TO PLAY** in the third quarter, fourth and inches on the Themala 35-yard line. Too far out for a field goal attempt from Arioch Morningstar, maybe too close in to punt. At any rate, a punt would give the Dreadnaughts the ball back. Up 13-7, if the Krakens could pick up another five or six yards, Morningstar could kick a field goal and make it a two-score game. Better to be aggressive and go for the first down rather than give up the ball.

Hokor called an off-tackle run up the middle. Coach held an old-school philosophy that if you couldn't convert at third-and-inches, you didn't deserve to be on the field. Quentin walked up behind center, saw all the linebackers cheating up. With the three-four defense, that meant seven players packed in tight at the line of scrimmage. Quentin wanted to audible to a pass play because aside from Yassoud's big first run, the guy hadn't done anything all day.

*Run the plays that are called.*

Quentin lined up under Bud-O-Shwek. He ignored his instincts. The linebackers cheated up even farther.

"*Green*, thirty-two! Hut-hut ... *hut!*"

He took the snap and turned left. Tom Pareless ran past, trailing a thin stream of blood that poured from a fresh cut on his left forearm. Quentin extended the ball. Yassoud took it, but without the *snapping* intensity he'd shown in the first quarter. Kill-O-Yowet and Sho-Do-Thikit drove forward. The Themala defensive tackle fought back hard as the Dreadnaught linebackers crashed in. The pile of sentients met at the line of scrimmage with a clattering *smash* of armor, yells of aggression and grunts of pain. Yassoud went down. Bodies stood, clearing the area. When the zebe flew in, picked up the ball and spotted it, Quentin could clearly see the Krakens were short by half a yard.

The Krakens hadn't converted on fourth down. The Dreadnaughts had the ball on their own 35, with a chance to drive the field and take the lead.

The Krakens had needed one damn *inch*, and Yassoud had actually *lost* ground. The offense ran off the field. Yassoud ran off slower than the others, limping, head down, arms hanging loosely. His jersey was torn in three places and blood sheeted down his left hand.

Quentin waved to Doc Patah, then pointed to Yassoud. The Harrah doctor flew onto the field, already examining Yassoud's arm as they came off the field together and moved to the bench. Quentin looked at the other Krakens players, at how *they* watched Yassoud. These weren't looks of admiration and support. They were looks of annoyance, perhaps a few of slight betrayal. Any tailback in the league should be able to pick up one *inch*, especially at such a critical juncture in the game. The fact that Yassoud had not picked up those yards?

Maybe he didn't have it after all.

An angry roar from the crowd drew Quentin's attention back to the field. Just as he looked, he saw Don Dennis, the crimson-helmeted Dreadnaughts running back, running up the sidelines right in front of the Krakens bench. Dennis was already past most of the Krakens defenders — only Berea and Perth had a shot at him. Berea closed for a tackle, but Dennis spun just as she jumped. She hit empty air, then the ground. She scrambled up, but even with her blazing speed, it was already too late.

Perth had an excellent angle of pursuit. She closed in as Dennis passed the 15-yard line. He ducked his shoulders in, out, then in again. The rapid-fire movement threw Perth off-balance a little. Instead of hitting him hard and clean, she awkwardly wrapped one tentacle around his chest, her other tangling in the back of his white jersey. Dennis was spun around, but he kept moving downfield, backpedaling now, his feet barely landing in just the right places to keep the stumbling body aloft. Perth fell but held on, her tentacles stretching as Dennis tried to pull away. She dragged along the ground behind him, sliding across the blue Iomatt. Dennis finally fell but broke the plane of the goal line just before he did.

Touchdown Dreadnaughts.

The extra point was good. Themala took the lead, 14-13.

**QUENTIN'S FACEMASK PLOWED** into the Iomatt, sending a spraying wave of moisture and dirt and blue bits of plant material into his face. He skidded along with a white-jerseyed Ki lineman and a white-jerseyed Quyth Warrior on his back.

After the touchdown that gave them the lead, the Dreadnaughts reversed their defensive strategy. They focused on pass coverage and blitzing, almost daring the Krakens to run. The few times Hokor took that dare, Yassoud couldn't move the ball.

Themala pinned their ears back and came after Quentin, blitzing on every play — sometimes with the inside linebackers, sometimes the outside, sometimes the corners, sometimes the safeties. They were also playing the short passing routes very tight, taking away the five- to ten-yard hook patterns, the inside slants and the out-patterns. That would have opened them up to the long ball if Quentin had had time to throw, but thanks to the weakness at right guard and the constant blitzing, time was something he did not have. He'd gone the first half with no sacks — the Dreadnaughts snagged him three times in the third quarter and now twice in the fourth.

He picked himself up off the ground and pulled a chunk of turf out of his facemask. He brushed the blue, circular leaves off his chest, his right hand smearing a long curve of blood across the 1 of his orange 10. Somewhere during the sack he'd lost most of the skin on the base of his thumb. Blood poured out of the wound, splattering on the blue turf and white yard markers at his feet.

That sack had come on a third-and-15. Fourth down. Quentin ran off the field, trailing blood as he went, looking up at the clock that read 4:23 left in the fourth quarter.

IT COULD HAVE BEEN a dramatic, come-from-behind victory ... if, that is, the Krakens defense had made a stop and got the ball back.

They didn't.

The Dreadnaughts put together a 55-yard drive that burned through the Krakens' three timeouts and the final 4:23 of the game. For the last two plays, Quentin had to stand on the side-lines and watch as the Dreadnaughts lined up with seven players on the line of scrimmage and three running backs packed tight next to and behind the quarterback — the "victory formation." For those two plays, quarterback Gavin Warren took the snap and immediately knelt down. The zebes blew each play dead, but the clock kept ticking away. After the last kneel-down, the clock ticked to zero.

The 1-and-1 Dreadnaughts jogged onto the field, elated at their win. The Krakens' sideline emptied more slowly, players filtering onto the field to greet their victorious foes.

Quentin walked out as well, first seeking out Gavin Warren, his counterpart on the Dreadnaughts. A slow, burning rage roiled in Quentin's soul. They'd had this game, *had* it, but it had slipped away.

The orange and the black was 0-and-2 and tied for last place.


### From the "Galaxy's Greatest Sports Show with Dan, Akbar & Tarat the Smasher"

**DAN:** To me there's no question which team is the biggest surprise. Gotta be the Bord Brigands. They went five-and-seven last year and now they start the season with two wins?

**AKBAR:** Dan, you're ignorant. I'm not surprised by that at all. Last year was a rebuilding year for the Brigands. They went out and got Athens, the biggest free-agent receiver out there, and now they are coming on strong.

**TARAT:** And they did finish last season with three straight wins, Dan, so I agree with Akbar that this is no surprise.

**DAN:** Idiots. I tell you, I'm saddled with *idiots* on this show. Fine, Akbar, who are *your* big surprises after the first two weeks?

**AKBAR:** The Yall Criminals, no question. They went eleven-and-one last year, they were the top seed going into the playoffs, favored to win it all. They lost that first-round playoff game to the Lu Juggernauts. Okay, that was a shocker, but it happens. Then they start this season with two straight losses?

**DAN:** Okay, I can agree with you there. Quite a surprise. Tarat?

**TARAT:** It's too early to focus on just win-loss records, but the team that surprises me is the Jupiter Jacks. They are one-and-one, which is nothing to worry about, but they just can't seem to throw the ball. They lost their top receiver on that game-winning catch in the Galaxy Bowl last year, and this season their second and third receivers just aren't stepping up.

**DAN:** I agree. Right now the Jacks can't beat teams with a strong pass defense, but what can they do about it?

**AKBAR:** They have to make a trade.

**DAN:** Oh really? And who is going to trade with the defending league champs? Tell me a team that wants to make them *better*.

**TARAT:** There are seven winless teams, Dan. I think any of them would make a trade. The Spider-Bears and Krakens are both winless; they would probably do anything to improve their game.

**DAN:** Hmmm, an intriguing conjecture, my Hall-of-Fame friend. The Krakens seem to have a lot of depth at receiver, and Quentin Barnes is getting his butt kicked. Maybe they trade for offensive line help?

**AKBAR:** I wouldn't be surprised to see that. Barnes has already been sacked *nine* times in two games, the most in the league.

**TARAT:** And that Human can move. If it was someone slower, there would be even more sacks, so that offensive line is really a shambles.

**DAN:** We'll see soon enough. The trade deadline is the Friday of Week Five. Come kickoff of Week Five, if the Krakens haven't made a trade, they are stuck with their horrible offensive line for the rest of the season. Let's see what the callers think. Line two, from Neptune, you're on the Space, go.

MESSAL THE EFFICIENT LED QUENTIN into the media room of Ionath City Stadium. There had been post-game press conferences in Tier Two, but they hadn't been mandatory. And, if you missed one, nobody *fined* you for it.

Quentin had seen the media room once, during a tour of the stadium, but it had been empty. It wasn't empty now. Messal led Quentin to a chair that sat behind a table. The tabletop was black. Orange skirting surrounded it, showing the Krakens logo in graceful folds. Behind the chair, a smart-paper wall faded logos in and out: the Krakens logo, of course, also the logos of Junkie Gin, Farouk Outdoor Wear, Ford Hovercar and some action movie starring Patuth the Muscular and Gloriana Wanganeen.

The table, chair and wall held little interest, however, because Quentin's attention focused on the bulletproof crysteel glass and the mass of sentients beyond it.

Reporters, packed so tightly you couldn't see the floor.

In that moment, Quentin knew what it was like to be an animal in a zoo.

As soon as he sat, they all started shouting at once, a single body made of fifty heads from a half-dozen species.

*Quentin! Quentin!*

He leaned back, not sure what to do. Then Messal was next to him, pointing to a reporter.

"Jonathan," Messal said. "Go ahead."

The fifty-headed monster quieted as a single Human stood.

"Jonathan Sandoval, Net Colony News Syndicate. Quentin, how does it feel to lose this close game?"

"Uh ... bad?"

*Quentin! Quentin! Quentin!*

"Kelp Bringer," Messal said, "go ahead with your question."

The monster quieted again. Quentin recognized the black-striped, blue Leekee he'd met during Media Day on the *Touchback*.

"Kelp Bringer, Leekee Galaxy Times. Quentin, you are in last place in the Planet Division. When you started the season, is that where you wanted to be?"

"I ... uh, *no*," Quentin said, trying to find the meaning of Kelp Bringer's question. Of course, the Krakens didn't want to be 0-and-2 ... the question couldn't actually be that stupid, could it?

"Quick follow-up question?" Kelp Bringer said. Quentin nodded, trying not to stare at a spindly, insectish symbiote using its tiny claws to pluck away at a yellow growth above Kelp Bringer's left eye. Kelp Bringer didn't even seem to notice.

"You lost by one point," Kelp Bringer said. "Would you have rather been blown out, like you were against the Isis Ice Storm? I mean, what's *worse*, the close loss or the blowout loss?"

Quentin felt himself shaking his head in annoyance, then stopped. *This is part of the game*, Don Pine had said, *this is part of the game*.

"Uh ... I guess a loss is a loss, you know? I ... um ... don't know that there's a difference. Next question?"

*Quentin! Quentin! Quentin!*

"Yolanda," Messal said.

Quentin's eyes snapped in her direction. Just like before, her beauty made everything else fade away. He hadn't seen her in the mass of sentients. She must have been blocked by the other reporters.

"Quentin, Yolanda Davenport, Galaxy Sports Magazine. You've gone two games in Tier One without throwing an interception. You're giving up an average of four-and-a-half sacks per game, but despite the pressure your decision-making seems to have improved from last year. To what do you attribute this?"

Finally, a real question. It was like a breath of planet-side air after a week in the *Touchback*.

"Well, I'm getting to know my receivers, and they're getting to know me. We practice route-throwing a lot, and I think I'm just getting used to the speed of the upper-tier game."

"Denver and Scarborough," she said. "Are *they* getting used to you?"

Quentin nodded. "Uh-huh. Next question?"

The fifty-headed monster started shouting again, but Yolanda's voice erupted, a roar that shouldn't have fit inside such a tiny body.

"Quick follow-up," she said. The monster's shout quickly faded to a surprised murmur.

"Uh, okay, go ahead."

Yolanda smiled and nodded a polite *thanks*. "Speaking of Scarborough and Denver, do you care to comment on the rumor that Ionath is going to trade them?"

Quentin froze. How did she know about that?

The fifty-headed monster paused only a second, then forty-nine heads shouted all at once, far louder than before, demanding an answer. Quentin leaned back. It almost felt like being under attack. Quentin didn't know what to do. He looked at Messal.

Messal met Quentin's wide-eyed stare, then turned to face the crowd beyond the glass.

"That will be all for Elder Barnes, thank you very much."

Quentin didn't wait for another question. He stood and left the media room, walking as quickly as he could without actually running.

## GFL WEEK TWO ROUNDUP
(Courtesy of Galaxy Sports Network)

| | | | |
|---|---|---|---|
| **Water Bugs** | 24 | Vanguard | 3 |
| Spider-Bears | 21 | **War Dogs** | 25 |
| Hullwalkers | 27 | **Astronauts** | 45 |
| Krakens | 13 | **Dreadnaughts** | 14 |
| **Atom Smashers** | 35 | Warlords | 17 |
| **Juggernauts** | 24 | Armada | 7 |
| Planets | 10 | **Ice Storm** | 20 |
| Scarlet Fliers | 14 | **Jacks** | 17 |
| Intrigue | 10 | **Brigands** | 17 |
| **Pirates** | 34 | Criminals | 30 |
| **Wolfpack** | 35 | Cloud Killers | 13 |

With Week Two coming to a close, four Planet Division Teams stand at 2-and-0: Isis, Lu, To and Wabash. Not to be outdone over in the Solar Division, the Bord Brigands, D'Kow War Dogs and New Rodina Astronauts also move into Week Three with unblemished records.

The Jupiter Jacks got back into the win column with a 17-14 thriller over arch-rival Neptune, while both newly promoted teams remain winless after Chillich (0-2) fell 25-21 to the War Dogs, and Ionath (0-2) lost a close 14-13 bout with fellow Quyth Concordia team Themala.

### Deaths
No deaths reported this week.

### Offensive Player of the Week
For the second week in a row, New Rodina quarterback **Rick**

**Renaud** wins PoTW honors. Renaud went 22-of-24 for 425 yards and six TDs.

### Defensive Player of the Week

**Cairns,** safety for the Shorah Warlords. Cairns had ten tackles, an interception and a sack in a losing effort against the Atom Smashers.

# 7

# WEEK THREE:
# SHORAH WARLORDS at
# IONATH KRAKENS

**PLANET DIVISION**

2-0  Isis Ice Storm
2-0  Lu Juggernauts
2-0  To Pirates
2-0  Wabash Wolfpack
1-1  Hittoni Hullwalkers
1-1  Mars Planets
1-1  Themala Dreadnaughts
0-2  Yall Criminals
0-2  Alimum Armada
0-2  Ionath Krakens
0-2  Coranadillana Cloud Killers

**SOLAR DIVISION**

2-0  Bord Brigands
2-0  D'Kow War Dogs
2-0  New Rodina Astronauts
1-1  Bartel Water Bugs
1-1  Jang Atom Smashers
1-1  Jupiter Jacks
1-1  Sala Intrigue
1-1  Shorah Warlords
0-2  Chillich Spider-Bears
0-2  Neptune Scarlet Fliers
0-2  Vik Vanguard

SINCE SOMETIME IN THE MIDDLE of last season, Quentin had known this time would come. The worst of all possibilities. Something that went totally against the teachings of his childhood, of his religion.

Was it killing another Purist Nation citizen? No.

Was it idolatry? Worshiping a false idol? Nope.

Sleeping with a woman before marriage? Nuh-uh.

Far worse than all of those — it was time to break bread with the Ki.

He shuddered at that term ... "breaking bread." He'd heard they didn't even eat bread. At least Don Pine was with him, there for both moral support and to caution against cultural faux pas.

"Just relax, kid," Don said as they walked down the corridor toward the Ki section of the ship. "It's going to be gross, but I'm sure you've seen worse."

"Really?" Quentin snapped. "And why is that? Because I come from the *Purist Nation*? Because I was *poor*?" Quentin was sick and tired of everyone thinking of him as a *hick*, as *backwater*. The Purist Nation wasn't great, but it had its good points.

Don rolled his eyes. "Hey, Q, you ever seen anyone burned at the stake?"

Quentin ground his teeth.

Don raised his eyebrows. "Well, have you?"

"Yes."

"How about stoned to death?"

"Yeah, sure," Quentin said.

"How about skinned to death? I hear that's a form of public torture."

"Well, yeah, but just one time."

Don laughed and held his hands palms up at shoulder height, a gesture that said *well, there you go.*

Quentin let out a long breath. Don wasn't his enemy here. It was a stressful situation, but Don was only here to help.

"Sorry," Quentin said. "When you grow up with it, you don't think it's strange. I guess I have seen some bad things."

"You have," Don said. "I wonder how long it will be before you realize just *how* bad. Maybe being around a normal life — if you'll pardon the expression — will show you just how truly messed up your homeland is. Hey, I heard you talked to Denver and Scarborough about the trade rumor going around the sports talk shows. What did you say to them?"

Quentin shrugged. "I told them it was just that, a rumor. I won't let them be traded."

"You said *that*?"

"I did," Quentin said, feeling immediately defensive. "I'm not going to trade them, and I told them so."

Don shook his head and sighed. "Wish you hadn't. What if you have to pull the trigger?"

"I won't," Quentin said just as they stopped at the door to the Ki wing of the *Touchback*. "No trades, and that's that. Now, can we get on with this?"

Don reached up and squeezed Quentin's shoulder. "Kid, you been in the Ki section yet?"

"Just the pool in the locker room."

"Ah," Don said. "Well, at least you know the smell. Some important stuff you need to know. Try not to flinch."

"Flinch at what?"

"At anything."

"Wow, that narrows it down."

"Just remember that nothing in here can hurt you," Don said. "Well, not that much, anyway."

Don pushed a button in the wall and the door slid up into a recessed housing in the ceiling. Quentin was somehow expecting things to fly out the door, but inside was just a small, empty room with another door on the other side. Don stepped in. Quentin followed. When Don pushed a button to close the first door, Quentin realized he was in an airlock.

"Hey Don, what does *not that much* mean, specifically?"

"It means don't be a baby." Don hit the button for the inside door. As soon as the door started to slide up into its recessed housing, a swarm flew out. Quentin ducked and swayed as the buzzing *things* hit his face.

"Ugh! What in High One's name is this?"

"Didn't I tell you not to flinch?" Don walked through the second door.

Quentin stood and waved his hands as he hurried to catch up to Pine. One of the flying creatures landed on his hand. He remembered Don's words and fought the urge to smash it. Quentin lifted his hand close to his face and examined the critter. It *sort* of looked like an insect, but none that Quentin had ever seen before. Soft, roundish body with four legs sticking out the bottom, pointy feet resting on the skin of Quentin's hand. A ring ran around the center of its body, kind of making it look like a little planet. The ring seemed flexible and strong, even though the diameter wasn't more than an inch from edge to edge. The ring fluttered and the bug rose up, hovered, then settled back down again. On top of the rounded body, Quentin saw five equidistant eyes — the same configuration as that of the Ki.

The little creature tensed, then sprang off his hand and flew up fast. Before it even passed the height of Quentin's head, something dove straight for his face. He ducked — again — and had a glimpse of something the size of his head, something with roundish wings and a pointy mouth that snatched the bug out of mid-air before flying off.

"Q," Don called. "Quit dinking around, we're late for dinner."

Quentin jogged after his teammate. It didn't look like he was in a ship at all anymore ... it looked like he was in a jungle. There were no corridors here, no hallways; as near as he could tell, it was just one big open space. On either side of a three-foot-wide path grew some kind of inch-high red moss, which itself quickly vanished under a mat of waist-high plants with broad, red leaves. He could see only about five feet from the edges of the path before long, thin, brownish-yellow vines grew up from the waist-high plants to cling to the ceiling, so thick they could have been crazy, angled prison bars of some forest jail. More red moss hung down from the vines, clinging to everything save for the hot lights mounted up in the twenty-foot-high ceiling.

"Don, this is really messed up right here."

"We need to hurry," Don said. "The appetizer is the only thing already dead, so you'll want to fill up on that."

They walked into a clearing of sorts, about thirty yards in diameter. At the outer edges, Quentin saw dozens of wide, silvery hammocks hanging at shoulder height. Five or six silver cables ran from each hammock and wrapped around one of the thousands of vines running from floor to ceiling. The long, tubular Ki were in some of those hammocks, multi-jointed arms dangling over the sides or held close to their head, holographic interfaces glowing in the air.

Scattered around the clearing, Quentin saw more of his Ki teammates sitting at what had to be workstations and holotables. The displays showed glowing images of football players wearing bright pink uniforms with dark pink polka dots and black numbers. The uniforms of this week's opponent, the Shorah Warlords.

"They're studying?"

"Yep," Don said. "That's pretty much all they do, study or eat."

"I'm surprised."

"Why?" Don said. "You study, practice, run or lift all the time, seems like. Why would they be any different?"

"Well, they're *linemen*. How much do they have to study the sentient they're facing off against?"

Don nodded, understanding. "It's not just brute strength, Q. There's a lot that goes into each snap, especially when it's Ki versus Ki. You ever watch the HeavyG wrestling leagues?"

Quentin nodded.

"It's like that," Don said. "Every snap, every play, there's a hundred moves and counter-moves being made. Your offensive line studies to make sure they are prepared, make sure they can keep you safe."

"Maybe they need some extra credit. My nine sacks says they're flunking all their classes."

"I heard that," Don said.

In the center of the clearing, Quentin saw what had to be the evening's focal point — a long, flat, stone table. A narrow trench ran around the outside of the table, just inside the edge. It only took Quentin a second to realize what it was — a blood trough.

"Don, are you *absolutely* sure I have to do this?"

Don didn't even turn his head to look at Quentin. Instead, he held up his right hand, fingers outstretched. The two Galaxy Bowl rings sparkled in the hot, bright lights.

Quentin nodded. "Okay, then let's get it over with."

The two quarterbacks walked forth from the edge of the clearing. Quentin's feet stepped on moss, leaves and sticks. Other than the lights above and the bits of ceiling still visible through the moss and vines, he would have no way of knowing he was in a spaceship.

As they approached the table, Quentin heard a heavy rustling from the surrounding jungle. Don stopped at the edge of the table, as did Quentin, who had to force himself to stay calm. Sure, these were his teammates, but they had only been his teammates for the past three months. For the nineteen years prior to that, he'd known the Ki as demons, as devils, as the eaters of men and the swallowers of souls. Now here he was, deep in some semi-artificial jungle, in their natural environment, *surrounded* by them.

They poured out of their silvery hammocks and scuttled to the table. Others actually *slithered* out of the underbrush, moving like huge snakes, legs tucked against their bodies. The Ki lined up around the table; ten long, tubular bodies bent up at the middle. The *smallest* Ki present — Gan-Ta-Kapil, the backup center — was eleven feet, eleven inches long. One of the Ki wore a strange back brace. It was Aka-Na-Tak, the injured starting right guard.

"Aka-Na," Quentin said, nodding to him. "We need you back this week, need you bad. Will you be ready?"

The Ki ripped off a bellowing roar of a sentence that lasted for fifteen seconds, then walked to the table.

Quentin nudged Don. "What did he say?"

"Basically, he said *uh-huh*."

"It takes that long to say yes?"

"It's a strange language."

Quentin watched the linemen moving in for dinner, then realized there were many "faces" missing, including Mum-O-Killowe. The Ki at the table were offensive line only.

"Where's the defense?"

"They live in separate quarters, remember?" Don said. "If they live together, they are too buddy-buddy in practice."

"We going to eat with the defense as well?"

"Later," Don said. "The offense is a little more ... civilized. I wanted to break you in easy."

The Ki surrounded the table. One of them — Quentin recognized him as Cay-Oh-Kiware, the backup left guard — carried a heavy black sack.

A black sack that *moved*.

Kill-O-Yowet also had a bag — a smaller bag that, thankfully, wasn't moving. He held the bag over the table and upended it, spilling its contents onto the stone surface. Shiny objects clattered, finally coming to rest in a scattered pile of candy-apple red.

Quentin recognized the creatures. Covered in clear, glossy candy shells, but he recognized them nonetheless — shushuliks, the little creatures that had drained the blood of Mopuk the Sneaky.

"Ew," Quentin said. "Don, I can't eat that."

"You will if you want to respect the Ki culture."

Quentin felt his anger rising. "You know what? Why do I have to respect every culture in the galaxy, yet no other culture seems to be required to respect *mine*? I can't dare to offend any sentient, but no sentient has a problem offending me?"

Don shrugged. "I don't know, kid. I guess some people just have to take the higher ground, or none of us would ever get along."

Don reached down and picked up a candied shushulik. He popped it into his mouth. It made a crackling sound when he bit down. "The Ki eat dessert first," he said as he chewed. "You'd do well to make a show of eating a *lot* of these things."

"Why?" Quentin picked one up. The candy shell started melting immediately, covering his fingertips in sticky red.

"Because then you'll be *full*," Don said. "I don't think you want a lot of room left in your belly when the main course starts to scream."

Quentin looked at the older quarterback to see if he was joking — he wasn't. Quentin shoved the stiff shushulik into his mouth, then bit down. The candy tasted sugary but also a little bitter. His teeth cracked through it into something soft. Soft, and also *crunchy*. His brain registered the word *bones* before that something popped and fluid shot out of his mouth, a gelatinous purple glob *hitting* his chin and dangling in a long streamer. He quickly wiped it away, then had to clench his teeth as his stomach started to rebel.

"Don't you *dare* throw up," Don said softly, glaring hard. "I kind of want to get out of this alive, if you catch my drift."

Getting out of it alive. Yes, that would be just fine. Quentin chewed, forced himself to swallow. He heeded Don's advice and reached for another. The Ki were scooping them up two at a time, popping them into their hexagonal mouths. They didn't seem overly concerned if the shushulik juice splattered all over. Within minutes, the table was covered with streamers of thick purple gloop.

Quentin picked up his sixth shushulik. He just stared at it. He couldn't possibly eat it and not hurl.

Sho-Do-Thikit let out a long, barking sentence.

Quentin looked at the Ki, wondering if somehow he'd offended his hosts. "He mad I'm not eating?"

"No," Don said. "Are you going to OS1 in the bye week or something?"

"Yeah. I'm taking John to his mom's place."

Don's shoulders dropped and his eyes softened with an expression of longing. "Tuna noodle casserole?"

Quentin nodded.

"Oh, man, I would kill a million sentients to swap out Ma Tweedy's TNC for *this*. Anyway, Sho-Do wants to know if he and Mum-O can ride along. They want to visit OS1."

"Uh, sure, I guess." He looked at Sho-Do. "Yeah, I'll take you guys."

The lineman grunted something Quentin could only assume was a thanks, then Cay-Oh-Kiware hefted his still-kicking bag.

"Here we go," Don said quietly. "You'll want to go to your happy place."

"What's a happy place?"

"A place you pretend to be so you don't realize where you actually are. Just tell yourself you're eating fish. Warm, salty, still-twitching fish."

"Uh … is it fish?"

Don sighed and sadly shook his head.

Cay-Oh-Kiware upended the bag. A multi-legged creature dropped out and hit the table. The first thought Quentin had was *furry crab*. The second thing was more coherent — *maybe that's what a small deer would look like if it had eight legs and lived on the seventh plane of hell.*

Even quad-sets of long Ki arms shot out, grabbing the creature's legs, its body, holding it firm to the table. Despite their overwhelming iron grip, the animal twitched and twisted spasmodically — it seemed to know that if it didn't break free, it was done for. The noise it let out, a cross between a siren and a bark, made Quentin want to turn and run.

Don took a deep breath. "I'm the elder, so I get to go first. You're the guest, so you go second. You need to do *exactly* what I do, okay?"

Quentin nodded, speechless.

Don reached down and put his hands on the squirming monstrosity. Its stubby head tried to turn and bite, but it couldn't bring its hexagonal mouth around. Three of its five eyes that could see behind it stared, wide and black, as Don bent his head toward the middle of its back.

A memory flashed through Quentin's mind, a nursery rhyme he was forced to memorize in his earliest years of school:

*What do I do if a Ki should attack?*
*I get behind him with my foot in his back*
*I bend him hard, his back gives a crack*
*Because the High One loves me, and I love Him back*

The Ki's spinal structure had a fatal flaw — if they were bent back too far, or struck in the middle of the back where their body bent, they could suffer paralysis or even die. Just as the throat was a weak spot in not just Humans, but in the majority of mammals, that spinal flaw must have been prevalent in many species from the Ki's home planet.

Pine grabbed the creature's spinal ridge with his strong hands, then bit down in the center of the deer/crab's back. The thing squealed louder. Don yanked his head backward once, twice, and on the third pull, a *kerrrrack* sound echoed through the clearing. Don stood, a chunk of the creature clenched in his teeth, black blood spilling down his chin and onto his chest. The deer/crab's eight legs spasmed sickeningly, stuck out stiff and motionless for a second, then started spasming again, uncontrollably, limbs just moving without direction.

Don spit out the chunk of creature's spine. It landed on the stone table, where it stuck with a wet *flop*.

The Ki linemen flipped the twitching creature on its back. Don reached down and sank his fingers into its abdominal area and pulled out a chunk of steaming, fur-covered meat. He gnawed at the exposed, black flesh, then nodded for Quentin to do the same.

"No shucking way," Quentin said. "That thing is *still alive*."

Quentin realized that the Ki linemen were staring at him, shiny black eyes locked and waiting. The only sound came from the creature's limbs scraping feebly against the stone table's surface.

Don took another bite of the piece of creature held in his gooey left hand. He raised his right hand and wiggled his fingers. One of his Galaxy Bowl rings sparkled in the light. The other didn't sparkle at all because it was covered with a glob of black blood.

Quentin breathed in deeply through his nose, then sank his fingers into the bloody, still-twitching muscle. Despite the inhumane approach, he tried to tell himself that every steak, every piece of fish, every ounce of animal flesh he'd ever eaten had once been a living thing. Well, it was one thing to *know* that information as you bit into a hamburger. It was another thing entirely to watch the animal die, to actually help kill it yourself.

*I think I'm going to become a vegetarian. But first, I have to finish what I started.*

Quentin curled his fingers and pulled back. The flesh resisted his pull. He had to re-grip, brace his free hand on the stone table, then *yank* a chunk out of the animal. He looked at it, looked at the dripping black blood, looked at the steam coming off the meat. Quentin met the eyes of each of the ten Ki linemen, then raised the mess to his mouth and sank his teeth into it.

It tasted warm and salty.

He closed his eyes and tried to think about it as "fish" and made a mental note to create a happy place as soon as possible.

## Excerpt from "The GFL for Dummies"
### by Robert Otto
### One game, fifty planets — how the GFL standardized the playing field

Following the 2682 season, the Empire Bureau of Species Interaction (EBSI) approved the application of another eight Tier Three teams, bringing the T3 total to 288.

Add in 76 Tier Two teams and 22 T1 squads, and you have 386 professional franchises under GFL management. With five species playing for nearly four hundred teams across fifty planets, how does the GFL guarantee a consistent playing experience and a uniform on-field product?

The answer to that question is in the GFL rulebook, under the heading "Standards for Playing Fields & Stadiums."

Just as the English language and the archaic Imperial Measurement System dominate football rules and culture, so, too, do the physical characteristics of the planet Earth dominate playing-field specifics.

For GFL measurement purposes, gravity is measured in units based on acceleration of 9.80665 meters per second, or the nominal acceleration at sea level on Earth. This constitutes one "G."

The other factors are temperature, air pressure and atmospheric composition. Almost all GFL stadiums are self-contained so that these parameters can be tightly controlled.

### Gravity Requirements

Playing field gravity is measured by official GFL scales and is based on a 350-pound weight, which is close to the average weight of a GFL player. Referees travel with their own 350-pound units, which are weighed before each game to ensure consistency.

**Max weight:** 1.06 standard gravity
(where 350 pounds on Earth would be 371 pounds)
**Min weight:** 0.94 standard gravity
(where 350 pounds on Earth would be 329 pounds)

## Temperature

Due to the varying physiologies of GFL species, temperature must be closely monitored. Most GFL stadiums are indoors with artificial atmosphere management in addition to gravity modifiers. Earth has the most outdoor stadiums, but temperature conditions must be met for GFL play.

**Max temp:** 26 degrees Celsius (78.8 degrees Fahrenheit)
**Min temp:** 14 degrees Celsius (57.2 degrees Fahrenheit)

## Air Pressure

This is strictly regulated due to potential effects on the dynamics of throwing the football. The league understands that an active passing game is often preferred by the majority of fans. Therefore, rules are in place to make sure air pressure will not overtly affect the throwing game.

The air pressure on Earth, at sea level, is 14.7 pounds per square inch, or "psi." This amount of 14.7 psi is known by the measurement term of "one atmosphere," or "atm." For GFL standards, stadium air pressures must fall within the range listed below:

**Max pressure:** 1.1 atm
**Min pressure:** 0.83 atm

## Atmosphere Composition

All of the five races that play football have similar atmospheric requirements. While this is a primary reason for endless galactic war as these five races seek to expand their territories, it is also the very glue that holds the GFL together. Many hypothesize that oxygen-breathing biochemistry is evolution's best choice for fast-moving, aggressive animal life. Sklorno, Ki, Quyth, Human and HeavyG are all oxygen-breathing animals.

There are, however, variations in the optimal atmosphere for each race (the exception being Human and HeavyG, who both prefer standard Earth atmosphere). In the interest of both fairness and consistency, the air composition breakdown is as follows:

75 to 78 percent nitrogen

18 to 21 percent oxygen

1 to 3 percent other

## Future Expansion and Races?

These strict parameters ensure that any team admitted to the GFL can play a fair competition against any other team of the Galactic Football League. But the standards will also impact the potential addition of future races to the league.

If additional sentient races are allowed to play, they will have to operate in the environment listed above. At this time, the GFL does not permit pressure suits, air tanks, air modifiers or any other device that modifies the environment for a specific race or player. All players *must* compete without assistance of any kind, the only exceptions being armor that protects against the kinetic energy of other players and skin-contact suits that regulate body temperature.

GAME TIED 10 TO 10, halfway through the third quarter. Third down and 18 on the Warlords' 45. The lights of Ionath Stadium blazed down on the blue field, illuminating the black jerseys, armor and helmets of the Krakens as well as the pink-and-black gear of the Shorah Warlords. The home crowd screamed before, during and after each play, just as loud between plays, hungry for that elusive first Tier One victory.

So much rode on this game. A loss would put the Krakens at 0-and-3. The Warlords were also facing the reality that they, too, were in a fight against relegation. A loss would put them at 1-and-2, near the bottom of the Solar Division. There weren't many wins in their future, and they needed this cross-divisional game against one of the weakest teams they would face this season — the Krakens.

As such, both teams were down for all-out war. Quentin had nanocyte tape wrapped around his neck, which did little to stem the flow of blood running down the inside of his armor. The Warlords All-Pro safety Cairns had caught him on a blitz — she'd tackled him with her tentacles, her big body and an illegal rasper wrap around his neck that the refs had conveniently missed. Her raspers had ripped off an inch-thick strip of skin all the way around, and a little muscle to go along with it. Doc Patah had said Quentin had come close to having his jugular ripped open, or some such garbage like that. Well, the jugular *hadn't* been ripped open — Quentin could still draw breath, and that meant he could still play.

Quentin walked up to the line. Just like the last play and all the plays before it, he felt a brief sense of relief when his gaze passed over Aka-Na-Tak. Even though the right guard was rusty and out of shape, he was a drastic improvement over Shun-On-Won. Not just an improvement in protection, but an improvement in morale. The other linemen were playing harder now that their squad-mate was back from injury.

The lack of a pass rush and Aka-Na's return was giving Quentin time to throw, and that was critical — once again, Yassoud Murphy's running game was anemic at best. 'Soud had carried the ball fifteen times for just twenty-two yards.

Quentin looked over the defense. Shorah had come into the stadium looking all clean and new, dark pink polka dots on bright pink jerseys, black letters spelling out WARLORDS above block black numbers. Their right shoulder featured the team's logo, a stylized Harrah done in — of course — pink and black. The same logo decorated either side of their hot pink helmets.

Their uniforms didn't look clean and new anymore.

Just like the Krakens, the Warlords' jerseys were ripped and torn, streaked with blue from the Iomatt plants, stained with three shades of blood. Pink polka dot arm and leg armor looked chipped, scratched and dented.

Pink was a strange color for football, but that pattern apparently represented the Shorah tribe. Pink, it seemed, was the color of Harrah blood, something Quentin had not yet seen.

He bent behind center, eyes locking on each player, automatically hunting for Cairns. He saw her, cheating up to the line, threatening blitz again.

Then he saw what she was doing.

All four armored eyestalks aimed right at him. She pointed her two raspers at him, wringing them together clockwise, then counterclockwise, like a twisting rope made of tooth-studded snakes.

Quentin stood straight and stared at her. Cairn's message was clear — Quentin's blood tasted good, and she wanted more. Whatever behavioral controls he'd developed, all his newfound *culture*, it all vanished, blown apart by an instant rage that curled his upper lip and furrowed his brow.

He pointed right at her and screamed. "Is that right? You want a second helping?"

He vaguely noticed the play clock counting down, his teammates looking back at him, confused. He reached to his neck and ripped off the nanocyte patch. He tossed it behind him, then rubbed his hands on his bleeding neck. He slid his palms and fingers over his helmet, feeling the blood spread across the chipped, scratched surface. He finished by pointing a bloody finger at Cairns, then pointing at his helmet — a message of his own, one that said: *You want it? Well, come and take it.*

He wiped his palms against his jersey, then settled in beneath center.

"*Greeeennn*, ten-eighteen!" he called out, audibling to a QB naked boot right. The Krakens knew their assignments and turned to face their foes. "Green, ten-eigh*teeeen!*"

Cairns was too smart to get drawn in by a naked boot. She'd see it coming, and that was exactly the plan.

Just before the snap, he stared at her again, his nostrils flaring, the rage in his chest bubbling up all wicked and lovely. She wanted to play in his world? *Well, if you want blood, you got it.*

"Hut-hut!"

The ball smacked into his hands. He opened to the left, putting the ball on Yassoud's belly and riding him into the line. Quentin pulled the ball free and spun on his right heel, away from the line, coming all the way around before he started sprinting to the right. A pink-clad Ki lineman reached for him, but only for a moment before the black-jerseyed Aka-Na-Tak upended the defender and crushed him to the ground.

Quentin tucked the ball into his right arm and ran, felt the air rush across his sweat-slicked face, felt it burning the torn skin of his neck, each step a surging rush of glory and life and immortality. Huntertown, the Warlords' left cornerback, saw the run and instantly crashed toward Quentin. Quentin adjusted his pace — Huntertown wasn't paying attention to the outside edge of the field, to Halawa, who was in at right wide receiver.

One thing most Sklorno receivers were not good at was blocking. Too many collisions took a toll, affecting a Sklorno's ability to catch the ball if not injuring her outright. So while they *would* block, they usually just got in a defender's way, forcing that defender to change direction. Sklorno receivers normally didn't hit with everything they had.

Halawa, apparently, was not most receivers.

In a fraction of a second, Quentin's chess-master mind calculated direction and velocity — he ran straight down the line, not changing his path, letting Huntertown come in fast. Just before she reached him, Halawa reached her. The oversized Sklorno receiver blindsided the cornerback, knocking her pink-spotted pink helmet clean off and sending her flying like a rag doll.

*BLINK*

The world downshifted to a speed where he was King, where he saw everything, heard everything, felt everything, smelled everything, tasted everything.

Halawa's hit not only left Quentin free to turn up the sidelines, it energized him. It was a burst of pure kinship, soul-binding with another species that played the game the way *he* played the game.

He ran down the sidelines. With Huntertown out of the way, Cairns was the only Warlord player in position to catch him.

*If you want blood ...*

On the snap, Cairns had dropped back into coverage and now streaked in with the blazing speed that only the Sklorno possessed.

"*Get out of bounds!*" Coach Hokor shouted in his headset. "*Slide!*"

No, not this time.

He tucked the ball tightly into his right arm.

The pink-and-black-and-white blur of Cairns shot in. Quentin reared his head back like a mountain ram, then screamed a primal scream as he brought it forward with all his strength, timing it to smash his enemy at the moment of impact. The hit *rattled* him. Still in his slow-motion mode, he felt the wiggle of his liver, the vibration of his stomach, the quiver of his kidneys. He heard something *snap* near his left shoulder, suffered a sword-stab of pain driving down into his lung.

He lost all sense of reality, of time and space and distance, but his feet kept moving, little hard-working creatures that had brains of their own. Quentin looked up into the stands as he ran. His watery eyes saw a blurry wash of orange and black — banners, flags, sentients — all melding together into one giant black monster with orange eyes that demanded sacrifice, *blood* sacrifice, and the monster must must *must* be appeased for the monster is High One himself.

He looked forward, saw the long, flat, black mouth of the monster, the High One, opening wide to *accept* him, to take him *home*. Quentin felt love and war-lust rage through his chest, bouncing off his wounds both internal and external, making the pain a distant thing, a thing to be felt by the weak and the damned.

He also sensed demons coming for him, things that would stop him from diving into the monster's welcoming maw. Not today, demons. His smart-feet moved faster, faster, pushing him across the blue Iomatt as if he were in a gravcar. He felt the heat of the demons, so close now. His feet launched him forward so that he *was* floating, he *was* flying, flying headlong into the monster's maw, into *freedom*.

*BLINK*

The sound of a whistle called him back and brought with it searing agony.

"Unnghhh!" was a semblance of the noise that came out of his mouth. He couldn't move his left arm, his *throwing* arm. He tried to get up but could not. His right arm still worked. He let go of the ball and blindly grabbed at a handful of Iomatt. He lifted his hand to his face and looked at the plants.

Painted black.

The black of the end zone.

He had scored.

Faces swarmed over him, the faces of his teammates, worried and excited and reverent.

He reached his right hand to his left shoulder, gently feeling for a second or two before realizing his shoulder pad wasn't there. The hit had cracked his indestructible armor, ripped it free. It felt like someone had driven a screwdriver down his neck and into his lung.

Quentin knew he was out of the game.

"Bring it home, boys and girls," he said, realizing that even *talking* hurt and not really caring about the pain. "Bring it home! Protect our house!"

Med-sled wires wrapped him and lifted him. Now he truly *was* floating. He didn't move a single iota when the sled carried him to the tunnel and back to the locker room.


**BROKEN COLLARBONES** hurt.

A brace under Quentin's chin isolated his head and kept it above the rejuvenation tank's pink gel. Even through high-anxiety concerns about his ability to heal, to play next week, he couldn't help but be fascinated by the process.

It was his first visit to the stadium's white-walled hospital. He'd seen the training room, sure. That room was just off the communal locker room. It had training tables, limb-sized rejuve tanks, surgical facilities for stitches and casts, the usual stuff. That was where he'd done his physical therapy and healing sessions after Yalla the Biter had torn his hand. The training room worked for small things like that. His new injury, apparently, required something bigger.

The hospital looked large enough to handle three or four critical patients at once. His tank alone was larger than his quarters on the *Touchback*, larger than all three rooms combined. Other than his head, his entire body was submerged. Doc Patah was actually *inside* the tank, gently undulating wings carrying him through the fluid. Quentin couldn't see below the neck brace. Holotank monitors on the wall let him watch Doc Patah's seemingly slow-motion flaps.

"Quentin," Doc Patah said. "Are you sure you want to watch this?"

Quentin started to nod before he remembered — for the hundredth time — that he couldn't move his head at all.

"I'm sure," he said. "I know your voice is coming through the speakers in the walls and all, but how the heck can you talk to me from in there, anyway? You're swimming in pink pudding."

"Harrah vocal inflections are made inside our chest cavity. The microphone inside transmits to my speakerfilm. I just routed the signal to the room's sound system. I'm going to touch a nerve cluster to make sure the pain blockers are working. Tell me if you feel anything. On a count of three, ready? Three, two, *one*."

Quentin watched the monitors. Doc Patah had opened up the skin from his shoulder to his neck. Through a pink haze, Quentin could see the jutting end of the broken bone.

Patah's right mouth-flap held a small metal probe. He poked it around the bone, trying different spots. "Do you feel anything?"

"Nothing," Quentin said. "Kind of weird."

"The nerve blockers are working. Excellent. The break isn't that bad. This will only take about an hour ... glue the bone, graft on brace strips that will dissolve on their own in a few days, sew you back up, then the cast."

"How long am I out?"

"Three days," Patah said. "You're young."

"So I can play next week?"

"I wouldn't recommend it."

"But I *can* play?"

Patah said nothing as he used clamps to pull the bone ends closer. "Yes, you can play."

Even though Quentin couldn't feel his body, he sensed the stress draining out of it. He *had* to play next week — the Krakens were traveling to the Ki system to play the undefeated To Pirates. The shucking *Pirates*, his childhood team. He'd risked public floggings to get pirated broadcasts of their games. Legendary quarterback Frank Zimmer. Quentin would be playing *against* Zimmer, on the *same field* as Zimmer.

Quentin couldn't stop his smile. At least his face muscles still worked. He'd delivered on his promise to win at least one of the first three games, and *without* trading Scarborough and Denver. Aka-Na-Tak was back, finally providing decent pass-blocking that would get better in a real hurry. Quentin had held out for his friends, and it had paid off.

He looked to the holotank again, watching Doc use some kind of small machine to fuse the broken bone together. Back in the Purist Nation, a broken collarbone would have put him out for weeks. Here on the *Touchback*, in Tier One? Three or four days. Amazing.

"Hey," Quentin said. "This the worst injury you've ever fixed?"

"Don't flatter yourself," Doc Patah said. "I used to be a ring doctor in the Intergalactic Fighting Association. I've repaired worse between rounds of a fight."

"Worse than *this?*" Quentin said, remembering the screaming fire that seemed to pour down his shoulder and into his lungs after the adrenaline had worn off. "You've repaired *worse* than this *between rounds?* Guys couldn't go out and fight if they had broken bones, could they?"

"I've seen sentients use their own broken bones as weapons, Quentin. I respect the toughness of you footballers, but there are athletes that make you look about as tough as a flyling."

Quentin started to shake his head but couldn't. He remembered the title fight between Chiyal North and Korak the Cutter. Chiyal *had* used a broken leg bone to stab Korak in the side. Such toughness, amazing.

"IFA, huh? You ever work for anyone I heard of?"

On the screen, he saw Doc Patah stop moving. The winged Harrah just floated there, perfectly still in the pink fluid.

"No," the Harrah said finally. "If you don't mind, Quentin, I'd like to stop talking with you and focus on your surgery. Shall I turn on the game highlights for you?"

"Sure," Quentin said. "That would be great. Can I watch from when I went out?"

The holotank monitor's image changed from his own surgery to a replay of the game broadcast. He saw himself being carted off the field. The announcers were talking about Quentin's touchdown run and how it changed the game's momentum.

"Hey!" Quentin said. "Chick McGee and Masara are commentating? I love those guys."

"Quentin, *please*. I asked for silence."

Quentin relaxed and watched the rest of the game. The Krakens' defense stopped the Warlords and forced them to punt. Relaxation turned to anxiety as Don Pine came in at quarterback. Quentin watched silently as Pine threw a third-quarter touchdown to Scarborough, then added an 85-yard, fourth-quarter strike to Denver.

The old man could still play.

Doc Patah said three days. Three days where Don Pine would be getting all the first-string snaps in practice.

Quentin promised himself he would be back on the field in two.

**"STAY BEHIND ME, QUENTIN,"** said Choto the Bright. "The club will be crowded, someone might bump your arm."

Gredok had allowed the Krakens players back into the city but still insisted his quarterback have a bodyguard wherever he went, even to one of the safest places in the city — Gredok's own club, the Bootleg Arms.

Quentin carefully adjusted the strap on his arm sling. One more day with this thing on, then he could start working out. Quentin followed Choto into the club. They were no more than a step inside the door when a familiar Quyth Leader voice rang out.

"Elder Barnes and Choto the Bright!" said Tikad the Groveling. "Welcome, welcome, *welcome!* We are so happy to have you here. Can we get you dinner? Drinks? Controlled substances? Human women? Females of other species?"

Quentin shook his head. "Not today, Tikad. The team leaves for Ki Imperial space tonight, so it's no time to drink. I came here to talk to Yassoud Murphy. Where is he?"

Tikad's eye turned a little green. "Oh, Mister Murphy isn't here, Elder Barnes, he —"

Quentin's hand shot out to grab Tikad, but no sooner had it reached the Worker than Quentin stopped himself. No. He wasn't on Micovi anymore, he didn't have to let his temper drive everything to a solution of violence.

Tikad flinched when Quentin reached, but Quentin just patted him on his pedipalp shoulder.

"I know he's here," Quentin said. "Just save us both the breath of arguing about it and take me to him, okay?"

Tikad seemed to think about it for a moment, then the green faded from his eye. "Of course, Elder Barnes. Right this way."

"Quentin," Choto said. "Should I join you for this conversation?"

Quentin thought about it for a moment, then shook his head. "No, I'll talk to him alone. I don't want him to think the team is ganging up on him."

"The team *needs* to gang up on him," Choto said. "Perhaps even apply physical encouragement. If your conversation fails, Virak and I may take it upon ourselves to help Yassoud understand the importance of running hard."

The thought of Choto and Virak teaming up for a beat-down made Quentin's stomach clench a little. Two veteran gangland toughs probably knew how to cause a lot of pain.

"I'll handle it," Quentin said. "Just hang out, okay?"

Choto walked to the bar.

Quentin followed Tikad through the nightclub, careful to avoid any of the wildly dancing patrons. All he needed now was an accidental bump that might cause him a few more days of recuperation. The fact that he was here at all infuriated him, but this conversation had to happen, and it had to happen *now*. Flashbugs popped in time to the music, filling the dark club with a spastic, colorful light. Tikad gestured to a booth that was obscured by a curtain. Quentin nodded. Tikad scurried away.

Quentin drew the curtain. Yassoud was in there, all right, slumped over, elbows on the table, both hands clutched around a mag-can of Miller. It was apparently the last of six — the other five were stacked in a little unfinished pyramid, a row of three with a row of two on top.

"Hey," Quentin said. "Mind if I join you?"

"I'm not here," Yassoud said. "I know this because I said to Tikad, I said, *Tikad, I'm not here.*"

Quentin slid into the other side of the booth. "Don't blame him, 'Soud. I was going to talk to you one way or another. Tikad chose the easy way." Quentin nodded toward the beer pyramid. "You know we fly out tonight and have practice tomorrow, yeah?"

Yassoud sank back in the seat, shoulders slumped, chin at his chest, the beer still clutched in his hands. "Thanks for the heads-up, hero. You want a brew?"

"No, I need my head clear because I'll be studying up on the Pirates tonight."

"Of course, you will," Yassoud said. "I don't know why you're bothering. The Pirates are gonna kill us."

Quentin chewed on his lower lip, wondering what to say. "You could study with me. We'll work out in the morning, VR against their defensive sets."

"At five a.m.? No, thanks. We can't all be machines, you know?"

Quentin felt a slight pang in his chest at the word *machine*, the nickname for their former all-star running back Mitchell Fayed. Yassoud sounded so dismissive, so ... *defeated*. Quentin could handle a lot of things in his teammates, but what he could *not* handle was weakness.

"Yassoud, maybe you should *try* being a machine. You're the starting running back for the Ionath Krakens, so you should work as hard as the starting quarterback."

"I'm working my butt off, man," Yassoud said, sitting forward so fast the mag-can pyramid rattled. "But come on, no one can live up to your standards."

"Shuck that, Murphy. Our running game is garbage."

"Hey, don't blame me because Gredok won't get an offensive line, I'm—"

"*Enough*," Quentin hissed. He realized his right index finger was pointed at Yassoud's face, the tip of the finger just an inch from the tip of his nose. "Don't you blame your teammates, you got me?"

"Get that finger out of my face, or we're gonna go."

A challenge, a *direct* challenge. Quentin sat back, controlled his automatic reaction. Even with one arm in a sling — literally — he could dust Yassoud. A month ago, maybe even a few weeks ago, he would have done exactly that. But not anymore.

"Time to be honest, 'Soud. You're not running hard enough and it's hurting the team."

Yassoud sipped his beer and looked off into the distance. "Maybe I'm running as hard as I can."

"You're not. Not even close."

"I *am*, Q."

Quentin leaned forward again. "This is your *shot*, man. You are a starting running back in Tier One. It's what every running back *dreams* of, and it's yours to lose. Why aren't you bleeding yourself dry to soak up every last minute of this opportunity?"

Yassoud shrugged. "Maybe I just don't have it, Q. Maybe I'm not good enough."

Defeat radiated off Yassoud, an emotion so thick and pungent it made Quentin sick to even look at him.

"You *are* good enough," Quentin said, knowing it might not be true even as he spoke the words. "This is your chance. If you don't start playing like your life depends on it, playing like I play, then you're going to regret it for the rest of your days."

"The rest of my days? There's more to life than football, you know."

"If that's what you think, then you don't belong."

Yassoud leaned forward again. "Right. Is that the wisdom of a nineteen-year-old?"

Quentin suddenly thought back to the one-armed boy on Micovi, the last person he'd talked to before driving to the spaceport for his flight to the *Combine*. The scrawny, malnourished boy with one arm, who clearly loved football more than anything. That kid would never even play the game, let alone have the kind of physical gifts that came naturally to Yassoud Murphy.

Quentin pushed the curtain aside, slid out of the booth and stood. "No, it's not the wisdom of a nineteen-year-old. It's the wisdom of a future Hall-of-Fame quarterback, a future MVP, a future Galaxy Bowl winner. It's the wisdom of a *man* that won't ever stop pushing himself until he's dead, crippled, or he's rewritten every record ever kept for his position. And if you don't have that attitude? If you're going to waste the talent the High One gave you by *not working hard enough* to develop it? Then you deserve to be nothing more than the drunk that you are."

Yassoud drained his beer, then completed the pyramid. "I really appreciate the pep talk, Q. I'm glad that when the chips are down, you come here and show what kind of friend you really are."

Quentin reached across the table and knocked over the beer-can pyramid. "I'm here *because* I'm your friend, you jackass! Friendship doesn't win football games. I will help you, but you have to help yourself first. And if you don't? I will find someone to replace you. Don't be late for the shuttle."

Quentin turned and left his friend sitting in the booth. Choto saw Quentin coming, shoved a spindly, nasty bit of deep-fried food into his mouth, then scooted ahead as they left the Bootleg Arms.

## GFL WEEK THREE ROUNDUP
(Courtesy of Galaxy Sports Network)

| | | | |
|---|---|---|---|
| **Armada** | 13 | Water Bugs | 10 |
| Brigands | 28 | **Cloud Killers** | 31 |
| **War Dogs** | 37 | Intrigue | 13 |
| Hullwalkers | 10 | **Pirates** | 46 |
| **Krakens** | 26 | Warlords | 10 |
| Atom Smashers | 6 | **Scarlet Fliers** | 17 |
| Jacks | 21 | **Astronauts** | 28 |
| Dreadnaughts | 15 | **Planets** | 24 |
| **Criminals** | 24 | Wolfpack | 13 |

Three weeks in and only five teams remain undefeated. The To Pirates crushed the Hittoni Hullwalkers 46-10 to move to 3-0, the D'Kow War Dogs (3-0) kept their record pristine by trouncing the Sala Intrigue (1-2), and the New Rodina Astronauts (3-0) won a nail-biter against the Jupiter Jacks (1-2).

The Isis Ice Storm and the Lu Juggernauts, who both had a bye week, are also undefeated at 2-0.

Over in the Quyth Concordia, the Ionath Krakens (1-2) made a statement that they will not go quietly into relegation with their 26-10 cross-divisional win over the Shorah Warlords (1-2). Krakens QB Quentin Barnes made every highlight reel in the galaxy with a spectacular, armor-shredding 45-yard touchdown run that put both he and Warlords defensive back Cairns out of the game. The Alimum Armada (1-2) got into the win column with a 13-10 overtime thriller over the Bartel Water Bugs (1-2).

Coranadillana (1-2) also ended their winless ways with a come-from-behind 31-28 upset over the Bord Brigands (2-1).

Wrapping up the week, the Neptune Scarlet Fliers (1-2) got

their first win of the season by topping the Jang Atom Smashers (1-2) by a score of 17-6, the Mars Planets (2-1) topped the Themala Dreadnaughts (1-2) 24-15, and the Yall Criminals (1-2) edged out the Wabash Wolfpack (2-1) by a score of 24-13.

## Deaths

Cusseta, second-year receiver for the Sala Intrigue, died on a hit from Pesac the Grinding. GFL officials ruled it a clean hit.

Huntertown, cornerback for the Shorah Warlords, died of complications resulting from a vicious crack-back block by Ionath Krakens rookie receiver Halawa. The Warlords have lodged a formal complaint that the hit was actually a clip and, therefore, illegal. Should GFL Commissioner Rob Froese rule the hit illegal, the Krakens will have to pay a death bounty to the Warlords.

## Offensive Player of the Week

To Pirates quarterback **Frank Zimmer**, who was a perfect 18-for-18 and threw three touchdowns.

## Defensive Player of the Week

Ionath Krakens middle linebacker **John Tweedy**, who had six solo tackles, an interception and caused a fumble.

# 8

# WEEK FOUR:
# IONATH KRAKENS at TO PIRATES

**PLANET DIVISION**
3-0  To Pirates
2-0  Isis Ice Storm (bye)
2-0  Lu Juggernauts (bye)
2-1  Mars Planets
2-1  Wabash Wolfpack
1-2  Alimum Armada
1-2  Hittoni Hullwalkers
1-2  Themala Dreadnaughts
1-2  Yall Criminals
1-2  Ionath Krakens
1-2  Coranadillana Cloud Killers

**SOLAR DIVISION**
3-0  D'Kow War Dogs
3-0  New Rodina Astronauts
2-1  Bord Brigands
1-2  Bartel Water Bugs
1-2  Jang Atom Smashers
1-2  Jupiter Jacks
1-2  Sala Intrigue
1-2  Shorah Warlords
1-2  Neptune Scarlet Fliers
0-2  Chillich Spider-Bears (bye)
0-2  Vik Vanguard (bye)

An excerpt from **Life in the Milky Way Galaxy**
*by Allison Rynne*

In the Modern Epoch of galactic history, fourteen planets have supported the evolution of sentient life.

Many experts consider this number to be small, considering

there are at least 200 billion stars in the galaxy and possibly as many as 400 billion. The number of explored star systems is currently around 500 million — just one-eighth of one percent of what might be out there. This 500 million *includes* efforts by non-sentient robotic systems.

By contrast, however, even more experts consider fourteen planets to be very high and well beyond the range of simple probability. A major point in this argument is the fact that all fourteen races evolved to sentience in a relatively narrow time span. The first two races to achieve faster-than-light punch drive technology were the Rewalls in 2345 and the Humans in 2387. The Leekee also developed the technology independently in 2470, followed by the Sklorno in 2502, the Grasslop in 2504, the Portath in 2530 and the Quyth in 2552. In a galaxy that is roughly 10 billion years old, seven races reached the FTL technology milestone within 207 years of each other. Some statisticians consider it an impossibility that two sentient races could have independently achieved FTL-level technology within 50,000 years of each other, let alone seven in just over two centuries.

Theories abound for this tightly cropped flowering of intellect, but thus far none have stood up to even the most rudimentary scientific scrutiny. What is known is that this "clustering" phenomenon allowed multiple sentient races to reach the stars, followed almost immediately by interstellar warfare. While conflict has seen three races become extinct (the Grasslop, the Takici and a race that possibly lived on Chillich), some astroanthropologists maintain that had any one race achieved FTL status several thousand years ahead of the others, that long time span of technological advantage would have resulted in *thirteen* extinct races, not just three. The fact that so many races reached the stars at the same time has, in fact, been a key factor in the continued existence of those races.

Another puzzling factor is the timing of the Givers' arrival in the Milky Way. The Givers first appeared around 2430, landing on the Harrah homeworld of Shorah in 2432. The Givers helped the Harrah achieve FTL status in 2448, then helped the Kurgurk do the same in 2478 and finally helped the Ki reach this goal in 2552 before they were massacred and eaten by those same Ki. That accounts for three more races reaching the stars at a time when not reaching the stars could result in extermination, as it did with the Takici and the unknown race on Chillich.

At this time, there are far more questions than answers. While the galaxy has lost three sentient races, it has also gained three in the HeavyG, the Prawatt and the HeavyKi. Population explosions and diaspora have all but ensured the fourteen sentient races are too numerous and spread out to be made extinct, as no species is confined to a single planet.

Are there still sentient races yet to be discovered or that might discover us? Exobiologists currently use a simple rule of thumb — if there are 200 billion stars, and 500 million explored stars have produced 14 life-evolving planets, then basic extrapolation means the remaining 199,500,000,000 stars could possibly hold 5,600 additional life-evolving planets.

It seems clear that the Milky Way holds many neighbors. It is only a matter of time before we are introduced.

## LIFE-EVOLVING PLANETS

| PLANET | RACE(s) |
| --- | --- |
| Chachanna | Sklorno |
| Chillich | Unknown (extinct) |
| Cretarak | Leekee |
| Earth | Human, HeavyG, Prawatt |
| Grasslop | Grasslop (extinct) |
| Ki | Ki, HeavyKi |
| Kurgurk | Kurgurk |
| Leekee | Leekee |
| Unknown | Portath |
| Quyth | Leader/Warrior/Worker/Female |
| Shorah | Harrah |
| Yall | Takici(extinct) |
| Yewalla | Rewall |
| Whitok | Whitokians |

• • •

## ARRIVAL AT FIRST KI PLANET

It took three days to reach the Ki Empire planet To. The *Touchback* had to punch from Ionath to Chillich, then the short punch to Chickchick in order to make a mid-range punch to Mallorum, then a long punch to Faso and finally a mid-range punch to To. The short punches took a half-day each to recharge the engines, while the long punches took over a day before they could continue on.

Five punches, five trips to the bathroom, five rounds of fear-induced vomiting. He could hold back the hurls when eating the most disgusting fare the Ki had to offer, apparently, but the safest form of travel in the galaxy had him spewing like clockwork. Instead of getting used to the trips, his fear of flying was growing progressively worse. True to form, though, he cleaned up and headed for the observation lounge, eager to see yet another new world, another new culture.

For the first time, he found the observation lounge filled with Ki — a big clutching ball of offense on the left side, a big clutching ball of defense on the right. Unsurprisingly, there were few other Krakens there to watch. The lounge still had plenty of room, but seventeen bodies at over five-hundred pounds each sure made it *feel* crowded.

He threaded his way through the thin space between the two writhing balls of Ki. He saw black eyespots lock onto him as he walked. They looked at him ... oddly. Was that *respect* in their eyes? No, this was something different. He knew their look of respect, as he'd earned that back in Tier Two with the win over the Sky Demolition. In that game, Yalla the Biter had torn Quentin's hand wide open. The wound should have put Quentin out of the game, but instead he'd had Messal the Efficient stitch up his hand using a machine designed to repair the Kevlar-fabric jerseys. Quentin had returned to the field and thrown the game-winning touchdown. After that, the Ki linemen had accepted him as a war leader. Yes, *that* was *respect*.

But this? This was different. The look in their eyes … it was one of *acceptance*. Acceptance, because he'd eaten dinner with them. It stunned Quentin just a bit to realize he could identify many emotions in the eyes of creatures he once thought of as soulless spawns of Satan.

He walked to the window. The two slithering piles contracted a bit, making room for him between them. When he reached the window, the balls expanded again, pressing lightly against the backs of his legs.

The Ki culture was all about physical contact. Both the offense and defense were touching him. They all felt like giant, muscled anacondas.

Quentin looked out onto a world of green oceans and yellow clouds. A single continent lined with three long mountain ranges. Between those ranges lay massive swaths of red. Even from orbit, he could see the sparkle of To's giant domed cities. The Ki could survive in the planet's open atmosphere, as could the Quyth and the Harrah, but other species had difficulty. Humans could acclimate, apparently, if they spent a week vomiting due to the noxious atmosphere.

[FIRST SHUTTLE, PREPARE FOR DEPARTURE]

Quentin turned. He pushed gently at the swarming, sliding Ki legs and bodies. They let him pass without incident. He walked out of the observation deck and headed for the landing bay, aware that first-shuttle riders Kill-O-Yowet, Mum-O-Killowe and Sho-Do-Thikit were scuttling along behind him.

**AS THE SHUTTLE APPROACHED** the city of ToPor, Quentin couldn't help but notice the similarities to Ionath City. Both were domed, the dome being the only thing that allowed a multi-species citizenry to interact on an otherwise unwelcoming planet. Both featured circle-and-spoke road design, and both featured a sports stadium in the dome's dead center.

The differences, however, were dramatic. First and foremost was the size — the ToPor dome was five times the diameter of

Ionath City and perhaps three times as high at the apex. New road spokes started at the eighth circle, then the fourteenth, then the eighteenth, and every four rings out from there. And where radio-active wasteland surrounded the Ionath dome, beyond ToPor was an endless vista of red jungle.

The final difference was rather odd — ToPor's city-center stadium was for the Ki's national sport of rugby, *not* gridiron football. The Ki had modified the game of rugby, starting with a larger ball they could clutch in all four arms. The sport perfectly fit the Ki body type. Gridiron, while popular, was a distant second.

Quentin felt a shoulder slam into him, pushing him to the left.

"Hey, John," he said, not needing to turn to see the culprit.

"Mighty Q," John Tweedy said. "You ever see a Ki Rugby League game?"

"Nope."

"The stuff is *crazy*, I tell ya. Crazy. We'll have to come back in the off-season and catch a game."

Quentin nodded, hoping there *was* an off-season, which they would get only if they stayed in Tier One.

The shuttle dove for the dome, which blurred open just like the dome of Ionath City. It closed behind them the same way.

"That's weird," Quentin said. "It's just like Quyth technology."

"Because it is Quyth technology," John Tweedy said. "Whatever the best tech is in any category, the Ki buy it. They've got the best of everything. You're in for a real treat, Q — world-class wine, women and song."

The mention of *women* and *song* set Quentin's thoughts spinning around the memories of Yolanda Davenport and Somalia Midori. When could he talk to Yolanda again? Not soon enough. And Somalia … did she *really* want to see him again, or was that some kind of showmanship thing? She couldn't actually be interested in *him*, could she? She was a famous musician, he was an orphan from Micovi.

The shuttle shot across the city. Quentin looked down, noting ToPor's perfection and order. He also noted the amount of greenery — or, in this case, "reddery" — that dotted the city. Every third ring was split into two thinner rings — the inner half comprised of perfectly formed buildings, the outer half filled with dense red jungle.

The shuttle circled the gridiron stadium. Open-air, like most dome-city stadiums. Quentin could see down to the red field with its black-trimmed white lines. The end zones were simple, both white with red words trimmed in black: TO in one end zone, PIRATES in the other. At the 50-yard line, the Pirates' galaxy-famous logo — a red Ki skull showing three eye sockets and bloody fangs, two black leg bones crossed beneath it.

Quentin's chest fluttered at the sight of that logo. When he was 9, he'd bought a black-market Pirates T-shirt. He'd kept it hidden in a floor crack during the day and slept with it under his pillow at night.

Six arcing towers curved in from outside the stadium, thick at the base and tapering to a point where they hovered high over the field. That design, that six-pointed design, it looked familiar. He'd seen it, but where? Then it hit him — six points, like the six sides of a Ki's pointy-fanged mouth. Quentin smiled, admiring the construction, the symbolism — the stadium was a gigantic maw waiting to gulp down its enemies.

"Yeah," John said. "Pirates Stadium, home of the five-time galactic champs. Pretty bad-ass, eh?"

Quentin nodded. "That it is, man."

"We have practice when we land, but tonight we're free. You want to hit the town?"

*Hit the town*, head out into a city full of To Pirates supporters, fans, players themselves, possibly, and — the thing Quentin wanted to avoid — team representatives. Perhaps that Creterakian civilian, Maygon. Maygon worked for Kirani Kollok, the Pirates' owner. That was the last thing Quentin needed, for the Pirates to try and recruit him again, get him to tank games as they had requested he do during the Tier Two season.

"Not tonight," Quentin said. "It's the To Pirates, man, I'll be studying."

"You sure? We have to leave right after tomorrow's game to

make it home for the Wabash Wolfpack next week. Tonight's your only chance to see a new city."

John was right. It killed Quentin to not see the sights of ToPor. If he just ignored the Pirates' efforts to recruit him, maybe that situation would go away.

"Thanks, but no," Quentin said. "You tear 'em up."

The shuttle dropped to the base of one of the tooth-towers, then slid into an opening. The shuttle landed, the door opened, and the Krakens players filed out for the customs inspection. Quentin went through the motions, now barely registering the fact that he was in the home of his childhood heroes.

The time for childish admiration was past. The To Pirates weren't his heroes anymore. They were an obstacle standing between him and his second win.

---

**IT HAPPENED MIDWAY** through the first quarter.

The first two drives were a slice of heaven. To even be *on* that red field, doing battle with the Pirates in their blood-red jerseys with the white-lined black numbers, the skull and cross-bones logo on both shoulders, their blood-red leg armor with the white-lined black stripe running from hips to black shoes, their blood-red helmets with the single white-lined black stripe down the middle, it was literally like living a dream.

He had protection now. Two drives where he had a chance to drop back, check through his routes and deliver a pass. He'd completed eight passes on twelve attempts in those drives, hitting orange jerseys right on the black numbers. His accuracy forced the linebackers to cover the passing routes, not cheat up to stop the run. This, in turn, gave Yassoud a little more room, a fraction of a second longer to make reads and cut accordingly. 'Soud carried the ball six times for thirty-two yards and a touchdown, his best first quarter of the year.

And then disaster struck.

It was on a boot right, Quentin rolling out so he had the option of passing, or — if the defense didn't respect his feet — just tucking and running. On that play Aka-Na-Tak had scuttled back just a bit then run to his right, down the line of scrimmage as a lead blocker for Quentin. Everything went fine until Bob Merrell — the To Pirates star linebacker — drove in hard and hit Aka-Na head-on. The big Human linebacker drove at Aka-Na's mid-section, the place where the Ki body bends from horizontal to vertical. A loud, *clacking* collision sent both players to the ground.

Even as Quentin hurdled the two fallen players, he saw Aka-Na's sickening twitches. Queanbeyan, the Pirates' strong safety, closed in and brought Quentin down for a short loss. Quentin almost *wanted* to be tackled, so he could finish the play and get back to his teammate.

When he did, he knew it was bad.


**THEY RUSHED AKA-NA-TAK** off the field. Shun-On-Won returned as right offensive guard, performing as ineffectually as he had for the first three games. Yassoud ran hard through the second quarter, but as the hits started to add up, his effort declined.

From there, just like he had the first three outings, Quentin spent the rest of the game either running for his life or flat on his back. The To Pirates' defense was just too good to not take advantage of the hole in the Krakens' offensive line. Quentin started trying to force the ball, to make something happen, and that's when the mistakes began. He finished with two touchdown passes (one to Crazy George Starcher, one to Scarborough), but also two interceptions and four sacks.

His counterpart for the Pirates didn't have those problems. Quentin watched from the sidelines as Frank Zimmer showed why he was still considered the best quarterback in the game. Zimmer picked the Krakens' defense apart, throwing for four touchdowns and 356 yards. The old man made it look effortless.

When the final gun sounded, the Pirates had doubled up on the Krakens by a score of 42-21. Quentin quickly shook hands and even hurried through the chance to talk to his boyhood hero, Frank Zimmer.

He had to get back to the locker room and check on Aka-Na-Tak.


**QUENTIN RAN INTO THE** visitor's locker room, hoping for the best. His teammates' mood told him he wouldn't get it. He'd seen this before, seen the entire team packed together in a communal locker room, Coach Hokor in the center by the holoboard, waiting for the last of the Krakens to filter in. He held a messageboard in his pedipalp hands. He waited for everyone to arrive because it was an announcement that no one wanted to make twice.

Messal the Efficient stood quietly by, a metal box in his middle hands. Quentin recognized that box. Inside was an engraving tool. The same one that Messal had used to carve Mitchell Fayed's name into the carapaces of the Krakens' Quyth Warrior players.

That was what the Quyth did when one of their teammates died.

"Krakens," Hokor said. "We have lost one of our warriors. Aka-Na-Tak suffered a recurrence of the injury that had kept him out of the lineup this season. The injury was severe. Doc Patah said he could have saved Aka-Na's life, but Aka-Na would have had paralyzed legs and would have been a sextapalegic. Aka-Na chose euthanasia."

Messal opened the box and took out the engraving tool. The Quyth warriors lined up, Virak the Mean in front, Choto the Bright right behind him.

"Wait a minute," Quentin said. "*Euthanasia?* What does that mean?"

Hokor looked at Quentin. "It means Aka-Na chose to die."

"*Chose* to die? What are you talking about? If Doc Patah could have saved him, why would he want to die?"

Sho-Do-Thikit let out a long string of unintelligible Ki language. Coarse, guttural, proud, yet carrying the weight of tragedy.

Then Don Pine was at Quentin's shoulder, listening to Sho-Do's speech. Don's uniform was immaculate, his jersey an unblemished, blazing orange. Quentin's, on the other hand, was stretched, ripped, streaked with red both from the field and from his own blood.

Sho-Do-Thikit stopped speaking.

Quentin turned to face Don, waiting for an explanation.

Don started to talk, then stopped and looked down. He was fighting back tears. Don's pause lasted a few seconds, then he nodded once and looked up, looked Quentin in the eyes.

"Doc Patah could have saved Aka-Na, even made him walk again," Don said. "But it would have required prosthetics, artificial nerves, implants. The injury was bad, Quentin, it wasn't just the legs, there was also damage to the digestive tract. Even with artificial implants, Aka-Na would have required constant care. He would have been dependent on doctors, nurses, his friends, his—"

"So *what?* So what if he would have needed help? What the hell is all this GFL money for if someone can't get help when they need it?"

Sho-Do-Thikit let out another short burst. Quieter than the first, slower. Quentin could hear a tone in those words he couldn't understand — a tone of patience.

The room's only sound came from the chitin chisel. Quentin looked to that sound, saw that Virak was finished. Messal was now engraving Aka-Na's name into Choto's middle left forearm. Killik the Unworthy was next in line.

Don put his hand on Quentin's shoulder. "Sho-Do said the Ki Warrior's way is to not be a burden. They feel it is better to die in battle than live life as a cripple."

Quentin felt his face turning hot again, tears blurring his vision. "But he could have *lived!* He didn't have to die. It's not right!"

"Quentin, Aka-Na didn't want a life without football. He didn't want to go from being a world-class athlete to an invalid. Right or wrong doesn't matter here, it was *his choice*."

Quentin tried to talk, but his throat locked up. Another teammate, dead. He roughly pushed past Pine, part of his mind hoping that Pine would take offense, start something, give Quentin something to *hate*, something to *hit*. Don just let him go. Quentin's thoughts melded into something incoherent, something that spun in all directions at once. He walked to the holoboard, lifted his helmet and started smashing it into the device. Plastic and glass shattered. He hit it over and over again until the helmet split against the harder machinery inside and a jagged piece of something drove into the base of Quentin's thumb.

Strong arms grabbed him, stopping him. Quentin turned, ready to do the one thing he knew well, *to fight*. Sho-Do-Thikit was there, black eyes staring, hexagonal mouth opening and closing to alternately expose then hide the pointy, back-slanting teeth. The Ki held Quentin with two of his arms. The other two arms held something up to Quentin.

Quentin looked down. A cup of black liquid. He didn't have to ask — it was Aka-Na-Tak's blood. Ki tradition, to mark yourself with the blood of your fallen comrade. Quentin dipped his left fingers into the cup, put them on his right shoulder and dragged diagonally to his left hip. Aka-Na's black blood streaked across the beat-up numbers "1" and "0" on the front of his jersey.

Quentin heard someone crying. He looked for the source and found it — John Tweedy. John's big head sat heavily in his big hands. The epitome of violence seemed unashamed of his tears. Through the fingers, Quentin could see letters flashing across John's face — IT WAS AN HONOR TO PLAY WITH YOU.

Seeing that message was the final straw. Quentin felt the tears pouring down his cheeks, dripping off his chin. The crowd broke up — there was nothing more to say. Quentin walked to the Human locker room, the weight of a galaxy making his cleated feet drag. He stripped off his armor and headed for the Ki baths.

**WITH A HEAVY HEART,** Quentin walked through the insane colors of the *Touchback's* Sklorno section. He'd heard that the Sklorno saw a wider range of the spectrum than Humans and also saw far greater detail in each color. A jersey might look "red" to a Human, but to a Sklorno, that single shade could look like twenty or thirty unique colors. The Sklorno knew they saw more than the other species and were constantly trying to communicate the splendor of their natural vision to the other races. That was the reason, presumably, for the atrocious uniforms of the Sklorno League in Tier Two, as well as those of the Alimum Armada, the Yall Criminals and the Chillich Spider-Bears.

This part of the ship looked vastly different than the simple, subdued tones and/or orange-and-black patterns of the Human, HeavyG and administrative sections. Maddening patterns of electric colors covered everything: blues, purples, reds, yellows, greens, oranges. Some colors were so thick and dark they looked nearly black, others were so bright you couldn't really look right at them without squinting. Such was the oddity of the Sklorno — clear bodies with no color, yet they surrounded themselves with a living and incestuous palette.

The colors did little to lift Quentin's mood. Yesterday, he'd had to say good-bye to a teammate. Today, time to say good-bye to two more. Aka-Na-Tak was dead. Shun-On-Won was a bust. The Krakens had no running game. Something had to be done.

Quentin walked to Scarborough's room. He'd called ahead and asked Denver to be there. Denver, of course, squealed with delight — as an official member of the "Church of Quentin," Denver would probably do just about anything Quentin asked.

He reached the oblong door to Scarborough's quarters. Quentin hung his head and closed his eyes. It wasn't too late to let Coach Hokor handle it. Just five minutes ago, Coach had said it wasn't Quentin's job to deliver such news. But Coach was wrong — Quentin's voice was the final decision, he would live with the consequences.

He lifted his head, squared his shoulders, then took a deep breath and let it out in a rush. He knocked on the tall, narrow door. He meant to knock three times, but the door opened after only two and his knuckles whiffed on empty air.

Scarborough stood there, shaking. Behind her, Denver bounced up and down, left and right, emitting unintelligible *chirps* of glee, or, maybe, of rapture. At least Scarborough could stay mostly still. The maturity of her age, perhaps.

"Quent ... Quent ... Quent ..." Scarborough said. She was too excited to pronounce his name. Her desperate intensity made him feel even smaller, even more like a backstabbing scumbag.

"Quentin Barnes!" Denver screamed from behind Scarborough. The younger wide receiver — just 9 years old — started bouncing off the left wall, then the right wall. "Quentin Barnes Quentin Barnes*QuentinBarnes!*"

"Okay, that's enough," Quentin said. "Denver, please calm down."

"Calmdowncalmdowncalmdown!" Denver said.

"Scarborough," Quentin said. "Can I come in?"

"Quent ... " she said, then turned and grabbed Denver, shoving the younger player further into the apartment. Quentin followed them in. The door shut automatically behind him.

He looked around, realizing that this was the first time he'd been *inside* a Sklorno's quarters. It had been such an accomplishment just to practice with them, to let them help him grow as a quarterback — actually socializing with them? Well, that would have been too much, too soon. Once again his mind reeled at how much he'd changed in such a short time and how those few short months actually felt more like a dozen years.

A mad amalgamation of colors coated the apartment walls. Patterns, textures, solids, stripes, dots ... there was no beginning and no end. Combinations ran from the wall to the floor, or the ceiling to the walls. Some of it might have been art, Quentin didn't know. Whatever the thought process behind the colors, the insane combination gave him an instant headache.

The high ceilings made him feel short, a nice break from many parts of the ship where he had to duck his head. He followed Scarborough through the hall into what must have been a living room to find not only Denver waiting, but also Milford, Mezquitic, Richfield, Stockbridge, Tiburon and even the massive Awa sisters, Wahiawa and Halawa. None of the Sklorno could sit entirely still. The younger ones didn't even bother trying, just jumped up and down, nine bodies with transparent skin showing the black skeletons and fluttering hearts beneath.

He'd come to have a talk and wound up at a church revival. His soul shriveled up a bit more. For the Sklorno, anything he had to say held the importance of life or death. Denver and Scarborough's friends had come to watch, to celebrate whatever glorious piece of information that Quentin was to bestow on the two.

But he wasn't here to bestow glory.

"Ladies," Quentin said. "I appreciate you all being here, but I need to speak to Scarborough and Denver alone."

Milford fell to the floor, maybe passed out, Quentin didn't know. Tiburon shook so violently that her raspers unraveled and started flinging drool all over the apartment. Quentin turned his head and held up his hands to block the spray.

"Okay, *okay*," he said. "That's enough. Everyone but Scarborough and Denver, out now, please."

The muscular, long-legged bodies started filtering past him down the hall and out of Scarborough's quarters. The Awa sisters carried Milford. Tiburon managed to make it on her own power.

Quentin heard the door hiss shut, leaving him alone with Scarborough and Denver, alone with a legendary receiver and the talented youngster that Quentin had met at the *Combine*. Here it was, not even halfway through his first Tier One season, and he had to say good-bye to both. They waited, each looking at him with four eyestalks that twitched in anticipation. He wanted to change his mind, but he couldn't — the future of the franchise rested on this decision. Time to get it over with.

"I have some … bad news," Quentin said. "You've both been traded."

Quentin would always remember that moment, remember the instant that through Scarborough's translucent skin he saw her blood *stop flowing*. The All-Pro receiver swayed for a second, then slumped to the ground.

Denver's four eyes looked at her, then swung back to Quentin.

"Quentin Barnes Quentin Barnes," Denver said, her big feet prancing in place. "We have been trained in what?"

Quentin watched Scarborough, wondering if he should call Doc Patah.

"QuentinBarnes!" Denver said. "Trained in what Quentin-Barnes*QuentinBarnes*."

There, a flutter. He actually *saw* Scarborough's oddly shaped heart restart, translucent blood once again course through her body. Her tentacle arms pressed against the floor, and she slowly pushed herself up to a kind of sitting position, folded legs all askew.

Denver looked from Scarborough back to Quentin. "Trained in what, QuentinBarnesQuentinBarnesQuen —"

"Stop," he said. Denver froze stiff, her only movement coming from the eyestalks that swayed like Medusa's living snake-hair.

"Not *trained*," Quentin said. "*Tray-ded*."

Even the eyestalks stopped moving. "Traded?"

Quentin nodded. "Yes, both of you. To the Jupiter Jacks."

Scarborough passed out again.

Denver started to shake. "CoachHokortheHookchest thinks I am unfit to catch the holy passes of QuentinBarnes?"

"No! No, Denver, you are totally fit to catch my holy ... uh ... to be a key receiver for us. Hokor doesn't hate you, and anyway, he's not making the decision alone."

She trembled. She stared at him with four sad eyes that had never looked more Human. "Then ... you ... you also want to trade us?"

He took a deep breath, let it out slowly, then nodded. "It's also my decision, Denver. It's what's best for the team."

"But ... what have I done to bring about the wrath of QuentinBarnes?"

"Nothing," Quentin said quickly, shaking his head. "No, Denver, you and Scarborough both, you are *amazing* receivers. It's just that we have that hole at right guard, and if we make this trade —"

"My life is over!" Denver screamed. She shook violently, every inch of her clear skin shivering. "I am not worthy of catching the holy passes! Oh my QuentinBarnes why have you abandoned me!"

"Denver, it's not like that, really, you ..."

His words trailed off as Denver started sprinting and jumping around the room, throwing herself into walls and furniture. Scarborough rose again, briefly, looked at Quentin with her four eyestalks, seemed to register his presence, then fell flat a third time.

"QuentinBarnesQuentinBarnesQuentinBarnes!" Denver screamed, sprinting around the room at top speed. "QuentinBarnesQuentinBarnes!"

They were devastated. He had done this to them. They would both flourish in the Jupiter Jacks' pass-happy system, yet Quentin had never felt so low in all his life.

The apartment door opened. The other Sklorno members of the Krakens rushed into the room, running to Scarborough, catching Denver and dragging her down, holding her still. There was much screaming, squealing and crying. It reminded Quentin of a funeral back on Micovi, of blue-clad mothers wailing in anguish over lost sons and daughters.

He felt a tug at his left sleeve. He looked down to see Coach Hokor.

"Hawick called me down here," Hokor said. "She knew what was happening when you sent the rest of them out of the room."

Quentin looked back at the wailing pile of Sklorno. "Coach, what do I do? This is *crazy*."

"Just leave, Barnes. The Sklorno have to grieve."

"*Grieve?* But … but it's just a trade, they still get to play."

"Barnes, do you believe in your High One?"

He nodded, unable to take his eyes off Denver and Scarborough. "Yes, of course."

"What if your imaginary friend … excuse me, what if your *god* came down from the sky and told you he was ashamed of you, he was banishing you to some other galaxy so he would never have to see you again."

"But Coach … you and I are not *gods*."

Hokor pointed a pedipalp at the Sklorno. "To them, we are."

"That's crazy."

"Defining it as crazy doesn't make it any less true, Barnes. Now, come on, leave them be."

Quentin took one more look at his teammates, both current

and newly former. No, it didn't look like the grief of a funeral ...
it looked *worse* than that.

Heart heavy with regret, he followed Hokor out of the apartment. Maybe they shouldn't have made the trade. Football was the
most important thing, and the franchise was the focal point of all
things football, but such *anguish*, such *heartbreak*.

Denver and Scarborough would never fully recover, and for
that, Quentin had no one to blame but himself.


**QUENTIN STOOD** in the docking bay, waiting for the visiting
shuttle to open its side door. The orange-and-black Krakens shuttle had left, ferrying Denver and Scarborough out to the Jupiter
Jacks team bus just a click away. Parked in its place was the gold-,
silver- and copper-colored Jacks shuttle.

As with any event welcoming a new player, most of the team
stood in the docking bay. This time there were more Ki than normal; the entire offensive line writhed in a big ball some twenty feet
to Quentin's right. Yassoud walked up and stood next to Quentin.

"Sorry to see Denver and Scars go," he said. "But I ain't gonna
lie to you, Q, it's about time we got some blocking."

Quentin sighed and nodded. While Yassoud was correct — the
blocking had been horrible on the right side — sometimes a running back had to create, had to make something out of nothing. If
that was a talent Yassoud had, he had yet to show it.

The shuttle's side door lowered slowly to rest on the docking
bay deck. Moments later, Quentin saw a man walk out.

"Whoa," Yassoud said. "I mean ... *whoa*."

Quentin played professional football, and as such, he had ample experience being around some of the biggest sentients in existence. Aleksander Michnik and Ibrahim Khomeni, the Krakens'
starting defensive ends, were both giant blocks of flesh at 525
pounds and nearly seven feet tall. Those two were big even by
HeavyG standards, but this man? Quentin had trouble even getting his head around what he saw.

Michael Kimberlin had to duck a little to step out of the shuttle, and when his huge feet *clonked* down the ramp, the sound echoed through the landing bay. His feet were the size of Quentin's whole foreleg, and his forelegs were the size of Quentin's thighs. Kimberlin reached the deck and just stood there. He wore a satiny Jupiter Jacks team jacket: copper-colored body, sleeves in silver with gold piping. On his right breast, the Jacks logo: a black-lined, eight-pointed, gold-and-silver star with a black letter "J" in the middle. He had a big silver and gold duffel slung over his shoulder.

"Hey, Q," Yassoud whispered. "Fifty bucks says that guy is over six hundred pounds."

"No bet," Quentin said. "I know you looked it up."

"And how would you know I did that?"

"Because if you don't know the answer, you bet twenty. If you know it, you bet fifty."

Yassoud looked at him. "I have a tell?"

Quentin nodded.

"Damn. Kimberlin weighs six-fifteen."

Quentin stepped forward and had to look up. This man, this massive, HeavyG man, was a full *foot* taller. Quentin actually felt small. He extended his hand. "I'm Quentin Barnes."

Kimberlin adjusted the duffel bag and shook Quentin's hand. "Ah, the boy wonder. You ready to get some work done?"

"I'm ready to be able to stand up and throw the ball."

"You just make sure that when I give you that time, and I will, you complete those passes."

Quentin looked down at his hand, which had vanished inside Kimberlin's, and wondered: *Is this what normal people feel like when they meet me?*

He looked up again. "I have to say, you are the biggest Human being I've ever seen."

Kimberlin's eyes narrowed. "How about you watch what you call me, Quentin," he said quietly. "We Homo pondus are *not* Human."

"Sorry," Quentin said. The HeavyG were always so sensitive about their race.

"Don't worry about it."

"After you meet the team, I'm happy to show you to your quarters."

Kimberlin smiled. "I'm offensive line, Quentin. I sleep where the offensive line sleeps."

The big man stepped past Quentin. Kimberlin quickly and politely met all that wanted to greet him, nothing more than a smile, a handshake and a nod. When he finished, he walked to the pile of Ki offensive linemen. Most people, including Quentin, would have stopped about three feet from the pile. Kimberlin did not stop. He dropped his bag and walked *into* the pile, letting his body lean up against the Ki. Quentin saw a few limbs touch Kimberlin, then heard a strange, unified grunting from the masses of vocal tubes. The Ki ball broke up into individuals that scuttled out of the docking bay, Kimberlin walking with them.

"Nasty," Yassoud said. "He's going to sleep in the Ki jungle? That is *disgusting*."

"That's unity," Quentin said. "It's what we need, 'Soud."

"Maybe that's what you need. Me? I need a beer."

"No, what you need is to practice. I'm going to the VR room to run routes with the Awa sisters. Halawa's our new number-three receiver, and I have to get her up to speed. Come and join us."

Yassoud stared at him. "We just finished team practice, man, and you want to go work out some more? Forget it." Yassoud walked out of the docking bay.

Quentin waved at the Awa sisters. They ran to him, not as crazily and dutifully as Denver would have, but Quentin had a feeling it wouldn't be long before they exhibited similar behavior.

"Are you ladies ready?"

Neither sister shivered or shook, but twitching eyestalks betrayed their excitement.

The three of them headed for the VR room.

## GFL WEEK FOUR ROUNDUP
(Courtesy of Galaxy Sports Network)

| | | | |
|---|---|---|---|
| **Cloud Killers** | 17 | Juggernauts | 14 |
| **War Dogs** | 31 | Atom Smashers | 22 |
| **Ice Storm** | 31 | Dreadnaughts | 0 |
| Planets | 10 | **Scarlet Fliers** | 24 |
| Astronauts | 10 | **Criminals** | 24 |
| **Intrigue** | 21 | Spider-Bears | 20 |
| Warlords | 35 | **Hullwalkers** | 42 |
| **Pirates** | 42 | Krakens | 21 |
| Vanguard | 3 | **Brigands** | 35 |

With the season one-third complete, the To Pirates are making a bold statement that this is the year for their sixth GFL championship. The Pirates (4-0) doubled up on the Ionath Krakens (1-3) 42-21 to remain undefeated.

But the Pirates aren't alone in lossless land — D'Kow moved to 4-0 with a win over the Jang Atom Smashers (1-3), and the Isis Ice Storm (3-0) stayed perfect coming out of their bye week thanks to a 31-0 drubbing of the Themala Dreadnaughts (1-3).

New Rodina (3-1) suffered its first loss at the hands of the Yall Criminals (2-2). The Lu Juggernauts (2-1) also put their first in the loss column, falling 17-14 in overtime to Coranadillana (2-2).

At the bottom of the Solar Division, only two winless teams remain — the Vik Vanguard (0-3) and the Chillich Spider-Bears (0-3).

### Deaths
Chillich Spider-Bears quarterbacks **Jason Houghton** and **Nelson McClintok**, both of whom died on clean hits from Sala

Intrigue defensive tackle Gum-Aw-Pin. This is the first time in the history of the GFL that one player has killed two members of another team.

Ionath Krakens offensive right guard **Aka-Na-Tak**, killed on a clean hit from To Pirates linebacker Bob Merrell.

More news out of Ionath, GFL Commissioner Rob Froese ruled that Shorah Warlords cornerback Huntertown's death was a clean hit delivered by Krakens wide receiver Halawa.

### Offensive Player of the Week

Cloud Killers kicker **Shi-Ki-Kill**, who was 5-for-5 in field goal attempts hitting from 54, 53, 48, 37 and 14.

### Defensive Player of the Week

**Ryan Nossek**, defensive end for the Isis Ice Storm, who had three sacks on Themala quarterback Gavin Warren.

# 9

# WEEK FIVE:
# WABASH WOLFPACK at
# IONATH KRAKENS

| PLANET DIVISION | | SOLAR DIVISION | |
|---|---|---|---|
| 4-0 | To Pirates | 4-0 | D'Kow War Dogs |
| 3-0 | Isis Ice Storm | 3-1 | New Rodina Astronauts |
| 2-1 | Lu Juggernauts | 3-1 | Bord Brigands |
| 2-1 | Wabash Wolfpack (bye) | 2-2 | Sala Intrigue |
| 2-2 | Coranadillana Cloud Killers | 2-2 | Neptune Scarlet Fliers |
| 2-2 | Yall Criminals | 1-3 | Shorah Warlords |
| 2-2 | Hittoni Hullwalkers | 1-2 | Bartel Water Bugs (bye) |
| 2-2 | Mars Planets | 1-2 | Jupiter Jacks (bye) |
| 1-2 | Alimum Armada (bye) | 1-3 | Jang Atom Smashers |
| 1-3 | Themala Dreadnaughts | 0-3 | Chillich Spider-Bears |
| 1-3 | Ionath Krakens | 0-3 | Vik Vanguard |

JUST LIKE the *Touchback* up in orbit, Ionath Stadium had a full Kriegs-Ballok Virtual Practice System. Tucked in a sub-basement somewhere beneath the home stands, the VR field let players work out against full, photo-realistic opposition. Quentin had arrived at 4:45 a.m., dead-set on beating Rebecca Montagne to the field. He had beaten her, but only by five minutes. If their budding work-ethic rivalry kept escalating, neither one of them would get any sleep at all.

They didn't speak to each other, just ran pattern drills until Halawa, Hawick and Milford arrived ten minutes later for the voluntary pre-practice workout. Over the next ninety minutes, they all worked up a sweat. Halawa was learning quickly, a combination of her natural skill and the nurturing of Hawick and Milford.

Rebecca Montagne would never throw a football in Tier One, but Quentin had to admit she had great hands. She wouldn't be mistaken for a world-class receiver, but she could catch and turn upfield almost instantly.

At 6:30 a.m., they all walked out of the VR room and headed to the main field for morning practice. They came out of the tunnel to a new sight — the rest of the Krakens sitting in the stands at the 50-yard line, packed together as if for a team photo.

"Hey, Q?" Rebecca said. "What's all this, then?"

Quentin shrugged. "Beats me, I've never seen this before."

Hokor's golf cart hovered at the fifty, right above the sidelines. The cart turned to face Quentin and the others.

"*Barnes!* Get over here. The owner wishes to address the team."

Quentin and his early-morning workout partners were apparently the last ones to report. Quentin and Rebecca started jogging to the sidelines. The Sklorno, of course, sprinted at top speed and were already up and in the stands before Quentin was even halfway there.

Gredok the Splithead stood on the sidelines, waiting. Quentin and Rebecca jogged faster.

At the back of the sideline section sat the stadium wall that, on game-day, separated the fans from the players and staff. Messal the Efficient stood at that wall, holding open a door that led up into the stands. Quentin walked through and up the stand steps, saw Yitzhak waving him over. Quentin sat next to the third-string QB.

"Zak, what's going on?"

"Gredok wants to talk to us, and now is not the time for your smart-ass attitude. Just be quiet and listen, cool?"

Yitzhak seemed very anxious, as if any untoward action from Quentin might result in serious repercussions.

"*Quiet!*" Hokor called out over his cart's speakers. "Gredok the Splithead is going to speak."

Gredok took a step closer to the wall. Morning sunlight radiated off his purple shirt and platinum jewelry.

"This week, we host the Wabash Wolfpack," Gredok said. "The Wabash owner is an old acquaintance of mine. And by *acquaintance*, I mean that a high point of my life will be to see her dead."

Gredok paused, looking over his team. Black clouds seemed to swirl in his one big eye. Even though the stadium was vast and open-air, none of the Krakens dared to make a sound. The silence added to the tension.

"Her name is Gloria Ogawa," Gredok said. "She is responsible for the death of my championship quarterback, Bobby Adrojnik. She was cleared by the GFL of any wrong-doing, but I do not care. She killed him. Since this franchise was relegated for the 2677 season, I have been waiting to play her team. Six ... long ... *years*, I have watched Wabash play in Tier One, while Ionath has toiled away in the shame that is Tier Two."

Gredok's eye flooded so black that the cornea looked like plastic. Quentin leaned back a little, noticed that other players were doing the same. Tiny and physically harmless, Gredok had a presence that made one *know* who was boss.

"If you do *not* win this week, if you *lose* in *my stadium*, in *my city*, I will be very ... *very* disappointed."

Gredok turned and walked toward the tunnel. The Krakens sat quietly, watching him go.

"Go team," Quentin said finally. "I don't know about you guys, but that's one whale of a pep talk."

A few nervous laughs filtered out of the Human players.

"All *right!*" Hokor screamed through his loudspeakers. "As if that wasn't enough motivation, we need a win to start climbing out of last place. First offense against practice-squad defense, and *no contact* — I don't need another injury."

Quentin and his teammates stood and walked onto the field. Today's practice would be light, just enough to keep in form before tomorrow's game.

Tomorrow's game, against what appeared to be the mortal enemy of Gredok the Splithead.


**THE HIT CAME** from his blindside, pounding the small of his back, driving him face-first into the blue field of Ionath Stadium. Quentin had held onto the ball too long, again, and had paid the price. He tried to get from his knees to his feet, but it was slow going. He hurt so bad. A big hand grabbed his arm and lifted him up as casually as a child picking up a rag doll.

Quentin was on his feet before he knew it, turning to look at Wabash Wolfpack defensive tackle Stephen Wardop. Wardop wore the Wolfpack away uniform: a pearlescent, white jersey with red letters trimmed in black and a red band that led from the underside of the sleeves down the flanks. The red band lined up with a matching one that continued down the white leg armor. A black-trimmed, red wolf head logo dominated the right shoulder, the wolf's snapping jaws ending at the left pec just above Wardop's number 90. The tip of that same logo ended on his back, just above the number there. The effect gave him one red shoulder, one white shoulder. Both sides of his red helmet carried that same logo.

"You can really fly, know that, Barnes?" Wardop said. "Hit like that, maybe you should think about insurance."

"You call that a hit?"

The big tackle laughed. "No, my friend, I call that a *launch*. I mean, you just *sailed*. Something flies that far, it ought to have a punch-engine in it."

Quentin rolled his eyes, slapped Wardop lightly in the helmet. Wardop had spent so much time in the Krakens backfield that he and Quentin now traded jokes like old friends. The sack had brought up fourth and fifteen. Quentin started jogging off the field as the punt team came on. As he ran, he couldn't help but looking high up above the sidelines, above the lower deck and into the luxury boxes of the rich, the famous, and the *owner*.

Even from down here, he could make out the tiny form of Gredok the Splithead. Standing right next to him, a Human woman. It was too far away to see their expressions, but he *knew* that Gloria Ogawa was smiling and that Gredok was doing everything in his power to keep his eye clear, keep his fur flat.

Midway through the fourth quarter, Wabash 35, Ionath 14. Yassoud wasn't running worth a damn. The Krakens had to pass to move the ball. Michael Kimberlin's individual protection was excellent, but he hadn't gelled with his fellow offensive linemen. Wolfpack defenders slipped through in the confusion. Wabash also kept dropping linebackers into coverage, taking away the short and underneath routes. That made Quentin hold onto the ball a bit longer, waiting for routes to develop, and when you held onto the ball, you were going to give up sacks.

Wabash was willing to take their chances on letting Yassoud break a big run. The gamble paid off with hits on the Krakens QB. Quentin had done something to his right knee. Or, rather, Wardop had done something to it. Quentin's lower-left ribs hurt, but only when he ran. Or walked. Or breathed.

Yassoud had racked up twelve carries in the first half for a whopping total of twenty-three yards before Hokor just gave up on him. In the second half, desperate for a solution, Hokor let everyone have a shot — Jay Martinez carried the ball five times for fifteen yards, Kopor the Climber had a rare four carries for ten yards, Tom Pareless notched eleven yards on three carries and even Becca "The Wrecka" Montagne got into the act, carrying four times for nine yards. Hokor needed someone to break out, to show something in a game that they had not shown on the practice field.

Hokor did not find what he was looking for.

Wabash quarterback Rich Bennett played well, not setting the world on fire but not turning the ball over, either. Wolfpack coach Alan Roark capitalized on his team's defensive dominance, using conservative play-calling aimed at ball control and field position.

Tailback John Ellsworth followed bruising fullback Ralph Schmeer into the holes, taking on all tacklers and always falling forward. When the Wolfpack did throw, Bennett kept his passes short, connecting to tight end Alexander Van Houten and wiry wide receiver Nakusp for eight yards here, ten yards there, chipping away at the Krakens' defense.

Against Ionath's anemic offense, the game plan worked like a charm. As the clock reached 0:00, Quentin heard something that set his soul on edge — the *boos* of the Ionath Stadium crowd, the *hiss* of Quyth Workers rubbing their pedipalps together in that species' favorite sound of derision and disappointment.

Quentin couldn't blame the fans, not one bit. Heading into their bye week, the Krakens were 1-and-4 and in last place. They weren't on a collision course for a Tier One championship, not anymore … now they were flying headlong toward relegation and a trip back to Tier Two.

And, perhaps even worse than that, they had disappointed Gredok the Splithead.

### From the "Galaxy's Greatest Sports Show with Dan, Akbar & Tarat the Smasher"

**DAN:** Okay, caller, you've now established that inbreeding runs in your family for at least six generations, possibly seven, so we really don't need to listen to anymore of your drivel. Sklorno *own* soccer, always have, always will. Humans can't compete.

**TARAT:** I just don't like that game, Dan.

**AKBAR:** You and me both.

**DAN:** All right, this is Sunday post-game review, so let's get back on the topic of the GFL. Two big stories today — Frank Zimmer's concussion and the passing of Sikka the Death, owner and founder of the Orbiting Death in the Quyth Irradiated League in Tier Two.

**TARAT:** Sad to see Sikka go. I played my last two years of football for him.

**AKBAR:** Hold on, hold on, big fella. Did you say *see him go?* Isn't that kind of a nice term for a shuttle crashing into his office, killing him and four other sentients?

**TARAT:** Accidents happen.

**DAN:** Yeah, Akbar, accidents happen.

**AKBAR:** Accident? Come on, guys, isn't it time we talked about the organized crime's influence over the game?

**DAN:** No, Akbar, it is most definitely *not* time to talk about that.

**AKBAR:** When is a good time? Next week?

**DAN:** Oh, I know! How about *never?*

**AKBAR:** You're just afraid the gangsters that run the league will get mad at you.

**DAN:** And why would I worry about *that*, Akbar? Maybe because a shuttle just flew into the office of one of those alleged gangsters? Do these really sound like the kind of sentients you want to anger?

**AKBAR:** I'm not afraid. These gangsters are ruining the game.

**TARAT:** I disagree, at least in the case of the Orbiting Death.

**AKBAR:** What? More Quyth Leader worship from a Quyth Warrior? Wow, what a surprise.

**TARAT:** It's bigger than that. Sikka founded the Orbiting Death. He built them into a quality Tier Two franchise that was always close to reaching Tier One. They never made it, but it wasn't for lack of trying. Sikka took chances on players that other teams wouldn't. Discipline cases like Ju Tweedy, or players that other teams thought were over the hill, like me. I know Sikka wasn't a model citizen, but it was his money and influence that resulted in the construction of Orbital Station One's first intergalactic-caliber sports facility, Beefeater Gin Stadium.

**DAN:** Don't you mean, *The Ace Hole?*

**AKBAR:** Hooo! That never gets old.

**TARAT:** I don't know why you Humans always laugh at that name. Anyway, that stadium, and its jet-black field, is a major cultural unification point for the sentients of OS1. Sikka the Death was a great owner and he built an excellent organization. I will miss him.

**AKBAR:** Well, you can shed a giant tear from your giant eye, Tarat, but I'm more concerned about how his death impacts the Orbiting Death franchise. Who owns it now?

**DAN:** Reports are that Anna Villani, Sikka's second-in-command, has taken over his ... uh ... his affairs.

**AKBAR:** What do you want to bet that she knows people in the shuttle-crashing business? So she has Sikka whacked, and now she owns a GFL franchise?

**TARAT:** Well, doesn't someone have to own it?

**AKBAR:** Sure, but should the league reward murder?

**DAN:** Hey, ho, slow down there, chief! Let's not go throwing the m-word around. Miss Villani might not appreciate that. Let's change the subject and talk about Frank Zimmer's concussion.

**TARAT:** Human brains are so fragile.

**DAN:** Despite all the protective gear technology, concussions continue to be a major source of injury.

**AKBAR:** I don't know why they can't just invent a better helmet.

**DAN:** It's not that easy, Akbar. There are physics involved.

**AKBAR:** What do you mean, physics?

**TARAT:** Physics is the science of matter and energy and interactions between the two, Akbar.

**AKBAR:** I know what physics *is*, Smasher. I'm asking why the great brains of the universe, those computerized egghead scientists of the League of Planets, why can't they make a better helmet?

**DAN:** Well, from what I understand, there is so much mass and force when a six-hundred-pound Ki nails you that your brain bounces off the *inside* of your skull. Helmets can protect the outside, but unless they put some kind of shock absorber between your skull and your brain? Not much can be done. Hence, the situation we have with another Frank Zimmer concussion.

**TARAT:** His seventh, I believe.

**DAN:** Yes, his *seventh* time, and this time Zimmer went down for the count. He took a vicious hit from Mars Planets safety Parbhani and was taken out of the game. The Pirates had been up fourteen to nothing, but with Zimmer out, the offense couldn't do anything. The Planets came back to tie it up in the fourth quarter, then win 17-14 in overtime. The Pirates' first loss of the season. And the concussion is apparently so bad that Zimmer will not play this week against the Isis Ice Storm in a battle for first place in that division.

**TARAT:** I think this puts the Pirates' entire season in question. Their backup quarterback is not at Frank Zimmer's level.

**AKBAR:** It's not like people didn't see this coming. Zimmer can't quarterback forever. Why didn't the Pirates go out and find a backup they could groom to take over?

**TARAT:** The rumor was that they were going after Quentin Barnes.

**DAN:** If that's true, the Pirates could still get their man. If Barnes stays in Tier One, the Pirates can't touch him this year or next due to league regulations. But if the Krakens drop down to Tier Two? Then Barnes is a free agent.

**AKBAR:** Why would Barnes leave the Krakens?

**TARAT:** My sources tell me that Barnes is making league minimum.

**DAN:** *What?* No way.

**TARAT:** My sources assure me it's true.

**DAN:** You heard it here first, Universe. Quentin Barnes, the quarterback of the Tier One Ionath Krakens, is making *league minimum*. Let's get some response to this. Line three from Orbital Station Two, you're on the space, go.

**QUENTIN SANK INTO** the healing warmth of a training room rejuve tank. Doc Patah hovered over him, checking readouts, positioning a clamshell fixture over Quentin's right knee.

"Is it bad, Doc? It hurts, but it doesn't feel *that* bad."

"You have a slight tear in your ACL," Doc Patah said. "In its current state, you could have easily shredded it. I admire your wanting to ignore pain, Quentin, but you need to tell me when you are hurting."

"I thought you said we footballers weren't tough, at least not compared to your fancy mixed-martial-arts fighters."

"Different sport. Fighters do not have backups that can spell them for a few plays if the doctor needs to make adjustments. They also have one fight every seven or eight months, not a season of eleven games. You're not a child anymore, Quentin, you are the focal point of a multi-billion-credit business."

Quentin opened his mouth to argue but realized he didn't have a counterpoint.

"At any rate, it is minor," Doc Patah said. "Twenty minutes in the tank, no strenuous activity tonight or tomorrow, you'll be fine."

Doc's mouthflaps called up the tank's controls. He moved icons, and the clamshell fixture closed on Quentin's knee. Quentin felt cold metal for a moment, then a poke as the nerve blockers kicked in, then nothing. He picked up some vibrations in his thigh — the echo of tiny machines burrowing into his knee to repair the damage. Quentin settled in, put his head back on the tank's rear lip and closed his eyes.

He wasn't sure how long he had sat there, or if he had fallen asleep, when he heard a voice he did *not* want to hear.

"You failed me."

Quentin opened his eyes and sat up, as much as he could sit up with his knee gripped in the fixture. Gredok the Splithead sat on a tiny stool just outside the rejuve tank. No one else was there.

Quentin felt a stab of tension, then forced it away. The rejuve tank's warm goo comforted him, relaxed him. He could use that to keep his emotions steady, not betray anything to the half-pint crime lord.

"I am humiliated," Gredok said slowly. "You are the quarterback, therefore, it is your fault."

Quentin nodded. "That's right."

Gredok stared at him for a moment. Quentin ignored the urge to talk, to fill the silence.

"I just said it is your fault I am humiliated, and you agree with me," Gredok said. "Most sentients would try to deflect my disappointment, knowing what might happen to them if they do not. Why do you not attempt to share the blame?"

"Because you're right. I *am* the quarterback. It's my team. Whatever the reasons for the loss, the buck stops with me."

They sat there for another long minute, perhaps two, neither saying a word. Quentin knew Gredok was measuring him, looking for tells, for signs, but this time there would be none to find — Quentin wouldn't pass the blame to anyone else that might suffer Gredok's wrath.

"Barnes, perhaps I have been wrong. I have been using threats to motivate you. What you Humans call *the stick*. Perhaps someone like you, someone who *chooses* to accept responsibility and ownership, perhaps you need *the carrot*."

Quentin waited, saying nothing.

"I know you are looking for your parents," Gredok said.

Quentin's heart hammered for a second, but he calmed himself, let the healing gel relax him. Now wasn't the time to show emotions. Did Gredok know about Frederico?

"Barnes, I am a powerful being. Very powerful. You know this?"

Quentin nodded.

"I have considerable reach, considerable resources. If I were to put those resources to work for you, you might find your family sooner."

"I would ... appreciate that, Gredok. But what's the catch?"

"The *catch*, Barnes, is that I have two goals for the season. The first was to beat Gloria Ogawa. You failed at that."

"And the second?"

"To *stay* in Tier One."

Gredok leaned forward, his softball-sized eye only a few inches from Quentin's. Quentin could see each individual hair in the silky black fur, see *through* the cornea to the small discs that lined the inside.

"So here is your carrot, Barnes. If you keep the Krakens in Tier One, I *will find* your family. I have police, judges, even *generals* on my payroll. Whatever the cost, I will find their whereabouts."

"And if I don't find a way to keep us in Tier One?"

Gredok stood and waddled away. He stopped halfway and turned.

"If you don't find a way, Barnes, then you will be back in Tier

Two. The entire galaxy will consider you a loser. Is there anything that would frighten you worse?"

Quentin slowly shook his head.

"Find a way, Barnes," Gredok said. "You find a way, and for this one thing, you will find out just what a powerful friend I can be."

Gredok left the training room. Moments later, the knee fixture beeped and released, snapping open, freeing his limb. Quentin stared at it for a moment, contemplated getting up, then finally put his head back down, closed his eyes and let the warm rejuve fluid carry him off to sleep.

## GFL WEEK FIVE ROUNDUP
(Courtesy of Galaxy Sports Network)

| | | | |
|---|---|---|---|
| Water Bugs | 10 | **Brigands** | 17 |
| Spider-Bears | 10 | **Dreadnaughts** | 21 |
| Cloud Killers | 28 | **Armada** | 31 |
| Krakens | 14 | **Wolfpack** | 35 |
| Atom Smashers | 28 | **Jacks** | 42 |
| **Juggernauts** | 27 | Criminals | 17 |
| **Planets** | 17 | Pirates | 14 |
| **Scarlet Fliers** | 21 | Ice Storm | 7 |
| Warlords | 47 | **Intrigue** | 52 |
| **Vanguard** | 20 | War Dogs | 18 |

A thrilling week of GFL action saw all undefeated teams finally suffer the bitter taste of loss. In a major upset, the previously winless Vik Vanguard (1-3) edged out the previously undefeated D'Kow War Dogs (4-1) by a score of 20-18. The Bord Brigands (4-1) moved into a first-place tie with the War Dogs in the Solar Division, thanks to a 17-10 win over the Bartel Water Bugs (1-3).

The To Pirates also dropped their first of the season, falling 17-14 to the Mars Planets (3-2). Things don't get any easier for the Pirates, who face the Isis Ice Storm (3-1) next week in a battle for first place in the Planet Division. The Ice Storm is tied for second with the Lu Juggernauts (3-1) and the Wabash Wolfpack (3-1).

### Deaths
No deaths reported this week.

### Offensive Player of the Week
Dreadnaughts quarterback **Gavin Warren**, who was 18-for-22 with three TD passes in Themala's 21-10 win over Chillich.

**Defensive Player of the Week**

Cloud Killers cornerback **Smileyberg,** who had five tackles and two interceptions, including one she returned 34 yards for a touchdown.

# 10

# WEEK SIX: BYE WEEK

**PLANET DIVISION**

4-1  To Pirates
3-1  Isis Ice Storm
3-1  Lu Juggernauts
3-1  Wabash Wolfpack
3-2  Mars Planets
2-2  Hittoni Hullwalkers (bye)
2-2  Alimum Armada
2-3  Coranadillana Cloud Killers
2-3  Yall Criminals
2-3  Themala Dreadnaughts
1-4  Ionath Krakens

**SOLAR DIVISION**

4-1  Bord Brigands
4-1  D'Kow War Dogs
3-1  New Rodina Astronauts (bye)
3-2  Sala Intrigue
3-2  Neptune Scarlet Fliers
2-2  Jupiter Jacks
1-3  Bartel Water Bugs
1-4  Shorah Warlords
1-4  Jang Atom Smashers
1-3  Vik Vanguard
0-4  Chillich Spider-Bears

**TWO HUMANS,** one Quyth Warrior and two Ki, and Quentin's yacht still had plenty of room. Aside from Don Pine stopping by his quarters to dish out advice, Quentin had never played the role of host before. He liked it.

In the galley, Quentin opened a bag of candied shushuliks and put them in a bowl. Disgusting, but it gave Mum-O-Killowe and Sho-Do-Thikit something to eat that didn't squeal. And, truth be told, shushuliks were not nearly as disgusting as what was in the other snack bowl. Quentin grabbed two mag-cans of Miller with his right hand, put the bowl of shushuliks on top of the other, scooped them both up and walked to the salon.

He had to laugh as he walked in. Not only was this yacht *his*, not only were they taking *his yacht* on an interstellar trip, but he had Mum-O, Sho-Do and Choto the Bright sitting in his salon watching the Galaxy's Greatest Sports Show with Dan, Akbar & Tarat the Smasher. Two of the "Satanic races," right here in his *home*.

He set the bowls on the table. Mum-O and Sho-Do immediately went for the shushuliks, while Choto looked into the other bowl.

"Spider snacks?" Choto said. "Thank you, Quentin."

Quentin gestured to the holotank. "They've been advertising them on GGSS. Nacho flavor. Tarat seems to dig them. Enjoy, just don't ask me to eat any."

"I will not, Quentin."

"And all of you, eat these whole, will ya? I don't want to have to clean up shushulik goo or spider juice off my floor."

All three of the aliens grunted, their mouths already full.

Was it strange that it felt so good to see his guests eating? Comfortable? Happy? He walked to the small control cabin and offered a mag-can to the "captain."

"Frederico," Quentin said. "Beer?"

Frederico shook his head. "Uh, no, Quentin. I don't feel like getting sloshed while I'm driving your rich-boy yacht."

Quentin shrugged. "Okay, that's cool. We all set for the trip?"

"Yep, you can quit worrying. Flight plan is confirmed. We're due in OS1 space in three hours. We already have a docking berth reserved."

"Will we have to do the customs search?"

Frederico shook his head. "Probably not. There are random searches, but it's not like the way the GFL searches everything. We're just another pleasure craft, taking a trip from one Concordia planet to another."

"Awesome. Thanks again for flying this for us. You sure you can't join us at Ma Tweedy's when we arrive?"

Again Frederico shook his head. "Look, I can fly you there, I can stay on the ship as long as no one knows I'm on board, but I *cannot* show my face on OS1, not now that Anna Villani is in charge of things. She and I don't get along."

"You have history with Gredok the Splithead and history with Anna Villani? You going to share any of this?"

"Don't hold your breath," Frederico said. "My business is my business. I'll keep my focus on finding your family, thanks."

"Any progress?"

Frederico half-shrugged, leaned his head to the right. "I've got a few leads. When we get back from OS1, I'm going to have to follow them up. You probably won't hear from me until after the season."

"That's like two months from now."

"You're a regular mathematician."

"I mean I won't hear from you for two months? You can't call?"

Frederico shook his head. "I think that's best. We don't want Gredok to know that I work for you, so calling is bad. I'll just take a guess that your private calls might not be so private."

Quentin opened his mag-can. Even if Frederico didn't find anything, the man was *trying*, which was more than Quentin could do. At least until the off-season. "So where are you going?"

"Where else? The Purist nation. At least for starters. These things take time."

A low beep sounded in the control room.

"Shuttle approaching," Frederico said. "John's landing. You should go greet him in the landing bay, Mister Yacht Owner."

Quentin smiled, set the extra can of Miller on a counter, then walked out.


**QUENTIN STOOD RIGHT WHERE** Manny Sayed had stood a few weeks earlier, waiting for the Krakens shuttle door to lower.

Quentin was genuinely excited about a home-cooked meal, spending a day or so away from football. So cool of John to invite him, even if John was doing it mainly so he wouldn't have to fly public transport.

The door lowered. John walked out. So did Rebecca Montagne. Quentin's smile vanished.

"Q!" John said. "We ready to get this bus rolling?"

"Rebecca," Quentin said. "I didn't know you were coming."

"Hello," she said, looking at him for only a second before looking away.

"She's comin' home to meet Ma," John said. "You don't mind, do you, Q?"

"No," Quentin said, fighting back his annoyance. A trip with John had turned into a big party, including a person he really didn't care to associate with. "Of course, I don't mind."

"Awesome," John said. "So, where're the guys?"

"Salon," Quentin said. He gestured to the door. John and Rebecca walked toward it. Quentin walked after them, unable to miss the fact that John reached out and held Rebecca's hand.


**Transcript from the "Galaxy's Greatest Sports Show with Dan, Akbar & Tarat the Smasher"**

**DAN:** We are back with breaking news. You heard it here first, sentients — Orbital Station One authorities are on the hunt for Orbiting Death running back Ju Tweedy, who is wanted for the murder of Grace McDermot.

**TARAT:** Just shocking.

**DAN:** That it is, Smasher. According to authorities, witnesses reported sounds of conflict in McDermot's apartment. Ju was seen leaving the scene. When neighbors went in just a few minutes later to check on McDermot, they found that she had been beaten to death.

**AKBAR:** That's horrible. Was this McDermot chick someone Tweedy knew?

**DAN:** Apparently they'd been dating, and the police say she may have been trying to break it off.

**AKBAR:** Well, even though Tier Two isn't in season, Ju is still on the Orbiting Death, which means he's got diplomatic immunity. I'm sure the investigation will go on, but he can't be detained, can't even really be questioned without going through a GFL intermediary.

**DAN:** That's true, Akbar, and we'll see ... wait ... the producer is sending me a message. Oh, my, what a *stunning* development. The Orbiting Death has *cut* Ju Tweedy.

**AKBAR:** What?

**TARAT:** Are you joking?

**DAN:** No, this looks valid. Orbiting Death owner Anna Villani just released a statement that says, and I quote, "The Death will not be associated with a murderer, nor will we allow criminals to hide behind diplomatic immunity."

**AKBAR:** A *crime boss* said that? Ridiculous.

**TARAT:** Then The Mad Ju can be arrested, put in jail.

**AKBAR:** They *cut* him? What does that mean?

**TARAT:** Cutting someone means he is no longer on the team roster, Akbar.

**AKBAR:** Smasher! I know what *cut* means, for crying out loud! What I'm saying is that Ju Tweedy is the best running back in football. Who cuts the number-one running back in football?

**DAN:** Apparently, the Orbiting Death. I have to say, if the allegations are true, I commend Villani for cutting him. Most owners would hide their player behind diplomatic immunity. They'd put football and money ahead of justice.

**AKBAR:** Oh, come on, Dan! Did you forget that Anna Villani is the owner of the Orbiting Death because she just assassinated the previous owner?

**TARAT:** That's a good point.

**DAN:** Hey, now, Akbar, we talked about this before. We can't just go throwing around accusations.

**AKBAR:** Dan, you can pretend you don't know what this league is all about, but I call 'em like I see 'em. A gangster like Villani doesn't cut the best running back in football because she wants *justice* for a nobody named Grace McDermot. There's something else going on here.

**TARAT:** You know, I seem to recall that name, Grace McDermot …

**DAN:** Oh, Tarat, I'm sure you're mistaken. Just the name of some poor girl that chased the wrong footballer, I think.

**AKBAR:** No, no, I think Tarat is right. I remember her name from somewhere.

**TARAT:** Hey, I remember. Grace McDermot, wasn't that the actress that dated Villani?

**DAN:** Come on, this isn't some gossip show.

**TARAT:** Oh, now I remember. McDermot was Villani's consort. I do not understand the strange breeding rituals of Humans, but I do remember that.

**AKBAR:** Wow, first Villani whacks Sikka the Death, then she—

**DAN:** Hey, time for another commercial break!

**TARAT:** But we just had a commercial br—

**DAN:** This segment brought to you by Ju-Ku-Killok Shipping. Remember, if you've got to ship it across the galaxy, don't you want to ship it with a Ki? We'll be right back after this.

**QUENTIN TURNED OFF** the holotank just as the Galaxy's Greatest Sports Show faded into commercial. Frederico and his teammates sat in the salon, all frozen, all looking at John Tweedy.

John stared at the now-empty holotank.

"John," Quentin said. "You okay?"

"No," John said. He looked up at Quentin, his eyes narrow, intense. "I have to go get him."

Choto stood up and walked over to John. "There is nothing you can do, John. Anna Villani is in charge of Sikka the Death's syndicate now. She controls the police, judges, maybe even parts of the military. I am sorry for your pain, but if you go after him, all you can do is get caught in the crossfire."

"I have diplomatic immunity," John said. "They can't touch me."

"They can if you are providing aid to a murder suspect,"

Choto said. "Even if you can get to your brother, you would still have to smuggle him out on a ship. Probably *this* ship. If you do that, you risk not only yourself, but your friends and the future of the Krakens. I am sorry, but I grew up on OS1, and I'm telling you there is no way we could get your brother off-planet. He doesn't have immunity anymore."

"Then we give it back to him," Quentin said. "We sign him to the Krakens."

John looked at Quentin and nodded. "Yeah. Yeah, that would work."

Becca stood up. "Are you crazy? John, your brother is a murder suspect."

"He's innocent," John said. "We have to protect him. Tell her, Quentin."

"Innocent until proven guilty," Quentin said. "But he won't have a trial. They'll just kill him. We have to do the right thing."

Rebecca shook her head. "The *right thing?* Oh, no, you don't. John wants to save his brother, sure, but as for you, Quentin? This isn't about protecting an innocent man, this is about *football.* He is a *murder* suspect, you idiots! That poor woman is dead because she couldn't possibly defend herself against someone of Ju's size."

"He wouldn't," John said. "I'm telling you, my brother is a jerk, but he isn't like me ... he's not a killer."

"Has he ever killed anyone on the field?"

"Well, he's never killed anyone outside of football."

"He's taken life," Rebecca said. "On the field, off the field, on purpose, on accident, it doesn't matter. He's a killer, like you, like me."

John shook his head. "You're *wrong*, Becca. And even if you're right, it doesn't matter. He is my brother. Quentin, have Frederico take us into the Madderch Shaft. I'm going after Ju."

Becca turned to Quentin. "This is your ship. Don't take us into Madderch. They'll be waiting for us."

"*No*," John said. "Look, we already had a flight plan filed, before any of this happened. That won't raise any suspicion. If I try to book commercial travel now, my name will show up somewhere because I'm the brother of a murder suspect. You guys don't have to go into Madderch with me, but at least get me there."

Quentin looked at Becca, then at John. John, who had tried to help Quentin find his family. John, who had secretly hired a bodyguard. John, whose brother just so happened to be the best running back in football. Was this about doing the right thing, or was Becca right — was it about the game?

"I'm going with John," Quentin said.

"But you can't even sign Ju!" Becca said. "You don't have that authority."

Quentin nodded. "Then I guess I'll have to find someone who does. Frederico?"

The detective stood. "Yes?"

"Get us ready to make the punch to Orbital Station One. We go as soon as I finish my call."

Quentin walked out of the salon and into his stateroom. He stood in front of the room's smaller holotank, called up the interface, then punched in a call to the *Touchback*.

**"BARNES!" HOKOR SAID,** his face slightly larger than life in the holotank. "You will *not* go to OS1! I'm sending the shuttle for you right now, you and your teammates will return to the *Touchback*."

Quentin crossed his arms and shook his head. "Can't do that, Coach. I can fix this. Just give me authorization to sign Ju Tweedy."

"Absolutely not, Barnes. Don't get involved with him, don't get involved with Anna Villani. Only Gredok can do something like that."

"But she'll kill John's brother!"

"You do *not* sleep with a gangster's concubine. John's brother played with fire. Now, he will pay the price. I will not have his idiocy damaging the players on *my team*."

"John is going to Madderch with or without your permission, Coach. I can't let him go alone."

"*Barnes!* Do not take John Tweedy to Orbital Station One. If you do, Gredok will rip your head right off your narrow, Human neck."

Quentin closed his eyes, tried to work through the possibilities. If Gredok was in Ionath City, he was a twenty-, maybe thirty-minute trip up to the *Touchback*. Would Gredok come after them? If Quentin were the owner, would he?

Yes. He would. An owner could not let five of his starting players get themselves killed. Quentin wasn't just a rescuer, he was also bait.

"Coach, we're going. If Gredok backs our play, we'll win. If he doesn't ... well, it's truly been an honor to play football for you."

"*Barnes!* Don't you—"

Quentin broke the connection and walked back into the salon.

"Well?" John said. "Is Gredok going to follow us in?"

"Absolutely. He has to. We're going, right now. Anyone wants out, take the yacht's shuttle and go to the *Touchback*. Our teammate needs us, so who is in?"

Mum-O-Killowe let out a horrid war cry and waved his upper arms. Sho-Do-Thikit snapped out an arm and flicked Mum-O in the vocal tubes. Mum-O yelped, then fell silent. Sho-Do then banged his upper right hand against his chest. The exchange told Quentin that the two Ki were in but that Mum-O had spoken out of turn — Sho-Do-Thikit was the alpha and wasn't about to let the juvenile defensive tackle forget it.

Quentin looked at Choto. "You're from OS1, Choto. We need you. Are you in?"

"I am tasked with protecting you," Choto said. "So if you are going, I have no choice."

That left only Becca. "Montagne, you want out? Then leave."

She chewed her lower lip, glaring at him. "You're a bastard, Barnes. We're one-and-four, you're heading into a dangerous situation, and you're taking our two starting linebackers, our left tackle, *and* our star defensive lineman."

Mum-O-Killowe let out a little bark.

"Don't mention it," Rebecca said. "Quentin, if this goes wrong, if anything happens, the Krakens are heading back to Tier

Two for sure. Not even Yassoud would bet against that, no matter what odds you gave him."

She was right and he knew it, but there was a bigger game afoot. They might get hurt, get killed, but he believed with utter conviction that if they didn't sign Ju Tweedy, the Krakens were headed for relegation regardless.

"Everyone here knows the risks," Quentin said. "They also know the reward. The situation isn't black and white, so make your call."

She glared at him with pure hate. He stared back. The battle of wills lasted only a few seconds before she looked down and away.

"All right," she said. "I'll go."

He nodded at Frederico. "Take us to Orbital Station One."

**QUENTIN MANAGED** to not throw up during the punch-in, an amazing feat considering that the smell of candied shushuliks still filled the salon. Three hours until punch-out into normal space: time enough to plan.

"Choto," Quentin said. "Madderch is your stomping grounds. What do we do?"

"The city has fifty million people," Choto said. "Unless John knows where his brother might be, we don't have a chance."

John rubbed his hands. His face tat spelled out gibberish. "A couple of seasons ago, I visited Madderch and went out drinking with Ju and his teammate Shi-Ki-Kill. We went for Chinese food. A couple of rowdies tried to rob the restaurant. Ju and I beat the crap out of them, rousted them out. No cops, no reports, no nothing. The owner said if we ever needed a favor, we could ask him for anything. If Ju is still on-planet, that's where he'll hide."

"Chinese food," Choto said. "You remember the name of the place?"

John nodded. "Chucky Chong's League-Style House of Chow."

"I know that restaurant," Choto said. "Excellent moo goo gai pan. But there is a problem. Chucky Chong's is two miles from the shaft opening."

"Two miles?" Quentin said. "That's nothing, we could grab a cab, even jog it in like twenty minutes."

"No," Choto said. "Your face is too famous, Quentin. And you as well, John. People may recognize you. If word gets out, the police or Anna's people will follow you right to Ju. I am a native son of Madderch, and as such, I am also too well known. There will be a sentient-hunt for Ju, so police will be all over the streets."

"We split up?"

John shook his head. "Unless my brother sees me, he won't go with anyone."

Quentin didn't have to know Ju to see the logic in that. Were he in Ju's shoes, there were only a few people he would trust. "Then, we all go together. Choto, can you make some calls when we come out of punch-space? There's got to be some way we can travel those two miles without being seen."

They waited as Choto considered this.

"I don't know anyone directly," he said finally. "I won't have my family move us around, it is too risky — sorry, John."

John nodded. "I understand."

"I haven't lived in Madderch for years," Choto said. "But my family has connections in the sanitation department. I will try to set something up. But whatever we do, success, if not our lives, will depend on Gredok arriving soon after us to sign Ju. He will come?"

Quentin nodded. "Yes, Gredok is coming. Trust me."

His teammates seemed somewhat relieved by this. They all trusted him. At least all but Rebecca Montagne. She stared at Quentin, anger and doubt in her eyes.

He just hoped that his plan would work and he could prove her wrong.

**SITTING ALONE IN HIS STATEROOM,** Quentin felt the reality wave break over the *Hypatia*, felt himself spreading, separating. Then almost as soon it started, it was over. He managed to keep down the snack he'd had during the short flight. Maybe he was finally getting used to space travel. That, or the fear of what he was doing far outweighed his fear of punch-space. Having one crime lord unhappy with him was bad enough. He was about to make it two. And that was the best-case scenario. The worst? He wouldn't make it off Orbital Station One alive.

He slowly breathed away the stress of the flight, then walked out of his stateroom and into the salon. His passengers waited for him: Rebecca Montagne, Mum-O-Killowe, Sho-Do-Thikit, John Tweedy and Choto the Bright.

Choto worked a palm-up display, pedipalp fingers touching and moving glowing icons. A message scrolled through the air, but Quentin didn't know how to read Quyth.

"Choto, what's the word?"

"We have transport," Choto said. "This is very short notice, Quentin, but my brother knows an OS1 native who can get us to Chucky Chong's."

"A Quyth Warrior? A Worker?"

"Human," Choto said. "The Concordia accepts all citizens."

Quentin nodded. He found it hard to remember that the other governments weren't like the Purist Nation and that in most systems, all species were welcome. Orbital Station One had native Human residents that could trace their roots back some two centuries, to ancestors who had emigrated from the Planetary Union, the League of Planets or even the Purist Nation.

Choto closed his left pedipalp hand. The holopalm blinked out. He turned to look out a view port window to Orbital Station One, the place of his birth. "Once this yacht moors to the shaft wall, we must all fit into the lifeboat. My contact will pick us up there. What we will do is dangerous. But to rescue John's brother, there is no other way I can think of. Quentin, are you *sure* that Gredok will come after us?"

"Absolutely," Quentin said, although he still had no idea. "He's got our back, Choto. You know it."

Quentin looked out the view port at the massive construct. Orbital Station One, or "The Ace," as it was frequently called. The planetoid was completely artificial, built over centuries by the

Quyth as an outlet for the excess population of their homeworld. Quentin had been here once before, during the Tier Two season. The pointy sphere reminded him of a massive medieval mace, a rock studded with blue, metallic points.

The "points" were actually crystalline spires probably two miles high, a mile thick at their base. They reflected a dull, metallic-blue color, their surfaces worn and pitted from space dust and debris. They were projections of the silica-based lifeform that made up the planet's ever-expanding framework. Centuries of terraforming had brought in countless asteroids, gradually building up mass. That same crystalline material made up most of the buildings, city streets, even the sprawling football stadium known as the Black Hole by the locals, and The Ace Hole by Human detractors throughout the rest of the Concordia.

Frederico flew the *Hypatia* straight toward a unique spire. Unlike the thousands of points that angled to a weathered tip, this one extended about a mile up from the uneven surface before ending in a two-mile-wide circular opening. This entrance led through the crust of OS1 and into Madderch, The Ace's main city center.

Frederico's voice came over the yacht's speakerfilm. "So far, so good. I'm sure Villani will have cops check registrations for incoming ships to see if any GFL players or staff are coming in, but I think they'll focus on flight plans filed after Ju got cut. We might escape notice long enough to get you all off the yacht."

"Might?" Becca said. "Well, that's comforting."

The players rode in silence as the *Hypatia* slid through the void toward the opening's edge. Quentin watched the changing view, mesmerized by the scale of what he saw. Starships, some twenty times the size of the *Hypatia*, noiselessly moved in and out of the two-mile-wide shaft.

The *Hypatia* slid over the shaft, bottom parallel to OS1's surface, then descended belly-first. Long rows of lights ran down the inside of the shaft, each light far larger than the yacht itself, a line of illumination reaching down and down to the buried civilization far below. Like the last time he'd been here, the long strings of lights reminded Quentin of the mines on Micovi, the mines he'd worked before a gangster discovered that he had a million-credit arm.

The *Hypatia* descended the shaft, the big ship suddenly small in the presence of the miles-long traverse. Bluish projections jutted forth from the walls, the same bluish material that made up the spires and most of OS1's framework. Thousands of small interstellar-capable ships were moored to these projections, running the gamut of sizes from small trucks, cargo tugs and yachts up to massive haulers far larger than the *Touchback* and something that made Quentin nervous — warships.

The Purist Nation had no warships, at least none that he'd ever seen. Creterakians restricted the navies of all the conquered systems. The Quyth Concordia, however, was not a conquered system and, as an independent system, had one of the galaxy's largest fleets.

The moored ships did not move, but the spires themselves showed countless spots of activity. Yellow, bug-like machines crawled the walls, along the piers, around the docked ships. The machines trimmed and repaired the always-growing blue silicate, keeping the semi-organic surface tidy, clean and ready for commerce. It was hard to focus on just one of the machines — they moved about in such numbers, it was like trying to see an individual ant amidst a swarming ant hill.

The *Hypatia* slowed, then shuddered as it moored to some long, unseen blue spike.

They had arrived.

"You better move fast," Frederico called out on the sound system. "I just got a notice from customs officials. We were tapped for a random inspection."

"Okay, team," Quentin said. "To the lifeboat. Let's go."


**AS A FOOTBALL PLAYER,** Quentin Barnes had gotten up-close and personal with all the races: Human, HeavyG, Ki, Quyth Warrior and Sklorno. The hitting, blocking and tackling usually involved physical contact with just one or two other beings. Fumble-recovery pileups, however, created a mass of twisted bodies all jammed together so tightly that the players on the bottom couldn't move until the whistle blew and the pile slowly broke apart.

A pileup like that seemed roomy compared to the lifeboat and the packed mass of sentients crammed inside. Quentin had somehow wound up against the inner hull — he felt metal grate pushing into his right cheek, the bony carapace of Choto's elbow pressing into his left. Rebecca Montagne's muscular body was pressed into his back, someone was damn near cutting off the circulation in his legs, and — worst of all — a Ki arm or leg was mashed right up against his lips. It wasn't racist to say that the Ki stank (because they did, and *bad*). Now, Quentin had firsthand knowledge that they tasted even worse.

Lifeboats were made for four normal-sized sentients or three GFL-sized ones. In this lifeboat, they had managed to pack in two Humans, a HeavyG woman, a Quyth Warrior and two Ki.

"Hey, Wrecka," John said. "Get your foot off my knee, will ya?"

"I can't move," Rebecca said. "And I don't think that's me on your leg."

"Well, someone's foot is on my knee," John said. "Hey, whose foot is on my knee?"

Quentin managed to bend his leg a little, then give a short stomp.

"Hey!" John said.

"It's my foot," Quentin said. "Mystery solved, Uncle Johnny, now shut up and deal with it like the rest of us."

The only advantage to Quentin's mashed-up posture was that his right eye was almost on top of an exterior monitor. His left hand was smashed against his chest, but he could wiggle his fingers enough to work the monitor's controls.

Speakerfilm inside the lifeboat emitted Frederico's voice, somewhat muffled by the two thousand pounds of tightly packed footballers.

"This is your captain speaking," Frederico's said. "I believe your local guide is en route."

Quentin looked at the monitor and saw what Frederico was talking about. A spiderish machine the size of an air-tank scuttled along the underside of the blue spire, moving with a jerky precision. Hooked feet dug into the slick, jewel-like surface, letting the machine practically sprint down the length. The gravity here was just a hair under standard, which meant that if the maintenance machine fell — unless it had anti-grav (and it didn't look big enough for that) — it would plummet two miles straight down the shaft to the city of Madderch below.

"Uh, Choto?" Quentin said as the machine rushed closer, filling up the tiny screen. "I don't know about this ..."

"It is the only way," Choto said. "And John, your feet smell like the rear-end of a giant greten fish."

"Hey!" John said. "You leave my feet out of this."

"If only I could," Choto said.

"Choto, *seriously*," Quentin said. The yellow crawler moved faster and faster, closing in. The pier shook just a little with each spidery step. "This is a *bad* idea."

"Just hold on," Choto said. "The ride is about to get bumpy. Quentin, please release the locks."

Quentin moved his left hand and hit a button, releasing the locks holding the lifeboat firmly in place. He then switched the view, letting him see it from a camera farther up the *Hypatia's* side.

As soon as he did, he wished he hadn't.

The yellow spider-machine reached one long arm into the lifeboat hold. The lifeboat rattled, then lurched. Quentin started to say something, and just as he did the whole lifeboat turned and the Ki arm (or leg) that had just been on his lips now slid into his mouth and pressed down on his tongue.

*Oh High One, why would you ever create anything that tastes as bad as this?*

Quentin bit down hard. He heard Mum-O-Killowe roar, then felt the limb yank out of his mouth. He clamped his jaws shut, hoping he would never experience something like that again as long as he lived.

There was no room for them to be thrown around by the spider-machine's rough handling, but their weight shifted and turned and pressed them against each other. On the screen, Quentin saw the machine arm pull the lifeboat out of the *Hypatia*, then bend the arm and press the lifeboat against its back. It turned in place and scurried down the protrusion.

As he lurched helplessly from side to side, Quentin switched camera angle again. The next view must have come from the top of the lifeboat because he wasn't staring at the protrusion or the spider-machine — he was looking straight down the seemingly bottomless, hollow spire. His stomach roiled. The view, combined with the pure-evil taste of the Ki limb, made him fight to stop from puking up that snack he'd so expertly held down after the punch-out.

The spider-machine moved fast toward the shaft wall, angled for a crack in the rocky blue material and crawled right inside. A sudden lurch and grinding sound told Quentin the lifeboat had smashed into something, probably the side wall. His brand-new lifeboat from his brand-new yacht, now probably all scratched and dented. And oh, great — the static on the small screen told him the camera had probably been torn away. He could see nothing more and really had no idea where the driver was taking them. If there even *was* a driver at all.

The Krakens players jostled heavily against each other for another few minutes, thrown this way and that but mostly *down* as the machine seemed to head for the city below.

Then a final lurch, a *gong*, and the lifeboat moved no more.

"Quentin," Choto said. "Open it up, please."

"*Please*," Rebecca said. "John's feet, oh, my *God*, please get the door open."

"Hey!" John said.

Quentin was now inverted at a forty-five-degree angle, head lower than his feet. He had to squirm a little, but he reached out and found the button to open the lifeboat.

The six teammates half-fell, half-crawled out. Quentin had a cramp in his right leg and he wanted very badly to brush his teeth, get that rancid dead-sparrow taste of Ki out of his mouth.

Quentin stood and stretched as he looked around. They were

in a small cavern, lit by glowing balls of various sizes that jutted partially out from the blue, translucent ceiling. The light illuminated cracks and veins of varying density. A second spider-machine crouched nearby, the back end of its left side taken off, parts spread all over the translucent blue ground. Racks of tools and other equipment ringed the parts.

As Quentin suspected, his new lifeboat was beat to crap. Scratched, dented, long gouges in the orange paint. He'd had it, what, four weeks? Nothing he could do about it now. The spider-machine that had carried the lifeboat gave off metallic groans as the legs folded in on themselves and lowered the body. The dented yellow head split, the bottom half descended to the ground. A man in a yellow jumpsuit and scuffed leather boots stepped out. Quentin couldn't read Quyth, but he assumed the large patch on the man's shoulder said something like *Madderch Sanitation and Maintenance*.

"Howdy, all," the driver said. "Shirop the Heavy-Handed told me you needed a local. The name is Jake. Jake Bible."

John stepped up quickly and shook the man's hand. "John Tweedy."

"I know who you are," Jake said. "I watched you Krakens guys beat the Death last year. The Krakens suck, by the way."

The fact that John didn't instantly hit Jake right in the mouth was testimony to his stress level, his focus on rescuing Ju.

"So how do we get to my brother?" John asked. "We've got to move fast, man."

"Depends," Jake said. "I can't get you to him until I know where he is."

John paused, then looked at Choto. "Can we trust this guy?"

"I do not know," Choto said. "I have never met this Human. But I am afraid we don't have a choice. Wherever your brother is, he can't hide for much longer."

"No kidding," Jake said. "Ju has like the most famous face in all of The Ace. Villani wants him bad, too — she's offered a reward of a hundred grand for info that leads to his arrest or capture or ..."

Jake's voice trailed off when he saw John staring with those crazy eyes.

"Say it," John said. "Or what?"

Jake took a small step back before answering. "Or his death. If you guys don't get The Mad Ju off this station fast, the only way he's leaving is in a coffin."

John nodded. "Okay, okay. I guess I have to trust you, Jake Bible. You get fifty grand if I reach my brother. Screw us, I'll kill you myself. But if you rat us out? Then I turn you over to *him*."

John pointed at Mum-O-Killowe, who let out a long, low, answering growl.

Jake took a good look at the twelve-foot-long Ki, then nodded. "Right," he said. "I get it. You guys make your point loud and clear, no need for any violent examples. So where do we go?"

"Have you heard of Chucky Chong's League-Style House of Chow?"

"The moo goo gai pan place?"

John nodded.

"I know it," Jake said. "I'll have us there in twenty minutes. It's close, but we'll have to take wall-crack paths. Cops are searching every vehicle in the city. So, everyone will be riding in the storage section of *that*."

Jake pointed to his spider-machine. Quentin sighed. Somehow he'd known that was coming.

**AFTER THIRTY MINUTES OF BEING** slammed around a storage space only slightly larger than the lifeboat, the maintenance machine's back hatch opened. Quentin crawled out into a dirty back alley, stepping over a wrongly folded Mum-O-Killowe in the process.

And he'd thought he felt beat-up after a game? That ride was like playing three games in a row.

Quentin had to assume the customs inspection hadn't been a coincidence, assume that Anna Villani knew he was here. A very real threat, yet he had been tucked away inside a maintenance ma-

chine, one that looked just like tens of thousands of other maintenance machines spread throughout the city. If he and his teammates
hadn't been spotted coming out of the *Hypatia*, then no one would
know exactly where they were. As GFL players, they couldn't be
arrested or detained — but if Anna owned the cops, they probably
weren't worried about filing reports and following regulations.

Jake Bible stepped out of the spider-machine and quickly
walked back to Quentin and the others, his head swiveling from
side to side as he looked around the alley for anything suspicious.
He carried two large duffel bags filled with something bulky, but
obviously light.

"This the place?" Quentin asked.

"No, but close," Jake said. "I had to park in an alley. A pier-
maintenance crawler too near a main street would draw attention."

"So you have a grav-car for us or something?"

"Nope. Now you walk."

"But we might get recognized," Quentin said. "You recognized
John right off."

"I brought you disguises," Jake said and tossed the bags to the
ground at Quentin's feet.

Quentin knelt and opened the first bag. He reached in and
pulled out a black jacket that had a blue-trimmed, metalflake-red
circle on the left breast.

"No way," John said. "You want us to dress up like Orbiting
Death fans?"

"It's perfect," Jake said. "Probably fifteen thousand sentients
in the city tonight wearing Death gear. It's just what people wear
here. Death football is like a religion. And a lot of *plus-sized* sentients are fans. You know, the GFL-wannabe types?"

Quentin started passing out the gear: jackets, shirts, jerseys
and — most importantly — hats. He and his teammates put on
the items.

Jake smiled. "Yeah, now you guys look good. I can get you
more gear when the Death wins the Tier Two tourney and moves
up to whip your fat Kraken butts next season."

John walked up and put his huge hand on Jake's neck, squeezed and lifted. "I let that earlier comment slide," John said. "And I'll let this one slide, too, because I need to get to my brother, but I'm starting to get offended."

I WILL BEAT YOU TO DEATH WITH YOUR OWN FOOT scrolled across John's face.

He set Jake down gently. The smaller man rubbed his neck. "Right, got it. Gooooo, Krakens, okay? Now, where's my money?"

"I get my brother, you get your money," John said. He walked to the end of the alley. Quentin followed and looked out into the streets, up at the buildings.

Madderch sat nestled inside a sprawling blue dome. Massive blue tinted crystals reached out from inside the dome, curving around themselves and intertwining with each other like some unfathomable concave beard.

The city's buildings were mostly made from the same blue metallic material, an organic substance that seemed bubbly, almost as if it was made by pouring water down a wall and letting it freeze, layer by layer, into a thick sheet of ice. Trimming maintenance vehicles, both flying and crawling, were always in motion, cutting away at spiraling growths that stuck out from buildings, streets and even from the long connections that linked the buildings together. Some of the buildings towered so high the eye and mind had trouble reconciling it, trouble making sense of top floors that were almost a half-mile above ground level.

The living crystal didn't limit itself to well-defined buildings. Spires, spurs and branches reached from building to building, curving over alleys, streets, even stretching out so far they arched over entire blocks. There were so many connections that by three or four blocks away, the buildings all looked like parts of an enormous sponge.

On one of the buildings, Quentin saw a fifty-foot-high animated image of Ju Tweedy jumping up and over clashing linemen to land in the end zone. Ju's face had to be ten feet high, if not bigger. Every being in the city of Madderch knew *exactly* what he looked like. And at 6-foot-8, 365 pounds, even if you *could* disguise that famous face, you'd have a hard time disguising the big body.

"Hey," John said. "That's the place."

Quentin looked to where John was pointing. The base of a towering building held many street-level businesses, but Quentin knew their destination when he saw it. Squiggly red symbols covered a white storefront, as did holos of Quyth Warriors repeatedly dipping pedipalps into square, white containers and pulling out bunches of long noodles. The sign above the restaurant read CHUCKY CHONG'S LEAGUE-STYLE HOUSE OF CHOW.

Hundreds of sentients walked up and down the street, staying on the sidewalks to avoid grav-cars traveling more than a little too fast. Other sentients — mostly Quyth Workers, but also Humans, some Sklorno, flapping Creterakian civilians and a few Ki — weren't really moving at all. They leaned against walls, sat on the sidewalk, hung from streetlamps and signs, all with postures that either radiated defeat or ached with predation. Quentin recognized their kind from many years of surviving on the streets of Micovi: petty thugs, street toughs, drug addicts, drunks, hookers and the refuse common to any big city anywhere in the galaxy.

"High-class place, John," Quentin said. "You and your brother really know how to pick 'em."

"The egg rolls are unreal," John said distantly, his wide-eyed gaze flicking from sentient to sentient. "They put shredded tenati mites in there."

Quentin shuddered at the thought, imagined that he might have been wrong — there might be something that tasted even worse than Ki leg. "All right. This burger ain't gonna cook itself. John, get the rest of the team. We're going in."

Quentin crossed the street, careful to avoid the cars. By the time he walked into Chucky Chong's, his teammates were right behind him.

The decor was a crazy mix of themes: Tower nautical and old-Earth China. A dozen sentients sat in cushioned red booths. Mostly Human, but there were a few Quyth Workers as well. One HeavyG man, his table covered with heaping plates. Everyone in the restaurant looked working-class: construction, maintenance, manufacturing, that kind of thing.

Behind the counter floated a white-skinned Harrah wearing a red backpack. Gold characters — which Quentin could only assume were Chinese — emblazoned the backpack's red enamel. The Harrah saw Quentin and the others, then flew out from behind the counter to stop in front of Quentin and John.

"Herro," it said to John. "It has been a rong time."

John nodded, smiled just a little. "Chucky."

Quentin looked from the Harrah to John. "*This* is Chucky Chong?"

"What?" the Harrah said. "You no think I rook Chinese?"

"I ... uh ... I wouldn't know what Chinese look like, Mister Chong."

"Rook rike me," Chucky said, then turned to face John. "Now, I go get your ... friend. You get him out of here, get him out safe?"

John nodded.

Chucky Chong's white wing-flaps fluttered. He gracefully shot over the counter and through a door that probably led into the kitchen. Seconds later, he came out, trailed by a massive Human wearing sunglasses, a thick black hat and a long, tan coat.

"Great disguise," Quentin said. "We'll get at least twenty feet before anyone recognizes him."

John either didn't hear the comment or ignored it. He walked quickly to his brother, reached his hands up and held both of Ju's shoulders.

Ju smiled with relief. "Big brother."

"Hey," John said. "Ready?"

Ju nodded.

Rebecca walked up fast and poked Ju in his chest. "Did you do it, Ju? Did you kill that girl?"

Ju stared down at her. "Who is this?"

"I'm the woman that just risked her life to save your ass," she said. "And you're going to look me in the eye and answer my question."

"Becca," John said, "of course, he didn —"

Becca turned on him, her eyes full of fury and even more intensity than she showed on the field. "John, *shut up*. A woman was murdered. We're not going anywhere until I believe Ju didn't do it."

The restaurant fell silent. Ju looked down at her for a few seconds more, then slowly shook his head.

"I didn't do it," he said. "I ... couldn't have done it. I loved her. They set me up."

Rebecca stared up at him, stared up hard. Ju did not look away. He had a sadness to his eyes, a fatigue. It seemed like a strange expression — a sense of loss combined with resignation, as if what was done was done and he already knew he had to move on.

"Becca," Quentin said. "We have to go."

"You're not going anywhere," a voice called from the front door. "At least not with *our* running back."

Quentin turned to see six sentients: a normal-sized Ki in front, only about 250 pounds compared to Mum-O-Killowe's 650, a Creterakian civilian on that Ki's shoulder, two GFL-sized HeavyG, an oversized Sklorno nearly as big as the Awa sisters and a Ki so big it was still trying to fit its body through the front door.

Chucky Chong shot through the air to hover in front of the new arrivals. "You no welcome heah! We crose! You go!"

The six ignored the Harrah restaurateur. All of them wore nondescript clothes, save for the Creterakian. His garish outfit was light yellow with blue polka dots.

The colors of the Coranadillana Cloud Killers.

"Crap," Quentin said.

Quentin recognized some of the Cloud Killer players, like the hard-hitting Sklorno cornerback Smileyberg and the HeavyG tight end Jesper Schultz.

John Tweedy stepped up to stand next to Quentin.

"Damn," John said. "I forgot that the Killers picked up Shi-Ki-Kill in the off-season."

Quentin pointed at the small Ki. "Is that Shi-Ki?"

John nodded. The kicker-sized Ki grunted. Things had just become much, much more complicated. Coranadillana was a city on the planet Satah of the Harrah Tribal Accord. Satah, which was even closer to Orbital Station One than Ionath was.

"Wanna know something, John?" Quentin said absently. "Considering that Shi-Ki is the only one besides you that could have possibly known Ju might hide here, and considering he plays for a Tier One team that is as bad off as we are, *and* considering that team has a bye week just like we do, John, it might have shucking helped if you'd remembered that."

"Sorry," John said.

Quentin shrugged. He hadn't come all this way to lose the galaxy's best running back to anyone, especially to a team that the Krakens played in just three weeks. "It doesn't matter anymore. We've got bigger fish to fry."

The small Ki barked a short, choppy sentence, his voice just as big and strong as that of Sho-Do-Thikit or Mum-O.

"Barnes," the Creterakian said. "Shi-Ki-Kill says that if that is a joke about his size, it's not funny."

"I don't care what he thinks," Quentin said. "Ju Tweedy is coming with us."

"Wrong," the Creterakian said. "My name is Molloya. I am the official representative of the warlord Yashahon, owner of the Cloud Killers and leader of the Yashahon tribe of planet Satah. I am here to offer Ju Tweedy a contract."

"How much?" Ju said.

John turned on him. "Ju! You can't sign with them!"

"Why not? I have to get immunity or I'm screwed."

"But we came to get you!"

Molloya flew overhead, just out of reach. The leathery, flapping noise reminded Quentin of his days back on Micovi, when the bats would "police" an area or a situation and people would die if they happened to move too fast. But he wasn't in Creterakian-controlled territory anymore, and this disgusting creature flying above his head was just another scumbag gangster.

"We offer league maximum," Molloya said. "Three seasons, guaranteed."

John's face turned white.

"Nice," Ju said. "But what about Anna Villani? Can you protect me from her?"

Molloya let out a horrid, screeching sound that must have been Creterakian laughter. "Villani's power is nothing compared to the glorious warlord Yashahon. Once we have you on Satah, you are safe."

Ju nodded, then turned to look at Quentin. "And what are the Krakens offering for a contract?"

"Are you *kidding* me?" Quentin said. "There is a price on your head. Everyone on The Ace is looking for you. If Villani finds you, you're a dead man, and you're *negotiating*?"

Ju shrugged. "Business is business. I'm a rare commodity. If you have an offer, make it. If not, I can live with three years max salary."

"We can match that," Quentin said quickly, having no idea if the Krakens could, nor having any idea what constituted *league maximum*.

"He lies!" Molloya screamed from above. "He is not authorized to sign a deal, Ju, and time is ticking away. Villani is closing the noose. Barnes can't make that deal, nor can any of his teammates. Ask him!"

Ju looked from Molloya to Quentin. The look on Ju's face was a mixture of calmness and greed. He felt safe now. His worst-case scenario was a trip to Tier One and a big paycheck. His best case was a trip to Tier One and an even bigger paycheck.

"Well?" Ju said. "You did bring a contract box, didn't you, Quentin?"

Quentin's hands clenched into fists. He hadn't thought another team could get here this fast. He should have checked the schedule, seen who had an off-week, who was in the area. There was nothing he could do now unless he wanted to start a brawl, and a brawl might land them all in jail. He'd lost.

"Know what, Ju?" John said. "I don't think it matters who brought the contract box, Ju."

"And why's that, big brother?"

"Because your only chance is to walk out of here with the last team left standing."

Quentin started to say *John, no*, but it was already too late. The bulky linebacker turned and shot toward the Cloud Killers players, crossing the restaurant with the kind of blazing speed only professional athletes possess. Quentin saw Shi-Ki-Kill's black eyes widen (perhaps that was a common fear response among all sentients) just before Tweedy slammed into him, driving him back, using him as a shield to crash through the other Cloud Killers players.

Mum-O-Killowe must have started running a split second after John because the young Ki followed John in, compressing and extending in a powerful, straight-line shot that took one of the HeavyGs right off his feet. Sho-Do-Thikit shot into the fray, as did Rebecca Montagne. The diner started to disintegrate. Tables and chairs shattered, counters cracked, dishes flew, and food sprayed in every direction.

"You no fight heah!" Chucky Chong screamed. "You go now!"

Jesper Schultz rushed at Quentin. Quentin side-stepped the big HeavyG's swing, then brought his own fist around in an overhand right that caught Schultz on the left cheek. Pain shot through Quentin's hand. It seemed to hurt him more than the HeavyG, who turned and swung a backhand left that caught Quentin in the mouth and threw him backward. He crashed through a table and landed on his back amidst broken wood and plastic, looking up at the pair of Sklorno dressed in all black.

"Quentin Barnes eats dinner with us!" the one on the left screamed. The one on the right simply sagged in her seat, shaking in rapture. Great, he'd been recognized.

A massive hand grabbed his foot and yanked him out from the wreckage. Now he found himself looking up at the HeavyG.

"No red jersey for you here, you pansy quarterback," the enormous Schultz said as he cranked his fist back to deliver a crushing blow. A blow he never landed because Rebecca Montagne dove in at top speed and put her shoulder into Schultz's exposed ribs. Quentin heard a *crack* and a deep cry of pain from the man.

Schultz stumbled and sagged. Rebecca landed on top of him, then started kneeing him in the face.

Quentin saw that Ju Tweedy was just standing there, smiling, watching it all go down.

"Ju is in there!"

That voice came from outside the diner, and Quentin recognized it — Jake Bible.

Quentin looked past the brawl, out the door. He didn't need to recognize individual sentients to know gangster enforcers when he saw them. Two Humans, a HeavyG and three Quyth Warriors, all dressed in expensive clothes, rushing across the street toward the diner, and all holding something in their hands.

Jake Bible had sold them out to Villani's goons.

"Krakens!" Quentin screamed. "Back door, now!"

"Don't you dare," the flapping Creterakian said. "The great Warlord Yashahon will—"

The bat didn't finish his sentence because Chucky Chong flew into him and knocked him through the restaurant's front window. Glass shattered and scattered.

Chucky turned and screamed at the Krakens players, his voice now fuzzy and distorted. "You forrow me, now!"

Chucky shot through the swinging door that led to the kitchen. The Krakens responded instantly, running or limping from the fight, following the flying Chucky Chong. Along the way, Quentin grabbed Ju's thick arm.

"You ready to be a Kraken now, Ju?"

Ju saw the gangsters rushing in, then looked at Quentin and nodded quickly. "Turns out you know how to negotiate after all."

"Then come on!"

Quentin followed his teammates, who were following Chucky Chong. He heard gunshots, felt a bullet whiz past his head as he ducked through a door and into the kitchen.

**QUENTIN SPRINTED DOWN THE ALLEY** of an alien world, armed gangsters not far behind. He jumped piles of rubbish. When he couldn't run over divider fences, he ran through them — not that many were left with his bigger teammates clearing the way. Every now and then he was just a little too late turning a corner and a bullet would hiss past his head or smack into a wall, sending up a shower of blue crystal shards. He kept everyone in front of him, including Ju, urging them on. Then he was out of the alley-maze, sprinting across traffic. Grav-cars extended street brakes, soft claws digging into the street surface below with a rubbery squeal. Some didn't stop fast enough and smashed into each other. A four-passenger cab hammered into Quentin's right hip, sending him careening across the street. He hit and rolled, started to come up, then threw himself flat on his back as a grav-truck roared over-head just inches from his face.

A strong hand grabbed his and yanked him up hard enough to dislocate his shoulder.

Rebecca. "Quentin, come on!"

"Where is everyone else?"

"We got separated, but come on, we have to *move!*"

She was bleeding from the left temple. Her right eye looked swollen, but these things did nothing to hide her animal intensity. This girl was a warrior.

She yanked him and he moved with the momentum, running off of the street and onto the packed sidewalk. He heard police sirens coming closer, then heard more gunshots. Just in front of him, a bullet connected with an elderly Quyth Leader's head, entering through the big, softball-sized eye and exiting out the back in a cloud of whitish meat. The Leader fell to the ground, already dead.

Quentin had to jump over the twitching body.

"Quentin, this way!" Becca ducked into another alley. He fol-lowed her in. They had to slow down thanks to a curly tangle of thick, blue crystal. The sculpture-like curves sliced into his Orbiting Death jacket as he picked his way through.

He stepped over one thin curl of blue only to put his foot down right on top of another. He felt the crystal slice into his foot just before he saw it poke out from the top of his shoe, bloody and gleaming in the thin light that filtered into the back alley. He bit back the scream — he didn't have time to bleed.

Quentin pulled his foot off the shard and started running. Bullets smashed into the blue crystal curves behind him, filling the alley with a cloud of flying splinters.

Suddenly, Chucky Chong flew next to him.

"Your friends are thees way! You run now!"

Chucky whizzed down a smaller alley on the right. Less crystal here, as if something had knocked it all down not long ago. Quentin saw boxes, blankets, more trash — a place where homeless and transients slept.

Chucky flew through the alley to an abandoned building. Quentin knew it was abandoned because of the plastic plates mounted over the doors and the windows, and the blue crystal spurs that curled around the openings and even through the plastic. An abandoned back alley apartment, or store, or whatever it was, quickly forgotten in a city where even the walls had to be constantly trimmed.

He ran, felt a hand grabbing his arm.

"How do we reach Gredok?" Becca said. "We're running out of options, where is he?"

"He's coming," Quentin said and prayed to High One that he was right.

He ran for the crystal-choked door, wondering how he would get in without cutting his hands to ribbons. Just before the door, he saw movement to his left — Choto, waving from an open window. Blue shards coated the ground below the window. One of his teammates had broken in and cleared the way.

Limping and trailing footprints of blood, Quentin ran to the window and climbed through.

QUENTIN STOOD INSIDE the abandoned storefront. His teammates had fared little better than he. Mum-O was clutching a lower left-arm wound that dribbled black blood through his thick fingers onto the dirty floor below. Choto the Bright bled from a gunshot wound to his shoulder, John had a fairly severe cut on his left thigh, Becca's eye had swollen shut, and Sho-Do-Thikit's front right foot was a shredded mass of orangish flesh and wet black blood.

Ju Tweedy, of course, looked fine.

Blue crystals grew up from the floor like budding trees. He and the others had to watch out for the sharp edges.

"Quentin," John said through heavy breaths, "where is Gredok?"

"He's coming. We have to keep moving."

"Move *where?*" Becca said. "Choto, you're from here, where do we go?"

"My family's bar," Choto said. "The Dead Fly. It is on the other side of the city. We need to steal a vehicle."

Ju rolled his eyes. "You guys call this a rescue? Are you *kidding* me? Damn, John, thanks for messing things up again."

Quentin lost it. He limped the three steps to Ju and threw a hard left cross. Ju bobbed back a fraction of an inch. Quentin's punch sailed through empty air. He never even saw the fist that smashed into his nose.

Quentin fell on his ass as the room blurred. He tasted blood. Wow, Ju Tweedy was *fast*.

John grabbed his arm and helped him to his feet. "Yeah, Ju is kind of like the best fighter ever," John said. "Taking a swing at him isn't such a good idea."

The crack of a gunshot.

Ju Tweedy looked down at his leg. Blood started to spread from a spot a few inches above his knee.

"Ouch," Ju said, then his legs gave out.

"Everyone stay real still," said a voice from the window. Quentin and his teammates turned ever so slowly to look at the small, Human gangster crawling through the window, his gun trained on the Krakens players the entire time. Four of his well-dressed associates followed him in.

"You guys shouldn't have come here," the little gangster said.

"We have diplomatic immunity," Quentin said. "You can't touch us."

The little gangster shook his head. "No, you shouldn't have come *here*. To this building. You should have stayed out in the public eye. You know, where there are witnesses?"

The gangsters stood there, each with a gun trained on a Krakens player.

"So?" John said. "So you can do whatever you want, what are you gonna do?"

"We're gonna wait," the gangster said. "Miss Villani wants a word with The Mad Ju."

Ju let out a moaning noise, then sat up and jammed his thumb into the new hole in his leg. He grimaced as he did, yet the move seemed as perfunctory as drinking a cup of coffee in the morning.

Ju smiled at the little gangster. "Hey, Smitty. How about I give you an autographed jersey and we call it even?"

The short gangster shook his head.

"Season tickets?" Ju said.

Smitty laughed, then shook his head again. "I'm gonna miss you, man. You always did crack me up. Now, shut your mouth."

They all stood in silence. A couple of minutes later, Quentin heard two sets of footsteps coming down the crystal-strewn alley. One heavyset with big feet and one that sounded different — the click-clack of high heels.

Quentin saw those heels — a sexy, dark red with six-inch stems — slide through the open window, followed by long legs clad in black stockings with a repeating pattern of skulls running up each side. A red leather skirt that clung tightly to wide curves below a narrow waist. She seemed to float through the window, until he realized her effortless movement came courtesy of the two gigantic hands holding her sides.

The big hands put the woman down. She stepped forward, resplendent in dark red leather and black lace. She wore dangling, black earrings and a small pin above her left breast — metalflake-red with a flat-black circle, the team logo of the Orbiting Death.

The dark outfit accentuated her white skin. Not pink, not tan, but *white*, as pale as fresh snow. She wore metalflake-red lipstick on big lips. Heavy black eye shadow covered her eye sockets and extended to her temples. The hair was jet-black, but that was a dye job — women with Tower heritage had hair as white as their skin.

By the numbers, she might have been the hottest woman Quentin had ever seen in his life, hotter than Somalia Midori, possibly even more beautiful than Yolanda Davenport. But there was something disturbing about this woman, an aura of coldness and lethality. If it was the person inside that really counts, he was looking at a walking corpse.

"Hello, Julius," she said. "Fancy meeting you here."

Ju stared at her, sadness and hatred in his eyes. "Why did you kill her? She didn't do anything."

Anna smiled at him, her perfect lips stretching into a soulless smile. "She betrayed me, Ju. You thought you were safe, could flaunt it right in my face, but you didn't think long term. And for that, you both have to pay."

For some reason, Quentin looked at Becca. She met his gaze, gave him a small nod of understanding — she had been wrong, Ju *was* innocent.

Anna walked around the room, looking at each Kraken in turn before her made-up eyes finally landed on Quentin.

"Ju," she said. "I see you brought me some new playmates. How considerate of you."

Quentin wiped blood away from his nose. "Miss Villani. Maybe we could just slow down a little bit, talk this out."

She walked toward Quentin, walked slowly, letting her high-heel echoes ring off the curled, crystal shards and empty walls. Quentin took a step forward to meet her and instantly realized it was a mistake when three more barrels pointed his way.

She wrinkled her nose and nodded. "You should probably stay still and all that, Barnes. Don't get ... twitchy."

She reached up a red-sleeved white hand, let her black fingernails trace down the right side of his cheek. He stayed perfectly still, ignoring the tingle her fingertips sent through his skin.

"Quentin Barnes," Anna said. "My goodness. You're even more of a specimen in person than you are on the news. Let me guess, you organized this ill-fated rescue attempt?"

Quentin looked at John, then back at Anna. "Yeah, sure," he said. "We wanted to save John's brother. We really didn't mean any disrespect, Miss Villani."

She smiled, now running her fingers through his hair. "No disrespect. Tell me, Quentin, how stupid are the women in the Purist Nation?"

Quentin didn't know how to answer the question, but he knew he'd said something wrong. "Uh … well, they're as smart as other women, I guess. I mean *people*. They're as smart as other people, I mean."

"Oh, I don't think so," Anna said. "Because I bet a pretty set of lips like yours can say anything to the girls back in the Nation, and they'd believe it. But out here in the rest of the galaxy? Maybe we girls aren't so malleable. Maybe they don't believe your lies."

"But Miss Villani, I—"

He stopped talking when her left index finger rested on his lips. "Shhhh," she said. "Quiet now. Best if you let me talk. You tell me you mean no disrespect, yet you come into *my* city, without so much as a *hello*, let alone actually asking for my permission. You come after a man that you know has wronged me. Wronged me so, *so* badly. Yes, Quentin, that *is* disrespect. You disrespected me. Now, what are you going to do about it?"

Quentin looked down into her cold eyes. "I … I don't know, Miss Villani."

She pulled her finger away from his lips. His red blood coated her white fingertip, almost matched her metalflake-red nail polish. She slowly traced the finger across her full lower lips — his blood gleamed on her lipstick.

She slid her finger under his chin. "Maybe if you give Anna a nice kiss, she'll forget all about this and let you go."

Quentin stared at her for a second, then looked at his teammates. He could discern no reaction from Sho-Do and Mum-O. Becca shook her head *no*, while John violently nodded *yes*.

Quentin looked down at her, saw the corners of her mouth lift up in a controlling smile. He bent and kissed her.

She only *looked* cold. Her lips were soft, warm and strong. She kissed him back a little harder than he kissed her. He felt every muscle in his face simultaneously relax and tingle, felt a warmth in his chest. He'd lost himself in the kiss when she gently pulled away.

Quentin opened his eyes. His blood had smeared across the pale white skin of her chin, the corners of her mouth. She stared at him with a quizzical look in her eyes, as if she were working out a puzzle.

"Hmmm," she said, then patted him twice on the cheek. "Sorry, Quentin, not good enough."

She turned on one heel and strode toward Ju. Quentin noticed that she stopped well out of Ju's reach. Even though he was wounded, Ju Tweedy was a big, dangerous, *fast* man.

"You flaunted her in my face, Ju," Anna said. "And for that, I'm afraid you have to go. Smitty? Take care of this for Anna."

Smitty walked forward, slowly raising his gun toward Ju's head. Ju took a deep breath. He didn't look away — he was going to watch his death coming. Quentin tried to think of something to say, but he had no words. Anna Villani's cold confidence made it clear that there was no talking to her, no getting Ju out of this. The Krakens would be lucky if *they* got out of this.

Smitty leveled his weapon, arm slanted down until the barrel was only a few feet from Ju's head.

Everyone jumped when a shot rang out.

Everyone, including Smitty, who took a half step to the right, then collapsed. He landed on his butt, fell to his back and lay flat, a blood stain spreading from a spot in the center of his chest.

"Drop your weapons."

Quentin and everyone else in the room looked to the window. There stood Virak the Mean, a smoking handgun clutched in his left pedipalp. Also in the window, down to his left and to his right, two Humans each holding handguns, aiming them into the room, three weapons ready to take out anyone that moved too quickly.

Anna's gangsters tensed, seeming to weigh their odds.

"Villani," came a voice from behind Virak. "Tell your people to put down their guns, and there will be no further issue. You have my word. If anyone points a gun at Ju Tweedy, they die."

The voice belonged to Gredok the Splithead.

**ANNA'S EYES NARROWED.** She drew a slow breath in through her nose and held it. Quentin could feel the rage radiating off her white skin. She let out the breath through her thick, lipsticked lips.

"Boys, drop the guns."

Her gangsters immediately complied. Quentin noticed that there was no backtalk, no debating — when Anna Villani spoke, her sentients snapped to action.

With the two Humans covering him, Virak the Mean stepped through the window. The two Humans came next, followed by another Quyth Warrior Quentin didn't recognize. Finally, Virak reached back through the window, lifted Gredok the Splithead and gently set the Quyth Leader down inside the room.

Anna Villani walked up to Gredok. At five feet, eight inches tall in her spike heels, she towered over the well-dressed, well-groomed Quyth Leader.

"Gredok," she said, venom dripping from her voice. "What do you think you're doing here?"

"Protecting my property," he said. "The situation I saw is your sentients pointing weapons at my players. Of course, I cannot allow that to happen."

"They came into *my* territory! That means I can do whatever I want."

"I believe you are getting ahead of yourself, Villani," Gredok said. "The Council has not yet recognized your authority."

Her face wrinkled into a sneer. A sneer that Quentin couldn't deny was even more attractive than her smile.

"Oh, please," she said. "I am in control of the OS1 syndicate, there is no doubt about this."

"You are wrong. Sikka the Death's passing means the OS1 syndicate is leaderless. You have to make your bid to the Council, Villani."

"Like they would dare deny me."

"If they *do* dare, you are out," Gredok said. "There are many ambitious young leaders in the galaxy that want this territory."

"Like who? Perhaps Stedmar Osborne?"

Quentin's eyes widened just a bit at the mention of his former boss, the owner of the Micovi Raiders.

Gredok nodded, his whole upper body moving back and forth twice to signify *yes*.

"If Osborne comes here," Anna said, her words cold and slow, "I will cut out his heart and feed it to him."

"Aside from the relative anatomical improbability of that act," Gredok said, "it would not be Osborne who would come first. If the Council denies your bid, and you were foolish enough to resist their orders, at least a dozen of the galaxy's best assassins would descend on Orbital Station One. They would be gunning for *you*, Villani. And if you were even more foolish as to *not* submit a bid and simply assume control — which, despite what you just told me, I am sure you *have not done* — well then, there would be more than a dozen. Many more."

She stared down at him, hate filling her face.

Gredok looked up at her, as calm as ever. "I always considered you smart, Villani. A smart leader would not assume control without a vote from the Council. So, are you in control of the OS1 syndicate?"

Her lips sneered again, then she relaxed them. Gredok had all the cards. Quentin was starting to understand the criminal hierarchy. With Sikka the Death gone and no leader in his place, Gredok had the right to kill any of these sentients — including Anna — without fear of repercussion.

"No," she said. "I have not assumed control."

"Smart," Gredok said. "I always thought you were smart. Since you are not in control, that means you must respect the requests of any *shamakath*."

"Gredok, if you think I'm going to swear fealty—"

"Nothing so crass," Gredok said. "I am simply going to take my players and leave."

Anna looked back to Ju, glaring at him, hunger in her eyes. "Just *your* players?"

"No!" John shouted. "Gredok, he's my brother, you can't just leave him!"

"*Silence!*" Gredok's scream could have come from a being twice, possibly three times, his size. A voice full of rage and power. "Another word out of you, John Tweedy, and I will not only start looking for a new middle linebacker, I will enjoy the process, because killing you here and now would provide me with immense satisfaction. You have pushed me as far as you dare. Your brother is wanted for murder. His own team cut him. He no longer has diplomatic immunity. Even if he is turned over to the police, we all know where he will end up. There is nothing I can do."

"Yes, there is," Quentin said. "You can sign him."

If the room had been still before, now it was frozen absolute-zero stiff. Gredok shuffled in place. The small clacks of his feet, the clink of his jewelry and the rustling of furry arms against a furry body filled the silent room. Then he stopped moving, and all fell silent again.

Gredok stared at Quentin. The leader didn't look upset, or even agitated. That is, unless you looked into his one big eye, which was flooded a deep, pitch black.

"Barnes," Gredok said. "I think that you are forgetting something."

"And what's that?"

"That you have a two-time Galaxy Bowl quarterback playing one spot below you. If I kill you now, the result on the field will be little different for the rest of the season."

Quentin wiped more blood away from his nose. He had to play this just right. Gredok didn't make idle threats. Quentin was as close to death as he'd ever been.

"We're not talking about *this* season," Quentin said. "We're talking about *next* season, and the season after that, and the season after that."

Gredok said nothing. Some of the black faded away. Now, he

was only mad enough to destroy a city, not sat-bomb an entire planet.

"Sign Ju Tweedy," Quentin said. "That gives him diplomatic immunity. Then the police can't touch him."

"I can touch him," Anna said. "And I will. No way I agree to this."

Gredok whipped around to face her. "Did I ask you if you agreed to it? Did I, Villani?"

Her lip curled again, but she shook her head.

Gredok stared for a second, then slowly turned again to face Quentin. "Barnes, Ju Tweedy is wanted for murder. There will be an investigation."

"The system police want to talk to him? Fine. They can come to the *Touchback* and question him. He didn't kill that girl, Gredok."

"Guilt or innocence doesn't matter."

"It does this time," Quentin said. "The investigation will find out he had nothing to do with it."

"Barnes," Gredok said, "you are playing a game that you do not know how to play. Do you really think all of this ... complication ... is worth it? Just to replace Mitchell Fayed?"

"Ju Tweedy isn't a *replacement* for Mitchell Fayed," Quentin said. "He is *better* than Fayed, and you know this."

Gredok stared, then walked forward until he was standing right in front of Quentin. The mob boss's right pedipalp reached up a little and curled inward, a gesture that said *get down here.* Quentin knelt on one knee.

"You played me," Gredok said, quietly enough that only Quentin could hear. "You called Hokor, knowing Hokor would call me. You knew I would find you because of your tracking bracelet. You knew I would come after you, possibly even want to kill you, because you put so many of my valuable players in danger. Did you also time it so I would make a dramatic, last-second entrance?"

"No," Quentin said. "The way I figure it, you're a little late."

Gredok's black fur instantly ruffled to full length, stayed puffed-up for a moment, then lay flat again.

"I would suggest you avoid provoking me," Gredok said. "At the moment, I am unable to tell you which would give me greater pleasure — winning the Galaxy Bowl trophy or shooting you in the stomach and watching you beg for death."

Quentin saw his own reflection in Gredok's cornea, saw his own eyes widen a little at the threat. Gredok wasn't joking. If Quentin pushed this any farther, it would be too much.

"I apologize," Quentin said. "I am grateful that you came after us, Gredok. But Ju Tweedy is worth it. You've seen him play. Right now, he is the best running back in all of football. We can have him."

"And make an enemy of Anna Villani, a Human I barely know? To make an enemy of her now is foolish."

"And how will it look if you don't sign Ju? Your players ran off without the approval of their *shamakath*. You had to fly to Orbital Station One and bring them home. It will be clear to the galaxy that you *could* have signed Ju Tweedy but did not. If you hadn't come here, that's one thing, none of the other crime bosses came ... but *you* did. Since you came, and you didn't sign Ju Tweedy, I think the other crime bosses can only assume one reason — that you fear Anna Villani. This is crazy, of course, and far from the truth, but it is what they will think. You will lose face, crime lords will think you are getting weak. The only way to avoid sending that signal is to sign Ju."

Gredok just stared. His eye flooded black again, even thicker than before. Quentin felt his pulse rushing, knew that Gredok could sense that, and yet this time it could not be stopped. This Quyth Leader could call for Quentin's head at any second.

"You are religious?" Gredok asked quietly.

Quentin swallowed and nodded.

"Then you had best embrace your primitive beliefs and pray, Quentin Barnes, *pray*, that you do not suffer an injury so grave it ends your career. Should the day come when you can no longer play for me, you and I will have some business to settle."

He turned and walked back to the woman dressed in dark

red. "Villani," he said. "I will be taking my players, and also Ju Tweedy as well."

"That *jackobath* doesn't leave this planet," she said quietly. "I don't care if everyone in this room dies in a blood bath, Ju Tweedy is mine."

"Very well," Gredok said.

"What?" Ju said. "What do you mean, *very well*?"

Gredok pointed a pedipalp at him. "Ju, I suggest that you do not speak again. If you do, I will take my leave immediately."

Ju stared, then hung his head.

"Villani," Gredok said. "I want to take Ju Tweedy with me, but I will leave the choice up to you, out of courtesy and respect."

"You *know* what my choice is."

"You haven't heard my offer," Gredok said, his voice rising and gaining intensity. Anna leaned back, just a little.

Quentin didn't just *watch*, he found himself *studying*. A room full of guns and deadly people, a wounded man, a corpse, a powder-keg that could blow up and kill everyone in a flash of gunfire. All of this, and yet Quentin could see Gredok's strategy, see him intentionally raising his voice at just the right time to gain more and more control over the situational flow. What Quentin did on the football field, Gredok the Splithead did in a game of death.

"My offer is simple," Gredok said, his voice again calm and barely audible. "I wish to offer Ju Tweedy a contract. In exchange for this allowance, I will speak on your behalf to the Council. I will endorse your bid to assume control of the OS1 syndicate."

Anna Villani blinked rapidly, almost like a ticker measuring off her thoughts. She hadn't seen that one coming. "You will endorse me?"

Gredok did his Human nod approximation again.

Quentin watched her face. He could see the want there, the lust for power. She hated Ju Tweedy and wanted him dead, but she wanted that power even more.

"All right," she said. "But if you can't reach an agreement with Ju, he is mine, and I still get the endorsement. Agreed?"

"Agreed," Gredok said. "Now, if you would be so kind as to leave us to our own devices, I will negotiate with Ju. I'm sure your people will be watching us depart. If Ju is not with us, you will know we could not reach an agreement."

Anna looked at Ju once more, hunger on her face. "I hope you run for it," she said, then she turned and looked at Quentin. "Don't think I will forget this, Barnes. A kiss is just a kiss, unless it is a kiss good-bye."

Quentin stared back at her and felt something that he rarely felt — fear. She was a reptile in Human disguise. A stunning, sexy reptile.

She walked to the window. Her massive HeavyG guard lifted her and delicately set her outside the window. Her guards followed her out, leaving Quentin, Gredok, Ju Tweedy and the other Krakens players alone in the abandoned building.

To an outside viewer, someone who didn't know the players in this particular game, the situation might have seemed comical — a room full of sentients ranging from two hundred and fifty pounds up past six hundred, some seven feet tall, some twelve feet long — the elite athletes of the galaxy and by any standard some of the most dangerous sentients in existence. And yet these big, strong sentients radiated nearly tangible fear in the presence of a three-foot-tall being that vaguely resembled a furry cross between a monkey and a spider.

"I am *not* happy," Gredok said. "The influence I just gave Anna Villani — for *free* — would have fetched a steep price. You have all cost me."

The black-furred Leader strode over to the still-bleeding Ju.

"Ju Tweedy. You will sign with the Ionath Krakens."

"How much?" Ju said immediately.

"League minimum," Gredok said. "For three years."

"*Minimum?* But I'm making—"

"You are making *nothing*," Gredok said. "You were cut from the Orbiting Death. You will sign, and now, or I will leave you here to fend for yourself."

"I'll run. Another team will sign me."

"Running will be difficult when you are missing a foot. Virak?"

The Quyth Warrior turned and fired a shot into the floor just left of Ju's knee. Concrete and plastic shot up in splinters. Ju winced as one of the splinters sank into his thigh. The Warrior changed his aim slightly — the barrel now pointed at Ju's right foot.

"I have made my offer," Gredok said. "Do you accept, or do you decline?"

Ju looked pained, and not from the fresh wound spilling blood down his thigh. He looked at his brother, John, who nodded violently. TAKE THE DEAL YOU IDIOT played across John's forehead.

Ju looked back to Gredok, then slowly nodded. "I accept," he said.

Gredok snapped his pedipalp fingers. Messal the Efficient hopped over the window, where he must have been waiting the whole time, a contract box clutched in his pedipalps. Gredok took the box, called up the holodisplay, poked a few numbers, then slid his middle left pedipalp finger inside.

Ju stood and limped to the box and put his right thumb inside. After a brief pause, the box gave out a *beep*, and the deal was complete.

"Choto," Gredok said. "If you aren't too busy following your new *shamakath*, kindly call the Orbital Station One system police and tell them we need an escort back to our ship. Full police protection as befits our diplomatic immunity."

## GFL WEEK SIX ROUNDUP
(Courtesy of Galaxy Sports Network)

| | | | |
|---|---|---|---|
| Armada | 24 | **Criminals** | 27 |
| War Dogs | 27 | **Water Bugs** | 28 |
| **Hullwalkers** | 31 | Juggernauts | 13 |
| **Ice Storm** | 22 | Pirates | 10 |
| Atom Smashers | 14 | **Dreadnaughts** | 18 |
| **Jacks** | 45 | Spider-Bears | 13 |
| **Astronauts** | 17 | Vanguard | 3 |
| Intrigue | 31 | **Scarlet Fliers** | 35 |
| Wolfpack | 21 | **Planets** | 28 |

At the halfway point of the 2683 season, the Isis Ice Storm (4-1) took sole possession of first place in the Planet Division with a 22-10 manhandling of the faltering To Pirates (4-2). The Mars Planets (4-2) won their third straight in a critical match with Wabash (3-2). The win puts the Planets into a tie for second with the Pirates.

The New Rodina Astronauts (4-1) moved back into first place in the Solar with a 17-3 win over the Vik Vanguard (1-4). The 'Stros are tied with the Bord Brigands (4-1), who had a bye week. Just a half-game behind both of those squads are the D'Kow War Dogs (4-2) and the Neptune Scarlet Fliers (4-2). The Dogs missed their chance at sole possession of first, thanks to a 28-27 loss to the Bartel Water Bugs (2-3), while Neptune moved up, thanks to a 35-31 shootout win over the Sala Intrigue (4-2).

### Deaths
Mars Planets running back **Daniel Dziubanski**, killed on a clean hit from Wabash defensive tackle Stephen Wardop.

### Offensive Player of the Week

Yall running back **Jack Townsend,** who carried the ball 23 times for 212 yards and a touchdown in the Criminals 27-24 win over the Armada.

### Defensive Player of the Week

Wabash defensive tackle **Stephen Wardop,** who had two sacks, six solo tackles and a fatality in a losing effort against the Mars Planets.

# 11

# WEEK SEVEN:
# IONATH KRAKENS at
# LU JUGGERNAUTS

## PLANET DIVISION

4-1  Isis Ice Storm
4-2  To Pirates
4-2  Mars Planets
3-2  Lu Juggernauts
3-2  Hittoni Hullwalkers
3-2  Wabash Wolfpack
3-3  Yall Criminals
3-3  Themala Dreadnaughts
2-3  Alimum Armada
2-3  Coranadillana Cloud Killers (bye)
1-4  Ionath Krakens (bye)

## SOLAR DIVISION

4-1  New Rodina Astronauts
4-1  Bord Brigands (bye)
4-2  D'Kow War Dogs
4-2  Neptune Scarlet Fliers
3-2  Jupiter Jacks
3-3  Sala Intrigue
2-3  Bartel Water Bugs
1-4  Vik Vanguard
1-4  Shorah Warlords (bye)
1-5  Jang Atom Smashers
0-5  Chillich Spider-Bears

**MEMO FROM THE DESK OF**
**GFL LEAGUE COMMISSIONER ROB FROESE**

**To:** Gredok the Splithead
**Subject:** The League's stance on the murder investigation involving suspect Ju Tweedy.

It is the Galactic Football League's official position that Ju Tweedy is now a member of the Ionath Krakens, and as such, he is afforded the full diplomatic immunity granted to any signed player. Ergo, he may not be detained by the System Police of Orbital Station One, nor may he be detained by any law enforcement agency during his travels.

The GFL will cooperate with the investigation into the murder of Grace McDermot, of which Ju Tweedy is a suspect. The Krakens franchise is also expected to cooperate fully. Further questioning of Ju Tweedy is required and will be performed on the Krakens' official team bus (the Touchback). Any efforts by the Krakens franchise to deny access to Ju Tweedy will result in the maximum fines and penalties available, at the Commissioner's discretion.

Unofficially, let it be known that I, Rob Froese, in my capacity as GFL commissioner, will get to the bottom of this. Ju Tweedy had the means, the motive and the opportunity to murder Grace McDermot. Witnesses put him at the scene of the crime. If he committed this crime, not only will he pay, but I will do everything in my power to have the Ionath Krakens franchise charter pulled for damaging the image of the GFL and for general abhorrent behavior.

The Creterakians may turn a blind eye to your criminal ways, Gredok, but I am watching. Sooner or later, you're going to get what's coming to you.

*Rob Froese*

Memo from the Desk of Gredok the Splithead

To: GFL Commissioner Rob Froese

Subject: A response to your memo regarding the Grace McDermot investigation

Dear Commissioner Froese,

The Ionath Krakens wish to thank you for your involvement in this delicate matter. We have full confidence that Ju Tweedy will be found innocent of this heinous and tragic crime.

And when — not if — Ju Tweedy is cleared of all charges, I will expect a full apology, in person, for your insolent tone. People far more important than you have asked my forgiveness for far less, of this I assure you.

Forgiveness, I should add, that most of them did not receive.

If you are looking for enemies, Commissioner Froese, may I respectfully suggest you shop elsewhere. The cost for dancing with me might be higher than you are prepared to pay.

Sincerely,

Gredok the Splithead

**QUENTIN HAD ALREADY SEEN** his first Ki Empire planet. That was fortunate because on the planet Lu, he would see the Juggernauts Stadium and nothing else.

Only the Ki members of the Krakens were allowed to go down early. The rest of the team — Human, Sklorno, Quyth Warrior, HeavyG, even Doc Patah and the support staff — were not allowed off-ship before Sunday's game. When Sunday came, they didn't even use the team shuttle to descend. Instead, Gredok hired an unmarked freighter to take the players down a mere four hours before kickoff. Quentin saw the inside of the landing bay and the visitors' locker room. As soon as he left the locker room, he'd see the stadium, play the game, do his press conference, then back on the freighter and back to the *Touchback*.

Gredok wasn't taking any chances. He wanted the team isolated from Commissioner Froese and any investigators. If Froese wanted his people to talk to Ju, Gredok would make sure it was on the *Touchback* and deny each and every meeting as long as possible. Gredok called it "laying low," a technique practiced by criminals from time immemorial. The longer Gredok stalled the investigation, the better it was for everyone.

In the Human locker room of Juggernauts Stadium, Quentin went through his ritual. He laid out his gear but also watched the Human Krakens players welcome Ju to the team. Quentin and John had spread the story of the showdown between Gredok and Anna, how Anna had revealed Ju's innocence. That, combined with Ju's status as the running back the Krakens so desperately needed, had everyone brimming with excitement. Sure, Ju was still wanted for murder, but his innocence would be proven — the only variable was time.

Ju was all smiles and charm, praising the organization, giving thanks and proclaiming his innocence, but only when asked. He didn't preach or push it on anyone. Everyone loved the man right off the bat — everyone but Yassoud.

Yassoud simmered with anger, frustration and failure. He'd had his chance. After five games of futility, he'd been replaced.

Unless Ju Tweedy was hurt or killed, Yassoud's running days with the Krakens were mostly over.

John walked around the locker room like a peacock, strutting-proud that his little brother had joined the team. Now that they were on the same team, their sibling rivalry had taken a step back if not vanished altogether.

Helmet in hand and already dressed for the game, John Tweedy saw Quentin and walked over. He didn't smile so much as he beamed, glowed. "I'm not going to forget what you did, Q."

Quentin shrugged. "You'd have done the same for me."

John nodded. "Yeah, sure, but that doesn't change the fact that you did it for me, did it for my family. And I want to show you something."

He reached into his helmet and pulled out a holocube, which he handed to Quentin. Quentin took the small piece of plastic and squeezed the sides.

A hologram of Ma Tweedy flared to life. She was still hunched over, ears in her shoulder, eyes squinting so tight she might have been blind. She didn't have the half-orange, half-black jersey anymore. She wore an orange Krakens away jersey with the number 50 — John's number. Her ballcap was also Krakens orange, with the Ionath logo on the bill and a 48 on the brim — Ju's new number.

"That's *my* jersey," John said, his smile still blazing and wide, MOM ALWAYS DID LOVE ME BEST scrolling across his face. "She said she was so proud of me for saving Ju. *My* jersey, Q! Not his, *mine*."

"Congrats," Quentin said and went to hand the cube back.

"No, it's for you," John said. "Hit play."

Quentin held the cube in his lap and hit the play icon. The image of Ma Tweedy moved, and her voice came out from the holocube's small surface.

"Quentin! Jonathan tells me that you saved my boy Julius. Thank you, Quentin. From now on, you're family. You always have a home with Ma Tweedy, honey. And don't forget to slide."

The playback stopped. Quentin laughed.

"Ma likes you," John said.

Quentin felt a lump in his throat. This woman that he'd never met had called him *honey*, had called him *family*, the kind of words a mother would use.

John gave Quentin's hair a quick ruffle, then walked off toward Ju.

Quentin put the holocube in his locker, then he looked at Ju, who was laughing and joking with his brother and with the rest of the Krakens. Quentin watched Ju's charm — genuine or fake? Quentin remembered the man in that life-and-death situation only a few days earlier, remembered Ju looking down the barrel of a gun and *negotiating* for a better deal. Quentin would have been grateful beyond measure just to play ball again, to be on a team again. Ju Tweedy? He seemed far more concerned about money.

Well, whatever Ju's motivations, Doc Patah had done his magic and repaired the running back's bullet wound. Ju Tweedy was ready to play. And yet, for all of Ju's skill, he had never played a down of Tier One football. This was his coming-out party. The galaxy would be watching, waiting to see if Ju could dominate at the highest level. Ju would be ready to show them that he could.

Quentin tuned Ju out, tuned everyone out. He started his ritual, putting the gear on one piece a time, mentally playing through the names, stats, tendencies and history of every player on the Lu Juggernauts.

Now he had an offensive line.

Now he had a running back.

The league was about to see just how good the Ionath Krakens could be.

**QUENTIN'S HAND HURT.** Hurt in the best way possible.

It hurt because every time he handed off to Ju Tweedy, the meaty running back snapped his arms down so hard it nearly broke Quentin's fingers. Ju ran full-speed toward the line, every play, every moment. He ripped his arms down to take the ball like it was some kind of enemy, like it was a threat to Ma Tweedy herself.

When Ju hit that line or went through a hole, High One help the first Lu Juggernauts defensive player that stepped up to stop him. When Ju dipped his battering-ram of a head, lowered his huge shoulders and slammed into that hapless soul clad in Juggernauts' steel-blue and gold, Quentin could almost see shockwaves.

For once, Quentin wasn't covered in stains from the field's plants. In this case, those plants were a coarse, tan grass, light enough to make the black lines and yard markers really pop in the afternoon sun. Quentin wasn't dirty because the Krakens just kept running the ball. That constant, punishing running style started to wear the Juggernauts down. Ju had twenty-two yards on seven carries in the first and another thirty-five yards on eight tries in the second, including a ten-yard touchdown run.

In the second half, that running game made the linebackers watch for Ju Tweedy, watch him every play. Quentin gave a ball-fake, those linebackers froze, waiting to see if they had to tackle the Human wrecking ball. That reaction, that freeze, gave Quentin another second, even two seconds, of time to throw. Combined with the excellent protection of Michael Kimberlin and the offensive line, for the first time that season, Quentin had time to drop back, step up and evaluate all of his receivers to find the open one.

That meant completed passes, and a lot of them. He hit Crazy George Starcher six times for eighty-eight yards and a touchdown. Hawick also had a TD, part of her five catches for an even hundred yards. The best part of the game for Quentin? One completion to Halawa — which just happened to be for a 36-yard touchdown.

The Krakens' defense didn't play great, but they did enough for the win. Running off the field to the violent, drum-line-like *clacks* of the mostly-Ki fans, the Krakens entered the locker room with a 28-21 win, a record of 2-and-4 and a new sense of optimism that permeated every ounce of their collective being.

• • •

**THE LOCKER ROOM** felt electric.

Things had felt good when the Krakens beat the Shorah Warlords in Week Three, but that had been more relief than anything else. Relief that they would not go the year without a win. This? This was different.

It was different because now they had a running game. Ju Tweedy finished the game with 103 yards on 28 carries. His punishing presence demanded defensive attention, giving Quentin more time to throw the ball. As a result, Quentin enjoyed his best game in Tier One: 15-of-20 for 235 yards and three touchdowns. With a healthy offensive line, a running game that kept the defense on its heels, three excellent receivers and a quarterback that wasn't half bad, Ionath had suddenly become very, very dangerous.

The Krakens players surrounded Ju, filling the central locker room with shouts, clacks, grunts and laughter. The team was still in last place at 2-and-4 but were just one game behind the Themala Dreadnaughts. Six games left in the season. If they won half of those, the possibility of staying in Tier One seemed very real.

Players congratulated Ju, welcomed him to the team all over again, happy to give him a slap on the shoulder pads, a handshake, a friendly push. He was the final piece of the offensive puzzle and everyone knew it.

Everyone except Yassoud Murphy.

Yassoud looked at the celebration. The bearded man wore his emotions on his sleeve, and in that moment it was plain that he wanted to be Ju Tweedy so bad it might as well have been a holo-sign floating above his head. Yassoud looked down and shuffled into the Human locker room.

John Tweedy stood at the edge of the central locker room, leaning his back against a wall, his helmet dangling from his fingers by its facemask. His sweaty, clumpy hair stood up in all directions. A steady rivulet of blood drained from his broken nose, out of his left nostril at an angle that curled just past the left corner of his mouth, down his chin to drip-drip-drip on his already-stained jersey. He hadn't bothered to stop the bleeding. Quentin wasn't sure if John even *knew* he was bleeding.

Quentin walked up to him, raised his fist and brought it down on John's shoulder pads.

"Uncle Johnny, what's up? Didn't you get the memo?"

"What memo?" John said quietly.

"The one that said *Krakens win*. Because we did win, you know."

John looked at Quentin and forced a weak smile. "Yeah, we won. That's good, I've just got other things on my mind."

John looked back to the circle of players still celebrating with Ju.

Quentin wasn't sure what to say. John had put in a monster of a game — five solo tackles, four more assists, a sack and an interception. He should have been dancing on benches and offending people with creative forehead tattoos.

"John, what's the matter? You were all fired up for your brother before, and *we won*. So, why aren't you happy?"

John shrugged. "I am. It's just ... well, Ju is being a good boy now because he just got here. We had to go get him and all, no choice there, but ... "

"But what?"

John wiped the back of his left hand across his broken nose, saw the blood smearing his knuckles. He grunted with mild surprise, then looked at Quentin, blood still smeared across his nose, lip and cheek.

"Just that a tiger can't change its spots," he said. "I love my brother, but he's a real jackass. I just hope he doesn't show his true colors until after the season."

John walked to the Human locker room, leaving Quentin to stare at the Ju Tweedy Fan Club and wonder how John could be so jealous of his brother that he didn't appreciate a hard-won victory.

## GFL WEEK SEVEN ROUNDUP
(Courtesy of Galaxy Sports Network)

| | | | |
|---|---|---|---|
| Water Bugs | 34 | **Astronauts** | 35 |
| Spider-Bears | 0 | **Pirates** | 54 |
| War Dogs | 15 | **Brigands** | 17 |
| Hullwalkers | 24 | **Armada** | 27 |
| Juggernauts | 21 | **Krakens** | 28 |
| Intrigue | 20 | **Jacks** | 42 |
| Vanguard | 7 | **Warlords** | 17 |
| **Wolfpack** | 24 | Ice Storm | 17 |
| Criminals | 10 | **Cloud Killers** | 28 |

A last-second field goal by kicker Howard Dinatale gave New Rodina (5-1) a 35-34 win over the Bartel Water Bugs (2-4), keeping the Astronauts tied for first place in the Solar with the Bord Brigands. The Brigands outlasted the D'Kow War Dogs (4-3) in a 17-15 nail-biter. This turn of events sets up a crucial first-place showdown next week, as the Brigands host the Astronauts.

In the Planet Division, the To Pirates stopped their two-game skid with a 54-0 devastation of the Chillich Spider-Bears (0-6). The win moved the Pirates back into first, thanks to the Ice Storm (4-2) dropping 24-17 to the Wabash Wolfpack. Isis and Wabash are now tied for second with the Mars Planets, who had a bye.

### Deaths
No deaths reported this week.

### Offensive Player of the Week
Ionath quarterback **Quentin Barnes**, who went 15-of-20 for 235 yards and three touchdowns.

**Defensive Player of the Week**

To Pirates linebacker **Richard Damge,** who had four solo tackles, five assists, a sack and and a fumble recovery against Chillich.

# 12

# WEEK EIGHT:
# IONATH KRAKENS at
# ALIMUM ARMADA

| PLANET DIVISION | |
|---|---|
| 5-2 | To Pirates |
| 4-2 | Isis Ice Storm |
| 4-2 | Wabash Wolfpack |
| 4-2 | Mars Planets (bye) |
| 3-3 | Alimum Armada |
| 3-3 | Coranadillana Cloud Killers |
| 3-3 | Hittoni Hullwalkers |
| 3-3 | Lu Juggernauts |
| 3-4 | Yall Criminals |
| 3-3 | Themala Dreadnaughts (bye) |
| 2-4 | Ionath Krakens |

| SOLAR DIVISION | |
|---|---|
| 5-1 | New Rodina Astronauts |
| 5-1 | Bord Brigands |
| 4-3 | D'Kow War Dogs |
| 4-2 | Neptune Scarlet Fliers (bye) |
| 4-2 | Jupiter Jacks |
| 3-4 | Sala Intrigue |
| 2-4 | Shorah Warlords |
| 2-4 | Bartel Water Bugs |
| 1-5 | Jang Atom Smashers (bye) |
| 1-5 | Vik Vanguard |
| 0-6 | Chillich Spider-Bears |

**QUENTIN SURVEYED** the holographic teams. His computer-generated Krakens offensive line squared up against the computer-generated Alimum Armada defense. The Armada had to have the ugliest, corniest uniforms in the GFL. Navy blue with three parallel coils of gold braid stitched around the sleeves. Thin, turquoise numbers trimmed in equal widths of green, royal blue and white, finished off with more gold braid. White helmets carried the Armada logo on each side: a blue and green anchor trimmed in black, set in a white circle surrounded with a turquoise circle of flame. The uniforms were supposed to resemble sailor outfits from some long-lost Earth military. Yet another Sklorno misinterpretation of the history of the birthplace of football.

The holographic stadium painted the picture of a football-crazed environment. Alimum's dark-green-lined turquoise turf was much-loved and much-hated throughout the league. The mostly turquoise-clad crowd waved white flags decorated with the Armada's anchor logo. Past the goalpost, Quentin could see a crysteel-encased end zone packed with madly jumping balls of black fur — male Sklorno, also known as "bedbugs." Watching the female Sklorno play football on the field aroused the males to the point where they had no self-control and had to be segregated from the females.

The holographic defensive line and linebackers wore those hideous Armada uniforms, but the cornerbacks were real Sklorno that wore Krakens practice blacks.

Real receivers in practice whites complemented Quentin's holographic offensive line. On the left, Milford lined up wide, covered by cornerback Perth. Halawa was wide right, squaring off against her twin sister, the cornerback Wahiawa.

"Hut-*hut*."

Quentin slapped the ball in his hands and dropped back five steps. Milford and Halawa shot down their respective sidelines, well covered by the corners. Quentin paused a second, then launched a long, arcing pass. The holographic Alimum crowd roared as the ball spiraled downfield. Halawa went up for the catch. Wahiawa jumped as well, but she was just a fraction of a second behind and she knew it — her tentacles ripped down on Halawa's in a blatant case of pass interference. Despite the rough handling, Halawa fought a single tentacle free. Nearly horizontal, falling back to the turf with three hundred pounds of defensive back pulling her down, Halawa pulled in the pass one-tentacled before she and her sister smashed into the ground.

Quentin sucked in a quick hiss of air and couldn't suppress a giggle that made him sound like a little boy hiding in a grown man's body. Damn, Halawa's potential seemed limitless.

The clapping of a pair of Human hands cut through the computer-generated crowd. Quentin turned to see a smiling, clapping Ju Tweedy, dressed in street clothes and walking into the VR room.

"Heck of a catch," Ju said. "*Heck* of a catch."

"Simulation off," Quentin said. The illusion of Alimum Stadium flickered, then vanished. "Hey there, Ju."

"They told me you'd be here, but I didn't believe them. I mean, we just had practice as a team, and you're in here for more?"

"That's right," Quentin said. "That's how we get better. I'd like to see you join us."

Ju laughed. "Practice? What are we talkin' about, man ... *practice?* Not a game, not a game ... we talkin' about practice? I save it for the games, Q."

Quentin didn't like that attitude but nodded anyway. After Ju's performance against the Juggernauts, Quentin was willing to go with whatever the man said. "Fair enough. Then what are you doing here?"

"I was hoping to have a word with you. In private." Ju reached into his pockets and pulled out two cans of Miller lager. "My brother tells me this is your favorite?"

Quentin smiled. "Yeah, cool. Ladies, practice is over. I'll see you tomorrow."

Milford and Perth shot out of the room, almost running Ju over. Halawa and Wahiawa always waited for each other, so they were a step behind.

"Halawa," Quentin said, stopping the sisters in their tracks. "That kind of effort is what I want to see. Keep it up, and there's a bigger role for you to play."

She shivered, just once, then turned and ran out of the VR room with her sister right behind. As soon as she left, Quentin realized he'd done that only in part to motivate Halawa. He'd also done it to impress Ju Tweedy.

Ju watched the sisters go, then tossed Quentin a beer.

"Thanks." Quentin popped the mag-can's top. "So, what's up?"

"I wanted to talk to you about the future of the team."

"We're rolling," Quentin said. "That win against the Juggernauts, that was huge."

Ju nodded, sipped his beer. "True, true."

"We've got a running game now. I think that's what we were missing."

Ju smiled and gave a theatrical bow. "Why, thank you, Quentin, I do what I can. But it's not just the running game. The offensive line is going to gel with Kimberlin, and you're going to have grade-A protection. I know Scarborough is gone, but I think Halawa is the real deal."

Quentin half-raised his beer in salute. "High One willing, she could really be something."

"Want my opinion, Q?"

"Isn't that what you came here to give me?"

Ju smiled. "You're not much for small talk, are you?"

Quentin just took another sip.

"I think this is the beginning of a championship team," Ju said. "I think the offensive pieces are in place. If Gredok and Hokor bolster the defense in the off-season, I think it could happen."

Quentin nodded.

"*Could* happen," Ju said. "That is, with the right leadership."

The words were polite but clearly a challenge — a challenge to Quentin's authority. Quentin felt his anger rising. "What are you saying, Ju?"

"I'm saying I'm used to being in charge."

"Excuse me?"

"In charge," Ju said. "I was the team captain of the Orbiting Death. I'm *always* the team captain. When I play on a team, it's my team. Like how the Krakens are your team now."

Quentin felt a coldness creeping up his arms, a trail of goosebumps marking its path. "That's right, Ju. The Krakens are my team."

"*Your* team is a losing one. I show up for one game, we win. Maybe you're not the right leader to take this franchise to the top. Maybe the team needs a change."

Quentin felt his hands itching to turn into fists, but he kept them still. He could handle this and in a mature way — after all, he wasn't on Micovi anymore. He shook his head, slowly. "No change, Ju. Sentients risked their lives to go get you. You should be walking in here and thanking me up and down, not telling me my leadership sucks."

Ju shrugged and looked away, as if he were bored with the conversation. "Don't think I'm ungrateful, Quentin, but that's in the past. A leader has to look to the future." He bent and set his beer can on the VR deck. "I'll tell you what. I hear you're a brawler. How about you and I have a go to decide it?"

"What ... *now?*"

"Sure," Ju said. "Man to man. You whip me, I follow your lead. I whip you, the team is mine."

Quentin's free hand clenched into a fist. A mixture of emotions tore at his thoughts: the urge to just attack Ju, take him up on his offer; the words of Yitzhak; Quentin's own desire to stop solving problems with his fists; and — the most disturbing one, perhaps — just how *fast* Ju had moved back in that abandoned building when he blasted Quentin in the nose.

Quentin shook his head. "That's not how we solve things here, Ju. I've gone through a lot to help put this team where it is. If it wasn't for me, you'd be dead, so how about you shut up and do your job?"

Ju smiled condescendingly. "I understand. I mean, I just got here. As long as we keep winning, the team will keep following your lead, right?"

Quentin nodded. "That's right."

Ju picked up his beer and raised it in a salute. "Well then. Here's to hopes of winning."

He drained his mag-can, then tossed it to the deck. Ju walked out as a bit of remaining beer spilled out onto the VR flooring.

Quentin felt a fist in his chest, a fist that made him want to lash out. Ju Tweedy wanted to be the man, and that did something to Quentin's soul he'd never felt before.

Once Quentin took over a team, no one ever challenged his leadership. At least, not until now.

One game in, and the real Ju Tweedy had arrived.

The tiger, it seemed, had not changed its spots.


**ANOTHER PUNCH-OUT,** another trip to the bathroom, another round of vomiting.

Quentin's eyes scrunched tight as his stomach fought for something to bring up. He'd tried to be clever, starving himself for the last twelve hours to cheat his stomach of material, hoping this might stave off the punch-out sickness his worrying mind brought on. Nice hypothesis, but the testing phase involved data collection — and what he was collecting was puke.

It seemed to last longer this time, almost as if his stomach was telling him *oh, did you think you were getting used to space travel? Nice try, smarty-pants, but I have the last laugh — next time have a burger so I can get some real work done, okay?*

Not that his stomach could talk. Talk? No. Make strange, choked noises? Yes, that it could do quite well.

This time it wasn't just the regurgitation itself that annoyed him, it was the amount of time it took — he was about to see his first Sklorno world, and he didn't want to waste a single second.

Finally, he felt his stomach relax. He stood and rinsed his mouth out in the sink.

He had been getting better at space travel. So why this gut-clenching relapse? Maybe it was the anger that he had to bottle up inside, anger at Ju Tweedy's arrogance. Three days since that encounter in the VR room, and Quentin couldn't quite get it out of his mind.

He dried his face on a towel, then threw it in the sink as he ran out of his bathroom, out of his quarters and down the corridor. He was about to see another new world, another new culture.

He ran onto the observation deck. The deck was packed with Sklorno, all fourteen Krakens of that species. They pressed against the view port windows, jumping up and down, their exposed raspers splattering the crysteel with spit, tentacle-arms pressed flat as if they were desperate to reach out for the planet itself. A few other Krakens were in the lounge — Don Pine, the kicker Arioch Morningstar and Ju Tweedy. Ju winked at Quentin, then turned his attention back out the lounge windows. Most of the players steered clear of the insanely jumping Sklorno. Only one window stayed free of the spastic celebration — because the wide form of Michael Kimberlin took up most of it. Rebecca Montagne stood to his right. As big as she was, she looked like a little kid next to Kimberlin.

Wait a minute, was she tucked in a little too close to Kimberlin?

Quentin shook his head. It was none of his business if Becca was dating Michael. Or John. Or whoever.

He walked up to that window, moving to the left side of Kimberlin. Quentin still hadn't gotten used to feeling *small*, which was exactly the way he felt when he was near Kimberlin anywhere other than a football field.

"Hey, Michael," Quentin said.

The big lineman looked down, then nodded a greeting and looked back out the window.

Outside the *Touchback*, the planet Chachanna loomed close. A big planet, much larger than those of the Purist Nation and maybe even a bit larger than Earth. Unlike the pale blue Earth, however, Chachanna almost glowed a suffused pink.

**ALIMUM, THE CAPITAL CITY** of Chachanna. Endless veins of small, moving lights represented vertical layers of traffic sliding between towering buildings, a pumping and pulsing that reflected the nighttime city's endless circulation of sentients. In that regard, Alimum looked familiar, but Quentin had never seen anything so ... *dense*. You couldn't tell where the city ended. It just *sprawled*, an endless mass of civilization. Normally a shuttle came in from an angle outside the city, then entered city airspace and flew toward the stadium. In Alimum, there *was* no "outside" the city. The shuttle entered the atmosphere over buildings that were all taller than Ionath's largest. As the shuttle moved toward the city center, the buildings grew progressively bigger and bigger.

And everywhere, *movement*. Cars, flying vehicles, little tiny specks that were sentients moving inside and on top of every building. The evening hour didn't seem to matter on Alimum.

The shuttle leveled out as a path of ever-larger buildings passed beneath. Some of them had to be three hundred stories, maybe even more. Off in the distance, Quentin saw the glowing sphere that was Alimum Stadium. His heart quickened at the sight of one of football's great palaces.

The dome had two layers of pure crysteel. Between those layers, a two-foot-thick moving wave of plasma suspended in a dome-wide mag field. The result of that technological magnificence: a spectacular surface that glowed like a million-facet diamond blazing in noonday sun, only the sun was *inside* the jewel.

But as the shuttle closed in, something else caught his eye. Thick columns of glowing pink smoke rose up all over the city, semi-illuminated from some fire at their base. The columns expanded as they rose, funnels that slowly merged into the clouds above.

"Anyone know what's with the smoke?" Quentin asked. "That like the Sklorno version of fireworks? Welcoming us or something?"

Kimberlin's head snapped around to look at Quentin, his eyebrows raised high, his mouth open. The lineman looked at Hawick and Milford, almost as if he was worried they had heard.

"What?" Quentin said. "Did I say something racially *insensitive* again?"

Kimberlin shook his head, but the eyebrows stayed high and the mouth stayed open. He walked over to stand next to Quentin.

"The smoke columns are part of a ... welcome ... for us. Of sorts. I know many of those cookeries run all day and all night, I've just never seen *all* of them running like this."

"Cookeries?" Quentin said. "Sso, they're preparing a feast or something?"

Kimberlin nodded. "Yes, it's a feast to welcome us. Or in honor of us, more accurately. You and Don Pine, in particular."

"Sweet," Quentin said. "I wonder if it's edible for Humans. What's the main course?"

Kimberlin blinked, then answered. "Sklorno."

"Right, a Sklorno feast, but what are they cooking?"

"Quentin, they are *cooking* Sklorno."

The words didn't seem to register for a minute. "You're messing with me, right?"

Kimberlin shook his head. "No. The Sklorno eat each other all the time. It's how they deal with overpopulation."

"By eating each other."

Kimberlin nodded. "There are eighty billion Sklorno on this planet. Alimum alone has five billion in just the city proper. It's difficult for them to control breeding. If there is even a minor statistical increase in the birthrate, they are looking at millions of extra mouths to feed."

"But that's barbaric," Quentin said. "Cannibalism? That's *insane*."

Kimberlin snapped his fingers. "*There's* the racially insensitive Quentin I've heard about."

He was trying to make a joke, to lighten the mood, but Quentin didn't appreciate the humor. "Screw you, man. They *eat their own*, that's just evil."

"You can't judge their culture," Kimberlin said. "This is their way as a species. They've been dealing with massive overpopulation for centuries, maybe a thousand years, and this is their solution. Do you know how many Sklorno are in the Dynasty?"

Quentin held up three fingers. "More than this many?"

"Just a bit," Kimberlin said. "The Dynasty's best guess is 263 billion citizens. The closest to that is the Quyth Concordia, with something just over 170 billion. There are rumors the Creterakians have more citizens than the Dynasty, but a bat is about one one-hundredth the mass of a Sklorno. And, those 263 billion Sklorno are packed onto just *five* planets. The Planetary Union, by way of comparison, has over 31 billion spread out over twelve habitation centers."

Quentin squinted at the big lineman.

"What are you looking at?" Kimberlin said.

"Looking *for*."

"Fine, what are you looking for?"

"The data link," Quentin said. "You got a computer in that melon of yours, or what?"

"It's called *education*, Barnes. You should give it a try."

"If I get one, can I use fancy phrases like *by way of comparison?*"

"For a quarterback, you are shockingly inerudite. How long did you go to school?"

"A couple of years," Quentin said. "Don't worry about it, big man, it's too late for me anyway."

"It's never too late to learn, Quentin," Kimberlin said. "I think you are intentionally obfuscating your intellect and wearing your ignorance as some misguided badge of honor. Knowledge is power. You ever decide to really leave your backwater heritage behind and understand the galaxy in which you live, let me know. I'd be happy to tutor you."

Quentin waved a hand dismissively. "Yeah, right. I got educated for my career and seem to be doing just fine at that. But if I ever need to figure out what *obfuscate* means, I'll be sure to look you up."

The shuttle banked a little, angling for the Crystal Dome. In doing so, it flew directly through a billowing column of pink smoke.

Quentin closed his eyes and hoped the shuttle's air system was entirely internal.

"You can open them now," Kimberlin said.

Quentin did.

"Just remember a few things while you're here."

"I'm already trying to *forget* things."

"You aren't just a player here, Quentin," Kimberlin said. "You're a religious icon."

"Oh, come on, not that *Church of Quentin Barnes* crap again —"

"It's not *crap*," Kimberlin said. "It's real, and you had better pay exceedingly close attention to it. Don, you want to tell him?"

Don Pine turned in his seat, gave Quentin a long look.

"Naw," Don said. "Mike, you used to handle this stuff for me back in '78 and '79, so help Quentin out."

Until just then, Quentin hadn't made the connection that Kimberlin and Pine had played together when Pine was with the Jupiter Jacks. Would have probably been Kimberlin's rookie season when the Jacks won the 2676 title. Kimberlin didn't wear his GFL championship ring from that year. Maybe he hadn't played much his rookie season, didn't think he deserved to wear it. So Kimberlin had been with Jupiter when Pine's career fell apart in '78 and '79, yet neither of them mentioned it. Interesting.

"Fine," Kimberlin said. "I'll share my knowledge in this domain. Sklorno are about as different from us as different can be. They started most of the galactic age wars. They caused the extinction of not one, but *two* sentient races. The planets the Sklorno couldn't conquer, they destroyed. Experts think it's only a matter of time before the Sklorno start another war."

"What's this got to do with me?"

"I'm trying to make you understand that this is a very different place. If you say the wrong thing, you could start a religious riot that would line the streets with dead. You could have a million sentients waging war in your name, or the same million sentients committing suicide because they misinterpreted the way you say *hello*. This is not some Human system of little difference from your own, this is a truly *alien* culture. Know the customs of the culture you are visiting, especially when they think you are an omnipotent being."

"That's funny," Quentin said. "I don't *feel* omnipotent."

Kimberlin looked up, sighed and shook his head. "Do try and leave your paltry attempts at humor on the shuttle, Quentin. I'm rather attached to living."

• • •

**THEY DISEMBARKED THE SHUTTLE** at the Crystal Dome's landing pad and lined up for customs inspection. Quentin stood in line with Don Pine on his right, Michael Kimberlin on his left, and John Tweedy next to Kimberlin. They waited for the customs officials to finish checking the shuttle. Quentin took advantage of that time to process — or at least try to process — an overwhelming assault of visual information.

The floor on which he stood was made of the same crysteel-sandwiched material as the stadium dome. Glowing, beautiful colors coursed through the floor, lighting him and his teammates from below like some nightclub special effect. Walls of non-illuminated crysteel — the boring, see-through variety — curved up and in from the landing pad's edges. Quentin saw scratches, scores and pock-marks on the outside of the armored walls, clearly the result of small arms fire and probably a few firebombs. Some teams, apparently, gave new meaning to the term "warm welcome." Nice.

Behind him, the glowing stadium dome arced up and curved away. The landing deck was part of the dome but almost seemed to float thanks to surrounding buildings that rose high overhead, blurring and then fading completely into pink clouds. Countless windows in those buildings reflected the waves of colored light cast up by the dome and the landing pad deck.

He could see five layers of elevated roads winding through the soaring buildings, carrying traffic in all directions. He suspected more layers wove unseen beneath his level. Between the suspended decks, small aircraft flew with abandon. Just five minutes after arriving he saw an accident: a twin-engine aircar tried to duck under a larger airbus, but it clipped the highway below, tumbled into a wheeled cargo-hauler — aircar and cargo-hauler alike plummeted out of sight.

Traffic rolled on as if nothing had happened.

And there was more to see. Creterakians whipping around the landing pad, a dense, moving cloud of a security force dressed in white with GFL logos on their backs, entropic rifles in their little hands. True to instincts bred over nineteen years in the Purist Nation, Quentin stayed stock-still.

"Know what you'll find funny?" Don whispered. "The bats hate it here."

"Why?"

"Sklorno think they're tasty. Seems the Dynasty is not quite as subjugated as the Creterakians would like."

Quentin did notice that the circling Creterakians didn't elevate above the armored walls, where they might be targeted by a passing road vehicle or aircar. The rulers of the galaxy were afraid they might get eaten by a subjugated race? Don was right — that was funny.

Quentin looked to the other sentients crowding the landing pad. A dozen Quyth Leaders, also dressed in white uniforms with GFL logos large on their small chests. And behind them, a line of Sklorno dressed in what had to be military armor. The gear gleamed of polished metal and looked far heavier than the football padding of his Sklorno teammates. Battle armor. Where his teammates looked *fast*, these Sklorno guards looked like killing machines.

"Hey, Q," Don said quietly. "Why wasn't Ju in the first shuttle?"

Quentin shrugged. "Maybe Hokor wants him to put in a few solid games first."

The truth of the matter was that Quentin had specifically asked Hokor to put Ju on the second shuttle. If Ju was having delusions of grandeur, keeping him off of the first shuttle would help show him his place.

Two Quyth workers pushed a grav-sled out of the shuttle.

"No explosives, no weapons."

The Leader in charge of the customs inspection waved the Workers out of the ship. "Good, now we can get out of sight and back into the compound." His pedipalps twitched in a strange way, and a touch of pink swirled across his cornea.

Quentin leaned over and whispered to Kimberlin. "The customs inspector looks nervous."

"I'm hardly surprised," Kimberlin said. "Apparently, the Sklorno think that Quyth Leaders are even more scrumptious than the bats."

Quentin felt his eyes widen. Cannibalism was one thing, but

where did this sentient-on-sentient predation end? "What about Humans? Where do we rate on the taste-o-meter?"

"I'll tell you if you like," Kimberlin said. "But trust me, it's not a ranking that will make you deeply trust your teammates."

"I thought you said knowledge was power."

"Most of the time, it is. But sometimes, Quentin, ignorance is bliss."

Quentin decided to take Kimberlin's word for it.

A Sklorno approached. This one did not have armor. Instead, she wore thick robes of orange and black that covered her clear skin from eyestalks to thick toes. Quentin saw an image on her chest, some kind of ceramic plate showing a Human face.

When she stopped just in front of him, he recognized that face.

Because it was his.

"Quentin Barnes," the Sklorno said. "I am the High Priestess of the Church of Quentin Barnes. It is my holy honor to welcome you to Alimum."

Quentin opened his mouth, but no words came out. The High Priestess of the Church of Quentin Barnes? What could he say to that? Should he say anything at all? This was madness ... a church dedicated to *him*?

She jumped, just once, just a few feet. "Quentin Barnes?" Don leaned forward and looked to Quentin's left. "Hey, Mike, you want to help him out a little?"

"High Priestess," Kimberlin said. "The Godling Barnes has decided to forgo speech. He is deep in contemplation and has asked me to speak on his behalf."

Quentin looked from the Sklorno to Kimberlin, who just raised his eyebrows in an expression that said *do you want me to bail you out or not?*

Quentin did. He turned back to the orange-and-black-clad Sklorno and nodded.

"High Priestess," Kimberlin said. "The Godling Barnes must prepare for the game. He wishes to be left alone. He is honored by your presence, High Priestess, and bestows upon you the thoughts of many passes and many catches."

Even with the heavy robes, Quentin saw her shiver. She walked backward, bowing over and over again.

"That should take care of it," Kimberlin said. "I believe you will be left alone for the remainder of your stay. Unless, of course, you want to leave the heavily guarded, armored and secure stadium facilities so you can go out drinking with your pal John Tweedy."

"No," Quentin said quickly. "No, I think I'll stay in the compound."

"Good idea," Kimberlin said. "Just follow me."

They walked across the pulsing, glowing floor toward the lifts. Quentin saw another robed Sklorno, this one dressed in gold, silver and copper.

"The Jupiter Jacks," Quentin said, nodding to the Sklorno. "What's up with her wearing those colors?"

"A teammate of yours first played upper-tier ball for the Jacks," Kimberlin said. "Recognize the face on her chest?"

Quentin did. It was the face of Don Pine. All of this was just too surreal. Maybe next season he would explore a Sklorno city, but for now, *heavily guarded, armored and secure stadium facilities* sounded just right.

He headed for the lifts, wanting nothing more than to get to his room, get a meal and lose himself in preparation for the upcoming game against the Alimum Armada.


**THE BALL BOUNCED ALONG** the turquoise field, the fumble's path unpredictable and panic-inducing. Quentin dove for it, thought he had it when his hands hit blood-streaked leather, but the ball squirted from his grip and sailed into the air. He started to scramble up for it, but a Ki lineman drove into his ribs and smashed him to the field.

A slew of orange-jerseyed, black-helmeted Krakens and blue-jerseyed, white-helmeted Armada players hit the bouncing ball at the same time, hiding the brown spot in a moving mountain of angry sentients. Pinned to the ground, Quentin watched as zebes flew in, whistles blowing madly, trying to pull players off the top of the wriggling pile.

Quentin waited, his heart in his chest, the knee of a Ki buried in the small of his back. Down 24-14 early in the fourth quarter, they'd had a sustained drive rolling along right up until Ju Tweedy fumbled.

The whistles blew again and the zebes pointed down-field — pointed the wrong way. Armada's ball.

The Ki lifted off Quentin with only a little extra push. Quentin climbed to his feet, picking chunks of turquoise-colored grass out of his facemask as he walked to the sidelines. The home Alimum crowd roared and performed their tradition of the "flag pass," handing multiple white flags from sentient to sentient as fast as they could, always to the left, so that a dozen or more of the white banner seemed to race around the stadium.

Quentin reached the sidelines and turned, praying to High One that the defense could make a stop. The Krakens were only down by ten points. It wasn't over. If they could get the ball back, they had a chance to win it.

**A TWEEDY HAD LOST** the ball, and a Tweedy got the ball back. Quentin had watched John Tweedy playing possum all game, pretending to be a little slower than he actually was, even letting Armada QB Vinson Nichols complete some short passes when John could have knocked them down. That was just how John played the game, thinking in terms of four quarters as opposed to one play.

The Armada had recovered Ju's fumble, then marched twenty-two yards, slowly chewing up the clock. With 5:32 to play, Nichols dropped back and threw what should have been a safe hook pattern to tight end Mark O'Leary. That was when John finally turned on his top speed. He dove and extended, his outstretched hands just an inch or two in front of O'Leary's. John intercepted the pass and fell to the ground, giving the Krakens the ball.

Quentin felt that adrenaline stab of momentum, of possibility.

He ran out to huddle with his offense. They had a first-and-ten at their own 37-yard line, down by ten points, 5:16 left in the game.

Hokor's face appeared in the heads-up holo.

"*Barnes!* We have time to win this, but we need yards fast. Single back, spread set. Do what you do."

"Coach?"

"Audible from the line," Hokor said. "No-huddle offense, you make it happen."

Quentin felt a rush of pride. Game on the line, the Krakens needed two scores, and Hokor was handing over the reins. The team would run a play, return to the line without huddling, then listen as Quentin called the plays from behind center.

The spread set put three wide receivers on the field: Hawick, Milford and Halawa. He also had Crazy George Starcher at right tight end and Ju Tweedy in the backfield.

Quentin's mind slipped into an automatic mode. He hit Hawick on an out-pattern for eight yards, throwing the ball just out of bounds where only she could catch it. The next pass, he hit Starcher over the middle for fifteen, then Halawa on an inside slant for ten.

On the next play, Quentin saw the blue-jerseyed Armada defense bunching in.

A blitz.

"*Green*, eighteen flash!" Quentin called, audibling to a screen pass. "Green, eighteen flash! Hut-hut!"

He dropped back five steps as his offensive line gave one hit, then pretended to let the defense beat the blocks. Four Armada Ki linemen scuttled toward him, as did a Quyth Warrior linebacker and the Sklorno left cornerback. Quentin kept backpedaling, looking downfield, then at the last second turned and threw the ball to his right where The Mad Ju was waiting. Ju hauled in the light pass. Kimberlin and Vu-Ko-Will had run to the right as soon as they'd let their defender past and now moved upfield to block for Ju.

It was a thing of beauty and savagery. Quentin's play had caught the Armada flat-footed. Their blitz left few defenders in the defensive secondary. Those that did react tried to reach Ju but had to try and go *through* Kimberlin and Vu-Ko because they were just too big to go *around*. Ju practically jogged, not going full speed, running just a bit behind his blockers. A linebacker tried to crash in, but Kimberlin laid him out flat. The cornerback drove in, trying to go around Vu-Ko's outside shoulder. Ju used that exact instant to turn on the jets, brushing past Vu-Ko's *in*side shoulder, then sprinting up-field. The safety tried to catch him at the ten, but The Mad Ju just bowled her over, then slowed down and actually walked into the end zone.

A perfectly called play, perfect execution. Arioch Morningstar's point-after made the score 24-21 in favor of the Armada. Three minutes and forty-two seconds left in the game. Now all Quentin could do was wait and see if the Krakens' D could get the ball back.

SOME THINGS WERE just not meant to be.

The Krakens did not get the ball back. Armada quarterback Vinson Nichols put together a sustained drive that slowly chewed up yards. Three third-down conversions kept the drive alive. The Krakens burned through their time-outs but couldn't force the Armada to punt. Quentin could do nothing but watch as Nichols lined his team up in the victory formation for the final play, then took a knee to let time expire.

Someday, *someday*, Quentin wanted to be the one taking a knee to end the game.

It had been a great contest, possibly the Krakens' best overall team effort yet. Quentin shook hands with the other players until he reached Nichols.

"Nice game, kid," Nichols said. "You're putting together a heck of a team."

"Thanks. Heck of a team, sure, but not good enough to take you guys yet."

Nichols shrugged. "I'm not looking forward to playing you next year, that's for sure. The Mad Ju was a great add; he killed us tonight. When he gels with your offense? Ionath will be hard to beat."

"Yeah, he is looking sharp."

"It's just turnovers," Nichols said. "Your interception and his two fumbles. If you guys clean up the turnovers for the last four games, you might win enough to stay in Tier One."

*... his two fumbles ...*

"Hey," Nichols said. "You okay? You're spacing out on me."

Quentin blinked and gave his head a quick shake to clear his thoughts. "Yeah, sorry. Great game, man. See you next year."

Nichols smiled and slapped Quentin's shoulder pad. "You better win two more games, brother, or I won't see you next year at all."

Nichols jogged to the tunnel. The remaining crowd saw him leaving the field and gave a hearty cheer. He waved his helmet at them, then was gone.

Quentin started the walk back to the visitors' locker room.

*... his two fumbles ...*

The knock on Ju Tweedy had always been that he couldn't hold onto the ball. Fumbles happened, to some guys more than others. Against the Armada, Ju had rushed for eighty-seven yards and a touchdown *and* caught three passes for forty-three yards and a second score. A great game, by any standard. But Ju's words back in the VR room rang through Quentin's head.

As long as we keep winning, the team will keep following your lead, right?

A win against the Armada would have made the Krakens 3-and-4, tied for last with the Yall Criminals. Instead, the loss made the Krakens 2-and-5, once again in sole possession of last place.

Last place ... was that where Ju Tweedy *wanted* them to be?

## GFL WEEK EIGHT ROUNDUP
(Courtesy of Galaxy Sports Network)

| | | | |
|---|---|---|---|
| **Armada** | 24 | Krakens | 21 |
| Brigands | 13 | **Astronauts** | 28 |
| **Cloud Killers** | 10 | Hullwalkers | 6 |
| **Ice Storm** | 44 | Atom Smashers | 14 |
| **Jacks** | 38 | Vanguard | 34 |
| Planets | 14 | **Juggernauts** | 17 |
| **Scarlet Fliers** | 44 | Spider-Bears | 10 |
| **Warlords** | 17 | Water Bugs | 14 |
| **Dreadnaughts** | 21 | Wolfpack | 17 |

With almost two-thirds of the season in the books, it's still anyone's game in the Solar Division. The New Rodina Astronauts (6-1) claimed sole possession of first place with 28-13 win over the Bord Brigands (5-2). The Brigands now find themselves in a three-way tie for second with the Scarlet Fliers (5-2), who topped the Chillich Spider-Bears 44-10, and the Jupiter Jacks (5-2), who beat the Vik Vanguard 38-34 in a last-second pass from Shriaz Zia to Denver.

Over in the Planet Division, the Isis Ice Storm moved back into a first-place tie, thanks to a 44-14 drubbing of the Jang Atom Smashers (1-6). Isis caught up to the To Pirates (5-2), who were off on a bye week.

The relegation alarms are starting to sound. Jang now finds itself right in the Solar relegation bubble occupied by the Chillich (0-7) and the Vanguard (1-6). Ionath (2-5) is at the bottom of the Planet Division, with the Yall Criminals (3-4) and the Hittoni Hullwalkers (3-4) just a game above.

**Deaths**

No deaths reported this week.

**Offensive Player of the Week**

Isis quarterback **Paul Infante,** who threw for 341 yards and two touchdowns against the Jang Atom Smashers.

**Defensive Player of the Week**

**Cian-Mac-Man,** defensive tackle for the Lu Juggernauts, who had four solo tackles, two sacks and a fumble recovery in a 17-14 win over the Mars Planets.

# 13

# WEEK NINE:
# IONATH KRAKENS at
# CORANADILLANA CLOUD KILLERS

**PLANET DIVISION**

5-2  To Pirates (bye)

5-2  Isis Ice Storm

4-3  Alimum Armada

4-3  Coranadillana Cloud Killers

4-3  Themala Dreadnaughts

4-3  Lu Juggernauts

4-3  Mars Planets

4-3  Wabash Wolfpack

3-4  Hittoni Hullwalkers

3-4  Yall Criminals (bye)

2-5  Ionath Krakens

**SOLAR DIVISION**

6-1  New Rodina Astronauts

5-2  Bord Brigands

5-2  Neptune Scarlet Fliers

5-2  Jupiter Jacks

4-3  D'Kow War Dogs (bye)

3-4  Sala Intrigue (bye)

3-4  Shorah Warlords

2-5  Bartel Water Bugs

1-6  Jang Atom Smashers

1-6  Vik Vanguard

0-7  Chillich Spider-Bears

### Excerpt from "Sky Gods: The Ascent of the Harrah"
### by Zippy the Voracious
### Chapter Four: The Givers

The year 2432 will always be remembered as the time that everything changed for the Harrah species. It was in that year that the Givers descended through in the thick atmosphere of Shorah to land on that planet's icy surface.

The Givers brought with them technology that stunned the tribes of Shorah, technology that was several centuries ahead of what the Harrah had themselves developed. By the time the Givers departed in 2448, they left the Harrah with the greatest of all modern-day technologies — gravity manipulation and the punch drive, providing the Harrah the ability to explore the stars on their own terms.

But was that technology given to the Harrah too soon?

When the Givers arrived, the Harrah were a tribal-oriented race. Two centuries later, little has changed. Tribal culture still forms the structure of the system's government. The Yashindi are currently the Accord's ruling tribe. Below them, each planet is ruled by a specific tribe, and underneath that, specific tribes rule each population center down to the smallest of towns. A tribe may never rule more than one area, city or planet at a time. Promotion to larger management areas or demotions to smaller ones are a common part of Accord politics.

The Grand Tribe Master of the Yashindi is the Accord's official figurehead, a position comparable to the President of the Planetary Union, the First Scientist of the League of Planets or the Emperor of the Ki Empire. However, the Grand Tribe Master's decisions are not law — all decisions must be approved by a majority vote of the five planetary tribal leaders. Before those leaders can vote, they in turn must get approval for their decision via a vote by the tribal leaders beneath them, and they must get *their* vote approved from the tribal leaders beneath *them*.

As you can imagine, this means it takes a long time for the Harrah to make decisions on anything.

While far from a democracy, this painfully slow process has produced historically prescient choices, including the bold intergalactic political moves that resulted in the acquisition of the planets Satah and Lorah from the Whitok Kingdom and the Planetary Union, respectively.

For all the benefits of this extrapolated tribal culture, however, there are also significant drawbacks. Power is still largely determined by strength. If a tribe wants to move up in rank and acquire a larger territory, it can do one of two things — wait for the tribe above it to vacate a territory by moving up and hope that the ruling powers grant advancement, or it can just wipe out the tribe above it and assume control. These internecine battles are a way of life in the Tribal Accord, continuing to this day despite efforts by the Creterakians to stamp them out.

In the Tribal Accord, a family rules by force, cunning, guile and brutality. Successful warlords hold massive amounts of power. Tribal alliances form, shift, break and re-form on an almost yearly basis, which makes it impossible to tell who is firmly in control and who is next in line. Vendettas are never forgiven. Many transgressions are payable only by blood, and often by death.

So, let this be a warning to all who travel to the Accord — do so at your own risk. The sky cities are a key part of intergalactic commerce, a popular tourist attraction and a growing force in the Galactic Football League, but the wrong thing said at the wrong time to the wrong Harrah — or even just wearing the wrong colors — and you could end up on the bad end of a flaying hook.


**QUENTIN HAD SEEN** many amazing things in his season-and-a-half with the Krakens. A prison station turned GFL player testing center, irradiated planets on the road to recovery, artificial constructs the size of small moons, each thing more staggering than the last.

But when it came to sheer size and scope, none of those things could compare to the planet Satah.

"Wow," Quentin said. "That sucker is big."

"Eloquent, as always," Doc Patah said. "You have such a way of turning sheer grandeur into the commonplace of the pedestrian."

"Is that an insult?"

Doc Patah's speakerfilm let out a heavy sigh. "No, not really, just a factual observation."

"Well, I don't care what you say, Mister Fancy-Pants — that planet is *big*."

And it was. Bigger than anything Quentin had ever seen. A swirling mass of yellow, orange and red. "Is that bigger than Jupiter?"

"By over thirty percent," Doc Patah said. "Satah is the largest inhabited planet in the galaxy, young Quentin."

"I wish you'd stop calling me that. I'm not that young."

"Hmmm," Doc Patah said.

The *Touchback* angled toward the city of Coranadillana. For once, they wouldn't have to use the shuttle — the *Touchback* could dock at one of the orbital city's massive piers. Coranadillana's scope and scale made Quentin's brain hurt. As big as the *Touchback* was, it moved toward a pier that might as well have been the tallest building in Ionath City turned on its side. And that pier was one of *hundreds*. In fact, if you took all of Ionath City and put it in orbit, you'd have a close approximation of Coranadillana. The piers radiated out from a yellow-tinted dome, inside of which Quentin saw the vague shadows of buildings.

"So, Doc," Quentin said, "you gonna give me the grand tour? I hear you're from here?"

The Harrah spun in place, not rising or falling from his hovering position seven feet off the ground. One second his flattish, rigid body was facing the window, his soft, undulating wings gently holding him in place, the next he had pivoted. His six deep, black sensory pits pointed right at Quentin's face.

"*Who* told you I was from here?"

Quentin took a step back before he knew what he was doing. "Uh … I don't know."

"*Who said it?*"

"Doc, I don't remember. It's just some talk that's going around, it's no big deal."

Quentin couldn't detect emotion from the sensory pits, or the curved mouth, or the long tentacles on either side of that mouth. Doc Patah's voice came from the speakerfilm mounted on his backpack — artificial, yet it carried all the emotion of any agitated Human.

"It is a big deal," Doc Patah said quietly. "It is an *extremely big* deal, and I would appreciate it if you would squash that *rumor* whenever you hear it. Can you do that for me, young Quentin?"

Quentin nodded.

"Thank you. We can't have loose lips sinking ships, now can we?"

"What does that mean?"

Doc Patah's wings waved. He spun in place again to stare out the window. "It means nothing."

Quentin took a step toward Doc Patah, then another, moving in rather close.

"I may be young," he said quietly, "but I'm not stupid. I will do what you asked, but I need to know if I'm telling the truth for you, or *lying* for you."

"Does it matter?"

Quentin nodded. "It does to me."

The heavy sigh again escaped the speakerfilm. "Young Quentin, the only word for you is *quaint*. Well, *naive* and *gullible* come to mind as well, but *quaint* specifically applies to your beliefs in truth and honor."

"Your Mister Big-Shot vocabulary means you are obfuscating."

Doc Patah spun to face him again, and this time, Quentin could have sworn he saw the sensory pits widen, just a bit.

"My goodness," Doc Patah said. "*Obfuscating?*"

"That's right," Quentin said quietly. "I looked it up. Now, answer my question."

Doc Patah paused for a moment. Quentin stared at him, making a mental note that he had to learn more about Harrah emotional cues. The Harrah weren't part of the on-field team, and as such, it had never crossed his mind to study up on them the way he studied up on the Sklorno, Ki, HeavyG and the Quyth. But that was an oversight — Harrah were part of the Krakens organization, and as such, he needed to know what made them tick.

"I will answer," Doc Patah said. "When you tell sentients that I am not from Coranadillana, you are lying for me."

"And why should I do that?"

"Because *not* lying could get me killed."

Quentin hadn't expected that answer. It seemed that Doc Patah, surgeon extraordinaire, had a past.

A soft shudder rolled through the *Touchback*. It had docked.

Quentin leaned in even closer and whispered. "I'll shut down that rumor, no problem."

"Thank you."

[KRAKENS PLAYERS AND SUPPORT STAFF, REPORT IMMEDIATELY TO ACCESS HATCH TWO FOR ENTRY INTO CORANADILLANA]

Quentin reached down, scooped up his duffel bag and slung it over his shoulder. "So, Doc, are you going to come into the city with us?"

"No," Doc Patah said. "Coranadillana is a place I can never go again."

Quentin started to walk away.

"Young Quentin," Doc Patah said.

Quentin turned and waited.

Doc fluttered away from the window, his wing-skin slowly propelling him forward. "You followed the advice on clothing and colors?" Doc Patah asked.

"I wouldn't call it *advice*, exactly. Gredok said all players can wear nothing but orange and black, and clothing must display the Krakens logo. Considering Gredok is less than pleased with me at the moment, I decided not to rock the ship. Fortunately, being on the team, most of my wardrobe is orange and black with a Krakens logo."

"I see," Doc Patah said. "Speaking of not rocking the ship, I know you had some trouble on Orbital Station One? Ran into some of the Cloud Killers players?"

Quentin shrugged. "We did what had to be done."

"True," Doc Patah said. "But remember that the Cloud Killers are owned by the Warlord Yashahon. If you should ever cross paths with her, or any sentient in her organization, can you do me a favor?"

"What?"

"Pretend to be someone else," Doc Patah said. "Pretend to be someone who does not have a cocky attitude, and show respect."

Quentin made a *pshhh* sound. "And why should I?"

"Because Yashahon is dangerous," Doc Patah said. "And she may not have as much respect for GFL diplomatic immunity as the rest of the owners do."

Still no emotional tell from the blank face, but there was something in Doc Patah's voice that carried heavy emphasis.

"Okay," Quentin said. "I'll take your word for it."

"You are wise beyond your years, young Quentin."

"I wish you'd stop calling me that."

"Hmmmm," Doc Patah said.

Quentin rolled his eyes and left the observation deck.


**CORANADILLANA FELT LIKE HOME** — the home Quentin wanted to forget. After the regimented order of Ionath City, the perfection of ToPor, the orbital city of Coranadillana seemed like encapsulated chaos.

A wheeled passenger transport carried the team through the streets. The lightly traveled road looked unkempt and generally dirty, as if it received little attention from the city staff. Most vehicles he saw were cargo-haulers. There were also many wheeled ground cars — no grav-sleds — customized for the race of the driver: long vehicles for Ki mostly, along with those built for Quyth Workers, and cars that seemed to adjust to both Humans and HeavyG. There were a few Sklorno vehicles, but mostly the long-legged creatures chose to walk, or rather, they ran. Nothing really got in the way of their sprinting full-out, as they were just about the only pedestrians Quentin saw.

Little road traffic and few pedestrians, which was no surprise, because if you wanted to see the populace of Coranadillana, all you had to do was look up. Thick clouds of Harrah flashed overhead, diving, spinning, banking and circling, so many that their constantly streaking shadows blocked out the sunlight and caused a constant, flickering, strobe-light effect.

Quentin had spent time with Doc Patah, seen Harrah referees, but he'd never really seen the race in its element. There was no way to count the Harrah that ranged through the domed city. They flew in all directions, so fast that if you tried to track one whizzing by you would get whiplash. It was so different from watching the Creterakians. The bats flew like a flock of birds, packed tightly together, moving almost as one multi-headed animal. The Harrah, on the other hand, were all individuals — individuals flying at insane speeds with built-in collision-avoidance systems that never seemed to fail.

And then the sky seemed to clear, at least a patch of it. Two Harrah entered the space, flying in tight, concentric circles around each other. One trailed fabric streamers, green with blue dots. The other trailed orange streamers covered in red-ringed green dots. They banked and swerved, maneuvering inside an instant, moving sphere of tightly packed Harrah.

"That's crazy," Quentin said. "Hey, Kimberlin! This some kind of mating dance or something?"

Michael looked up through the bus's clear glass roof, then shook his head. "I'm afraid not. That looks like an honor flight."

Quentin watched them banking, marveling at the control, the dexterity — living things just shouldn't be able to move that fast. "Sweet. Like a fly-off or something?"

The two fliers split, seemed to hit the edges of the living sphere, then came back at each other at blinding speed. As they passed, Quentin saw something pink spray into the air. The two creatures hit the sphere walls, banked and came at each other again. At the last moment, the one with the blue-dot streamers banked just a bit to the right.

The one with the red-tinged green dots fell from the sky like a rock, trailing long, liquid splatters of pink that caught the flickering sunlight. The lifeless body hit the sidewalk just to the right of the passing ground-bus. Thin, pink liquid splattered against the sidewalk, the street, and some of it even hit the bus's windows.

"Oh," Quentin said. "*That* kind of honor flight."

He sagged into his seat. Like so many things in so many places, death never seemed to be far away.

The ground-bus ran over a bag of trash, then turned a corner, giving the Krakens their first view of Cloud Killer Stadium. It looked only a bit larger than the open-air stadiums he'd played in back in the PNFL.

"It's small," Quentin said, happy to lose his thoughts in football and try to forget the brutal, primitive display he'd just witnessed.

"Seats about eighteen thousand," Kimberlin said.

"That's all? We've played in front of almost two hundred thousand. I can't believe a Tier One team has only eighteen thousand at a game."

Kimberlin smiled. "I said it *seats* eighteen thousand. The actual attendance is a bit more. You'll see soon enough."

Quentin nodded and closed his eyes. Soon enough indeed — they would play in less than four hours. He settled into his seat and started to mentally run through the Cloud Killers' roster, recalling the memorized list of names, positions, statistics and tendencies.

The Cloud Killers were 4-and-3, but they were beatable. If, that was, Ju Tweedy decided to hold onto the ball.

QUENTIN TRIED TO FOCUS, tried to block out the constantly flickering shadows playing across the yellow field. A bright yellow with black lines.

He looked up, like he did before and after every play. He knew he had to stop doing that, but he couldn't help it. Tens of thousands of Harrah swarmed overhead, high enough to be completely out of the vertical playing area required for long passes and punts. They were so thick they looked like a living, moving dome. That, apparently, was how they watched the game — by flying over it.

He forced himself to look down again, to survey the defense. The game had turned into a dogfight. Late in the fourth quarter, the Krakens were down 16-to-14. Krakens offensive players bled through ripped orange jerseys and the cracked armor beneath. The Cloud Killers' defense looked no better, blue-polka-dotted yellow jerseys torn and stretched, coated with different colors of blood. Quentin didn't know if there had been a rivalry before the bar fight, but there sure was one now — he felt pure hatred on both sides of the ball.

Ju had fumbled twice, but he'd also scored two touchdowns. Was he tanking on purpose? Quentin still didn't know and couldn't say as much to Coach Hokor. The Krakens were on the Cloud Killers' 34-yard line — another first down would put them well within the range of Arioch Morningstar's foot. A field goal would put them up 17-16 with only a couple of minutes left to play, if that.

A field goal would possibly win the game.

Quentin slid his hands under center. He had Ju Tweedy behind him in a single-back set. Starcher was the right tight end. Five yards outside of him, Halawa was a yard off the line of scrimmage. Milford was lined up wide left — Hawick had taken a late hit from Smileyberg earlier in the quarter and had yet to return.

Smileyberg, the Cloud Killers' left cornerback, was playing a good eight yards off of Halawa. Griffith didn't want to get beat deep by Halawa's speed. If the defender was that far off, though, Halawa was supposed to read that coverage and run a shallow slant-in. Would she adjust her route on her own? Did he need to audible to make sure she ran the slant?

"Blue, forty-one!" Quentin called down the line. He looked at Halawa, who looked back with two of her eyes. Both eyestalks quivered, only for a split second, and in that split second, Quentin knew what route she would run. He felt a lightning-bolt thrill ripple through his chest, all the way down to his knees.

"Blue, forty-one! Hut-hut ... *hut!*"

He took the snap, raised the ball as he turned his shoulders and launched a laser-shot to his right. The only way the ball could be caught was if Halawa came off the line at a forty-five-degree angle downfield and toward center.

And that was exactly what she did.

Five steps in, the ball hit Halawa dead in the chest. She never even broke stride. Quentin felt another burst of that lightning sensation ripple through his stomach, his skin — in that flicker of time he knew that short pass was the perfect union of quarterback and receiver. Halawa caught the ball and turned upfield. Smileyberg had run with her, accurately covering the inside slant, but a ball thrown that perfectly could never be defended. Smileyberg wrapped her tentacles around Halawa's shoulder pads — too high to bring down the huge rookie receiver. Halawa half-jumped, raised her right foot to Smileyberg's facemask, then *stomped* down hard. The safety's helmeted head drove into the yellow field. Halawa kept on going. She tried to cut to the sidelines, but the safety and strong safety reached her and drove her out of bounds after a fifteen-yard gain.

First-and-ten on the 19. A chip-shot for Morningstar. Quentin looked at the clock — 1:16 to play.

Coach Hokor's face appeared in the heads-up holo. "*Barnes!* Dive right. They only have two time-outs left, let's force their hand and grind this out."

Quentin nodded. That was the right strategy. Run the ball, chew up the clock, maybe get one more first down and kick the field goal with time expiring. If they couldn't get a first down, then take the lead and leave the Cloud Killers with only fifteen or twenty seconds to play. Running the ball was basic football strategy ... so why did Quentin's instincts scream at him to not do it?

"Coach, let me run a quarterback keep-out. I promise I'll slide."

"No," Hokor said. "Give the ball to Ju."

"But Coach, I—"

"*Run the plays that I call!*"

Quentin felt pulled in multiple directions. All Ju had to do was slam the ball into the line and the Krakens had the game wrapped up.

Quentin huddled his players. "Okay, forty-one dive on two, on two. We run three times, take the field goal and we win this thing. Ju, you hold onto the ball, you got it?"

Ju stood, pointed his index finger at Quentin, then winked and flipped his thumb down twice. *Bang-bang.* "You got it, *captain*," he said.

They walked to the line accompanied by the sound of a deafening drumbeat, thousands of flying Harrah pounding their hollow chests. The terrestrial fans were also shouting, screaming and clacking, loud but barely audible over the Harrah's thunder.

The Cloud Killers knew it was a run, and they crowded the line, daring Quentin to put the ball in the air where they might have at least a chance of a bobbled pass, a tipped ball, something that would stop the inevitable game-winning field goal.

*Run the plays that are called.*

"Red, forty-two! Red, forty-two! Hut-*hut!*"

The ball slapped into Quentin's hands. He pivoted to the right, extending the ball for Ju. Ju's giant arms clamped down, but clamped down too soon. Quentin felt the ball squirt away. It hit the ground and bounced in front of the big running back. Ju reached for it one-handed, slapped it, and the ball sailed forward, arcing over the offensive line to the defense beyond.

Killers defensive end Jesper Schultz reached his big hands up and caught the ball in the air. He curled his body around it, then fell to the ground in the HeavyG equivalent of a fetal position. Sho-Do-Thikit was the first to reach him, drilling the tucked-up defensive end with a full-on extension shot, but Schultz just skidded across the yellow field.

The whistle blew. Zebes flew in.

Despair and denial swept through Quentin's soul as he looked up at the scoreboard. One minute, thirteen seconds to play,

Krakens with only one time-out, Cloud Killers with the ball and ahead by two.

It was over. All Coranadillana had to do was take a knee three times.

The chest-cavity-pounding drumbeat hit such an intensity that Quentin felt his eardrums vibrating in complaint. They'd had the game won, but a Ju Tweedy fumble had let it slip away.

Quentin walked off the field, seeing the same dejection that he felt hanging from the shoulders and heads of every Krakens player.

Everyone except Ju, who still had his head up high.

Quentin's upper lip curled into a sneer.

**BRIGHT LIGHTS BLAZED,** making it hard to see the assembled reporters packed into Cloud Killer Stadium's small press room. But the lights didn't stop Quentin from hearing them, from hearing their inane questions.

"Quentin! Quentin! Kint the Fabulous, ESPN. Ju Tweedy had another mixed game for you, going for over a hundred yards and scoring two touchdowns, but do you think his three fumbles were a factor in the loss to the Cloud Killers?"

Quentin glared in the reporter's general direction, able to make out only a little bit of his face through the lights.

"Yes," Quentin said. "We lost sixteen to fourteen, by two points. So, yeah, I think three fumbles, including two in the red-zone, *might* have had an impact."

His words rang with sarcasm, but the reporters didn't seem to register that. He'd barely finished his last word before the voices erupted into annoying and endless shouts of his name until one of the peons shouted down the others.

"Quentin! Quentin! Sara Mabuza, Earth News Syndicate. How does it feel to know that you're in last place?"

"How do you *think* it feels?" Quentin said. He heard his temper slipping, then controlled himself. This was part of the job, he had to lighten up. "It feels like crap, but we can come back from this."

There were more than a few laughs heard through the endless shouts of his name. His fingers curled into fists.

"Come on," Mabuza said, barely able to hide her own laughter. "The Krakens are two-and-six with four games left, including one against the Jupiter Jacks."

"We win two games, we're safe," Quentin said quickly. "We still have to play the Hullwalkers, who are only one game ahead of us. And we're only two games behind the Criminals and the Planets. We play them both as well. Any of those three teams loses the rest of their games, including their game against Ionath, and we win two? That would do it for us."

There was still a little laughter, but also a few murmurs of approval. Perhaps the reporters didn't think a football player could do math?

"Quentin! *Quentin!* Kelp Bringer from the Leekee Galaxy Times. Are you saying that you *really* think the Krakens are still in this, that you're not already on your way back to Tier Two?"

Quentin stood up. "That is *exactly* what I am saying. We have the offense to win those games if we can hold onto the ball. The Krakens can, and *will*, stay in Tier One. I see my *mandatory* twenty minutes for answering your idiotic questions has expired, so I'm done with this."

He stormed away from the table and back toward the visitors' locker room. His own words already rang in his ears. Had he just guaranteed the Krakens would stay in T1? Yes, yes, he had. And he was right about one thing — they *could* stay in Tier One, *if* they could hold onto the ball.

Ju Tweedy couldn't get what he wanted, so he was fumbling on purpose. Quentin had to find a way to get Ju to play to win, or it would be Tier Two all over again.

## GFL WEEK NINE ROUNDUP
(Courtesy of Galaxy Sports Network)

| | | | |
|---|---|---|---|
| Water Bugs | 17 | **Jacks** | 35 |
| **Spider-Bears** | 24 | Atom Smashers | 23 |
| **Cloud Killers** | 16 | Krakens | 14 |
| **Juggernauts** | 24 | Ice Storm | 14 |
| Planets | 17 | **Armada** | 31 |
| **Astronauts** | 28 | War Dogs | 7 |
| Warlords | 38 | **Brigands** | 44 |
| Pirates | 14 | **Dreadnaughts** | 16 |
| Vanguard | 20 | **Scarlet Fliers** | 24 |
| **Wolfpack** | 23 | Intrigue | 12 |
| **Criminals** | 17 | Hullwalkers | 10 |

There is only one word to describe the Planet Division playoff race, and that word is "madness." A tumultuous week ended with *seven* teams tied for first and another two teams only one game out. The Alimum Armada (5-3) grabbed a share of first place with a 31-17 win over the Mars Planets (5-3). The Lu Juggernauts upset the Isis Ice Storm 24-14, leveling both teams' records at 5-3. Wabash also moved into first by beating the Sala Intrigue 23-12, and don't look now, but here come the Themala Dreadnaughts. After starting the season at 1-3, the Dreads (5-3) have won four straight, including this week's 16-14 win over the To Pirates (1-7).

In the Solar things are a little more clear. New Rodina (7-1) won its fifth straight to stay in first, beating up on the War Dogs by a score of 28-7. D'Kow began the season at 4-0, but four straight losses move them to fifth place in the Solar. The Astros need to keep winning to stay ahead of the Jupiter Jacks (6-2), who beat

Bartel 35-17; Neptune (6-2), who topped the Vik Vanguard 24-20; and Bord (6-2), who beat the Shorah Warlords 44-38.

The Chillich Spider-Bears (1-7) earned their first win of the season with a 24-23 victory over the Jang Atom Smashers (1-7). Chillich, Jang and Vik are now all tied at the bottom of the Solar Division.

**Deaths**

No deaths reported this week.

**Offensive Player of the Week**

Jupiter wide receiver **Denver**, who caught five passes for 112 yards and three touchdowns in a 35-17 win over the Bartel Water Bugs.

**Defensive Player of the Week**

Atom Smashers linebacker **Mike Dowell**, who caused two fumbles and had six solo tackles in a 24-23 loss to the Chillich Spider-Bears.

# 14

# WEEK TEN:
# YALL CRIMINALS at
# IONATH KRAKENS

**PLANET DIVISION**

5-3  Alimum Armada
5-3  Coranadillana Cloud Killers
5-3  Themala Dreadnaughts
5-3  Lu Juggernauts
5-3  To Pirates
5-3  Isis Ice Storm
5-3  Wabash Wolfpack
4-4  Yall Criminals
4-4  Mars Planets
3-5  Hittoni Hullwalkers
2-6  Ionath Krakens

**SOLAR DIVISION**

7-1  New Rodina Astronauts
6-2  Bord Brigands
6-2  Neptune Scarlet Fliers
6-2  Jupiter Jacks
4-4  D'Kow War Dogs
3-5  Sala Intrigue
3-5  Shorah Warlords
2-6  Bartel Water Bugs
1-7  Jang Atom Smashers
1-7  Vik Vanguard
1-7  Chillich Spider-Bears

From the *OS2 Tribune*

## Orbiting Death Owner Makes Bold Roster Moves

*by* SHAKA THE IMPERSONATOR

ORBITAL STATION I (Galaxy News Service) — New owner Anna Villani has wasted no time in putting her stamp on the Orbiting Death football team.

Villani became the Death's new owner after the tragic passing of Sikka the Death just a few short weeks ago. While Villani publicly mourned Sikka's passing, she also had a job to do — how could she get the Death ready for the upcoming Tier Two season *without* all-star running back Ju Tweedy? Tweedy, who recently signed with the Ionath Krakens, is the prime suspect in the murder of OS1 citizen Grace McDermot.

Offensively, Villani immediately changed the Death from a running team to a passing one with the signing of quarterback Condor Adrienne, formerly of the Whitok Pioneers. The Pioneers finished 6-3 last year, with all three losses occurring when Adrienne was out with a leg injury.

"I was surprised to get the news," Adrienne said. "I mean, well, we re-ally have a good thing going in Whitok. I love it here in Whitok, and I wanted to take the Pioneers to a Tier One championship. I don't know why [Pioneers owner] Shag-En-Bah sold my contract, but well, I'll make the most of it with the Orbiting Death."

Villani also signed Quyth Survivors running back Chooch Motumbo to replace Tweedy, but it was on the defensive side of the ball that she shocked the Quyth Irradiated Conference with the addition of Sky Demolition All-Pro linebacker Yalla the Biter. Yalla is the all-time GFL leader for fatalities, with eight during his seven-year career.

"We are going to Tier One," Villani said of the roster additions. "These players are what were missing from last year's lineup. Whatever it takes, we *will* win the T2 Tournament in 2683. I have some scores to settle in Tier One, and you can bet that I will settle them."

*"Whatever it takes, we will win the T2 Tournament in 2683."*

— ANNA VILLANI, ORBITING DEATH OWNER

**A FLYER FOUND IN PISSAGATA,** second-largest city on the planet Yall of the Sklorno Dynasty.

★ ★ ★

# ATTENTION!
## All members of the CoQB!
## A PILGRIMAGE!

The CoQB is booking group passage on a ship to Ionath, located in the Quyth Concordia, to see His Holiness Quentin Barnes give his blessings live!
This affordable trip includes transit fare, travel to the planet's surface and official church robes in "the orange and the black," the official colors of His Holiness Quentin Barnes. A limited number of tickets are available for the football game of the Ionath Krakens game against the Yall Criminals. Those that cannot attend the game will join us on the streets of Ionath City, jumping, singing songs and shouting praises in honor of His Holiness Quentin Barnes.

Basic food is included, but pilgrims should feel free to bring a friend if fresh meat is desired.

Yes, you can see His Holiness at his home Temple of Ionath Stadium. The truly devoted will assuredly make this pilgrimage. Full members, acolytes and those interested in converting are all welcome.

**Join us in holy worship!**

★ ★ ★

**JU TWEEDY HADN'T FUMBLED** the entire game. Quentin had to wonder if the only reason for that was because the Krakens were down 42-21.

Late in the fourth quarter, down by three touchdowns, the home crowd booing the Krakens once again. Well, not the *entire* home crowd. At least ten percent of the stadium was filled with Sklorno females, clad eyestalks-to-toes in orange and black wrapping or robes. Those Sklorno squealed, chattered and chirped every time Quentin touched the ball, which — considering he was the quarterback — happened on every Krakens offensive play.

Apparently, the Church of Quentin Barnes had traveled en masse to Ionath. No matter what Quentin did, they cheered. Many season-ticket holders in those sections had dressed in rain gear or outdoor wear — they were prepared for ten thousand Sklorno females in religious rapture, raspers dangling long and flinging drool when the females jumped with joy at each completed pass.

The city streets were full of Sklorno, and not just the females. Bedbugs, the male of the species, were all over the place, an estimated five thousand of them milling about with the females and generally getting underfoot. For Quentin's safety, Gredok had confined him to the Krakens building and the stadium for the entire week. Quentin hadn't minded that edict at all — the whole thing was overwhelming, embarrassing and a little bit frightening.

He walked back to the forming huddle. He'd just thrown another incompletion, forcing a ball into coverage. The pass probably should have been picked off, but Hawick had knocked the ball out of the defensive back's tentacles.

The Criminals kept five defensive backs in — a "nickel" package — instead of the normal four. They were playing the pass, making sure the Krakens couldn't get a long ball for a quick score that might put them back in the game. Quentin had already given up two interceptions, throwing into double and even triple coverage as he tried to make something happen. With only four minutes to play, the odds of a three-touchdown comeback were slim.

"*Barnes!*" Coach Hokor popped up in the heads-up holodisplay. "Stop forcing the ball. We can't win if you just give them the ball back."

"Coach, we need points."

"We also need to work for the rest of the season and not needlessly put our receivers in jeopardy with the kind of passes you are throwing. X-set formation, run the draw."

"A draw play? You wanna run the ball?"

"That's right."

"But Coach, we need to pass, we—"

"*Run the plays that I call!*"

Quentin kicked the ground, then walked to the huddle. Hokor had given up on the game and wanted to turn the last four minutes into real-time practice. The Krakens would try to put a drive together, see if they could get one more touchdown, build experience for the next three games so they could score when it mattered, score in a game they could win.

"X-set draw," Quentin said to the huddle. Tired faces looked up at him. His teammates didn't want to run the ball, they wanted to go for the win no matter how improbable it might be.

"Just run the damn play," Quentin snapped. "X-set draw on two, on two, ready? *Break!*"

Quentin walked to the line. The X-set put four receivers on the field — two wide to the left and two wide to the right — with Ju Tweedy as the single back behind Quentin. The defensive backs moved into woman-to-woman coverage, with a good seven- to eight-yard cushion off of Hawick, Milford, Mezquitic and Halawa. The linebackers spread to the sides of the line — they would be playing a short zone, trying to disrupt inside slant patterns. If Quentin audibled, he could get Hawick or Halawa to sprint out ten yards and turn on a hook pattern, then hit either of them right there.

But a ten-yard pass wouldn't get points. So, he might as well just run the plays that were called.

He looked over the Criminals' defense. White jerseys with purple numbers and purple splashes on their shoulders. White helmets decorated with their purple "ball-and-chain Sklorno" logo. Purple leg armor. Shoes that had started the game as white were now streaked with stains.

"Red, twenty-two!" Quentin called out. "Red, twenty-two! Hut-*hut!*"

Quentin dropped back and raised the ball to his ear, eyes scanning for a pattern. The four receivers sprinted downfield, forcing the defenders to move back as well. The linebackers also backpedaled into their zone positions. Five steps into the drop, Quentin stuck the ball out to his left, where Ju Tweedy tore it out of his hands.

The linebackers had to stop their backward momentum before they could come forward. In that brief pause, Ju reached the line. Michael Kimberlin had let his defensive tackle penetrate past the line of scrimmage but had pushed him to the right, to the outside. The tackle couldn't stop his momentum as Ju ran inside, keeping Kimberlin between the tackle and himself. Ju shot through the line at full speed. A Quyth Warrior linebacker attacked, but a head-and-shoulders fake left that linebacker grabbing at air as Ju went by him, cutting outside and heading for the sidelines. A cornerback angled for him, trying to shake off Halawa's downfield block. Instead of cutting, Ju just lowered his head and shoulders and ran her over. He high-stepped through the tackle, reached the sidelines and cut upfield.

Quentin watched, hearing the home crowd roar as Ju chewed up the yards. The safety and strong safety's speed let them quickly close the distance. Ju reached the 10-yard line, then slid out of bounds just as the strong safety hit him.

Quentin felt a rage wash over him. Ju could have lowered his shoulder, taken the strong safety on, tried for the touchdown. But instead, Ju slid out of bounds just ten yards shy of a score. In one play, Ju had shown his moves, his physical power to run sentients over, *and then* showed that — sometimes — he chose not to use that physical power. His team was down by three scores and needed a big play, yet he ran out of bounds.

● ● ●

**THE KRAKENS GOT THAT TOUCHDOWN** three plays later when Quentin hit Crazy George Starcher for six. With only two and a half minutes to play, down by two touchdowns, Arioch Morningstar tried an on-side kick. The Criminals got the ball back. They then notched two first downs and proceeded to run out the clock.

Once again, Quentin had to watch the opposition's victory formation, their quarterback taking a knee to end the game.

Quentin shook hands with the Criminals players, a rage building inside of him even as he nodded and passed out the obligatory good game congratulations.

Ionath was now 2-and-7. Two and a half games behind the next closest team, the Mars Planets, who were 4-and-5. Three games remained in the season. The Krakens had to win at least two, if not all three. Quentin's bold claim that they would stay in Tier One looked like just that — a bold claim.

Something had to be done. Something drastic. Ju wanted a man-to-man fight, winner take all? Well, then maybe that had to happen. But before it could, Quentin needed to take Ju out of his game.

He needed to get inside Ju Tweedy's head.

## GFL WEEK TEN ROUNDUP
(Courtesy of Galaxy Sports Network)

| | | | |
|---|---|---|---|
| Armada | 13 | **Ice Storm** | 22 |
| Brigands | 28 | **Jacks** | 34 |
| **Hullwalkers** | 23 | Wolfpack | 16 |
| Krakens | 24 | **Criminals** | 35 |
| **Atom Smashers** | 12 | Vanguard | 9 |
| Planets | 17 | **Cloud Killers** | 23 |
| **Scarlet Fliers** | 22 | Water Bugs | 17 |
| **Astronauts** | 63 | Spider-Bears | 10 |
| Warlords | 14 | **War Dogs** | 17 |
| **Dreadnaughts** | 28 | Juggernauts | 7 |
| **Pirates** | 20 | Intrigue | 10 |

The drama continues in the Planet Division. With just three games left in the season, it's a four-way tie for first between teams with matching 6-3 records: Coranadillana, Isis, Themala and To. Isis stayed in first by knocking Alimum (5-4) down to second place with a 22-13 win. Themala also knocked a team down to second, thanks to a 28-7 win over the Lu Juggernauts (5-4).

New Rodina (8-1) won its sixth in a row to stay in first place. The Astronauts recorded their highest point total of the season, winning 63-10 against the Spider-Bears (1-8). Both Jupiter (7-2) and Neptune (7-2) remain hot on New Rodina's heels for the Solar Division title.

And speaking of things on heels, the relegation monster is closing in on Ionath. The Krakens (2-7) are two full games behind the Planets (4-5) and the Hullwalkers (4-5).

In the Solar Division, four teams remain on the relegation

bubble: Bartel (2-7), Vik (1-8), Chillich (1-8) and Jang (2-7). The Vanguard and the Spider-Bears go head to head next week. The winner is guaranteed to avoid relegation.

## Deaths

Alimum Armada wide receiver **Tenny**, who was killed on a late hit from Mars Planets linebacker Doug St. Cyr. Cyr was injured in an altercation following the hit and will be out for the rest of the season.

## Offensive Player of the Week:

Dreadnaughts quarterback **Gavin Warren,** who threw for two touchdowns and ran for two more in a 28-7 win over the Lu Juggernauts.

## Defensive Player of the Week

Neptune free safety **Tulsa,** who had three interceptions and four tackles against the Bartel Water Bugs.

# 15

# WEEK ELEVEN: HITTONI HULLWALKERS at IONATH KRAKENS

**PLANET DIVISION**

6-3  Coranadillana Cloud Killers
6-3  Isis Ice Storm
6-3  Themala Dreadnaughts
6-3  To Pirates
5-4  Alimum Armada
5-4  Lu Juggernauts
5-4  Wabash Wolfpack
5-4  Yall Criminals
4-5  Mars Planets
4-5  Hittoni Hullwalkers
2-7  Ionath Krakens

**SOLAR DIVISION**

8-1  New Rodina Astronauts
7-2  Jupiter Jacks
7-2  Neptune Scarlet Fliers
6-3  Bord Brigands
5-4  D'Kow War Dogs
3-6  Sala Intrigue
3-6  Shorah Warlords
2-7  Bartel Water Bugs
2-7  Jang Atom Smashers
1-8  Vik Vanguard
1-8  Chillich Spider-Bears

### Excerpt from "Third Best: A Comprehensive Catalog of the GFL's Tier Three Franchises"

*"In the short and violent history of interaction between our sentient races, there has never been anything approaching the phenomenon of gridiron football."*
— Ratak the Postulating, 2664

Ratak said those words on the eve of the third GFL expansion, which took the league from fourteen teams to eighteen. That was nineteen seasons ago, and his words have never rung more true. While broadcasts of Tier One and Tier Two gridiron football dominate galactic sports culture, the game's real spread is seen in Tier Three. To the uninitiated, the numbers are shocking — 23 individual T3 leagues contain 288 teams.

The "Grandaddy of Them All," as it's known, is the National Football League, or NFL. The galaxy's longest-running professional football league, the NFL has operated with almost no interruptions for seven and a half centuries. Originally founded as the American Professional Football Association in 1920 (ErT), the league changed its name to the National Football League in 1922.

In 1922, there were eighteen teams concentrated in an Earth area known as the "American Midwest." Today, the NFL is the largest T3 league, boasting 51 teams across four planets: Earth, Mars, Jones and New Earth.

But, of course, gridiron football is not limited to just Human-centric worlds. Both the Ki Gridiron League (KGL) and the Chachanna Football Collective (CFC) boast eighteen teams, and another thirteen T3 leagues each have ten teams or more.

While some leagues are single-species, like the Human-only Purist Nation Football League, most actively seek multi-species rosters. Tier Three leagues not only provide a constant supply of players to the upper tiers, they have also been instrumental as a focal point for species integration and cross-cultural interaction.

And, perhaps most important of all at least from the Galactic Football League's perspective, T3 leagues have greatly increased an understanding of and a desire for the game of gridiron football. As the popularity of upper tier football continues to explode, GFL officials know full well that the "third best" is a major part of that success.

## GFL-AFFILIATED TIER 3 LEAGUES

| LEAGUE | TEAMS | SYSTEM | NAME |
|---|---|---|---|
| NFL | 51 | Planetary Union | National Football League |
| KGL | 18 | Ki Empire | Ki Gridiron League |
| CFC | 18 | Sklorno Dynasty | Chachanna Football Collective |
| TAGA | 16 | Tri-Alliance | Tri-Alliance Gridiron Association |
| S6GL | 16 | League of Planets | Satirli 6 Gridiron League |
| GAT | 15 | Harrah Tribal Accord | Gridiron Accord of Tribes |
| PNFL | 12 | Purist Nation | Purist Nation Football League |
| WG | 12 | Quyth Concordia | Whitok Gridiron |
| CFL | 12 | Sklorno Dynasty | Chillich Football League |
| TFL | 12 | Tower Republic | Tower Football League |
| YFL | 10 | Sklorno Dynasty | Yall Football League |
| KREFL | 10 | Ki Rebel Establishment | Ki Rebel Establishment Football League |
| QGA | 10 | Quyth Concordia | Quyth Gridiron Association |
| T3GL | 10 | Planetary Union | Thomas 3 Gridiron League |
| W4GL | 10 | League of Planets | Wilson 4 Gridiron League |
| WGL | 10 | Sklorno Dynasty | Withrit Gridiron League |
| JNSV | 8 | Planetary Union | Jupiter, Neptune, Saturn and Venus |
| CGA | 7 | League of Planets | Capizzi Gridiron Association |
| W6GL | 7 | League of Planets | Wilson 6 Gridiron League |
| V3GL | 6 | League of Planets | Vosor 3 Gridiron League |
| R2FL | 6 | Planetary Union | Reiger 2 Football League |
| WKFL | 6 | Whitok Kingdom | Whitok Kingdom Football League |
| RPL | 6 | League of Planets | Rodina Planetary League |

• • •

**Live feed from UBS GameDay holocast coverage**

"Hello again, football fans, and welcome to Ionath Stadium. I'm Masara the Observant, and with me as always is everyone's favorite color commentator, Chick McGee."

"Thanks, Masara, your class is only outshined by your intellect."

"You know it, Chick. We welcome those viewers joining us after watching the Isis Ice Storm's thrilling 27-24 overtime win against the Coranadillana Cloud Killers. Here in Ionath the action is already underway. Chick, fill the viewers in."

"Well, Masara, the Hullwalkers took their first drive forty-five yards into the Krakens' red zone but had to settle for a field goal. Richfield gave the Krakens good field position on their own thirty-seven. We're waiting for the end of a commercial time-out. The visiting Hullwalkers are resplendent in white jerseys with the dark blue and crimson sleeves and numbers, crimson armor and dark blue helmets with the famous Hullwalkers boot logo. Ionath, the home team referred to by loving locals as *the orange and the black*, are ready for their first possession. Down three to nothing, let's see what Quentin Barnes and the rest of the gang can do."

"The Krakens come out of the huddle, Chick, and ... wait ... what's this? Quentin Barnes isn't lining up under center. He's standing there, staring at running back Ju Tweedy."

"Is Barnes confused, Masara?"

"I don't know, Chick. And The Mad Ju doesn't seem to know what to do. He's halfway into his stance, he just held up his hands as if *say hey, what's going on?*"

"Yes, that's why you're the play-by-play genius that you are, Masara. Wait, Barnes is raising his right arm. Just his right arm, and ... now he's pointing to the Ionath sidelines. Still staring at Ju and pointing at the sidelines."

"Chick, is he telling Ju to get off the field?"

"Maybe he's pointing to a spot on the sidelines and saying, *Right over there is where I floated an air biscuit.*"

"Chick! That's not appropriate!"

"Then maybe he said he kicked a fifteen-yard stink-goal?"

"*Chick!*"

"Sorry, Masara, sorry, folks at home. The play clock is ticking. Barnes is standing there, pointing. The offensive line is looking back, as are the receivers. The orange-and-black-clad Krakens faithful in the stands have no idea what's going on. And Ju Tweedy, most of all, hasn't a clue."

"Chick! The play clock is ticking down and Krakens coach Hokor the Hookchest looks beside himself on the sidelines."

"Hokor looks like he's miles from the bathroom and the super squirts are making him do the brown dance, Masara."

"Chick!"

"Sorry, Masara, sorry, folks at home, but ... yes, Hokor just called a time-out! He's storming onto the field, waving over both Barnes and Tweedy. Masara, we can only imagine what will be said during this time-out."


"BARNES! WHY ARE YOU just standing there like that?"

"I didn't think Ju was up for the play, Coach. I pointed at the sidelines to tell him it was time to get off the field."

"What?" Ju said. "What do you mean *not up for the play?* It was a damn off-tackle run."

Quentin shrugged. "I looked into your eyes and didn't see that killer spirit, Ju."

Hokor ripped off his little baseball cap and threw it down on the blue field. "*Barnes!* What is this, a day at the zoo?"

"No," Ju said. "Not a day at the zoo, Coach, it's amateur night."

Quentin laughed. "Hey, that was pretty good."

"*Barnes!* Can you look into his eyes again and tell me if you see the killer soul?"

"Killer spirit, Coach."

"Fine, *fine!* Can we just play football?"

Quentin gently reached out and held the sides of Ju's helmet. Quentin turned Ju's head a little bit, tilted it, making a big show out of examining Ju's face. Ju stared back, eyes wide and crazy like his brother's.

"Done?" Ju said. "See what you need to see?"

Quentin let go of the helmet and nodded. "Yep, you look like a regular killer, Ju."

"Fine," Hokor said. "Now, go run the play that I called."

"Sounds like fun," Quentin said, and he jogged back to the huddle. Ju stared after him for a second, then followed.


**"WELL, CHICK, WHATEVER IT WAS,** it seems to have been sorted out."

"If Hokor finds a bathroom, maybe."

"Chick, *please!* This has nothing to do with bodily functions."

"It does when I'm sitting next to you, Masara."

"Chick!"

"Sorry, Masara, my bad. The Krakens break the huddle, the offensive line takes positions."

"Barnes walks up behind Bud-O-Shwek, the center, he bends down and ... he's standing up again. Barnes turns, and ... what is this?"

"Masara, he's staring at Ju Tweedy again, and he's pointing to the sidelines again. I think the message is clear — Barnes wants Ju Tweedy off the field."

"Chick, Ju is looking to the sidelines, he doesn't know what to do. The play clock is ticking again. Either the Krakens call a time-out or they will be penalized five yards. Why wouldn't Barnes want his best player on the field?"

"I don't know, Masara, but I'll get to the bottom of it. What's this? Hokor is sending Yassoud Murphy onto the field! Murphy is sprinting out, he's gesturing madly for Ju Tweedy to get to the sidelines. If Ju doesn't hurry off, the Krakens either get that delay of game or they get penalized for twelve men on the field."

"Ju is standing there, Chick, and the crowd is starting to boo."

"This is strange indeed, Masara. Barnes is lining up under center, Murphy is in a three-point stance behind him."

"And there goes Ju, Chick. Ju is sprinting for the sidelines. He's off, and the ball is snapped. Murphy takes the handoff and plows forward for three, no, four yards. Chick, can you explain this bizarre behavior?"

"No, Marasa, but I think we won't see Ju Tweedy for rest of this drive. Clearly, there is some bad blood between Barnes and Ju."


THE KRAKENS MANAGED two first downs, then had to punt. Quentin ran to the sidelines to find several sentients waiting for him: Don Pine, John Tweedy and Coach Hokor.

"Q," John screamed as Quentin ran off the field. "What are you *doing*, man?"

"Don't worry about it," Quentin said, pushing past him. "Don't you have a defense to run?"

"Yeah, but Q, you're making my brother look like an idiot!"

The crowd roared, then subsided. It sounded like the Hullwalkers punt return team almost broke it open. Quentin looked at John, then nodded to the field. John looked, saw the punt team coming off and his defense running on. He gave Quentin an expression that said *we're not done with this*, then pulled on his helmet and ran onto the field. "Barnes!" Hokor screamed. "On the bench, *now! Ju*, Murphy, Pine, you too. Move!"

Hokor stomped off, his fur fully extended.

Pine grabbed Quentin's arm, more to get Quentin's attention than to pull at him. Pine leaned in as they walked to the bench. "What are you thinking, kid? You cost us a time-out."

"Don't worry about it," Quentin said. "I know what I'm doing."

"Good, then fill me in."

Quentin shook his head. "I can't. You just remember what I did for you, you got it?"

Don stopped short. "What?"

"You heard me," Quentin said. "You *remember* what I did for you, and you *do not* replace me unless I say so."

"But Quentin, if Coach wants —"

Quentin poked his index finger against Don's armored chest. "You heard what I said."

Quentin pushed past him, found Hokor stomping around in front of the bench, then sat down to the right of Ju. Ju's scowl had nearly pinched his two eyebrows into one. Yassoud sat on Quentin's right, his eyes alive and alert with excitement, his jersey already torn. It was the first time Quentin had seen that much joy on Yassoud's face since the end of the Tier Two season. Pine sat on Ju's left.

Hokor stomped up and stood in front of them, still having to look up with his one big eye even though the four Human players were seated.

"Now," he said, "will someone tell me what's going on?"

Ju jerked his right thumb at Quentin. "Ask him."

Quentin shrugged. "Beats me."

"*Barnes!* Why did you want Ju off the field?"

Quentin shrugged again. "I love having Ju on the field, Coach. He runs very hard."

Hokor stared at Quentin, then turned to Pine. "Well?"

Don Pine held up both hands, palms out, and shook his head. "Hey, I have no idea, Coach."

"Pine, you *always* know what's going on with your team."

"It's not *my team* anymore," Pine said. "Really, Coach, I got nothing."

Hokor turned on Yassoud. "And *you*. Is this your doing?"

Yassoud laughed. "Are you kidding me? Why would I be involved?"

"Because you've been on the bench for the last four games and you want to get back on the field."

Yassoud blinked. "Yeah ... I guess I do want back on the field." He shook his head, as if to clear it. "But, I just got called in to run the ball and I did, Coach. That's it."

Hokor again turned to face Quentin and Ju, staring at each of them in turn.

"It will be hard for us to win this game," Hokor said, "but we can win it. Whatever you two have going on, it ends now, understood?"

Quentin nodded, then turned and offered his hand to Ju. "What do you say, pal? Ready to go win one for Hokor?"

Ju eyed the hand suspiciously, then met Quentin's gaze. "Sure," Ju said, and shook. "Just knock that crap off, got it?"

"I got it."

The Ionath Stadium crowd roared.

"Fumble!" someone on the sidelines shouted. "We got the ball!"

Hokor's fur instantly fell flat, as if he'd forgotten all about the incident. "Our ball! We're going to run it. I-formation, get Montagne to do isolation blocks, Ju, you follow her in. I want to maintain this field position and at least tie it up."

Quentin stood, gently slipped past Hokor and walked onto the field.

**"WELL, CHICK, THE KRAKENS** have the ball in scoring position. The offense is huddling up. I wonder if we'll see any more hijinks."

"Hijinks? Is that even a word?"

"Yes, Chick, it's a Human word."

"Well, I'm Human, and it's news to me."

"Chick, come on —"

"Masara, look! The Krakens blockers and receivers are on the line of scrimmage, but Barnes is doing it again! He's just standing there, pointing to the sidelines."

**JU TWEEDY STORMED** forward, hands clenched into fists. Quentin just smiled. As he'd suspected, Rebecca stepped between the two men, her hands on Ju's chest.

"Hold on," she said, "take it easy."

Ju pointed over her shoulder at Quentin. "I'm gonna *kill* him!"

Quentin said nothing, he just kept pointing to the sidelines.

Ju tried to walk forward again, but Becca stayed in front of him. Then the offensive linemen were there, subtly blocking any path around Becca that Ju might take to get at Quentin.

Ju stopped pushing and glared. "You're making a mistake, Barnes."

"Get off *my* field, Ju," Quentin said. "And send in Murphy. He actually wants to win."

Whistles blew and flags flew. Delay of game.

"*Barnes!*" Hokor in the VR display. "I've had it! Get off the field!"

"Sorry, Coach," Quentin said. "I can't do that."

"What do you mean *you can't do that!* I want you off!"

Quentin shook his head. As the zebes marked off the five-yard delay of game penalty, he walked with his team back to the new huddle.

Even over the angry roar of 185,000 fans, Quentin heard the faint trace of Hokor screaming for Don Pine. Helmet in hand, Pine ran to Hokor, listened, nodded, then started running on the field. He stopped in his tracks when he saw Quentin.

Quentin was staring at Pine. Staring and pointing to the sidelines.

Pine paused, took one step forward, then shrugged and ran back to Hokor.

Quentin didn't know if Quyth Leaders could have heart attacks. If Hokor lived through his messageboard throwing, tiny-hat-ripping, headphone-smashing, turf-kicking temper tantrum, well, then probably not.

Yassoud ran onto the field, sprinted to the huddle and waited, his eyes wide and alert with excitement.

Quentin looked each of his players in the eye or eyes. "Everyone ready to have some fun?"

They nodded and grunted.

"Okay, I-formation, off-tackle right on two. And Murphy? Do me a favor, and run hard, will ya?"

"You got it!"

"On two, on two … ready? *Break!*"

• • •

**IN A PERFECT GALAXY** or in a heroic holo, the Krakens would have won the game without Ju Tweedy running the football.

It was not a perfect galaxy.

Yassoud ran harder than he ever had, including his days in Tier Two. The defense had to pay attention to him, but without The Mad Ju in the game, the Hullwalkers keyed on Quentin. They blitzed as often as possible, double-covering Hawick and Milford. Even with excellent protection, his line couldn't always hold back the assault. He finished the game 22-for-35 for 235 yards, no TDs, two interceptions and four sacks.

The last sack — of course — was the worst. Although he had to admit to himself it wasn't really a *sack*. He'd felt pressure, tucked the ball and ran. Instead of sliding for a three-yard gain, he lowered his head and tried to pick up the five yards needed for a first down. He hadn't really been thinking, just reacting, doing what he'd always done through five seasons of football. The hit had cracked a rib, apparently, and once again he sat in his now-familiar post-game perch in the rejuve tank.

"I should skip the nerve blockers," Doc Patah said. "I should let you feel this bone-stitching."

"Aw, come on, Doc-P. Why would you do that?"

"Because you've *got* to learn to slide. If you get hurt, the franchise can't win a Tier One title. I am not interested in working for a team that can't take the belt."

Quentin looked around the training room. Everyone was gone, just him and Doc Patah. If he was going to ask, now was the time.

"The belt," Quentin said. "I like how you compare everything to fighting."

"It is my first love. I consider it the third phase of my life. This, possibly, is the fourth."

"You liked being a ringside surgeon for fights, then?"

"It presents challenges unlike anything else medicine provides. I love the crowds, the smells, the sounds, the sights. I love the months of target-specific training, of watching sentients spend a significant portion of their short lives preparing to briefly take on another sentient. There is a purity in fighting, in locking two sentients inside a cage and letting them decide who is better. It is primitive, to be sure, but a highly refined and elevated kind of primitive. To me, organized fighting is the embodiment of our growth as sentients, to take that which makes us barbaric and to channel it, turn it into a ceremony, a religion of the instincts that let us all beat out the other species on our respective planets."

Quentin nodded. If someone asked him if he liked football, he would probably just say *yeah*. Doc Patah, apparently, was far more eloquent.

"So why stay with the Krakens?" Quentin said. "Why not get back into it?"

Doc Patah was silent for a moment. Quentin waited, wondering how to phrase the question he really wanted to ask.

"I have a past, Quentin," Doc Patah said. "I will not get into it, but that past has caught up with me. I am here, and I don't have a choice. Gredok the Splithead saw to that."

His was an artificial voice, interpreted and refined by the speakerfilm on his backpack, and yet Quentin could hear the bitterness in those words.

They sat in silence until Doc Patah took the lead. "You have something you want to ask me," he said. "Something — unsavory — I think. I suggest you get it out in the open."

Now or never.

"When you were a trainer, did you ever help your fighters ... cheat?"

Doc fell silent. Quentin waited, feeling ashamed it had come to the point where he even had to talk about it.

"I had situations," Doc Patah said. "Situations that called for creative solutions. Why do you ask?"

"Because I may need a creative solution."

"This involves Ju, does it not?"

Quentin fumbled for the words. Eloquence was the domain of doctors, not quarterbacks.

"Quentin, what is it you want?"

"Ju is killing the team, Doc. He wants to be the captain. He wanted to fight me for it, one on one. I refused."

"Why?"

"Because that's not who I am anymore," Quentin said. "I'm learning you can't solve every problem by punching it."

"An honorable stance," Doc Patah said. "Quite civilized. But can I give you some advice, young Quentin?"

Quentin nodded, for once not offended in the least by that ubiquitous question.

"Being civilized is honorable," Doc Patah said. "But sometimes, civilization fails. You have to decide if this is one of those times."

"We have two games left. We have to win them both. To win them, I need Ju Tweedy running hard. To get that, I need to convince him it's my team, *not* his. And to do that, I have to fight him, but there is too much on the line. If I lose and honor the bet, the team will be very confused, confusion that will cost us. They follow me now because I've *earned* it out on the field. If I lose to Ju, I think we lose the last two games and drop out of Tier One. I'm willing to do anything to stop that, even ... "

"Cheat," Doc Patah finished. "You want to rig the fight."

Quentin felt his face flush red. To hear Doc Patah say those words, it brought the situation into focus.

Quentin nodded.

"I see greatness in you, Quentin," Doc Patah said. "I see in you the cage fighter that will do *anything* to win. I may be stuck with the Krakens, but that doesn't mean I don't want the championship. With Ju's leadership, the Krakens will flounder in Tier Two. But you? Someday soon, you can take us to the title fight. And I should also say that I do not like Ju. He is arrogant. Spoiled by his abilities. I will help you. When do you need this ... assistance?"

"Probably about fifteen minutes after I get out of the rejuve tank."

Doc Patah paused. Quentin could have sworn he heard the speakerfilm give out a very Human sigh.

"How do you think he will fight?"

"I made him mad," Quentin said. "I think he'll come at me all wild, enraged."

"I see," Doc Patah said. "Just sit there and let the bone-stitcher do its work. I'm sure the repair will last all of ten seconds once you start your idiocy with Ju. I will prepare what we used to call the Neptune Neck Kiss."

"Do I have to kiss him?"

Another sigh. "No, Quentin, you do not have to kiss him. However, I hope that you are not afraid of needles."

Doc floated off to his station, mouthflaps sorting through bins of equipment.

Actually, Quentin *was* afraid of needles, but he wasn't about to say anything. He put his head back on the tank's edge, closed his eyes and started to sort through his memories of how Ju Tweedy moved.

**THE HUMAN LOCKER ROOM** had emptied. Quentin sat in front of his locker, fingertips probing the skin above his just-repaired rib. Doc Patah had said the wound would be healed in a few days — if, that was, Quentin didn't get, say, punched in those same ribs by a world-class professional athlete.

Quentin had sent Messal with a message for Ju — *meet me in the VR room*. Right or wrong, it had come to this. Quentin had tried to do the right thing, but violence had found him yet again. He didn't like it, not one bit, but the team came first.

And for the team, Ju Tweedy needed to get knocked the hell out.

Someone walked into the room. Quentin looked up, assuming it would be Ju and that the fight would go down here, not in the VR room.

But it wasn't Ju. It was his brother, John Tweedy.

"Hey, Uncle Johnny."

John started to talk, then choked up for a second. He cleared his throat and pressed on. His face carried an expression of internal pain, and his face tattoo scrolled gibberish.

"I hear you're going to fight my brother."

Not *Ju*, but rather, *my brother*. Even if John thought Ju was a selfish jerk, they were still family — no question where John's true loyalties fell.

"I've got to do something, John. He's fumbling on purpose."

John's eyes squeezed tight, his head turned away.

How had John found out about the fight? Maybe the team knew this was coming, maybe not, but John's arrival just minutes before the fight ... Ju had told him. Just as Quentin was trying to get in Ju's head, Ju was trying to get in his.

"Quentin," John said, "I feel real bad, 'cause I think we're friends and all —"

"We are friends. And nothing you have to do for your family is going to change that."

John smiled, then nodded. "Thanks. That means the world. I can't let you fight my brother. Ma wouldn't like it. I'll stop you right here if I have to, but I don't wanna have to."

Quentin stood and offered his hand. "Look, John, if you don't want me to fight your brother, I won't."

John looked suspicious. "Really? You mean it?"

Quentin smiled. John reached out and took Quentin's right hand. As soon as he did, Quentin yanked him forward and landed a powerful, short left on John's jaw, right where it met his skull. John Tweedy dropped to the locker room floor.

"Sorry, John," Quentin said. "Fighting one Tweedy is work enough. Two is more than I can handle."

He hoped John would forgive him for the sucker-punch. John probably would, but if not, well ... the team came first.

Quentin headed for the VR room.


**QUENTIN FELT** a calm coldness as he walked into the VR room. Ju Tweedy was waiting for him. Ju still had his leg armor on, his wrists were still taped — he must have been waiting here since the end of the game, as if after Quentin's on-field antics he'd known the fight would go down. Ju wore a sweaty, gray "Property of Krakens" T-shirt with the collar ripped out and the sleeves cut off. His thick, muscular, exposed arms gleamed with sweat.

He looked at Quentin with an expression that was part eagerness, part rage, part respect.

"I didn't think you'd show," he said.

"Yes, you did," Quentin said. "That's why you came here right after the game."

Ju thought for a second, then nodded.

"You embarrassed me out there today," Ju said. "You embarrassed me in front of a hundred thousand sentients."

"Actually, one hundred, eighty-five thousand, three hundred and twelve," Quentin said. "I checked the attendance. Thought you'd like to know exactly."

Ju's smile faded. His eyes widened. In that moment, he had never looked more like his brother.

"That was just in person," Quentin said. "Don't forget the broadcast audience. We're talking at least five hundred million sentients that have seen it already, with another quarter-billion as the signal is relayed through the shipping channels. By the time replays are done, Ju, our little escapade will be seen by close to a trillion beings. Nothing like an audience, eh?"

Ju's chin dipped down. He glared out, eyes visible just under the ridge of his hairy eyebrows. This was the face captured in highlight holos and advertisements, the face of the *real* Ju Tweedy when he actually came to play.

"And your brother won't be bothering us," Quentin said. "I just kicked his ass. I already sent a message to your ma because Doc Patah is taking John to the hospital."

The eyes widened further. Maybe Ju was a self-centered jackass, but his reaction spoke volumes about his love for John. There was a soul in there after all — Quentin just had to beat it out of him.

"You for real with this?" Ju asked, his voice calm and slow. "Winner take all?"

Quentin nodded. He rubbed his hands together, fingers tracing the inside of his right wrist. He felt the needles embedded under his skin. Maybe he wouldn't need them.

Ju twisted to the left, then to the right, his spine cracks echoing through the VR room.

"Gonna bust you up," he said.

Quentin waved him forward. "Go for it."

Ju walked in. He didn't run, didn't come in off-balance. Maybe he was infuriated, sure, but not enough, not yet. Quentin had to push more buttons, get the guy so enraged he would make mistakes.

Quentin fell into his fighter's stance: right foot forward, left foot back, open right hand out in front, left fist just in front of his left cheek — both to protect and to be ready to strike. His left was the hand that could throw a football eighty miles per hour, the hand that had ended almost every fight Quentin had ever been in.

Ju closed the distance. Quentin shuffled back a couple of steps, drawing the bigger man in, then planted on his right foot and pushed forward, snapping out a right jab. The fist caught Ju in the temple, popping his head back. Quentin was already in motion, whipping his shoulders and twisting his hips for a vicious left hook. He had the briefest moment to think the fist would land right on the hinge of Ju's jaw, ending the fight in a one-two combo, then Ju ducked the punch and drove a right hook of his own into Quentin's ribs.

The same ribs Quentin had broken during the game.

Ju's first punch felt like a gunshot.

The blow had so much power it knocked Quentin sideways. Ju's big left hand followed it up, coming for Quentin's chin, but the younger man shuffled back. The knuckles hissed past so close, he felt a puff of air tickle his skin.

Ju threw a right but telegraphed it. Quentin stepped inside the punch, Ju's inner forearm hitting harmlessly on Quentin's shoulder. Quentin brought his knee up — hard — landing it square in Ju's testicles, lifting the big man up off the ground.

Ju let out a grunt of surprise and pain. His feet seemed to slip as he came back down. He landed on his knees. Quentin had a moment — a brief, *idiotic* moment to think he'd ended it — then

Ju threw his right elbow down in a short, savage arc. The tip of his elbow hit the top of Quentin's toes. Quentin heard and felt the *snap* of something giving way just before molten-metal pain raged through his foot.

Quentin fell backward, following the instinct to get away. He landed on his butt, both hands clutching his broken toes.

"Shuck … er …" Ju said, forcing out the words. He was tucked into a fetal position, both hands at his groin. "Fight … *dirty* … "

"You … know it … " Quentin said, trying to focus through the pain. "Fight … to … *win*."

Ju rolled to his hands and knees. If Quentin could have pressed the fight, it would have been over, but he couldn't rise. But Quentin knew he *had* to get up, *had* to *attack*.

He struggled to stand, hopping on just his right foot. Even that motion jarred his left toes, making them feel like the flesh was sliding across broken glass. Quentin hopped toward his foe.

Just as Ju started to rise, Quentin reached him and threw a hard overhand left. The blow caught Ju on the temple, instantly ripping open a long gash. Ju's head snapped down but popped back up. Quentin reared back and landed a second left, this time cutting Ju's cheek. He raised his hand for a third, but Ju's right hand grabbed the back of Quentin's right heel and *yanked*.

Quentin's foot shot out from under him. He landed hard on his back. Instinctively, he brought both fists up over his face, elbows tight to his ribs. Ju straddled him in an instant, blood sheeting off his enraged face, dripping down in streams rather than spatters.

The first right hit Quentin's left shoulder, concussive force ripping through his chest. Then a left that Quentin blocked, then a right he also blocked, then a short left elbow that somehow slipped through and caught him in the mouth.

More *snaps*, this time, from his teeth. Blood and bits of tooth filled his mouth. Quentin couldn't see, he could only *feel*. He felt Ju sitting back, rearing up high — the big right hand would be up at his ear, ramping up for an all-in haymaker.

Quentin waited for that first sensation of movement, then arched his hips high as hard as he could. Ju's hard punch was already bringing him forward — Quentin's bucking motion threw the big running back off-balance. As both of Ju's hands hit the ground to catch his fall, Quentin reached his left hand behind Ju's head and grabbed a handful of thick hair. Quentin planted his right foot and twisted hard to the left, pulling Ju's hair in the same direction.

Ju flew away, partially from his own movement, partially from Quentin's. Ju rolled once, then came up on his knees, head low, glowering eyes peeking out from beneath his eye socket ridges.

Quentin stood on his one good foot, blood pouring out of his mouth. He spat once. His right front tooth landed on the deck in a glob of blood. Damn, why was it always *that* tooth that got knocked out?

Quentin held up his left hand to show a bunch of Ju's hair, the ends still clinging to a small chunk of flesh that had come out with it.

Ju's eyes widened. His hands felt at the back of his head, his fingertips came away bloody.

"What's the matter, Ju?" Quentin said. "They don't teach you rich boys how to fight for real?"

Ju screamed and shot forward like a sprinter coming out of the blocks.

*BLINK*

Like his best moments on the football field, Quentin's world slowed to a crawl. Ju, his face sheeted with blood, his eyes wide with rage. This had been the effect Quentin had wanted, for Ju to be out of control. In his fast-processing mind Quentin thought of the old folk saying *be careful what you wish for*.

Quentin felt the bones in his foot grinding against each other, felt the stub of his right front tooth stinging with each breath. He'd blasted Ju *hard*, yet the big running back kept coming.

Quentin had to use what Doc Patah had given him.

He dove forward, the two footballers smashing into each other like a head-on linebacker blitz without pads. As they collided, Quentin slid his right wrist across the left side of Ju's neck.

The needles were set up almost like sand paper, a dozen or more of them packed closely together. A quarter-inch long, they drove deep into Ju's skin and immediately began to dissolve. The dissolving was the important part, Doc Patah had said — anyone testing after the fight wouldn't find needles and would only discover the cheat if they were checking for that specific drug.

*BLINK*

Quentin flew backward, realizing that Ju's arms were around his back, Ju's shoulder in Quentin's chest. Quentin reached over and grabbed Ju's waist as he fell back, twisted hard to the right, throwing Ju off of him. They both landed hard on their sides. Ju let out a grunt of pain, as if he'd landed on something the wrong way.

Both men slowly stood.

Ju raged forward again, blood-smeared lips curled back from exposed teeth, eyes wide and wild. As he came in, Quentin saw Ju's right hand drop.

An opening.

Ju seemed to stumble, just a bit. Had he slipped in blood? Was it the drug?

Quentin timed it perfectly. As Ju rushed in, head down, right hand at his chest instead of up by his cheek, Quentin bent on his good leg and hopped *forward* and *up*. Ju automatically lifted his head in reaction, just a bit, but it was exactly what Quentin had hoped for.

As Quentin flew through the air, he put his right hand out and drew it back, twisting his shoulders and hips, driving his left fist forward. The punch slid over Ju's lowered right fist and hit the bigger man on the tip of the jaw.

Quentin felt a knuckle break, but he knew, he *knew*, that the punch had ended the fight.

Quentin landed on his broken foot and dropped, screaming in pain.

Ju stumbled once, then fell forward and landed face-first, not even bringing up his hands to block the fall. He hit and stuck.

Ju Tweedy did not move.

• • •

QUENTIN BARNES LIMPED down the corridor, his left arm over Ju Tweedy's shoulder. Ju supported much of Quentin's weight, so Quentin didn't have to step on the broken toes. Blood still poured out of the cuts on Ju's face, staining the corridor with a splattery red trail.

"So," Ju said, "what did you throw to knock me out? I remember coming at you after you hip-tossed me, then nothing."

Quentin nodded. "It was a Superman punch."

Ju groaned, and not from his obvious physical pain. "Oh, for real? Are you sure?"

Quentin nodded.

"Damn," Ju said. "That's the kind of thing you use to knock out amateurs. How did you land that?"

"You got mad," Quentin said. "You dropped your right hand, I came in over the top of it."

"Man, that's weird," Ju said. "I always keep my guard up. I'm not bragging, either. I mean that's something I always do no matter how tired I get."

Quentin kept limping along, not saying anything. He'd used the needles, sure, but he'd won that fight fairly … hadn't he? The drugs couldn't have kicked in *that* fast. It had been only seconds.

They reached the locker room and helped each other into the training room. Doc Patah was waiting for them.

He was a non-Human and usually very hard to read, but something about his demeanor froze both Quentin and Ju in place.

"Look at you," Doc Patah said. "Such idiocy, such risk of team assets. I wish I owned the Krakens myself, so I could legally vent you both."

"Well, you *don't* own the Krakens," Ju said. "So we need some fixin' up."

That heavy sigh from the Harrah doctor's speakerfilm. "Fine. Which one of you will be first?"

Ju smiled and slapped Quentin's right shoulder. Even that hurt.

"Q first," Ju said. Oddly, his voice seemed louder than usual, prouder than usual. "He's my team captain. I can wait."

His face still a sheet of blood, Ju helped Quentin to the first rejuve tank.

*He's my captain.*

And just like that, Quentin knew the ordeal of Ju Tweedy's intentional fumbling was over. As ridiculous as it seemed, a basic street brawl had settled their differences.

It was Quentin's team. *Period.*

The only question was, would Ju run hard enough for the Krakens to win their final two games?

## GFL WEEK ELEVEN ROUNDUP
(Courtesy of Galaxy Sports Network)

| | | | |
|---|---|---|---|
| Brigands | 10 | **Scarlet Fliers** | 24 |
| Spider-Bears | 10 | **Vanguard** | 14 |
| War Dogs | 28 | **Jacks** | 31 |
| Krakens | 10 | **Hullwalkers** | 25 |
| **Ice Storm** | 27 | Cloud Killers | 24 |
| **Atom Smashers** | 35 | Intrigue | 0 |
| Juggernauts | 14 | **Water Bugs** | 28 |
| **Astronauts** | 24 | Warlords | 3 |
| **Dreadnaughts** | 27 | Armada | 20 |
| **Wolfpack** | 14 | Pirates | 13 |
| **Criminals** | 17 | Planets | 13 |

With only two games remaining in the GFL's 25th Anniversary season, a pair of teams are closing in on a Planet Division title. Themala (7-3) is peaking at just the right time, winning its sixth straight to move into a two-way tie for first with the Isis Ice Storm. Isis (7-3) knocked off a fellow first-place holder for the second week in a row, this time edging out Coranadillana (6-4) by a score of 27-24. The To Pirates (6-4) dropped to second, thanks to a hard loss to the Wabash Wolfpack (6-4), who is still hungry to claim a playoff spot. The Yall Criminals (6-4) want a shot at that playoff berth as well, winning their third straight by topping the plummeting Mars Planets 17-13.

The top three in the Solar continue to rack up wins. New Rodina (9-1) remains in first, still just a single game ahead of Jupiter (8-2) and Neptune (8-2). With this week's wins, all three of those teams mathematically locked up playoff berths.

The fourth and final Solar Division playoff spot is down to a race between the Bord Brigands (6-4) and the D'Kow War Dogs (5-5). The Brigands beat the 'Dogs in Week Seven, which means for D'Kow to make the playoffs, they have to win their last two while the Brigands lose their final pair.

In Solar relegation land, the Chillich Spider-Bears (1-9) are still alive despite a 14-10 loss to fellow cellar-dweller Vik Vanguard (2-8). The Jang Atom Smashers (3-7) picked the perfect time to come alive, landing a 35-0 knockout on the Sala Intrigue.

In the Planet Division, the Mars Planets (4-6) just need one more win or one more Ionath loss to stay in Tier One for another season. That looks most likely, as Ionath travels to Jupiter to face the 8-2 Jacks. Ionath must win that game *and* beat Mars in Week Thirteen *and* see the Planets lose next week's game against the Hittoni Hullwalkers (5-5).

## Deaths

No deaths reported this week.

## Offensive Player of the Week

New Rodina quarterback **Rick Renaud**, who threw three touchdowns in an 18-for-26, 278-yard performance.

## Defensive Player of the Week

Vik defensive tackle **Ar-Cham-Balt**, who had four solo tackles and eleven assists for the Vanguard.

# 16

# WEEK TWELVE:
# IONATH KRAKENS at
# JUPITER JACKS

| PLANET DIVISION | | SOLAR DIVISION | |
|---|---|---|---|
| 7-3 | Isis Ice Storm | 9-1 | x-New Rodina Astronauts |
| 7-3 | Themala Dreadnaughts | 8-2 | Jupiter Jacks |
| 6-4 | Coranadillana Cloud Killers | 8-2 | Neptune Scarlet Fliers |
| 6-4 | To Pirates | 6-4 | Bord Brigands |
| 6-4 | Wabash Wolfpack | 5-5 | D'Kow War Dogs |
| 6-4 | Yall Criminals | 3-7 | Bartel Water Bugs |
| 5-5 | Alimum Armada | 3-7 | Jang Atom Smashers |
| 5-5 | Hittoni Hullwalkers | 3-7 | Sala Intrigue |
| 5-5 | Lu Juggernauts | 3-7 | Shorah Warlords |
| 4-6 | Mars Planets | 2-8 | Vik Vanguard |
| 2-8 | Ionath Krakens | 1-9 | Chillich Spider-Bears |

(x = playoff berth clinched, y = division clinched)

### Excerpt from Sorensen's Guide to the Galaxy
### The Jupiter Net Colony

At the turn of the 25th century (ErT), the Planetary Union had reached an exploratory standstill. Massive governmental investment to develop infrastructure on the Mars Colony, Capizzi and Satirli 6 had driven Union tax rates to over fifty percent. Taxes on "the rich" actually exceeded *sixty* percent. The heavy demands on business and wage earners were needed to prop up the then-nonexistent economies of those three worlds.

Oppressive tax rates shut down business expansion and investment. As businesses stopped spending, a recession set in. When that recession dove headlong into a depression, President Carmella Abreziad initiated two dramatic acts that forever changed the Planetary Union.

Her first bold decision was the cultural and technological exchange with the Harrah Tribal Accord. The Harrah wanted peaceful access to Jupiter and Saturn, both to develop resources and as a colonization zone for its people. The Harrah had achieved FTL capability just sixteen years earlier in 2448. They wanted to start stretching their wings, no pun intended, but were too new of a space-faring race to field a navy or a colonization fleet. The technology exchange gave the Harrah access to Planetary Union shipbuilding capability, while the Harrah shared their skills for developing resources on gas giants.

The President's second move branched directly off the first by creating the Sol System Free Trade Zone. The SSFTZ, or S-Fitz, as it came to be known, opened up Venus, Saturn, Neptune and Jupiter as tax-free areas for business development. Private enterprises were welcome to create orbiting stations around any of those planets. Permanent land settlements were not allowed, but temporary land leases were granted, allowing for the mining of natural resources. Abreziad also opened up work visas for Harrah citizens, allowing private companies to hire them almost at will.

It was a shocking policy: four planets instantly opened up to both private enterprise and an alien workforce. This created a

25th-century "gold rush," where businesses large and small, inventors, entrepreneurs and fortune seekers flocked to the S-Fitz. Rapid-fire growth ensued. The tax-free status allowed business to pour money into development of orbital stations and mining developments. While development on Mars Colony stagnated, the S-Fitz flourished.

Within two decades, all four of the planets had hundreds of orbital stations. Those hundreds grew to thousands; stations ranging from the size of small towns to million-plus habitations like Jupiter's Red Storm City. The sheer number of orbitals led to the need for centralized, planet-local governance.

In 2488, President Abreziad signed the Net Colony Act. All four of the outer-system planets were awarded full voting rights in the Planetary Union. Because the vast majority of the population lived in orbital stations, the "Net Colony" term referred to the shell of orbitals interlinked by trade, travel and tourism.

Now nearly two centuries later, the majority of the Net Colonies' inhabitants still live in orbit. Surface habitations are few in number and are considered to be temporary settlements under the control of their respective Net government. Large flocks of free-roaming Harrah populate all four planets. Most of the Harrah in these systems are third- and even fourth-generation Planetary Union.

Jupiter and Neptune Net Colonies each have populations of over 275 million. Saturn Net Colony boasts 185 million, while the scrappy citizens of the Venus Net Colony number 15 million.

The largest cities of the Net Colonies are Jupiter's Red Storm City, with 1.8 million, and Neptune's Trident City, with 1.7 million.

Those two cities also happen to field successful GFL franchises. The rivalry between the Jupiter Jacks and the Neptune Scarlet Fliers is considered to be among the best and most storied in the league. The Jacks have won three GFL titles, something that the residents of Jupiter Net Colony never hesitate to remind those from Neptune.

• • •

**THE GROUND BUS ROLLED** through the streets of Red Storm City. The whole team onboard. No shouting, no jokes, no playing and no "grab-assing," as Coach Hokor would call it. A team full of hard-hearted sentients, every last mind on the challenge awaiting them in a few short hours when the Ionath Krakens went to war with the Jupiter Jacks.

The 8-and-2 Jupiter Jacks.

The defending champion Jupiter Jacks.

Even if there had been noise, Quentin wouldn't have heard it. Tiny earphones filled his ears with the sound of one of the heaviest, meanest, most glory-inspiring songs he'd ever heard. A new track by Trench Warfare, so new that maybe ten people in the entire galaxy had heard it. Somalia had sent it to him, a rough mix of a song called "Heart of Steel." A song of the ancients, apparently, first sung some seven centuries earlier. She had sought out a song from the early days of football, a way of showing her appreciation for the risks he had taken just to hear her music.

The lyrics called to him, perfectly capturing the moment to come. *Always one more try, I'm not afraid to die, stand and fight.* He'd met her for all of five minutes, but there was no question that Somalia Midori understood *exactly* who he was, and *exactly* why he put his life on the line with every snap of the ball. Even if he never saw her again, he knew he'd found a kindred spirit.

Quentin listened to the song over and over again, absently staring out at Red Storm City. Total déjà vu, although there was nothing strange about that sensation — Red Storm City was a damn-near exact duplicate of Coranadillana. Harrah sailed overhead, but not nearly as many. Here, most of the citizenry stayed on the ground.

Red Storm City had been built shortly after the technology exchange between the Union and the Harrah Tribal Accord. Just like for the game against the Cloud Killers, the *Touchback* had docked at a massive pier jutting out from the city's edge. The Krakens had boarded a bus and driven through the city. If you took Coranadillana, mopped up the pink blood (both dried and wet), picked up all the trash, added thousands of sentients on the sidewalks waving silver, gold and copper flags as the bus drove through, then you'd have Red Storm City.

He should have been thrilled to see Jupiter for the first time, but the fact was that he really didn't care. He'd marvelled at enough new worlds for one season. All he saw now were visions of the game he was about to play, the passes, the runs, the defense, the hits, the pain and the blood.

The war and its warriors.

*Always one more try, I'm not afraid to die.*

Somalia really knew her music.

The bus turned the corner. Just as it had on Coranadillana, the football stadium rose majestically before them. Almost an exact copy, save for one additional deck. Rolling Rock Arena seated some 35,000 sentients. Just like Cloud Killer Stadium, the open top would allow thousands of Union citizens of Harrah decent to watch the game from above.

The song ended. Quentin played it again. The bus approached the stadium. So many fans waving flags or holding up replicas of the Galaxy Bowl trophy. The Harrah that sailed overhead did so with attitude, insolently trailing silver, gold and copper streamers from their tails.

Fans of the Jupiter Jacks.

Fans of the *enemy*.

Quentin stared at them all, knowing the disappointment they would feel when he beat their heroes into the ground.

**QUENTIN PIVOTED BACK** on his right foot, turning to the left and spinning all the way around to pitch the ball to Ju Tweedy. Ju caught the ball in motion, moving right, parallel to the line of scrimmage. Rebecca Montagne was out in front of him, and Michael Kimberlin out in front of her. Kimberlin clearly had no problem going hard against his old team — he loved playing smash-mouth football and didn't seem to care whose mouth he smashed.

The Jacks linebackers pursued while Xuchang, the corner

back, crashed from the outside to try and turn the play back in. Orange and black collided with gold, silver and copper. Ju made one move to duck the outside linebacker, then lowered his head as the inside linebacker and the safety crashed into him.

Four-yard gain, which brought them up third and two.

The Krakens ran back to the huddle. Quentin saw doubt in the eyes of his teammates. He couldn't blame them — the Krakens were down 14-7 against the defending galactic champs, and he'd already thrown one pick. There was a reason the Jupiter Jacks were 8-and-2, and that reason was their defensive secondary. Two All-Pro cornerbacks in Morelia and Xuchang, a hard-hitting free safety in Luxembourg and the free safety Matidi, the one who had the pick. Those four blanketed the Krakens' receivers. Hawick couldn't get open against Morelia, and when Xuchang couldn't cover Milford, she got help over the top from Matidi. Quentin had time to throw, but the excellent coverage made him wait too long for receivers to get open.

Ju was the last one back to the huddle.

"They're keying on me big-time, Q," he said. "I ain't got no room to run out there."

"I know, I know," Quentin said. The Jacks' defensive backs were so good they could handle most of the pass coverage and let seven players — the front defensive four and the three linebackers — focus on the run.

Hokor's head popped up in Quentin's helmet holo.

"*Barnes!* Dive left. Slam it up there, we need this first down."

"Coach, we've run up the middle on the last three third-and-short situations. They'll be waiting for it."

"*Run the plays I call, Barnes.*"

Quentin rolled his eyes and tapped off the holodisplay,

"Dive left on two, on two," he said to the huddle. "When this play is over, you *sprint* back to the line. We're going no-huddle, I'll audible from center. Got it? Ready? *Break!*"

The Krakens moved to the line. Quentin grabbed Ju's arm and leaned in near his helmet.

"I need a big fake out of you."

"We're not doing the run?"

"We are, you're just not getting the ball," Quentin said. "I have to soften up the defensive backs, and I'm doing it the old-fashioned way."

"The Human sacrifice way?"

"Think of it as a Sklorno sacrifice."

Ju smiled an evil smile. "That's my boy, Q. *Smash*-mouth."

Quentin walked up behind Bud-O-Shwek. Rebecca lined up at fullback, Ju behind her as the tail back. Quentin looked at the defense. As he'd suspected, the linebackers were leaning in, ready to take on the run.

Quentin tapped a quick left-right-left *ba-da-bap* on Bud-O-Shwek's pebbly behind, then bent to take the snap.

"Red, fifty-two! *Red*, fifty-two! Hut-*hut!*"

Quentin pushed off his right foot, stepping back with the left. Rebecca rushed by, murder in her eyes. Ju was two steps behind her. Quentin put the ball in his stomach. As the big arms closed, Quentin pivoted forward in time with Ju. At the last second, Quentin pulled the ball out just as Ju smashed into the hole.

Quentin put the ball on his left hip, hiding it from the defense, and sprinted down the left side of the line without a single blocker to protect him. The Jacks' right defensive end had bought the play fake, crashing in to get a piece of Ju. Quentin was by the defensive end before the guy knew what was happening.

The outside right linebacker figured it out faster, but he had also rushed in to stop Ju and was a step too late. Quentin cut up field, the Quyth Warrior linebacker trailing close behind.

Quentin was ten yards downfield before Luxembourg saw him. She sprinted in, the field lights reflecting off her copper helmet, her gold jersey with the silver sleeves and copper numbers. She looked like a fighter jet made from precious metals.

Quentin didn't cut, didn't spin, that wasn't what he wanted. He was here to go old-school.

Just before contact, he *snapped* his head forward, bringing all his weight and momentum, turning himself into a weapon. Luxembourg did the same thing, the two players colliding like butting mountain rams. Quentin felt the jaw-shaking impact through his whole body — it slowed him down, but he kept moving forward.

The linebacker brought him down from behind.

Quentin hit the ground, then looked to the sidelines. Fifteen-yard gain. First down, Krakens.

**"CHICK, THAT'S SOMETHING** we haven't seen much of in the past few weeks, Quentin Barnes using his size and speed like a running back."

"Masara, Barnes just laid the lumber on Luxembourg."

"She looks shaken up, Chick. She's slow to get back to the huddle. I wonder if the Jacks will sub her out ... wait a minute, what's this ... the Krakens are going no huddle, Chick!"

"They'll go after Luxembourg, Masara. She looks like she was hit by a drunken Purist Nation cop with a free pass for cross-species police brutality."

"Chick! This is not—"

"And the snap! Barnes drops back, he's got time. Woman-to-woman coverage. Halawa is going deep, going right past Luxembourg, Barnes is going for it all ... and it's ... it's caught! Touchdown, Ionath! Quentin Barnes ties up the game on a 66-yard strike to Halawa."

**QUENTIN RAN OFF THE FIELD** to cheering teammates and choruses of *nice run!* or *nice hit!* or *great pass!* He still didn't know if he could throw deep against Morelia or Xuchang, who would guard the Krakens number-one and number-two receivers, respectively, but from the first snap, he'd known that if Luxembourg slowed down even a little, she couldn't hang with Halawa. So, Quentin had *made* Luxembourg slow down.

"*Barnes!*"

Quentin's eyes flashed to his helmet holoscreen before he realized it was a living voice, not his helmet speakers. He looked down at Hokor, expecting the coach to be a puffy furball of anger. Hokor's fur looked smooth.

"Down here, Barnes!"

Quentin knelt. Hokor put a pedipalp on his shoulder. "Great call," Hokor said. "If we can get some more punishment on their safety and free safety, slow them down, I think Halawa can keep getting open. You agree?"

Quentin nodded. "She can as long as Luxembourg is in woman-to-woman coverage. If they want to cover Halawa, they'll have to switch to zone coverage. They do that, and I will carve them up."

"Good, we'll run more passes to Starcher, try to use his big, crazy body to wear them down."

"No, Coach, it should be me. A couple of naked boots, I can get to them and put them down."

Hokor waited while the crowd roared for the kickoff. Quentin didn't have to look, he could tell by the level of the cheering that the Jacks had returned the ball to their own twenty, maybe their thirty.

"Barnes, that hit worked, but you've been hurt several times this year. You go head-hunting for a top-level safety and free safety, you're asking for a major injury. You understand that?"

"We lose, we're out," Quentin said. "I'm willing to take that chance."

Hokor stared, then nodded. "Well, then I guess we are going medieval on their posteriors. We'll do it your way, Quentin."

Hokor walked away. Quentin watched him go, marveling at the exchange — it was the first time, ever, that the coach had called him *Quentin*.

Quentin stood and watched the game. He'd missed a play. Second and three on Jupiter's twenty-six. The Jacks broke the huddle. Quentin watched as Denver ran toward him, taking up her position at wide receiver not even five yards away from his spot on the sidelines. So strange to see her in copper, silver and gold instead of the orange and the black. Stockbridge lined up to cover her woman-to-woman.

Denver's eyestalks bent toward the Krakens sidelines, and she saw him. Her eyestalks quivered. "Quentin Barnes Quentin Barnes!"

"Hey, Denver, how you doing?"

"I love Jupiter!" she said. "Love lovelove! Thank you for trading me!"

Quentin hadn't known how much guilt he'd been carrying until that moment, until those genuine words set him free.

Jacks quarterback Shriaz Zia started calling the signals.

"I'm glad, Denver."

"Quentin Barnes Quentin*Barnes!*" she said, screaming now, her raspers dangling, her body shaking with excitement. "I play like you watch me watch me *watchme!*"

Zia took the snap as the two teams ripped into each other. Denver shot off the line like a bullet. The young receiver did a right-left-right step-cut that was so fast Quentin almost couldn't track it, so fast that Stockbridge stumbled — and Denver was off to the races. The ball was in the air before she'd cleared fifteen yards. She caught it in full, blazing stride at the fifty. Davenport and Perth, the Krakens' strong safety and free safety, respectively, closed on her immediately. The home Jacks crowd roared like the sound of High One. Denver did her right-left-right cut a second time — Perth stumbled, and Denver was by her. Davenport reached out for the tackle. At that moment, Denver turned toward Davenport, lowering her copper helmet and *smashing* forward. Davenport stumbled backward, grabbing with tentacles, raspers, even her tail, but Denver had all the momentum and would not be stopped.

Denver regained her balance and sprinted into the end zone for a 74-yard touchdown.

"Damn," Quentin said, wishing he had her back.

**IT TURNED INTO** a shoot-out. Quentin managed two more sneaky runs that let him go head to head on the defensive backs, once with Luxembourg and once with Xuchang. That second hit on Luxembourg had felt great. He'd leveled her, put her out for two series. The tangle with Xuchang didn't go as well. Quentin had hit her so hard, it cracked her helmet, but when he tried to get up, he felt a stabbing pain in his hip.

Doc Patah needled in to see if he could fix it, numbed it up some, but Quentin couldn't run for crap. He spent the rest of the game handing off and doing what he was *supposed* to do, which was drop back in the pocket and look for receivers.

He found them.

He picked up another touchdown to Halawa against Luxembourg's backup, then finally hit Hawick for a long strike when the Jacks switched to zone coverage.

Halawa wasn't the only young Sklorno to have a big game.

Denver burned the Krakens for another long score, this one a 44-yard pass. No wonder she loved-loved-loved Jupiter. The Krakens just couldn't cover her, not with Zia's laser-accurate arm. Denver finished as the game's MVP: eight catches for 156 yards and two touchdowns.

Scarborough also produced a big play for the Jacks. The former Krakens standout receiver caught just two passes on the night — one for twelve yards, the other for a seventeen-yard touchdown.

Yes, it was a shootout, but the Krakens had more bullets. Quentin had time to throw. He found his rhythm, using his short-pattern passing to hit Starcher, Mezquitic, Kobayasho, Richfield and Rebecca Montagne. By the time the game ended, Quentin had thrown for 312 yards, four touchdowns and completed passes to nine receivers. Yassoud was one of those receivers — he seemed thrilled with his one catch for eight yards and was happy to tell everyone on the sidelines about it in intricate, repetitive detail.

The Jacks finished the game with the ball but were unable to score on their last drive. The Krakens' D held until the clock ticked zero and the final score blazed bright for all to see.

Ionath Krakens 38, Jupiter Jacks 35.

After the game, Quentin limped out to the 50-yard line to shake hands. As he did, he looked up at the end zone's holographic scoreboard, which was flashing results from around the league.

What he saw was almost as thrilling as his four touchdown passes — the Mars Planets had held the Hittoni Hullwalkers to just *ten points* ... but had scored only nine themselves.

The Planets had lost. That loss made them 4-and-7.

The Krakens were 3-and-8.

If the Krakens beat the Planets in Week Thirteen, both teams would be 4-and-8, but the Krakens would win the tiebreaker.

It all came down to the final game of the season. The loser would be relegated, while the winner would get to stay at least one more season in Tier One.

## GFL WEEK TWELVE ROUNDUP
(Courtesy of Galaxy Sports Network)

| | | | |
|---|---|---|---|
| **Armada** | 27 | Brigands | 23 |
| **Water Bugs** | 28 | Atom Smashers | 20 |
| Spider-Bears | 13 | **Warlords** | 24 |
| **Hullwalkers** | 10 | Planets | 9 |
| Jacks | 21 | **Krakens** | 24 |
| **Scarlet Fliers** | 24 | War Dogs | 21 |
| Intrigue | 22 | **Astronauts** | 34 |
| **Dreadnaughts** | 24 | Cloud Killers | 14 |
| Pirates | 10 | **Juggernauts** | 13 |
| **Wolfpack** | 42 | Vanguard | 16 |
| Criminals | 16 | **Ice Storm** | 24 |

At least in the Solar Division, the playoff contenders are set. New Rodina (10-1) continues to roll, locking up a Solar Division title, thanks to a 34-22 win over the Sala Intrigue (3-8). Neptune (9-2) finished off the playoff hopes of D'Kow, beating the War Dogs in a 24-21 thriller. That result finalizes Bord as the fourth seed in the Solar playoff, despite the Brigands losing 27-23 to the Alimum Armada (6-5). The only question in the Solar playoff picture is where will the Scarlet Fliers and the Jupiter Jacks play? Ionath registered a stunning 24-21 upset over the Jupiter Jacks (8-3). Because the Jacks beat the Scarlet Fliers head to head, if both teams finish with the same record the Jacks will have the second seed and host the game. If the Jacks lose their final game against the Shorah Warlords (4-7) or if Neptune wins its final game against the Astronauts, the Scarlet Fliers will claim the second seed and host their arch rivals.

In the Planet Division things are not so clear. Isis (8-3) and Themala (8-3) both won to wrap up playoff berths. Isis pummeled the Dreadnaughts 31-0 in Week Four, meaning that the Ice Storm wins the division if it defeats the Hittoni Hullwalkers (6-5) next week. Themala faces the Yall Criminals (6-5). If Wabash (7-4) wins next week against the Lu Juggernauts (6-5), the Wolfpack is in. As we head into the final game, Lu, Coranadillana, Hittoni, Alimum, To and Yall all have a mathematical shot at the playoffs.

Chillich's 24-13 loss to Shorah means that the Spider-Bears (1-10) will be relegated at season's end.

Ionath (3-8) stayed alive, thanks to their upset win over the Jacks and thanks to Mars' 10-9 loss to Hittoni. The Krakens and the Planets square off in the season's final regular season game, with the loser heading back to Tier Two.

### Deaths

**Kin-Ja-Tan,** offensive right tackle for the Yall Criminals, on a clean hit by Ryan Nossek.

### Offensive Player of the Week

Armada tight end **Brandon Rowe,** who caught seven passes for 112 yards and two touchdowns.

### Defensive Player of the Week

**Ryan Nossek,** defensive end for the Isis Ice Storm, who set a GFL record with five sacks in one game. Nossek also recorded a fatality.

# 17

# WEEK THIRTEEN: MARS PLANETS at IONATH KRAKENS

**PLANET DIVISION**

8-3  x-Isis Ice Storm
8-3  x-Themala Dreadnaughts
7-4  Wabash Wolfpack
6-5  Alimum Armada
6-5  Coranadillana Cloud Killers
6-5  Hittoni Hullwalkers
6-5  Lu Juggernauts
6-5  To Pirates
6-5  Yall Criminals
4-7  Mars Planets
3-8  Ionath Krakens

**SOLAR DIVISION**

10-1  x-New Rodina Astronauts
9-2   x-Neptune Scarlet Fliers
8-3   x-Jupiter Jacks
6-5   Bord Brigands
5-6   D'Kow War Dogs
4-7   Bartel Water Bugs
4-7   Shorah Warlords
3-8   Jang Atom Smashers
3-8   Sala Intrigue
2-9   Vik Vanguard
1-10  Chillich Spider-Bears

(x = playoff berth clinched, y = division clinched)

**TO AN OUTSIDE OBSERVER,** to someone ignorant of the culture of sports, the sight might have looked comical. A teenager — huge and strong, but a teenager nonetheless — surrounded by sentients from five races.

This teenager wore black armor, a black helmet with a bright orange splash at the forehead. An orange jersey covered this armor: white-trimmed black letters spelling out KRAKENS on the chest above a white-trimmed black number 10. The shoulders of this jersey proudly displayed the six-tentacled team logo.

The sentients surrounding him wore matching black armor, helmets, and orange jerseys, their gear custom-fitted for different body styles. Some of these sentients were twice his age, a few even three times his age, yet they all hung on his every word. They followed him, *believed* in him, believed that he would lead them to victory. Or if victory could not be attained, he would leave his lifeless body on the field of failure.

Age did not matter. What mattered was that this teenager, this *general*, worked harder than anyone else, *played* harder than anyone else, would risk anything and everything to win.

On the sidelines of Ionath Stadium, they packed in around him, a team jumping as one, chanting as one. Beyond the team, the stadium itself, the sun blazing down on 185,000 crazed fans, a living reef of orange and black that screamed, that jumped, that waited and watched. The crowd's roar was the roar of a warship firing all guns, the blast of a star being born, the shuddering power of continents colliding and mountain ranges rising into the sky for the first time.

So loud was the crowd's thunder that they could not hear him, could not hear their idolized teenage superstar-in-the-making, but his voice reached the players packed around him. His voice reached them, and it carried tangible power, the timbre of a soul that would not be denied.

"This is it," Quentin Barnes said, his voice full of gravel and rage and the intensity of an exponential chain reaction. "This … is … *it*."

His eyes, wide and alert, *piercing*, sought out the eye or eyes of each of his teammates in turn. When eyes met, those teammates felt a *connection*, felt spiritually attached to this general. He asked nothing more than what he was willing to give himself — his life, his *soul*.

"Last week, we beat the defending Galaxy Bowl Champions," he said. "The *defending champs*. Why did we beat them? Because we *are* that good. We are champions in the making. We are the future greatness of this league. Each and every one of you, believe this, *believe* that next season we are going to tear this league apart and that *everyone* will *know ... your ... name*."

The team packed closer, hands and tentacles reaching out to him, to each other. Petty differences and deep hatreds fell away. They were *one*.

"That is next season. But to reach that goal, we must first destroy our enemy. It's all or nothing today, Krakens. All or *nothing*. The winner takes the glory, the loser is gone. *Today* we manifest our true destiny as champions. The Mars Planets don't think you are champions. The Mars Planets think you are *nothing*. But they made a mistake, didn't they?"

"Yes!" Screamed John Tweedy, who had already all but forgotten that same teenager had sucker-punched him a few days earlier. All is fair in love and war. "Yes, they came into *our house!*"

"That's right," the teenager said. "*Our house*, a temple built with the sweat and blood and bodies of those who came before us, built with *our* sweat and blood. From this moment on, Ionath Stadium is *sacred ground*. How do we defend sacred ground?"

"With our lives!" barked Virak the Mean, his cornea swirling with yellow and black. "We destroy transgressors!"

"Our stadium," Quentin said, his voice lowering. "Our sacred ground. Our home. Our *house*."

He raised his right fist high. The teammates did the same, reaching for his, limbs slanting up to make a pyramid of unity. The Krakens players joined him in a guttural cheer.

"Where are we?" Quentin said. "Whose house?"

"*Our house!*"

"Whose house?"

"*Our house!*"

"What law?"

"*Our law!*"

"Who wins?"

"*Krakens!*"

"Who wins?"

"*Krakens!*"

"This is our championship game. Now let's go play like champions!"

**THE KRAKENS WON THE TOSS** and chose to receive.

Mars lined up, white uniforms blazing in the afternoon sunlight. Blue numbers trimmed in gold decorated their chests and backs. The jerseys had blue sleeves, striped in white-trimmed gold, with their bold blue-and-gold "M" logo splayed large on the shoulder pads. That same logo decorated the sides of their blue helmets and the front of their blue thigh armor.

The crowd reveled in the opportunity of the day. This wasn't the Galaxy Bowl, but it might as well have been for the intensity that roiled through the stadium. The ground began making a unified sound as the Planets kicker raised his hand.

*Ohhhhhhhh …*

The zebe blew his whistle, and the kicker dropped his hand.

*OHHHHHHHH …*

The kicker ran forward, the crowd's roar culminating as his foot connected.

*OHHHHHAAAAHHHHH!*

The ball sailed through the air and the game was on. Richfield returned the opening kickoff to the Ionath thirty-five. The crowd roared so loudly Quentin felt the skin on his face tingling.

Quentin ran onto the field with his offense. He looked over his huddle. This wasn't the same team he'd had to start the season, not even close. So many familiar faces gone from the starting lineup, faces like Aka-Na-Tak, Shun-On-Won, Scarborough, Denver, Yassoud Murphy, Tom Pareless, Yotaro Kobayasho. New players had taken their places: Michael Kimberlin, Ju Tweedy, Rebecca Montagne, Crazy George Starcher, his face painted green. And another new face, Halawa, the number-three receiver waiting on the sidelines until she was needed.

Quentin also saw the starters who had been there since the season began, yet these starters looked somehow ... different. Hawick, now the team's number-one receiver and she knew it, thirteen years old and just entering her athletic prime. Milford, last year's rookie receiver now with two full seasons under her belt, still giddy and jumpy like the nine-year-old that she was, but growing more confident on every play. And the four living roadblocks that made up the rest of his offensive line: left tackle Kill-O-Yowet, left guard Sho-Do-Thikit, center Bud-O-Shwek, right tackle Vu-Ko-Will. Something about their black eyes, their body language, said that they no longer viewed Quentin as a fragile Human. To them, he was a Ki soldier in all but name.

There were many more players that would help in the years to come, but *these* ten, these were his brothers and sisters in arms, the sentients that would fight and bleed with him, the sentients that he would lead to the promised land.

"No more pep talks," Quentin said. "Time to sing for our supper. Everyone ready?"

Two Human and two HeavyG heads nodded, two Sklorno hopped and chittered, four Ki clacked arms against their chest armor.

"Here we go," Quentin said. "Right in their teeth, smashmouth. Off-tackle left on three, on three, ready? *Break!*"

The team ran or scuttled to their positions. I-formation, Rebecca right behind him, Ju behind her, Crazy George Starcher lined up as a left tight end. Hawick wide left, Milford wide right. Quentin took a long look as he walked up behind Bud-O-Shwek. The Krakens had begun the year horribly but had grown stronger as the season progressed. The Mars Planets, on the other hand, had started out the season 4-and-2 but had lost five straight to find themselves in this do-or-die situation. Injuries had riddled them, particularly season-ending damage to their starting inside linebackers.

Quentin stared down the replacement linebackers, Scott Pond and Morow the Devastator. The over-named Devastator was once an All-Pro, but that had been years ago. His physical skills were failing him — he now played with brains far more than brawn. Pond was 6-foot-4, 265 pounds, with good speed but had a bad rep for not wanting to tackle big running backs head-on. Neither of those middle linebackers were suited to stopping a big, strong, *angry* running back, which was the exact description of The Mad Ju.

"Red, twenty-two! *Red*, twenty-*two! Hut*-hut ... hut!"

Quentin pivoted to the right. Rebecca shot by and he handed the ball to Ju. Ju clamped down so hard Quentin winced, imagined he could hear Ju's forearms *clacking* together like the jaws of a bear trap. Michael Kimberlin knocked the opposing Ki defensive tackle backward, opening up a huge hole. Becca ran through that hole and put her shoulder into the Devastator's midsection. She wasn't as big as he was, wasn't as powerful, but brute strength wasn't Becca the Wrecka's game — she simply put a helmet and a shoulder on defenders — then nudged them a few feet or just got in their way to make space for her running back. Ju was behind her, waiting for her block, and when she pushed the Devastator just a smidgen to the right, he stepped left, directly into the path of Scott Pond. Pond attacked, but flinched at the last second, pulling back ever so slightly.

The Mad Ju bowled him over, high-stepped on by and was suddenly in the defensive backfield. Matsumoto, the free safety, rushed in and dove at Ju's legs. Ju was the league's biggest running back and a total bruiser, but what made him special was his quick feet and his crazy athleticism — he *hurdled* the diving Matsumoto, who grabbed nothing but air and got a facemask full of Iomatt for her troubles.

The safety, Parbhani, came in fast. Instead of going low, she went high. Big mistake. Ju lowered a shoulder and hit her hard. She bounced off him like a rock thrown against a boulder.

The two cornerbacks gave chase, but they were being harried by Hawick and Milford and they couldn't make a straight line to Ju. By the time they freed themselves from the receivers' downfield blocks, Ju had slowed to a walk at the 5. He strolled into the end zone as casual as you please.

The Krakens' first play from scrimmage, a 65-yard touchdown run for Ju Tweedy.

Quentin knelt and plucked some of the circular Iomatt leaves. He sniffed deeply, inhaling the cinnamon scent, then tossed the leaves aside and ran to the sideline.

**THE MARS PLANETS WERE** just too beat-up to make a game of it. They had no answer for Ju Tweedy. The Mad Ju ran wild, scoring a second time on a 44-yard run and finishing the day with 161 yards. The trade for Michael Kimberlin had been critical, but after watching Ju play — for *real* — for two full games, Quentin knew the words he had spoken to Gredok back on Orbital Station One were no lie: Ju Tweedy was even better than Mitchell "The Machine" Fayed.

Up 24-10, Quentin stood on the sidelines and watched his defense try to shut down the Planets' last-ditch efforts. With just 42 seconds to play, the Planets were on Ionath's 17-yard line. No time-outs, they had to score, get the onside kick and score again to tie it.

Loki Nightbreed, the Planets' quarterback, brought his team to the line. The Planets still had a very real chance, and they weren't giving up. Loki faced an end zone full of fans madly waving orange-and-black flags. In two full seasons, Quentin had never heard such noise.

He saw Loki cup his hands to his mouth, shout down the line of scrimmage. An audible.

Quentin turned to face the crowd and started waving his outstretched arms, palms up, the reverse of someone imitating a flapping bird.

"Come on!" he screamed. "Louder!"

He had never before interacted directly with the stadium crowd. Perhaps not until that moment had he realized how 185,000 spectators could react to him, as if he were a conductor of the galaxy's largest and most raucous symphony. As loud as the crowd had been, it instantly raged even louder. The fans knew that at that moment they were more than spectators — they were *part* of the game.

His teammates on the sidelines took up his efforts, waving to the crowd, urging them to ear-splitting levels.

Quentin turned back to watch the action. As a quarterback, he knew that stadium noise could wreak havoc with audibles. Loki actually looked up at the stands, for just a second, first left, then right, as if he didn't quite believe it.

Everything was happening so fast, all in the span of a few seconds. The play clock ticked down to seven, six — if Loki didn't run the play soon he'd be called for delay of game. Quentin hoped John Tweedy and company saw what he saw, saw the confusion. John did — he walked forward from his middle linebacker position to stand almost at the line of scrimmage, right between Mai-An-Ihkole and Mum-O-Killowe. John was showing blitz.

Loki looked at John, then tried screaming down the line again for a second audible. The crowd sensed his desperation like a shark smelling blood. The sound grew so overwhelming, so *hurtful* that Quentin instinctively put his hands to his ears.

Mars Planets players looked at Loki, the quick snap-glances of confusion. Loki looked up at the play clock.

*Three ... two ...*

The ball snapped and the lines erupted. Loki turned to hand off to running back Kirk Bastek, but Bastek wasn't looking — he thought it was a pass and was already running a route. Loki reached out with the ball. It hit Bastek in the arm, then dropped free. The ball hit the blue turf and bounced, just once, rising up in the air where Loki snatched it again. The quarterback stopped and turned, looking to make something happen. He didn't get the chance.

John Tweedy raged through the line, tilted so far forward he was damn near horizontal, big legs driving, big arms pumping. Just as Loki turned to look downfield, John launched himself. The orange flash of his helmet hit right under Loki's chin. Quentin winced at the hit's violence — Loki's head snapped back and his feet came right off the ground. The ball flew out of Loki's hands, but John continued through the hit. His big arms wrapped around Loki's back, big arms that *squeezed* even as all of John's weight drove the enemy into the ground. When they landed, both sets of feet were in the air.

The ball hit the ground again. The stadium literally shook from the noise, a tremor of possibilities. Players reacted, diving for the squirting pigskin. Quentin thought he saw Mum-O-Killowe dive on it, but the defensive tackle vanished beneath a savage pile of black and orange, white and blue.

Whistles blew, barely audible over the crowd's insane cacophony. Quentin held his breath. He felt someone grab his jersey — Yassoud, staring out at the field and all but hanging on Quentin's shoulder, his eyes bright with hope, his smile blazing in the afternoon sun.

Yassoud yanked Quentin left and right as they both watched the pileup. Zebes dove in. Players pulled each other off the pile.

Pushing.

Shoving.

Whistles.

One of the Harrah refs dove *into* the pile, slithering between larger, armored sentients. Only the ref's tail remained visible for a second, then he wiggled out and flew into the air.

He faced the other direction and pointed one mouth-flap.

Krakens' ball.

Quentin screamed and pulled at Yassoud's jersey, both of their feet dancing like little kids' at Giving Day. The sideline erupted with yelling, laughing and roaring Krakens players and staff.

"*Barnes!*"

Hokor in his heads-up.

"Barnes, stop grab-assing and get out there. Finish this."

Quentin kept laughing as he ran out on the field, pulling his helmet on, his offense following him out. They huddled, then broke the huddle and lined up. Quentin knelt behind Bud-O-Shwek. Rebecca Montagne was just a foot to Quentin's right, Ju Tweedy just a foot to his left.

The victory formation.

"Hut!"

The ball slapped into his hands. He clutched it tight, tucking it in both arms as if he were running right up the middle. No way he'd drop the ball now. He backed up two steps as the offensive and defensive lines half-heartedly pushed against each other.

Rebecca Montagne stood on his left, eyes alert, still ready to trade blows with anyone who came after her quarterback. The right sleeve of her jersey had been torn off sometime late in the second quarter, leaving chipped, scratched, black shoulder armor exposed to the sunlight. Dried blood caked the right side of her neck, the result of a hit that had somehow torn her ear.

Ju Tweedy stood on Quentin's right, standing up straight, hands at his side, his attitude arrogantly inviting in anyone who wanted one last tangle.

No one did.

Ball still clutched tight, Quentin Barnes knelt and touched his left knee to the blessed blue turf.

Whistles blew, zebes flew in. Both teams stood and started exchanging shoulder-pad slaps, congratulations and condolences even as the clock ticked down. The 185,000-strong capacity crowd started chanting off the final seconds.

Pride filled his heart. He kept the ball tight in his right hand as he reached out and grabbed Rebecca's helmet with his left, pulling her in for a quick head-butt.

"Hey!" she said.

"We did it," Quentin said. "Good game, Becca."

She smiled, then gave him a quick head-butt back. He laughed, feeling on top of the world, feeling like nothing could touch him. Big arms wrapped around his shoulders and lifted him.

"Congratulations!" Michael Kimberlin's voice. "You saved me from an insufferable season of Tier Two!"

A final, crushing roar from the crowd told him that the clock had ticked down to zero. The Ionath Krakens had beaten the odds ... they had stayed in Tier One.

More hands, more tentacles, more congratulations. The Krakens sideline emptied, players rushing out to the middle of the field as if they had just won the Galaxy Bowl. Quentin took more hits from his own teammates than he had during the entire game against the Mars Planets.

Quentin laughed, took the slaps to the head, the shoulder nudges, the chest bumps, took them all and smiled. He had a whole off-season to recover from any damage. An off-season that he could spend training, practicing and — most importantly — hunting for his family.

He found each member of the team, even those who hadn't played. He thanked and congratulated them individually. The last sentient he came to was the shortest of them all — Ionath's diminutive coach.

Hokor's cornea blazed bright yellow, the color of excitement, of happiness.

"*Barnes!* Get down here!"

Quentin knelt, seeing that Hokor had, for once, lost the headset. He still wore his tiny team hat. His fur looked smooth and glossy, like he hadn't a care in the world.

"Barnes! Great game. We live to fight another day."

"Thanks, Coach. I can't describe how good this feels."

"As good as getting promoted to Tier One?"

Quentin shook his head. "Even better. This is ... I can't even describe it. Everyone wrote us off."

"And we proved them wrong," Hokor said. He put both pedipalps on Quentin's shoulder pads. "And if you think this feeling is amazing, Quentin, wait until you raise that Galaxy Bowl trophy high."

Quentin's eyes widened. He felt a rush of adrenaline and a tingle in his stomach. His goal had *always* been the title. Because of the way the Krakens had played in the last two games, he now dared to believe that it could actually happen.

"Coach, you really think we can?"

Hokor nodded in that weird, no-neck way the Quyth nodded.

"We've got all the tools. We need to get better, *much* better, and we need to do something about our defense, but we can win it all with the team we have right now. That is, if we have a quarterback that can lead us there."

Quentin laughed, reached out and ruffled up Hokor's fur. "Just gimme the ball, Coach. Just gimme the ball."

Quentin stood and walked away from his celebrating teammates. He found the few Mars Planets players left on the field and wished each one of them well in Tier Two. Those players had a hard road in front of them, a road of two seasons back to back, a road Quentin and his Krakens understood far too well.

With that done, Quentin ran off the field, to the retainer wall that held back the crowd. He ran along that wall, reaching up to slap hands, pedipalps and tentacles of the orange- and black-clad fans reaching down. As he ran, he noticed that Ju Tweedy was behind him, doing the same, with other Krakens joining the train. The crowd went wild at the recognition.

He circled the entire stadium, then started walking to the tunnel that led to the locker room. The crowd continued to cheer and roar — fifteen minutes after the clock ticked zero, and they were all still here, celebrating a moment of pride for Ionath City.

As Quentin walked into the end zone, the crowd's roar picked up, reaching a volume almost as intense as what came before the opening kickoff. He stopped and turned, wondering what they were cheering at. He looked up at the big holoscreen in the field's opposite end zone and saw a huge image of himself: wide smile, bruised face, sweat-matted hair sticking out in all directions. Why was the on-field camera showing that?

And then it registered — the crowd was cheering for *him*.

One hundred and eighty-five thousand sentients, all raising their voices in a chorus of praise, of acceptance, of thanks for a strong finish, for making them proud of their team, of their city, of themselves.

Quentin Barnes, the dirty, orphan miner from Micovi, the teenager who only a few months ago had never met an alien in person, raised his battered helmet in salute.

He would be back.

The *Krakens* would be back.

And the galaxy would know his name.

Because the Ionath Krakens were on a collision course with a GFL Championship, and the only variable was time.

## GFL WEEK THIRTEEN ROUNDUP
(Courtesy of Galaxy Sports Network)

| | | | |
|---|---|---|---|
| **Water Bugs** | 20 | Spider-Bears | 16 |
| **Brigands** | 35 | Atom Smashers | 10 |
| Cloud Killers | 17 | **War Dogs** | 20 |
| **Krakens** | 24 | Planets | 10 |
| Ice Storm | 16 | **Hullwalkers** | 25 |
| **Jacks** | 21 | Warlords | 20 |
| Juggernauts | 18 | **Wolfpack** | 20 |
| Scarlet Fliers | 17 | **Astronauts** | 38 |
| Pirates | 21 | **Armada** | 24 |
| Vanguard | 0 | **Intrigue** | 10 |
| Criminals | 7 | **Dreadnaughts** | 21 |

Themala won 21-7 over the Yall Criminals (6-6) to complete an amazing turnaround. The Dreadnaughts started the season at 1-3, then won their next eight games to take the Planet Division title. Wabash's 20-18 win over the Lu Juggernauts (6-6) gave the Wolfpack (8-4) the second seed in the playoffs, while Alimum won 24-21 over the Pirates to claim the fourth seed.

New Rodina finished with a 38-17 win over fellow playoff team Neptune (9-3). Jupiter (9-3) grabbed the second Solar seed and a home playoff win thanks to a 21-20 thriller over the Shorah Warlords (4-8). Bord (7-2) grabbed the final playoff spot in the Solar by topping the Atom Smashers 35-10.

**Deaths:**
No deaths reported this week.

**Offensive Player of the Week:**

Ju Tweedy, running back for the Ionath Krakens, who gained 161 yards and two touchdowns on 23 carries.

**Defensive Player of the Week:**

John Tweedy, linebacker for the Ionath Krakens, who had six solo tackles and caused the fumble that ended the game against the Mars Planets.

# BOOK THREE:
# POST SEASON

# 18

# FINAL STANDINGS

## PLANET DIVISION

9-3   y-Themala Dreadnaughts
8-4   x-Wabash Wolfpack
8-4   x-Isis Ice Storm
7-5   x-Alimum Armada
7-5   Hittoni Hullwalkers
6-6   Lu Juggernauts
6-6   To Pirates
6-6   Yall Criminals
6-6   Coranadillana Cloud Killers
4-8   Ionath Krakens
4-8   Mars Planets
       (relegated, via tiebreaker)

First Tiebreaker: head-to-head
Wolfpack beat the Ice Storm,
giving Wolfpack the #2 seed.

Armada beat Hullwalkers,
giving Armada the #4 seed.

## SOLAR DIVISION

11-1   y-New Rodina Astronauts
9-3    x-Jupiter Jacks
9-3    x-Neptune Scarlet Fliers
7-5    x-Bord Brigands
6-6    D'Kow War Dogs
5-7    Bartel Water Bugs
4-8    Shorah Warlords
4-8    Sala Intrigue
3-9    Jang Atom Smashers
2-10   Vik Vanguard
1-11   Chillich Spider-Bears
        (relegated)

First Tiebreaker: head-to-head
Jacks beat Scarlet Fliers,
giving Jacks the #2 seed.

(x = playoff berth clinched, y = division clinched)

## From the "Galaxy's Greatest Sports Show
## with Dan & Akbar & Tarat the Smasher"

**DAN:** And we're back. Thanks again to our sponsor Galactic Pictures, who proudly present *Øverlord Doom: 2øø2*, the new movie starring Patuth the Muscular and Gloriana Wanganeen.

**AKBAR:** I saw it at a screening, Dan, and I have to say it's even better than Part One *and* Part Two.

**TARAT:** I can't wait to see it.

**DAN:** And I as well, Tarat, but we're here to talk about the end of the regular season and a very sad moment for a pair of teams.

**TARAT:** If you're a professional football player on one of these teams, Dan, this is a really horrible time. I can't describe how terrible it feels. All of these teams and players worked so hard during the season, but a pair of franchises are heading back to Tier Two.

**AKBAR:** One of those teams was no surprise. The Chillich Spider-Bears had a very difficult year, winning just a single game to finish one and eleven. They finished last in the Solar Division, so relegation drags them back down like a sand-pitter takes its prey.

**DAN:** It just seemed things were stacked against the Spider-Bears this year, guys. Injuries, deaths — it's hard enough to make it as a newly promoted team without losing all those starters.

**TARAT:** Overcoming injuries and deaths is part of the game, Dan.

**DAN:** I know that, Smasher, but you have to feel for those guys a little bit.

**AKBAR:** Well, I can tell you one Solar Division team that is happy the Spider-Bears had injuries, and that's the Vik Vanguard. Just *two wins* this season, and they get to stay in Tier One. They really have to get their linebacker situation figured out or they could get relegated next year.

**DAN:** And speaking of staying in Tier One, I think we have to give the big GGSS salute to the Ionath Krakens for their late-season run.

**AKBAR:** I couldn't agree more, Dan. An amazing turnaround. They win their last two games to finish with four wins, *including* a victory over defending champion Jupiter? Astonishing. The final win, of course, came against the Mars Planets. The Planets and Krakens both finished four-and-eight, but the Krakens win the head-to-head tiebreaker, so bye-bye, Planets.

**DAN:** Smasher, you were once a team captain when Mars was sent down. How did that feel?

**TARAT:** I was with the Planets when they were relegated in 2677. It's going to be a sad time on Mars, Dan. That's the smallest market of any upper-tier team. Amazing fan support, but it's a close-knit community and there will be great anguish and despair. I will say that they deserved to get relegated. They started out the season at four-and-two, then lost their last six games.

**AKBAR:** A galaxy-famous choke, for sure.

**DAN:** So the Krakens live to fight another season in T1. What do you think, guys, can they stay alive next year as well?

**TARAT:** I think so, Dan. They have three of the most talented young receivers in the league and a strong offensive line.

**AKBAR:** They also have that criminal, Ju Tweedy.

**DAN:** What do you mean, *criminal?*

**TARAT:** *Criminal* means someone who breaks the law, Dan.

**DAN:** I know what *criminal* means, Smasher! Akbar, Tweedy hasn't been *convicted* of anything.

**AKBAR:** Right, and those murder charges were just fabricated. Listen, Dan, Ju has money and the connections of Gredok the Splithead. He's guilty as sin, but he'll get off.

**DAN:** Sometimes I can't believe my life involves being around you every day.

**AKBAR:** If you want to call what you've got *a life*, go for it.

**DAN:** Moving on to the Tier One playoffs. It looks like a shoot-'em-up in the Solar Division. The New Rodina Astronauts should beat the seven-and-five Bord Brigands, then move on to face the winner of the Jupiter Jacks and the Neptune Scarlet Fliers. I think the Astronauts' great defense sets them up for a run at their fourth GFL title.

**TARAT:** Don't write off the Planet Division, Dan. Just because the Dreadnaughts, the Ice Storm and the Wolfpack have four losses each doesn't mean they can't win if they reach the title match.

**AKBAR:** I just don't see that happening, Tarat. Those Planet Division teams beat each other up too much during the regular season.

**TARAT:** I'll call it now, a Planet Division team will upset the Astronauts in the Galaxy Bowl.

**DAN:** All right, smart guy, if you're so confident, who's going to win it all?

**TARAT:** I pick the Wabash Wolfpack. Coach Alan Roark has them peaking at just the right time.

**DAN:** Improbable, at best. Akbar, how about you?

**AKBAR:** I'm going with the Jupiter Jacks. I think they have the capacity to upset the Astronauts in the second round, then win out from there.

**DAN:** And I'll stick with my pick, the New Rodina Astronauts. The 'Stros only have one loss this year, they've beaten all the good teams, and I say they'll take it. But who cares what we say, let's go to the calls. Line four from Hittoni, go.

**CALLER:** Yeah, Smasher, how can you say the Wolfpack will win it? They lost four games this season. What are you, stupid?

**TARAT:** Stupid? Why don't you just tell me where you are so we can meet, talk about it in person?

**DAN:** Smasher, now take it easy—

**TARAT:** I'll cut open your belly and show you all the black stuff you've got inside there, I'll—"

**DAN:** Okay! Moving on! Line three from Rodina, go!

# MEDIA COVERAGE OF TIER ONE PLAYOFFS AND CHAMPIONSHIP GAME

484  S C O T T   S I G L E R

From *Galaxy Sports Magazine*

---

# GFL Playoff Parings, Relegations Announced

---

*by* YOLANDA DAVENPORT

---

NEW YORK, EARTH, PLANETARY UNION — The 25th GFL season has come to a close, and with the final regular-season game begins the road to Galaxy Bowl XXV. There are no easy routes to reach D'Kow Stadium, the host of the GFL's grand dance. While there are clear favorites, the title is truly up for grabs.

In the Solar Division, the New Rodina Astronauts earned the top seed with a dominant 11-1 record, their only loss coming in a fourth-week loss to the Yall Criminals (6-6). In the opening round, the 'Stros will host the fourth-seeded Bord Brigands (7-5). The Jupiter Jacks (9-3) landed the second seed, earning them a home game against the Neptune Scarlet Fliers (9-3). Bitter rivals, the Jacks beat the Scarlet Fliers in the second week to notch home field advantage via the head-to-head tiebreaker.

On the Planet Division side, the Themala Dreadnaughts (9-3) earned the first seed. Themala hosts the Alimum Armada (7-5). Wabash and Isis finished with identical 8-4 records, but, thanks to 24-17 win in Week Seven, the Wolfpack get the home game based on the head-to-head tiebreaker.

# PLAYOFFS 2683

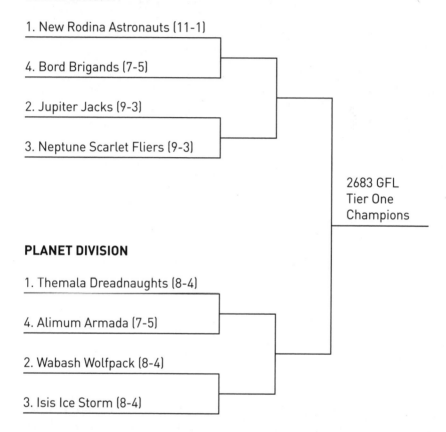

**SOLAR DIVISION**

1. New Rodina Astronauts (11-1)

4. Bord Brigands (7-5)

2. Jupiter Jacks (9-3)

3. Neptune Scarlet Fliers (9-3)

2683 GFL
Tier One
Champions

**PLANET DIVISION**

1. Themala Dreadnaughts (8-4)

4. Alimum Armada (7-5)

2. Wabash Wolfpack (8-4)

3. Isis Ice Storm (8-4)

## RELEGATIONS ANNOUNCED

While it's no surprise, the official report is in from the GFL head office. The Chillich Spider-Bears (1-11) and the Mars Planets (4-8) have been relegated to Tier Two. As for their replacements, we will have to wait for the completion of the upcoming Tier Two season and the subsequent T2 Tourney.

From the *Leekee Galaxy Times*

# Astronauts, Dreadnaughts dominate in first round of GFL playoffs

*by* KELP BRINGER

NEW RODINA, WILSON 6, LEAGUE OF PLANETS — Where there were eight, now there are four.

The New Rodina Astronauts completely dominated the Bord Brigands, earning a first-round 21-0 shutout. The Astronauts' defense controlled the game, holding the Brigands to just 213 yards of total offense.

---

*Where there were eight, now there are four.*

---

The 'Stros are now one game from the Galaxy Bowl, where they hope to represent the Solar Division. To make that trip, New Rodina has to defeat the Neptune Scarlet Fliers. The Fliers shocked the galaxy with a 14-10 first-round upset over their archrivals and de-fending GFL champs the Jupiter Jacks. Word from Neptune is that the parties are still raging a full day after the game.

On the Planet Division side, the Themala Dreadnaughts doubled up on the Alimum Armada, 28-14. The game was never really in question as running back Donald Dennis posted a banner day, carrying the ball 24 times for 134 yards and all four Dreader touchdowns. In the other Planet Division game, the Wabash Wolfpack topped the Isis Ice Storm 28-21. Wabash's fullback Ralph Schmeer seemed to be their secret weapon, unexpectedly scoring three touchdowns. Schmeer scored on runs of 1 and 2 yards, and he hauled in a 4-yard Rich Bennett pass with eighteen seconds left in the game to give Wabash the win.

Themala now hosts the Wolf-pack, with the winner earning a trip to the Galaxy Bowl.

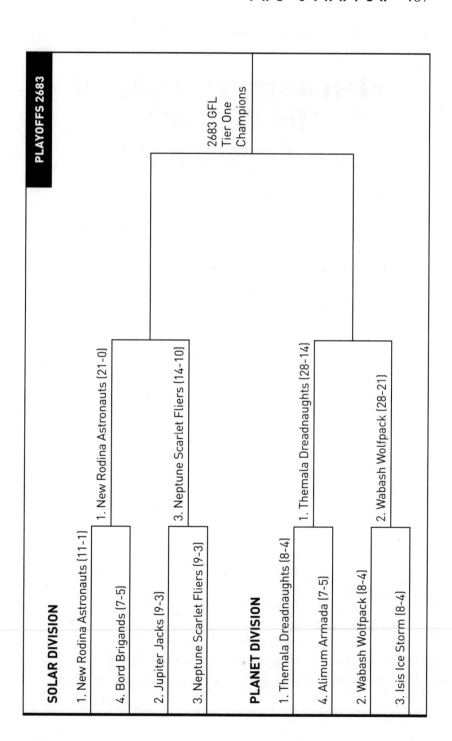

PLAYOFFS 2683

2683 GFL
Tier One
Champions

**SOLAR DIVISION**

1. New Rodina Astronauts (11-1)

4. Bord Brigands (7-5)

1. New Rodina Astronauts (21-0)

2. Jupiter Jacks (9-3)

3. Neptune Scarlet Fliers (9-3)

3. Neptune Scarlet Fliers (14-10)

**PLANET DIVISION**

1. Themala Dreadnaughts (8-4)

4. Alimum Armada (7-5)

1. Themala Dreadnaughts (28-14)

2. Wabash Wolfpack (8-4)

3. Isis Ice Storm (8-4)

2. Wabash Wolfpack (28-21)

From the *Net Colony News Syndicate*

---

# Astronauts vs. Wolfpack for the 2683 GFL Championship

*by* JONATHAN SANDOVAL

WABASH, FORTRESS, TOWER REPUBLIC — The invitations are sent, the RSVPs received, and we now know the two attendees of the big dance.

New Rodina manhandled the Neptune Scarlet Fliers, 38-21. New Rodina linebacker Douglas Glisson had a legendary game with seven solo tackles, four assists, two interceptions and three sacks on Fliers QB Adam Gurri.

That win is New Rodina's thirteenth of the season, and by all accounts the 'Stros look damn near unstoppable.

Here in Wabash, the Wolfpack defense put on a surprising show, holding the pass-happy Themala Dreadnaughts to just one touchdown in a 17-7 win.

"This is what we play for," said Wolfpack owner Gloria Ogawa. "We're bringing the hardware home."

The Wolfpack will become only the fifth team in GFL history to play in at least three Galaxy Bowls. Wabash won it all in 2669 but lost to the Ionath Krakens back in 2665.

This is New Rodina's fourth Galaxy Bowl appearance. The Astronauts are 3-and-0 in the big dance, winning the GFL title in 2660, 2663 and 2679.

The Astronauts are favored by eight points in the championship game.

*"This is what we play for.
We're bringing the hardware home."*

— GLORIA OGAWA, WOLFPACK OWNER

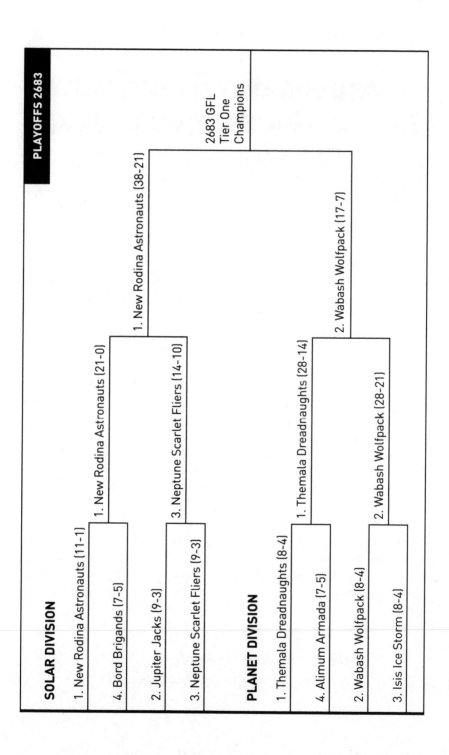

PLAYOFFS 2683

**SOLAR DIVISION**

1. New Rodina Astronauts (11-1)

1. New Rodina Astronauts (21-0)

4. Bord Brigands (7-5)

1. New Rodina Astronauts (38-21)

2. Jupiter Jacks (9-3)

3. Neptune Scarlet Fliers (14-10)

3. Neptune Scarlet Fliers (9-3)

2683 GFL
Tier One
Champions

**PLANET DIVISION**

1. Themala Dreadnaughts (8-4)

1. Themala Dreadnaughts (28-14)

4. Alimum Armada (7-5)

2. Wabash Wolfpack (17-7)

2. Wabash Wolfpack (8-4)

2. Wabash Wolfpack (28-21)

3. Isis Ice Storm (8-4)

From the *UBS Sports*

---

# Wolfpack Win Galaxy Bowl in Double-Overtime Shocker

### *by* PIKOR THE ASSUMING

D'KOW, NEW WHITOK, WHITOK KINGDOM — In a game that may go down as the greatest Galaxy Bowl of them all, the Wabash Wolfpack left no question that they are the champions of the universe.

"If you want to be the best, you have to beat the best," said Wolfpack coach Alan Roark. "Well, the Astronauts were the best. We wanted the title, we had to go through them to take it, and take it we did."

An amazing, double-overtime game saw the Wolfpack claim the GFL championship with a 23-17 victory. The Wolfpack won on a trick play when quarterback Rich Bennett pitched wide left to running back John Ellsworth. Ellsworth ran to the sidelines, only to stop and throw all the way across the field to Bennett for a 45-yard touchdown pass.

"It was meant to be," Ellsworth said. "I give thanks to Jesus, because clearly, Jesus loves the Wolfpack and hates the Astronauts. Thank you, Jesus!"

In what has become a pattern and a hallmark for victory, the Wolfpack had zero turnovers on the night. The Astronauts, on the other hand, gave up the ball three times: twice on interceptions by quarterback Rick Renaud and once on a fumble by running back Steven Schacknies.

"Our three turnovers were the difference," Renaud said. "We didn't take care of the ball. I think we're a better team, but we weren't tonight. The Wolfpack earned the win. They are the champs."

This is the second GFL championship for Wabash. They also become only the fifth team in league history to earn more than one Galaxy Bowl title.

*"If you want to be the best, you have to beat the best."*

— ALAN ROARK, WABASH WOLFPACK COACH

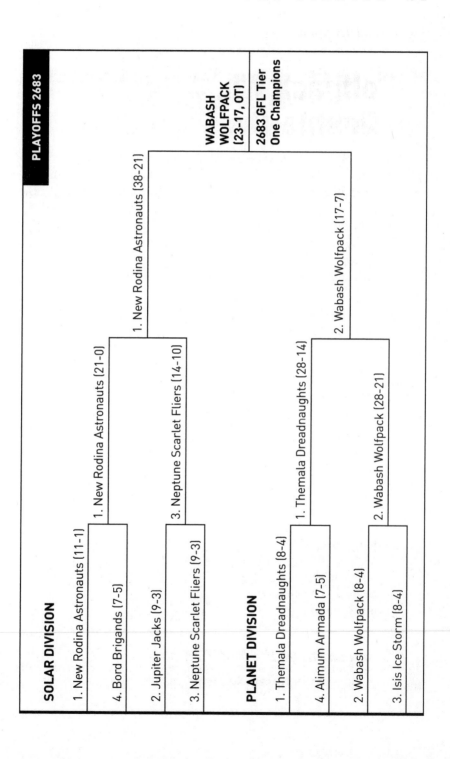

PLAYOFFS 2683

**SOLAR DIVISION**

1. New Rodina Astronauts (11-1)

4. Bord Brigands (7-5)

2. Jupiter Jacks (9-3)

3. Neptune Scarlet Fliers (9-3)

1. New Rodina Astronauts (21-0)

3. Neptune Scarlet Fliers (14-10)

1. New Rodina Astronauts (38-21)

**PLANET DIVISION**

1. Themala Dreadnaughts (8-4)

4. Alimum Armada (7-5)

2. Wabash Wolfpack (8-4)

3. Isis Ice Storm (8-4)

1. Themala Dreadnaughts (28-14)

2. Wabash Wolfpack (28-21)

2. Wabash Wolfpack (17-7)

**WABASH WOLFPACK (23-17, OT)**

**2683 GFL Tier One Champions**

From the *OS2 Tribune*

---

# Orbiting Death win the T2 Tournament, advance to Tier One

*by* SHAKA THE IMPERSONATOR

HUDSON BAY, EARTH, PLANETARY UNION — Tier One, say hello to metalflake-red and flat black.

The Orbiting Death won the Tier Two Tournament with a 14-10 victory over the Texas Earthlings. Death quarterback Condor Adrienne played the first half of the game, completing twelve passes on sixteen attempts with one touchdown, before Ganesha Fritz came in for the second half. Fritz completed eight passes on sixteen attempts and was intercepted twice by Earthlings linebacker Alonzo Castro.

On the defensive side, Yalla the Biter continues to be the Death's top player. Yalla racked up seven tackles and two sacks, including one that put Earthlings quarterback Case Johanson out of the game. Texas relied heavily on running back Peter Lowachee for the rest of the game. Lowachee gained 114 yards on 17 carriess and picked up the Earthlings' only touchdown.

The championship completes an amazing and surprising season for the Death. After losing dominant running back Ju Tweedy to legal complications during the off-season, most analysts thought the Death couldn't win the Quyth Irradiated Conference. Death owner Anna Villani, however, made key personnel acquisitions that gave the team a new identity.

"Signing Condor Adrienne was my biggest stroke of brilliance," Villani said. "He's the best quarterback in football right now, far better than that scrub [Quentin Barnes] from Ionath. And Yalla the Biter revitalized our defense. His aggressive play embodies the Orbiting Death philosophy."

Yalla the Biter finished the season with two more confirmed kills, extending his record-holding status as the GFL's all-time most-lethal player.

By playing in the Tier Two Tournament championship game, both the Orbiting Death and the Earthlings earned promotion to Tier One. The Death will play in the Planet Division, replacing the demoted Mars Planets. The Earthlings will play in the Solar Division, replacing the demoted Chillich Spider-Bears.

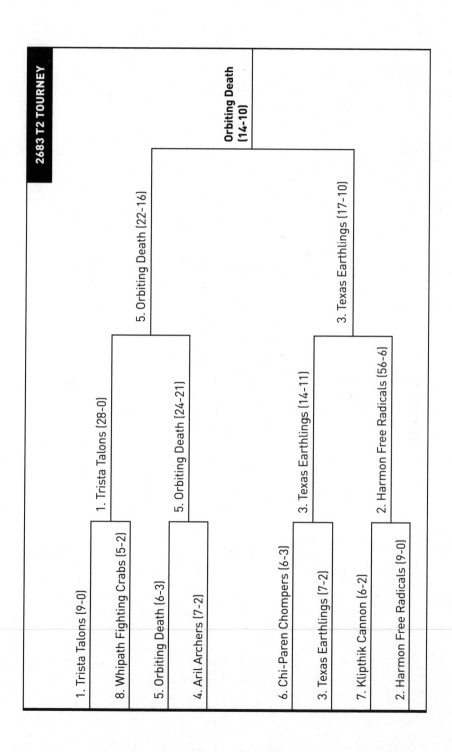

2683 T2 TOURNEY

Orbiting Death (14-10)

5. Orbiting Death (22-16)

3. Texas Earthlings (17-10)

1. Trista Talons (28-0)

5. Orbiting Death (24-21)

3. Texas Earthlings (14-11)

2. Harmon Free Radicals (56-6)

1. Trista Talons (9-0)

8. Whipath Fighting Crabs (5-2)

5. Orbiting Death (6-3)

4. Aril Archers (7-2)

6. Chi-Paren Chompers (6-3)

3. Texas Earthlings (7-2)

7. Klipthik Cannon (6-2)

2. Harmon Free Radicals (9-0)

# THE END

## *About the Author*

*New York Times* best-selling novelist Scott Sigler is the author of **NOCTURNAL, ANCESTOR, INFECTED** and **CONTAGIOUS,** hardcover thrillers from Crown Publishing, and the co-founder of Dark Øverlord Media, which produces his Galactic Football League series: **THE ROOKIE, THE STARTER, THE ALL-PRO,** and **THE MVP.**

Before he was published, Scott built a large online following by giving away his self-recorded audiobooks as free, serialized podcasts. His loyal fans, who named themselves "Junkies," have downloaded over fifteen million individual episodes of his stories and interact daily with Scott and each other in the social media space.

Photograph by Amy Davis Roth of Surlyramics.com